Australian author **Ally Blake** [...]
strong coffee, porch swings a[...]
beautiful notebooks and soft, [...]
inquisitive, rumbustious, spectacular children are
her exquisite delight, and she adores writing love
stories so much she'd write them even if nobody
read them. No wonder, then, having sold over four
million copies of her romance novels worldwide,
Ally is living her bliss. Find out more about Ally's
books at allyblake.com.

Suzanne Merchant was born and raised in South
Africa. She and her husband lived and worked
in Cape Town, London, Kuwait, Baghdad,
Sydney and Dubai before settling in the Sussex
countryside. They enjoy visits from their three
grown-up children and are kept busy attempting
to keep two spaniels, a dachshund, a parrot and a
large, unruly garden under control.

DATING DEAL WITH THE ITALIAN

ALLY BLAKE

BEST MAN'S SECOND CHANCE

SUZANNE MERCHANT

MILLS & BOON

First published in Great Britain 2025
by Mills & Boon, an imprint of HarperCollins*Publishers* Ltd,
1 London Bridge Street, London, SE1 9GF

www.harpercollins.co.uk

HarperCollins*Publishers*, Macken House, 39/40 Mayor Street Upper, Dublin 1, D01 C9W8, Ireland

Dating Deal with the Italian © 2025 Ally Blake

Best Man's Second Chance © 2025 Suzanne Merchant

ISBN: 978-0-263-39675-1

03/25

DATING DEAL WITH THE ITALIAN

ALLY BLAKE

MILLS & BOON

This book is dedicated to "great legs",
"blame the fingerprints", "smells like grape" and the
#winerywednesday crowd. You know who you are.

CHAPTER ONE

SUTTON MAYBERRY BOPPED along with the demo album of an indie band she was considering managing as she drove along the gently curving country road.

She smiled as she tipped her face to the sunshine dappling the windscreen of her rental car. Yet, when the GPS informed her that she would soon be turning left in order to "reach her destination," for the briefest of moments she considered driving on.

Which was silly. It had been her choice to hop on a plane and fly halfway across the world on a whim, and she was willing, nay, delighted to be there.

As if deciding to gift Sutton one more layer of delight, the forest she'd been driving through cleared, giving way to a view that had her blinking in enchantment. Pretty green paddocks dotted with fluffy white sheep nestled up against small, neat farmhouses boasting windmills and water tanks, and hillside after hillside covered in striations of fantastically twisted grape vines.

When instructed she did take that left, and found herself driving beneath a large, arched, wooden sign reading Welcome to Vermillion: You Are Entering Wine Country.

The Main Street of Vermillion was straight out of a romcom. Shop fronts with pretty striped awnings, cottage gardens bursting with roses bordered in old stone fences covered in moss, picture windows glowing with golden inner lights.

Handmade signs boasted local cheeses, cosy cafés, vintage clothes, bric-a-brac, homegrown vegetables, and baskets of grain ready for milling.

And if the "welcome" sign hadn't made it clear she'd entered "wine country," the grape carvings on every shop sign, and the grape vines curling around lampposts and drooping elegantly from pergola rooves, sure did the trick.

Sutton slowed to a stop at a pedestrian crossing as a pair of old ladies crossed the road, nattering happily, arms intertwined. She took the chance to let the window down and breathe deep of the soft spring air. It smelled sweet, floral and crisp. A million miles from the drizzle, and crowds, and hustle, and sticky pub floors, and loud music she'd left behind in central London a little over twenty-four hours before.

She smiled at the apologetic mother of a young toddler who'd started across the road, then stopped to pick up treasures along the way. Then her heart felt a little yank. Rewind time and that curious, curly-haired toddler might have been her.

For it was here, in this grape-laden hamlet, that her parents had first met. Fallen in love at first sight, no less. Her father been a backpacker, working behind the bar in a local pub, when the door opened, "bringing with it a shaft of sunlight, and within the beam the most beautiful woman he'd ever seen."

She could hear her father's voice; the storied tale of high romance having been narrated to her so many times over the years she could recite it by rote.

It had ended tragically, her mother dying when only a few weeks older than Sutton was now. Heartbroken, her darling father had whisked their small family back to London, turning Vermillion into a fairy-tale land in her mind, rather than a real place.

Until now.

A car behind her beeped. With a wave out the window,

Sutton rolled the car through the empty crossing and looked for a place to park.

Before she found a place to stay, she wanted to check in with her bands, let them know she'd arrived safe and sound. And her dad? *Not yet*, she thought, a frisson of guilt skittering up the back of her neck.

For all that he talked so fondly of Vermillion, it was inextricably tied up in the loss of her mother, whom he mourned, to that day. She didn't want to do anything to exacerbate that. So, she'd let him imagine her in Amsterdam with the Magnolia Blossoms, or Belgium with the Sweety Pies—he loved to keep track of where her bands were playing, even if his taste went more to Bowie than it did to modern punk, or jazz-funk.

He'd be thrilled she'd finally made the pilgrimage; she was *sure* of it. She'd just wait to let him know once she had something to share.

Now, having forgotten to grab an Australian sim card at the airport, finding a place with free Wi-Fi was key. And... there! A spot.

She pulled into the angled park, then looked up to find herself outside a yarn store. The sign read Swirl & Purl Craft Corner. On the left of it was a small old-timey cinema—the Hollywood and Vine—boasting a twilight showing of *Calamity Jane*. On the right was a gift shop called Wine Not?

Sutton huffed out a laugh. While her tastes ran more to indie horror, black jeans and T-shirts, and dark craft beer, she could see how her dad would have found such pleasure in this place.

Grabbing her slouchy black leather backpack from the passenger scat, she hopped out of the car, twisted back and forth a little to stretch out the kinks, then looked up the street.

Her gaze landed on a classic pub sign hanging from a horizontal pole high up on the outer wall of a big black brick building a few doors up. *Excellent*, she thought as she strode up the path. She'd grab a coffee, a bite to eat, and the Wi-Fi password, find a place to stay, and fend off jet lag as long as she could.

Rather imposing, the place was, up close and personal. Especially when compared with the twee architecture on the rest of the street. Tall, old brick, the facade painted matte black, bar the double-story windows along half the wall.

The sign above the door read Vine and Stein. She wondered if the inhabitants of the town were simply all delightful, pun-loving people, or if some town provenance made it compulsory.

Then, reaching to push open the door, she stopped at the last when some wave of energy, like déjà vu only stronger, swept over her. Her hand whipped back to hold the strap of her bag.

What if this was the pub in which her parents had first met? She flicked through her memories, but couldn't say if father had mentioned the *name* of the place, preferring to focus on the fairy tale, high points of falling in love.

She could message her dad and ask, but that would mean telling him where she was.

That could all come later, once she'd found her feet in the town in which she was born, a few weeks off the same age her mother had been when she'd died.

She'd lived with a ticking clock in the back of her head her entire life, born of the knowledge that it could all be taken without warning. It had been the impetus to throw herself at any opportunity that came her way.

No point holding back now, she thought.

Then she reached out and opened the door.

Dante Rossi had come to the conclusion that choosing to curse in Italian or English made no difference when attempting to feel less aggrieved about doing something he did not wish to do.

Far too big to be wedged beneath the Vine and Stein bar, shoulder on the verge of popping from its socket as he attempted to unscrew the bolt welding the vintage cash register to the bench above, that realisation came far too late.

I missed harvest for this, he thought, wrenching with all his might. Without result.

Autumn festivals, popular throughout Umbria, and the resultant uptick in vineyard tours, the influx of people in general, he could miss. But that handful of days when the delicate balance between allowing a crop to ripen to perfection and deciding the exact right moment to reap—that was pure magic.

"Al diavolo tutto," Dante swore through gritted teeth, cursing this place, this town, and his agreement to have anything to do with either of them when he ought to be back home, answering only to his own conscience.

"Ah, hello?"

Dante flinched at the unexpected voice, knocking his elbow against the underside of the bar. As numbing sparks shot up his arm, he let his eyes drift closed and imagined the hum of bees, the twitter of small birds the only sound for miles—

"Hello, down there?" the voice called again.

Dante twisted his head out from under the bar so that he might glance toward the office, and shout, "Chrissy! *Sei qui?*" in the hopes the day manager, who had disappeared some time ago, had returned.

"Back in a tick!" Chrissy had said the moment he had arrived. Dante had assumed "a tick" meant a short amount of time. Clearly it was yet one more Australianism he did not understand, as silence, bar the staticky, electric hum of the refrigeration system, gave him his answer.

He heard the scrape of a shoe and stilled. "Chrissy?"

"Nope!" said the dismembered voice, cheerfully. "I'm Sutton. Are you okay down there? Do you need some help?"

Dante did not need help. Not the kind the voice was suggesting, anyway.

Rewind a month, to when Zia Celia had called, begging him to come to Vermillion, to save the family vineyard—that was when *help* might have been of use. Some voice that reminded him why he stayed on his own estate and left the world to its own devices.

"Look, I think I should come back there—?"

"No," he growled. *"Il bar è chiuso.* The bar is closed."

Back home—what with siestas and long lunches and time at the vineyard linked more to sunshine and seasons than to clocks—it would not occur to him to give a damn. But here, every misstep added interminable additional time to his burden.

Using his rising ire, Dante white-knuckled the arm of the wrench, and pulled. His arms shook with exertion, the muscles between his shoulders screamed. He could do this; whatever it took to rid himself of any last vestiges of the remorse his aunt had used to get him there, and then he could go home.

"Are you sure?" asked the voice. "The sign on the door says 'open.' And when I gave the door a push, I was clearly able to enter."

Dante let the wrench fall to the floor with a clang, then lay back, breathing hard, and came as close to laughing as he had done in weeks. A laugh built on frustration—with this place, and with himself.

A bead of sweat trickled down his neck and he wondered when he might get time to shower, rid himself of whatever filth he was lying in. Hell, maybe he'd shave his head and burn all his clothes.

But first… He considered his nemesis. Not Australian. English? Female, most definitely. Obstinate, or wilfully obtuse.

"Note," he said, slowing his cadence, "the chairs atop the tables. The fact we are on emergency lights only. And if you look around you will see no other people in here bar yourself. I suggest those points back up my assertion."

When he heard nothing more from the other side of the bar, he assumed the intruder had moved on. He wondered if he might allow himself to take that as having managed to achieve one thing that day.

At the clearing of a nearby throat, Dante sent a short, sharp, tempestuous message to the gods, then heaved himself out from under the bar, enough to have a partial view of the owner of the voice leaning over it.

Dark silhouette, sunglasses atop long dark hair, backlit by the weak sunlight pouring through the street-side windows.

His choices came down to a) insisting the woman leave, b) ignoring her if she did not, or c) as his cousin Niccolo liked to say, *act like a human person* and help her with whatever it was that had sent her into the place, and *then* move her on, so he could get this one damn thing done right.

He gripped the edge of the bar and used it to leverage himself out from under the cabinetry. Sitting up, he wiped his hands on the knees of his jeans, tugged at the shirt stuck to him in several places—with sweat or old beer—then uncurled himself to standing.

"What is so important that—" Dante stopped, his next words drying up in his throat.

For the silhouette had moved with him, tipping back as he stood, revealing a face so lovely, so luminous, he could not recall what he'd been about to say. Drinking her in, he noted dark hair falling about her shoulders like ribbons, skin like sunshine on cream, cheekbones for days. Soft blue eyes, *bedroom eyes*, he thought, before he could stop himself.

Then she smiled and something pinged inside his head. Like a beacon. Or a warning.

"Wow," she said, laughing, her eyes sparking with light, "you're an absolute mess. What were you doing down there?"

He swallowed, surprised to find himself parched; like a man who had stepped out of the desert to find himself yearning not for water, but for a 1967 Leroy Musigny Grand Cru. Yet, Dante was not a man who *yearned*. His life—bar the last two weeks spent in this time-sucking, quicksand of a place—was exactly as he'd curated it to be. And far better than he deserved.

Certain he must have stood up too fast, for it was the only explanation for his discomfiture, Dante rolled his neck, ran sticky fingers through his tangled hair, then went to rest his knuckles on the bar, only to find they were covered in grease.

Crossing his arms, hands curled into fists, he looked into the woman's twinkling blue eyes and said, "What is it that you want, Ms....?"

"Mayberry," she said. "Sutton Mayberry." Smile widening as she looked around the bar, she added, "Don't you think bars and pubs feel strange when it's this quiet. It's as if this building is holding its breath, waiting for music and people to spill in through the cracks and fill the place with noise and light and grit and life."

Dante, who had seen at most a hundred people come into this white elephant of a business over the course of each day since he'd been there, felt tired imagining the scene she described.

Seeming to take his silence for agreement, the stranger lifted her sunglasses off her head to slip them into a soft leather backpack she'd dropped onto a barstool. She grabbed another barstool, sat, and said, "Well, are you going to offer me a drink?"

"A drink," he parroted, feeling warmth creep into his skin, his bones.

Elbows on the bar, she smiled up at him "This *is* a bar, right?"

"Si," he allowed. Then glanced right, to the big carriage clock on the wall between the front door and the kitchen. "It's eleven in the morning."

"Which makes it happy hour somewhere."

She was right, only it made his thoughts turn once more to home. He calculated it was around three in the morning at Sorello, the vineyard he owned and ran. All would be quiet there, bar the skitter of mice, and the groan of old wood—the comforting sounds of night in a three-hundred-year-old villa.

Brow tight, he looked back to find the intruder watching him. Long, dark lashes swept against her cheeks when she blinked, slowly, making his fingertips prickle, as if his blood was slipping and pooling in places it wasn't used to.

Needing space, he moved to the sink to scrub his hands clean. Then grabbed the hand towel and twisted it around his fingers to ground himself. He motioned to the bottles lined up in front of the mirror behind the bar, and asked, "What'll it be?"

"Are you kidding? It's eleven in the morning." A quick irreverent smile, then, "I've been on a plane for most of the past twenty-four hours, so would give anything for a coffee."

As one they looked to the machine that sat cold and still down the other end of the bar; not yet switched on for the day.

Because the Vine was closed.

When Dante did nothing to rectify the fact, the woman laughed, a soft husky sound, before saying, "How about a glass of water?"

"Still or sparkling?"

"Sparkling," she said, lifting her hands to hold them under her chin as she sparkled with all her might.

It was dazzling. She was dazzling. But Dante was not to

be dazzled. He could only hope that the flat stare he offered in return made that perfectly clear.

When she dropped her hands, her front teeth, a little longer than the rest, caught on her bottom lip with a slow drag.

And Dante... Dante needed this over and done with.

He reached for a glass from the rack above, filled it with ice, then poured her a glass of sparkling water on tap.

Habit born of weeks spent learning the ins and outs of the pub—trying to figure out why it was not pulling its weight within the Rossi portfolio of investments—had him turning to the cash register, only to remember it was broken. And heaviness pressed down on him once more.

He slid the drink in front of her. "On the house."

"Oh. Are you sure? Because—" One hand reached out to clasp the glass—short fingernails, shiny black polish—while the other tapped a finger on the bar.

"Was there something else? Perhaps you'd like me to cook you a three-course meal, wash your car, do your taxes..."

"That would be all amazing, but honestly, just your Wi-Fi password would suffice." It came with a smile that had no doubt gotten her what she wanted on any number of occasions.

Dante pointed to a laminated sign over the bar—username and password printed thereon. "If that's all?"

"It is," she promised, sliding off the barstool, grabbing her backpack, and slinging it over one shoulder. "I'll just... find a spot back there in the dark. Stay out of your way. Let you get back to..."

Tipping up onto her toes, she leaned over the bar, and waggled her fingers at the floor. When she looked back up, she was close. So close Dante felt a wash of softness, like sunshine on dust motes at the corners of his vision.

He could not have been more relieved when she gave him a nod of thanks, then made her way to a table near the farthest window, where a slab of sunlight poured into the bar. She took down the chairs, arranging them neatly, then sat on one in a slump of long limbs.

After looking out the window for a long moment, sighing, then running her hands over her face, she reached into her bag, pulled out a phone, and was soon lost to whatever it was his Wi-Fi helped her to do.

Not *his* Wi-Fi.

It was Zia Celia's. And his cousin Niccolo and cousin Aurora, who was getting up to mischief overseas. They, along with Dante's uncle Giacomo, had left Italy decades before, moving to South Australia to run the Vermillion Hill vineyard, and much of the real estate in town along with it. At the behest of Rossi Vignaioli Internazionali. Or, more specifically, Dante's father, who back then had run it all.

This responsibility Dante currently held for this place came by way of tendrils of duty and guilt, ancient turmoil that stretched all the way from the other side of the world. And back through time.

Once he had done as his aunt had requested, and found a pathway to bring the Vine and Stein back into the black, he could leave behind the twee shops and familial pressure, and return to the scent of olive trees, and old wood, and Italian earth. He could go home.

Laughter carried across the large near-empty space, as the intruder read something that tickled her. The sound curled inside him, warm and soothing. And while he did not wish to, Dante moved to the coffee machine and switched it on.

The thing let out a loud hiss as the water began to steam, and over the top of the machine, he saw the intruder look up. Sit up. Her face filled with hope.

"How long?" she called.

"Half hour to warm up," Dante responded.

"I'm pretty sure I can survive just that long. Black, please, when you're ready. Bitter is fine. And extra hot. If you're worried it might burn the roof of my mouth, it'll be perfect."

If Dante needed one more thing to convince him the world beyond his borders was a wild and unruly place, the thought of someone searing their taste buds, deliberately, rendering them unable to fully enjoy the pleasure that was a grape weathered by the elements, delicately plucked, liquefied, fermented, curated, stored, and turned into a life-affirming drop was it.

"Heathen," he muttered, as he set a series of espresso cups atop the machine in order to warm them.

Catching sight of the sleeve of his shirt, the smear of dirt thereupon, he glanced to the mirror behind the bar. Grease smeared his cheek, his hair was tangled with sweat, his brow deeply furrowed. He looked a wreck. He felt it too. As if his very marrow was suffering.

A small spark of light in his day thus far, Dante remembered he had spare clothes in the office, stashed there in case he ever needed to sleep on the small couch, if staying with his aunt and cousins became too much.

He considered letting the customer know he'd be off the floor. Then looked to the ancient cast-iron register. If she wanted it, she was welcome to it.

Emails and DMs checked, follow-ups sent, local shop from which to grab an Australian sim card sourced, bands advised she was back on deck, Sutton sent her dad a quick, "Have to postpone next week's lunch. Fill you in soon!"

Then dropped her phone to the table as if it might burn.

Fine. She was being a scaredy-cat. Still, better to fill her dad in once she'd seen more of Vermillion, so that she could lean into nostalgia rather than the "this was where you last saw Mum" angle. Right? Right.

Sutton reached for her espresso only to find she'd finished it.

The grumpy barman had—grudgingly—done a bang-up job of giving her exactly what she'd asked for. *Hot and deliciously bitter.* The coffee, that was, not the grumpy barman. Though as descriptors went…

She looked up, hoping to catch a glimpse of him hunched over the bar, mumbling becomingly. Alas he was nowhere to be seen.

Big, he was, and tall, and broad with it. All dark eyes, tortured brow, scruffy stubble and thick wavy hair that fell over his face; a gruff, swarthy kind of hot. Add that deep, Italian drawl—a velvet rumble any singer would kill for—and the tragic air of a wintry moor, a crumbling castle, a fallen angel, when he'd hauled himself up from beneath the bar it had been a *moment*.

Eyes unfocused, as she looked into the middle distance, Sutton felt the yawn coming before she could stop it. If she stayed put in the sunshiny window, she'd likely fall asleep where she sat.

Gathering her things, she made her way through the labyrinth of tables. The chairs had all been taken down by then, a handful of patrons had come in, the scent of lunch was on the air. Other staff now loitered behind the bar—a woman with a vibrant blue pixie cut absently dried glasses, a guy with a man bun appeared to struggle with the cash register drawer.

And while she felt a flicker of disappointment that she'd not get one final glance at the hot, bitter barman, Sutton wasn't in Vermillion looking for *that*. *Was she?* No.

The strange crackle she'd felt in the air when their eyes had met had to be down to the fact she'd walked into the place thinking about her parents, and how *they'd* met. Nothing more.

When Man Bun looked up, she waved and called out her thanks, then headed back out into the soft South Australian sunshine happy to put the Vine and Stein behind her.

* * *

Sutton walked the length of Main Street, passing a thrift shop, Corker of a Deal; a menswear store, Vine and Dandy; and noting other eateries in which she might be able to sit for a bit and work each day.

Living out of her suitcase, following her bands around the world for most of her adult life, she was used to renting tables in cafés for the price of coffee and a bite to eat. No point getting used to a home office when she'd never settled into any place long enough to call it "home."

She was looking at the menu of massages and facials on a sign outside the Wine Down Day Spa, wondering if it had existed when her parents had lived there, when someone cleared their throat.

A blonde woman in a fitted red dress and red stilettos, a pastry half hanging out of her mouth, arms filled with books, gave her a deadpan stare, and Sutton realised she was blocking the footpath.

"So sorry!" said Sutton with a self-deprecating laugh, as she hustled out of the way. "Daydreaming."

The woman tugged the pastry from her mouth and said, "Best way to spend one's time." Then her book pile began to slip.

Sutton leaped forward and grabbed the top book. Then the next few as well.

The woman popped the pastry back between her teeth, then tipped her head sideways toward the building next door—a darling, whitewashed wood cottage with black shutters and window planters overflowing with colourful pansies.

It was adorable. Until one stepped inside, and things took a turn. The walls were still a bright white but everything else— lush velvet couches, huge fluffy cushions, gilt-framed art— was a riot of bright pink, blood orange, and deep aquamarine.

All of which was in service of tightly packed rows of

floor-to-ceiling bookshelves chock-full of books, the covers of which woke Sutton faster than an espresso ever could. For there were half-clad Vikings, swoony cartoony rom-coms, beefy highlanders in short kilts, long-haired, muscular, lusty-looking men with wings, or fangs, or both.

"Feel as if you've stepped through a portal," the woman asked, reading Sutton's mind, "leaving behind the whole-some dreamscape that is Vermillion?"

"A little bit," Sutton admitted, looking at one of the books she'd carried in to find what appeared to be a naked space cowboy on the cover. "What is this place?"

"A haven for women who love fairies and dragons and dream of the men who morph into them. I'm Laila. Book pusher. Pleasure enabler."

"Sutton Mayberry," said Sutton. "Manager of indie bands. Pleasure enjoyer."

Giving Sutton's black leather jacket over black jeans over black Vans a once-over, Laila said, "I'm guessing you're not from around here."

"Well, I kind of am, actually," said Sutton. "My parents met here, in Vermillion. Fell in love, had me. Though we moved away when I was a toddler and I've not been back since."

Laila leaned her hip against the sales desk. "Vermillion is the setting of your origin story."

"I guess it is," Sutton said, quite liking how that sounded.

"Flying visit, or sticking around?" Laila asked as she flipped out a small stepladder, then clicked at Sutton to hand her the books she'd carried inside so she could place them on a shelf behind the counter. Tucked in between two rather spicy-looking bookends.

"Staying," Sutton said. "For a little while, at least." She wasn't sure how long, or what she hoped to find there, or much really, bar the fact she'd had to come.

"Here with anyone?" Laila asked, as she bobbed her way back down the ladder.

"Nope. I'm all alone." Sutton laughed at herself. "And that sounded more forlorn than I meant it to."

"Would you like it to be otherwise?" Laila asked, an eyebrow lifting suggestively.

Oh, thought Sutton, not having picked up that kind of vibe. "That's terribly sweet, but I'm straight, sorry."

Laila's eyes widened before she burst into laughter. "As am I, honey. As am I."

Sutton slapped a hand over her eyes in mortification. First the thing with the grumpy bartender—she was certain now that she'd stared at the veins roping up his sizeable forearms when he'd crossed his arms at her, and sighed, out loud, when he'd shaken his hair off his face only for it to fall instantly back over his brow in a Byronic sweep. Then assuming Laila had hit on her?

The "my parents met and fell in love here" thing was clearly doing a number on her!

"I'm so sorry," she said. "You found me out there, attempting to walk off jet lag before finding somewhere to stay. My people skills are clearly halfway between here and London."

"It's all good," said Laila, waving a hand over her face. "What about him—he your type?"

Sutton flinched. Then blinked to find Laila motioning to the book cover she'd rested her other hand on—a woman was entwined, intimately, with what appeared to be some kind of half man, half octopus.

Sutton curled her fingers into her palm. "My taste tends toward humans."

Laila laughed. "I was talking fiction, not real life. But since you brought it up—what's your jam? Brunettes? Blonds? Beefcake? Mamma's boys?"

When Sutton opened her mouth, then closed it again, unsure as to how the conversation had turned that way, Laila grinned.

"When I found you on the street you weren't the only one daydreaming. I was tinkering with an idea I've been playing with for some time—a fun way for young single locals to meet up." She pointed to herself. "And there you were, *all alone*, like some sign from the universe."

Octopus men, maybe not. But timing, connection, kismet—Sutton was fine with all of that. In fact, most of her greatest adventures were due to following breadcrumbs the universe had set down. All the while, the ticking clock in the back of her head, urging her on.

Laila held up both hands and moved around behind the sales desk. "Let's start fresh. You said you were looking for a place to stay?"

"I'll find something," Sutton assured her. While going with the flow wasn't for everyone—give her the day and time and she could tell you exactly what her dad would be doing—it was her normal.

"How about I'll do you a deal," said Laila. "I can hook you up with a room in a really sweet place, if you meet for me brunch tomorrow. Be my sounding board for the idea I was toying with when I banged into you."

Sutton opened her mouth to say she could sort herself out, but a yawn came out instead. "I might have to take you up on that."

Laila grabbed a notepad and scribbled something down using a pen with a fluffy pom-pom atop. "I know Barry, the owner of a local B&B. Between us, I'm his secret supply of Minotaur romances, so he'll never do me wrong."

Sutton looked to the notepaper. "The Grape Escape?"

Laila's lip curled. "I know. It's an epidemic."

Sutton looked around. "What have you called this place?"

Laila, phone now to her ear, smiled irreverently. "Well,

has that been an adventure. I believe I've chosen the perfect name—with a wink to wine, which the local establishment all but insists on—but they do not agree."

"The local establishment?"

"This town is run by a single family. I've been here three months now and their *representative* has popped in at least twice a week since, ostensibly to check if I am a happy little renter, while offering alternatives such as Pages and Pinot. Romance and Riesling." She rolled her eyes at both.

"As opposed to…"

Laila held up a finger. "Barry!" she said into the phone. "It's Laila from Forbidden Fruits."

Sutton laughed. Yeah, she could see how the Swirl & Purl Craft Corner crowd might not be au fait with that one. Less than half a day and this place was already turning out to be all kinds of fun.

When a minute later, Sutton was assured she had a room as long as she needed it, she wondered if she should buy something, to pay Laila back for the favour. Slightly terrified she might then read something she could never unsee, she said, "How does late lunch sound, in case I sleep through brunch? My treat."

"That'll work."

Picturing the bakery with the great-looking meat pies, the lovely café with the mouthwatering pastries, Sutton found herself saying, "I had pretty great coffee just now, at the pub up the road. The Vine and Stein?"

Something flashed across Laila's eyes before she said, "Sure. Why not?"

"Okay." Then, as she reached the door, Sutton turned back. "Laila?"

Laila, who had already opened a book with a man covered in green fur on the cover and started reading, looked up. "Hmm?"

"Have a list of alternative names at the ready, for when the 'establishment' next comes around."

"Such as?"

Sutton, who'd had a lot of experience helping her clients settle on band names over the years, had a quick think and suggested, "Kink and Cabernet?"

Laila barked out a laugh, then, eyes twinkling, grabbed pen and paper, writing madly as Sutton went out the door.

A half hour later, Sutton dragged her suitcase into the attic room of the Grape Escape.

"This suffice?" asked Barry, thin moustache twitching, as if the fact she was an acquaintance of Laila's meant she might take off with his candlesticks.

The roof was so slanted she had to duck. The bedspread was covered in big pink cabbage roses. The wallpaper was so fussy it made her feel a little dizzy. And she'd probably not have noticed the Minotaur lamp if not for Laila's inside info.

"It's perfect," she assured him. "Truly. I'm all appreciation."

Barry blushed red. Then, bowing slightly, backed away. "Breakfast is six till eight every day, bar Tuesdays. Fresh towels and bedding twice a week. We can organise any number of winery tours at reception."

"I'm not really a wine drinker, but thank you."

At that, Barry's eyebrows disappeared into his hairline.

Then he left her to fall face down on the softest bed that ever existed.

A minute later, after marvelling that she was really there, in Vermillion, Sutton was fast asleep.

CHAPTER TWO

THE NEXT MORNING, Dante was at the bar trying to make sense of the Vine's internet banking, when he heard the front door bump, a half hour before opening time.

He braced, bodily, blood thickening in his veins.

Only instead of a British brunette sidling inside, smiling at him in a way that made him feel an urge to bare his teeth, a big guy in a dirty emergency services uniform sauntered in, strode to the bar, and straddled a stool.

Dante shoved his phone into his back pocket, grabbed a bar towel, and set to wiping down the bench as if punishing the thing. When the customer reached over the counter to grab a donut from beneath the glass cloche, Dante took some solace in smacking the guy's hand with a precise whip of the towel.

"Seriously?" cried Nico, Dante's cousin, cradling his hand, while looking as if he was about to leap over the bar and wrestle Dante to the ground. Then, realising they were no longer eight years old, Nico went for the donut again instead.

This time Dante let him.

The donuts, and the building in which they resided, belonged to the man after all. The Australian contingent of the Rossi clan owning the Vermillion Hill vineyard and most of Main Street too.

"Where's Chrissy?" Nico asked around a mouthful of pink icing and sprinkles. Then he winced as he lifted the donut to his mouth again.

"Apparently her pet parrot is sick," said Dante, watching his cousin carefully now.

"Chappell or Sabrina?" Nico asked.

Dante hoped his flat stare made it clear he neither knew nor cared. Then when Nico winced again, hissing as he gently rolled his shoulder, Dante asked, "What is wrong?"

"Hmm?"

Dante motioned to Nico's uniform, not liking how beat up it looked. Or the scent of ash Nico brought in with him. Dante had hoped the years he'd spent away from family had inured him to worrying about them, yet his voice was rough as he asked, "Where were you just now? Someplace dangerous? Are you *hurt*?"

Nico cricked his neck. "Nope. Just training."

Dante's hackles shifted from high to medium alert.

His cousin had entertained a knight-in-shining-armour complex since the first time they'd watched *Superman* together as kids. Dante must have been eight, or nine. Nico, a couple of years younger, made a cape out of a tea towel, climbed atop a shed, and tried to fly.

Dante remembered the aftermath—Zia Celia, with Aurora a babe in arms, running after him, screaming, even though Nico had landed in a crouch, then bolted, not a scratch on him. While Isabella—three then, or four—had jumped up and down, cheering him on...

The moment Isabella appeared in his mind's eye, Dante shut the memory down. Before it took him down. Gripping the bar, he wondered what his aunt had been thinking, begging him to leave his sanctuary. What had he been thinking, agreeing?

"Kent!" Nico called, waving a second donut at the bartender, who was chatting up the builder who'd come in early that morning to remove the old cash register.

Kent looked up, smiled, flushed, fixed his hair, and said, "Hey, Nico."

Nico, clearly used to flustering people simply by existing, smiled and asked, "Coffee?"

"Too early, sorry," Kent called back, before glancing at Dante, his smile dropping.

"That your doing?" Nico asked Dante.

"Kent's quivering?"

Nico laughed. "I meant the coffee. But sure. Let's go with that. Do you always have to be such a surly bastard?"

"Not a case of 'having to be,'" said Dante. "More…preference."

Nico laughed again, only this time on the back of it came a frown. His mouth opened as if about to say more, but then a look came over his face.

The look, Dante called it. The one that told him the exact moment people remembered why he was irascible, how he'd done his best to survive the events that had led to it. Then decided it was best to pretend "the look" hadn't happened at all.

The truth of it was, he was fine with opening the Vine earlier. It could do with a portion of the flourishing Main Street bakery and café crowd. Only Zia Celia had shut the idea down. Cannibalising other businesses who paid them rent apparently not an option.

For someone who had rung him in tears a month ago, begging for his assistance, lest the entire family business collapse, she had plenty of decided opinions now.

"If you disagree with my methods," said Dante, taking a step back, "you're welcome to take my place."

"Ah, no. As you can imagine, I have been forced to work in every part of the family business since birth. We agree my skills are better served elsewhere." With that, Nico swallowed the last mouthful of donut, wiped his hand across the back of his mouth, and stood. "On that note, I am off to see if our tenants need anything fixed, loosened, collected from a high shelf. No rest for the sainted."

With a wide toothy grin, Nico strode to the door, stopping to hold it open when a herd of grey-haired gents wandered inside. He bounced on the spot, a mass of restrained energy, even as he happily chatted to each and every one.

Dante was eighteen months older than Nico, but in that moment it felt like eighteen years; his bones brittle, muscles hardened, mind fractured with bitterness.

Then, Nico looked back at him, clicked his fingers and said, "Hey, did you see the brunette who breezed into town yesterday?"

And Dante's next breath in came quick and sharp.

"Female," Nico, oblivious, went on. "Mid to late twenties. Rented gas-guzzler. Dark sunglasses, dressed all in black. I saw her when I was cruising past Forbidden Fruits."

"Forbidden Fruits?" asked Dante, finally finding his tongue.

Nico's brow lowered, his voice with it. "The R-rated book-store down the road."

"There's an R-rated bookstore down the road?" one of the older men asked, and the rest stopped and turned.

"Well, not R-rated, exactly," Nico said, looking to Dante for help.

Dante figured he was giving Nico's family more than enough help, so he crossed his arms, and motioned for Nico to go on.

"More *adult*," Nico explained, looking pained. "Spicy, lovey-dovey stuff. Place looks like rainbows and unicorns on the outside but is filled with stories that'd set your hair on fire."

Dante was about to ask how Nico knew what kind of stories they sold, when every one of the older men turned and walked back out the door.

"Wait. Come back!" Nico deplored. "That wasn't an advertisement."

Dante coughed. "Don't need a lack of morning coffee to keep people away, you're doing just fine on your own."

Nico flipped Dante an internationally recognisable hand signal.

When his cousin made to leave, Dante found himself calling out, "So, what did this brunette do? Jaywalk? Murder for hire? Drink an open bottle of non-Vermillion Hill wine in the street?"

Nico rolled his shoulder once more. "Nothing. Yet. Only she and the bookstore owner seemed awfully chummy. In cahoots."

"*Casa è* 'cahoots'?"

"Ah, *combutta*," Nico translated. "*In collusione.* I smell trouble."

Trouble, Dante thought. "Lot of passers-through. Probably long gone by now."

"Probably," Nico agreed, then with a wave over his shoulder, he left.

Only for Sutton Mayberry to walk through the front door of the Vine and Stein not five minutes later.

Her hair was up this time, in a messy bundle atop her head. Her jeans were ripped at the knees, and an oversize Pogues T-shirt and fluffy black cardigan half fell off one shoulder. She was well rumpled, like an unmade bed.

Imagining this woman in bed was enough to set off the claxon inside his head.

Then she looked up, her eyes catching on his. They brightened before a smile followed. Her shoulders lifted in a manner that Dante read, in some deep-down place inside, as delight. Upon spying him.

Dante considered calling Nico, hauling him back so that he might tell this woman the town wasn't big enough for the both of them.

"Hey," said Sutton, pointing at him as if they were old friends.

"Good morning," he said, pointedly, keeping his gaze level, even when her cardigan slipped at her shoulder again.

"I'm not that early, am I?" she asked as she plopped onto a stool, all long limbs and strangely compelling grace.

"You are," he grouched. Even though he'd had staff set the tables already that day. "What's your excuse?"

"Excuse?" She blinked at him, pink sweeping into her cheeks, as if caught.

Dante pointed to the Wi-Fi sign.

She laughed softly. "Ah, yes. Actually, I was hoping I might be able to set myself up at that table back there again. Only if I'm not in the way. This time I'm paying for the coffee. And one of those donuts would be fabulous."

Dante made to move. Only Kent swept past him, winking as he said, "Stay, keep chatting. I've got this."

"I love super-hot," Sutton said to Kent. "And bitter."

"Amen," said Kent, who kept his head down when Dante shot him a look.

When his gaze once again met Sutton's, her warm eyes smiling up at him, Dante felt as if the floor tipped under him. He pressed his boots harder into the ground and commanded himself to get a grip.

"The B&B is far too quiet to get any work done," said Sutton, leaning on the bar. "I prefer bustle, white noise. I get antsy when it's too quiet. Don't you?"

Dante loved the quiet. Olympic-level quiet. In low season, he'd been known to go days without hearing a voice, not even his own.

Yet, he found himself asking, "So, you *are* staying in town, then?"

She tilted her head in question.

And Dante realised he'd spoken as if she'd been in on Nico's conversation. "We... I assumed you were passing through," he adjusted. Only making it *clear* he'd been thinking of her. Which he had. More than was in any way rational.

A soft smile curled about her lips, before she looked down at her hands, then back up again. "Nope," she said with a shrug. "I'm staying. For a bit. I've taken a room over at the Grape Escape."

Dante nodded, as if he had a clue where that was. He'd worn a path from Vermillion Hill to the Vine and Stein and back again. Seeing no need to venture beyond that route. The sooner he found an answer as to how to make this great white elephant profitable, he'd be on a plane home.

"It is nice there?" he asked, when the alternative was allowing the silence to stretch like a bubble around them.

A sound came from the other end of the bar, where Kent was hovering by the coffee machine as it warmed itself up. A sorry, snorting sound.

"Oh, it's darling," said Sutton, clearly unworried by any of it. "The roof is gabled, so I have to duck if I get too close to the walls. The wallpaper has teeny-tiny grape vines with deer and hedgehogs and rabbits hiding in among the leaves. I've never seen so many scatter cushions in one building, much less one room. But the bed is like a cloud. And the pillows—"

She brought her fingers to her mouth, and sent a kiss into the ether to punctuate her delight.

As Dante's gaze stayed, stuck, on her pouting mouth, a buzzing sound began in the back of his head. When he lifted his gaze, it was to find her eyes on his, the pink in her cheeks a deep rose.

"Anyway," she said, clearing her throat, "*this* place is much more my scene."

"This place?"

She motioned around her.

Dante struggled to believe the Vine with its dark dusty corners, and excess of space, could be anyone's "scene."

"Why is that?" he asked. It was, after all, his duty to wrangle it into profit. Since his suggestions kept getting blowback, outside opinions could not hurt.

"Lots of reasons," she said with a slight shrug, enough that her cardigan slid slowly off her shoulder once more. "The high ceilings. Those gorgeous windows. The great coffee. The potential. I manage indie bands, back in London, so dark and shady, with a dollop of poetic tragedy, is my jam."

She hitched her cardigan sleeve, when it reached her elbow. The roll of her shoulder, the slow stroke of her fingers up her arm so inadvertently sensual Dante pressed his nails into his palms.

"I also love the feeling that if I take up a table for a couple of hours, I won't be in the way." She said that with a cheeky smile.

Dante grunted in agreement.

"That's a yes?" she asked, sitting taller.

"That table is yours."

"Great!" she said. "Great. Um, should I head over now, or wait here for the coffee and donut—?"

"Go," Dante asserted. "Kent will bring it over."

Kent looked up from the cloche, where he was scooping a donut onto a plate using the supplied tongs. "Are you sure? You can— Nope, seems that's my duty. Hi, I'm Kent."

"Sutton," said Sutton, lifting out of the chair to reach over and shake Kent's hand. "And this time, I'm paying."

Only when Sutton shot them both a smile, then left the bar to make her way to her table did Kent ask, "This time?"

"Long story."

Kent crossed his arms. "I have nothing but time."

Dante's returning look had Kent leaping back to work.

Dante remained behind the counter as Kent delivered Sutton's order. He watched the weak morning sunlight slanting through the large window, raining over Sutton's open laptop, the papers she had stacked on the chair beside her, the wide smile she gave Kent as he slid her plate onto the table, the way she leaned forward sniffing the coffee and grinning.

When his belly contracted with a strange kind of ache, Dante turned away. Once Kent was back behind the counter, he removed himself to the office, where he stayed for the rest of the morning.

It had taken Sutton a minute to remember where she was when she'd woken that morning. Not unusual, considering the number of nights she'd spent in motels, on tour buses, friends of friends' couches.

She'd spotted the brochures on her side table—historical tours, winery visits, forest walks—but it was the Minotaur lamp that had made it all come back to her.

Now, two coffees and two amazing donuts in, she found herself wondering which of the things in the brochures her parents had done together. Had they held hands while walking down Main Street? Made out in the back row of the cinema? Gotten lost together on the way to some waterfall?

Her belly tugged at the thought, only she wasn't sure if it was a *want* to know which of those might be true, or *want*, period.

She'd had relationships, just never *that* kind—all-romance, all-consuming. Far too busy enjoying other big experiences life had to offer. For what if she was anything like her father, and something went wrong…

She shook her head and went back to her laptop. She was making headway on the European summer tour she'd been finagling for the Sweety Pies, a jazz-funk trio she'd discovered a few years before. The logistics of keeping her bands relevant or, better yet, flourishing, kept her more than busy enough.

And boy did Sutton love being busy. No time to think too far into the future when one had to hustle, every single day.

She reached for her coffee. Made and delivered by Kent of the man bun, it was fine, but not quite hot or bitter enough. The one the other guy had made the day before had been far better.

The other guy. Grumpy Bartender.

She couldn't keep calling him that, not if she planned to come in here every day. His name was probably something classic, strong. Giovanni. Or Massimo. Or something deeply poetic, like Romeo. Or...

When her phone—with new Australian sim card installed—rang, Sutton was glad of the distraction.

"Hey!" said Bianca, lead singer of the Magnolia Blossoms—the first band Sutton had ever signed, back when she'd been a restless law student who'd grown up listening to her dad's beloved vinyl collection.

They were also the only one of those early bands she still represented. As great as she was at spotting potential, she was aware of her limitations. As a single-person management team, she was more than happy for them to migrate to larger management groups if they outgrew her. When a tour, or a show, was over, so many of the crew went their separate ways—moving on was a part of the gig.

"Where are you?" Sutton asked, trying to pin the source of the raucous music in the background.

"A punk joint in Leidseplein. Zhou's in the mosh pit. It's chaos!"

Sutton could picture it all too well. After several weeks spent touring small towns throughout Germany and Belgium, the Magnolia Blossoms were spending their autumn in Amsterdam, immersing themselves in the local scene, working on an album, and playing a spate of intimate club shows to test out new sounds.

The rare gap in Sutton's schedule had felt like another

sign it was the exact right time for her to finally make the trip to Vermillion.

"So, is wine country adorable as all heck?" Bianca shouted. "Or are you bored out of your mind yet?"

"It's so sweet I'm in constant danger of getting a tooth-ache!" Sutton shouted back, then mouthed an apology when customers a couple of tables over looked her way. Taking her voice down a notch, she said, "Though so far I've spent most of my time in the local pub."

"Naturally. Describe it to me." Bianca was a dedicated aficionado of great venues.

"It's quite a beautiful building, actually. No stage, alas. Kind of feels a little neglected." Sutton looked up, past the heads of the lunchtime crowd starting to fill the tables nearer the bar, to find the Grumpy Bartender was yet to reappear. "There's this bartender—"

"*Now* we're getting somewhere."

"I was going to say he makes great coffee."

"Honey, we've known enough bartenders in our time to know it's never about how well they pour drinks."

Bianca had a point. Bartenders were often consummate flirts, but the hulking Italian was not of that ilk. In fact, she couldn't quite pin what ilk he was. She'd always been a fast judge of character, had to be in order to keep up with the flimflam she dealt with in her line of work, but he was hard to pin down.

Not that she wanted to pin him, down or otherwise.

"This bartender makes superb coffee and is a total grouch," she blurted as she tried to wipe *that* image out of her mind.

"Sutton's got a cru-ush!"

"Please," she said, but it was a half-hearted effort. "The man looks at me like he's wondering what I taste like."

A beat later, Bianca made a choking sound. Then Sutton

heard her yell, relaying the information to someone nearby in a very loud voice.

"Gimme the phone," a new voice said. Francie, the Magnolia Blossoms' bass player. "Was there a piano involved when this tasting occurred? I always love a piano scene."

"What? No!" Realising she was all but shouting again, Sutton ducked her head and pressed her mouth to the phone. "I meant in a big bad wolf kind of way. And there's no piano here that I can see."

Though one would fit nicely in the back corner, she thought.

She really should cool it with the fairy tale angle. Her parents had been all about that—eyes meeting across a crowded room, et cetera. And while for her father, being so drawn to her mother was a highlight of his life, Sutton couldn't see how it was worth the pain of what came after.

Not that she was *drawn to* the Grumpy Bartender. Except, considering how much bandwidth she'd given the man, maybe she sort of was.

If something romantically inclined *were* to happen to her while she was in the town in which her parents had fallen in love, was that an objectively bad thing? Or the perfect place to open herself up to the one great adventure she'd steadfastly avoided thus far?

The thing was, while she'd found herself thinking about his large hands, and rough stubble, he'd neither said nor done a single thing to make her think such thoughts went both ways.

Flattened by that realisation, Sutton said, "Now the club, the Liefdescafé—are you happy with the setup? Anything you need me to manage?"

Bianca gave Sutton the rundown of the series of shows they'd contracted to play in a fabulously cool club on the bank of the Amstel over the northern autumn. Only Sutton found herself listening with half an ear as Grumpy Bartender appeared behind the bar.

Kent of the man bun and the blue-haired pixie with the undercut and sleeve tattoos listened intently as his hands cut through the air in that elegantly expressive manner Italians seemed to be born with.

"Have you told your dad where you are yet?"

Sutton blinked back into her conversation. Bianca had met her dad, adored her dad, and understood the complication. "Not yet."

"Just tell him you've met a grumpy bartender who works in a run-down bar but owns no piano. He'll be on cloud nine."

Sutton let her face fall into her hand, as she pictured her father with a hopeful smile on his face. He was so proud of her work, but didn't understand that looking for "the one" had never been her driving force. She could hardly tell him he was the reason why.

Just then, Sutton spied a familiar blonde in a poison-green '50s sundress hovering near the Vine's front door. Laila of the spicy fairy bookstore. Laila to whom she'd promised to buy lunch.

"Bianca," said Sutton, pushing back her chair. "I have to go. Liefdescafé follow-up tomorrow, okay?"

Hand over her eyes as if she was squinting into the abyss, Laila spotted Sutton, waved, then made a beeline.

Bianca rang off as Laila reached the table. After air kisses, and hellos, Laila sat down, dumped the book she'd been carrying on the table. Sutton side-eyed the muscular half man, half bear clinging to a lithe young woman in a torn dress on the cover, while Laila looked around as if waiting for the boogeyman to jump out from behind a table.

"So," said Laila without preamble, "you know the man who has been trying to make me change the name of my store? He came into Forbidden Fruits this morning, with another 'perfect alternative' for the name of my haven for women who own their desires. Wait for it." Laila held up both hands. "Stories with a Side of Shiraz."

Sutton coughed out a laugh.

"I'd like to give him a 'side of shiraz,'" Laila muttered. Then, "Anyway, his name is Niccolo Rossi. The Rossi family own this place, as well as the vineyard up on the hill. They own the entire town, practically. The punny shop names is *their* thing—a way to create a point of difference from the high-tech grape regions nearby, the German strongholds, and the venerable old-money labels."

"Sounds positively feudal."

"Right? A grape is a grape is a grape as far as I'm concerned. A cocktail, on the other hand, now that's something worth crowing about."

"Fair," said Sutton. "But you have to admit this building is pretty wonderful. So atmospheric. The architectural detail is gorgeous."

Laila looked around. "Agree to disagree. Now, who do I have to do to get a coffee around here?"

Sutton's gaze went straight to the bar. Only to find Grumpy Bartender watching her. Even when he shifted and looked away almost instantly, she felt the touch of his gaze like a sunburn.

"Ah," said Laila, twisting on the chair. "The 'architectural detail.' Now I get it."

Laila held up a hand, miming a request for a menu, then turned back to Sutton. "Now, before the hot woodchopper lumbers over here, let's get straight to it. I prefer keeping my 'back in ten minutes' sign up at the bookshop for half an hour, max."

"Okay," said Sutton, along for the ride now. Especially if the universe was about to put some new venture in her path. "Let's."

Laila sat forward, holding Sutton's gaze as if about to give her the answer to life, the universe, and everything. "We had not known one another five minutes before you told me three things—you had come halfway across the world, you were single, and this was where your parents met and fell in love."

Sutton was pretty sure she'd said other things too, but Laila was clearly following a thought.

"I believe," said Laila, "that's because you are hoping lightning will strike in the same place twice."

"By lightning you mean…?"

"Love lightning!" Laila said, her expression making it clear Sutton was acting dim. "You are craving it. I can see it written all over your face."

Sutton placed both hands on her cheeks. While *craving* was a strong word, she couldn't help remembering the strange sense of longing she'd felt, imagining her parents walking the same footsteps. Together.

"*This* is where it's going to happen for you, Sutton. I can feel it." Laila looked around, and shuddered. "Well, maybe not *this* place, but this general geographical area."

Sutton knew she could shoot down Laila's theory—claim nostalgia, a love of adventure, any number of excuses for making the trip. But what if that's all they were—excuses?

The ticking clock, her mother's age when she'd died, her lifelong desire to squeeze every ounce out of the opportunities her life gave her—that *had* led her to this place. Stuck with the truth that the only one of life's greatest adventures that she'd deliberately avoided was opening herself up to the possibility of falling in love.

Belly filled with butterflies, Sutton shuffled to the front of her chair, and kept her voice low. "Could you really see all that in me?"

Laila smiled. "Honey, however many romance novels you

think I've read in my lifetime, triple it. The signs are all there. The stars have aligned. Consider me your fairy godmother."

"So, what are you suggesting I do about this...this love lightning?" Sutton asked, right as a shadow fell over the table.

She looked up to find the Grumpy Bartender looming over them, holding a pair of menus. He refused to meet her eye, as if he'd heard every word of her last sentence.

"Why, hello," Laila said, holding out a hand, palm down, as if waiting for the thing to be kissed. "I'm Laila Vale. And who might you be?"

Grumpy Bartender's right eyebrow flickered north. "Dante," he said in that deep rough burr of a voice. "Dante Rossi."

So, his name is Dante, Sutton thought. Then, *Of course it is*.

"You're a Rossi?" said Laila, pulling back her hand. "Related to *Niccolo*, I presume? Yes, I see it now. In the eyes. The stubborn jawline. The air of entitlement."

Lines formed around Dante's warm brown eyes and for a second Sutton thought he might actually smile. In the end he merely huffed out a hard-done-by sigh. "Nico is my cousin," he said. "Younger. Do not hold it against me."

Laila perked up. "I'll consider it." Then she held up a finger as she looked at the menu.

When Dante the Grumpy Bartender waited, impatience rolling from him like a fog, and still he did not look her way, Sutton might have felt miffed, if not for the chance it gave her to take him in.

With the sunlight slanting over half his face, he looked like something out of a Michelangelo painting. If he lost the flannel button-down shirt, and dark jeans, that was. Not that Sutton was picturing how he might look minus shirt and jeans. Only now that she'd thought it, she was. In rather impressive detail. She imagined he'd be hard, beneath the clothes, bulky, all slabs of muscle, enough that she was left feeling hot and sparky and all kinds of upended.

"Flat white," said Laila, eventually. "Drizzle of caramel, whipped cream on top." She held out her menu and Dante took it.

Sutton opened her mouth to quickly request coffee number three.

Only for Dante to say, "Yet another espresso for you?"

The fact that he still did not look her way set something off inside her. "That all depends."

And Dante's gaze finally slid to hers. If she thought she'd felt a case of sunburn earlier, it was nothing compared with the heat that crawled into her face in that moment.

"On?" he asked, somehow making the word last longer than it had any right to last.

She leaned forward, resting her chin in her palm, and said, "Who's making it?"

His brow knitted, all "bear disturbed in the middle of a long winter sleep." Then he flicked his hair from his face, in a way that deserved to be in slow mo. "Would you care to put in a request?"

"Kent tried, twice. But they had nothing on the one you made for me yesterday."

Dante tucked the menu beneath his arm, and turned to face her more fully. "You are ruining your taste buds, you know."

"Lucky for me, they're mine to ruin."

The deep frown was back, the one that said "I am here under protest." Only this time she swore she saw a spark in his eyes. Heat. The thrill of the battle.

When he turned to leave, she found herself saying, "Thanks, Dante."

He paused, emitted a sound much like a growl, then stalked away.

It wasn't until he had made it all the way back behind the

bar, where he ignored someone asking for assistance, instead moving straight to the coffee machine, that Laila spoke up.

"Pass me a fan, because what was *that*?"

"That was *Dante*," Sutton said on an outshot of breath.

"Oh, no," Laila said, eyes bright, "that was a whole lot of hot, yearning, deeply delicious flirtation, threatening to set this place alight."

Sutton blinked, then reached over and picked up Laila's book. "I think you've read too many romance novels."

"There is no such thing as too many romance novels," Laila assured her. "Now, if you're sure you've not already been struck—"

Sutton shook her head, heartily enough that Laila stopped midsentence. And Laila kindly didn't make some comment about her protesting too much.

"Okay, then. Back to Mission: Find Sutton's Love Lightning."

"Ironic, I know, but any chance we can change the name?"

"Fine. But no wine puns."

"Deal. So, where do you imagine we start?"

"We start by hosting the biggest singles night this PG town has ever seen!"

CHAPTER THREE

"A SINGLES NIGHT," Sutton repeated, feeling a flicker of excitement. Or was it dread?

"It is literally the best idea I've had in ages," Laila gushed. "And that's saying something. You will find the perfect someone with whom to embark on a grand love affair. I will expand my mailing list. Win-win."

Sutton laughed. "You're not doing this for your *mailing list*."

"I'm a single business owner. Don't mock the mailing list."

Sutton gave her a look.

"Fine." Laila's shoulders slumped. "I'm not a complete mercenary. I'm relatively new to this town and while the business is going pretty great, meeting other locals, my age, with similar interests, would be nice."

That Sutton understood. "I'm in!" she said. "If only to help you make friends."

Laila poked out her tongue, then realised Sutton had agreed to her plan. "Oh, my gosh! We're doing this!"

Laila went on to talk crowd—half her customers were tourists, a good portion regular visitors from Adelaide way. "We are ripe with backpackers on working visas, and I imagine there are any number of lonely grape farmers...or whatever one calls them. As for location—I've considered hosting at Forbidden Fruits, but we are on the cosy side and I have no desire to have my wares pawed over by nonbelievers."

"What about here?" Sutton asked.

Laila screwed up her nose. "Very funny."

"I mean it," Sutton said, feeling definite excitement now. "Picture it, the tables all moved to the sides, opening up the centre for people to mill, gather, maybe even dance. Music playing from hidden speakers, warm faux candlelight everywhere glinting against the windows, the polished wood floor. I wonder if we can get them to drop the chandeliers, all tucked up into that high ceiling."

Sutton again imagined a stage at the far end of the space. There'd be room behind for storage and green rooms. Speakers and lighting rigs above. The roof was high enough they could easily add a mezzanine...

Okay, so not *now*. But it was something the place should consider.

"Lean into the dark and seedy?" said Laila. "It would add a certain edge to the event. In fact, it could be kind of fabulous. Okay, I'll take charge of the invites, and since you're friendly with management, you can look after logistics."

Sutton came back into her own body with a *phwump*. "Friendly? I wouldn't go that far."

Laila grinned. "Friendly/circling one another with lust in your eyes. Tom-ay-to tom-ah-to." Then, "Of course, if you're hesitating because you already have your eye on a certain lumberjack, then—"

"No," Sutton said. "I don't. It's not... It's fine."

Laila leaned forward, her cool hand wrapping around Sutton's warm one. "You are about to meet the man of your dreams. I will make a million new friends. If not, then at least we can both score great shags we can look back on in our old age with fondness."

And that was when Kent appeared then with their coffees. He placed Laila's down first, a grin hovering at the corner of his mouth.

"You know what?" said Laila, looking at her phone. "I'm going to have to take this to go."

Kent looked at the fancy swirl of whipped cream atop the thing, imagining getting it into a takeaway cup, and winced.

"It all looks the same once it hits your belly," said Laila, gathering her things. "Lock this place in, Sutton. No time to lose. This is going to be the wildest thing this town has seen in years."

"Wildest thing?" Kent asked, watching Laila sashay toward the bar with her mug.

"It seems we are hosting a singles night," Sutton said.

"Where and when?"

"Soon. We're hoping here."

Kent's smile dropped. "Good luck with *that*. Then again..." He glanced over his shoulder before putting Sutton's coffee in front of her. "He did make your coffee twice, to make sure he got it just right."

"He..." Sutton looked up to find Dante behind the bar. "He did not."

"Cross my heart," Kent sing-songed as he backed away. "Get this thing off the ground and count me in."

Sutton could only offer a quick thumbs-up.

It was a little over twenty-four hours since she'd arrived in Vermillion, and she'd been assured of a "grand love affair" if not love lightning. While it all sounded fantastical the moment she wasn't caught up in Laila's vortex, now that it was out there, in the universe, she could feel the pull of it, tugging her in that direction.

She hadn't realised she was staring into the middle distance until her focus cleared to find Dante watching her, again.

She lifted his coffee to her mouth, took a sip, found the flavour strong, lush, just on the verge of hot, but not enough to sear. It was gorgeous.

Dante cocked his head in question.

Sutton smiled, and mouthed, *Perfect*.

Dante nodded. Then for the longest of moments, they simply looked at one another.

When someone stepped up to the bar, and eye contact was lost, Sutton slumped back in her chair. That man was most definitely not on her list of possibilities—she was considering dipping a toe into romantic waters, not diving off a cliff.

Dante lay on the couch in Chrissy's office, eyes closed, feet hanging off the edge. Dean Martin crooned softly from a record player atop the filing cabinet, as Dante attempted to give his mind a five-minute reprieve.

He'd been in Vermillion for over two weeks, and the light still felt wrong, the air smelled different, the tap water tasted strange. Sleep had been hard to come by. And whatever bad thoughts might plague a person in daylight, without distraction they only came back louder at night.

He shifted so that his shoulders found a slightly less uncomfortable spot, breathed out, breathed in, long and slow, an approach to quieting the mind he'd found online late one night. Thankfully, the clouds of rest began to infuse the edges of his vision—

"Oh, sorry," a voice cut through the fog.

Dante opened his eyes. Slowly. Moving the arm over his eyes to cradle his head, he looked to find Sutton Mayberry standing in the office doorway.

As ever, the mere sight of her did something to him. Her loveliness, her *vitalità*, the fact she kept showing up—whatever it was, strong, physical reactions stirred in him when she was near. He fought them, gamely, as one song ended, the needle sliding into a groove between songs, and another began.

"Can I help you?" Dante asked, expecting she'd taken a wrong turn.

"I… Chrissy sent me back here."

Did she, now? The fact that he'd given Chrissy an official warning for arriving late, again, that morning a likely cause.

With a groan, Dante curled himself to sitting, then reached over to turn off the record player. The sudden silence in the room felt heavy, weighted, as if without it there was no masking the tension between them.

When he looked up, it was to find she'd not moved. In fact, she was white-knuckling the doorjamb, her gaze zeroed in on his chest.

He looked down. Ah, the bright purple T-shirt sporting the Vine and Stein logo into which he'd been forced to change, after one of the kitchen staff had walked through the wrong kitchen swing door, running smack bang into him, planting a plate of pasta to his chest. His backup shirt having been utilized the day before, he'd had no choice but to rummage through an old box of uniforms he'd found in the corner. The thing was a good two sizes too small.

Running a hand through his hair, he looked up again to find Sutton still staring. And something came over him, some gremlin making him sit a little taller, roll his shoulders. He might even have flexed, just a smidge.

Her mouth popped open on an outshot of breath. Which told him all he needed to know, and far more than he wanted to. Which was that this tension, this wild energy he felt in her presence, was not only on him.

"Sutton," he growled.

She blinked, furiously, her gaze lifting guilty to his. "Sorry, you were clearly taking a break. I'll come back later."

"No," he said. No point now. He went to ask again what she wanted, when the office landline rang. He waited for someone out front to pick it up. And waited.

"Scusi," he apologised, then, standing, picked up the phone and barked, *"Pronto."*

"Dante! So nice to hear your lovely voice," his aunt cooed with beautifully couched sarcasm, before tripping into instant Italian. She asked after his day, asked if he'd seen Niccolo, told him Zia Carlotta, in Sicily, a relation he'd never heard of, had come through her operation. She chatted as if this was how things had always been. As if he'd not been a family pariah for over a decade.

This he noted absently, distracted as he was by the sight of Sutton now moving about the space. Her fingers running over open boxes of cardboard cups, teetering piles of napkins, she paused at the box of purple Vine and Stein shirts, then moved to glance over the swathes of paper on the desk.

She stopped in front of the wall covered in old band flyers, Post-it notes so ancient they were curling at the corners, and the large, framed aerial photograph of Vigna dell'Essenza, the very first Rossi family vineyard, where he and Isabella had grown up.

When she moved past it, Dante let out a ragged breath.

When she reached the record player, she looked to him, asked with her eyes if she could start it up again. He nodded, and Dean was back.

She flicked through the box of old vinyls—all Italian, or Italian-adjacent. She pulled one from the box, gaze roving over the old-fashioned font and imagery. Her bottom lip, he noted, was slightly fuller than the top. Her nose had a slight bump on the end. Her hair was a sun-kissed dark brown.

He wondered if the monastic silence had not been safer than having "Memories Are Made of This" as the soundtrack to his wayward thoughts.

"Dante!" his aunt chided, as if it wasn't the first time she'd said his name.

"Si."

Then, in English, "Are you the one with the mushroom allergy?"

"No," he said. "That was Isabella."

The moment the words were out of his mouth his aunt made a sound, a kind of gasp and gulp in one. A sound that had haunted him enough that he'd left his entire family behind so that he'd not have to hear it again.

"No matter. *Non ci sarò per cena*," he said. He would not be back for dinner. For he would not walk through the door and see the apology, the agony, in his aunt's face.

"I must get back to work. *Ciao*," he said, then hung up the phone.

Pulse thudding behind his ears, he placed the phone in the cradle, and rubbed both hands over his face, before delving them into his hair. When he looked up, Sutton was watching him, her expression curious. Concerned.

Blood up, he snarled, "Why did Chrissy send you back here?"

"Because I asked where you were," she shot back, as if she'd felt the chill in the air and refused to let him turn it on her.

She slid the record back into the box, then leaned back against the filing cabinet, crossing her arms. "Where *will* you be?"

"Scusi?"

"You told your…your friend that you won't be home for dinner."

"Not *home*," he said. Home was a long way away. "I told my *aunt*, to whom I was speaking, I won't be eating at hers tonight." Then, "You speak Italian?"

"Un po'," she said, holding two fingers close together. "I'm a band manager, so lots of back-road European tours. Small venues in out-of-the-way towns where not everyone is able, or willing, to speak English. One of my bass players— Francie from the Magnolia Blossoms—is from Positano, so we've toured Italy quite a bit."

"What does a band manager do?" he asked, glad to move the subject on.

"Different things on different days. Line up gigs, marketing, negotiating contracts, schmoozing, strong-arming bar managers." She shot him a quick smile. "I can be very persuasive on that score."

As he well knew. "And you can do all that," he asked, "from a table by the window?"

"I can do it anywhere."

Her eyes flickered as the accidental double entendre bounced between them, and something dark shifted beneath Dante's sternum. Like a great dragon that had lain slumbering through a century-long winter, wakening after a deep sleep.

Yet rather than end this—for the longer she stayed, the more things she touched, the more of her energy, her scent, she would leave behind—he found himself saying: "You do know that nobody is actually *from* Positano."

Sutton blinked, then burst into laughter. The sound husky, bringing with it a wide smile that sparked glints in her night-dark eyes. "That's gold. I've met Francie's family, by the way, in their home, in Positano, but I am so saving that. It'll make her head explode. Are you from near there? Originally, I mean."

"Siena," he said, glancing at the framed photograph of Vigna dell'Essenza before he could stop himself. The hills, the driveway lined with pencil pines, the villa with its brick red roof—the likes of it could be found all over Italy. But this configuration any Rossi would recognise as theirs.

At the edge of the shot was the very tip of a dam. It was enough for Dante to look away.

"Now," he said, "my home is Montefalco, in Umbria."

"So, you don't live here, then? In Australia."

"I do not." He could have stopped there, but that face, those warm eyes compelled him to add, "I'm here helping family. Once my work is done, I will be gone."

Her brow knitted a moment, before she began moving about the room once more. "So, if you are not a South Australian pub manager, what is it that you do?"

"I make wine."

"Plenty of vineyards around here, I've noticed."

"Not like mine."

"How so?"

"Different grapes, different varietals, different history. Different seasons and soil, sunrises and sunsets, rainfall and timing. Different levels of management expertise."

"So, a grape is not simply a grape."

"A grape is not simple at all."

"No?" she said.

And if he was not so attuned to the slightest movements in her expression, he might have missed the teasing note in her eyes. Might not have felt the tap of it against his chest, and the warmth that spread from that point out to his very extremities.

Choosing to take her question at face value, he explained, "We grow several varietals at Sorello—my vineyard—the primary being the Sagrantino, a grape indigenous to the region. It flowers early, yet requires a long, hot season if it is to ripen as we'd like. Low-yielding, thick-skinned, broody, high tannins—picked too soon it leaves the mouth grippy, dry. Yet when nursed into perfect fruition, it yields the lushest inky, earthy, plummy delight."

Her tongue darted out to wet her lower lip before she dragged her teeth over the spot. "Sounds yummy."

"Yummy," he repeated, gaze caught on the sheen on that bottom lip. Plump, lovely. Off-limits.

"I can only assume so," she said, "since you looked like you were having a religious experience just now."

He looked up, humbled by what his expression must have given away.

"I'm not a wine drinker," she said with a shrug. "So, I wouldn't know."

Dante breathed out in relief. She'd been referring to his enthusiasm when talking about wine, not when his attention had been on her mouth. Only... Back up a moment.

"Did you just say you are *not a wine drinker*?"

"Yep."

He leaned against the back of the couch. "By that you mean you are no expert?"

"By that I mean I drink coffee. Lager, when out. Cocktails on occasion. I've tried wine, but to me it tastes kind of...sour."

Dante's hands lifted in the air before floating back to grip the chair. Such words from anyone else would feel like a knife to the heart, but the way the woman drank coffee, she clearly did not know what she was missing.

"I could change your mind," he said.

She looked over her shoulder, her gaze connecting with his. "My will is strong, and I know what I like."

The words *lasciami provare* tripped to the edge of his tongue. *Let me try.* He swallowed them back, teetering between knowing his limits and wanting things he simply could not have.

She held out her hands in surrender. "I'm sure your wine is amazing, in the grand scheme of wines. I can't imagine it would dare be anything less, with you in charge."

Dante bowed, accepting her words as true.

Then she smiled, nose scrunching up at the edges, lines fanning from the edges of her eyes. It looked so right on her it was clear she smiled a lot.

"Sutton," he said.

"Yes?" she said, adding "Dante," a beat later.

And the dragon inside him roared.

"Why did you come find me?" he asked.

Her eyes widened. "Right! I have a proposal for you. Well, for the manager of this place. Which I've just discovered is *not* you."

"It is not," he assured her. "And yet, propose away."

He folded his arms, noted the way her gaze dropped to his biceps, where the sleeve of the too-small T-shirt cut into his flesh. This time he did not flex. He was not Nico, prancing about like he was Prince of Vermillion. In fact, he could shake his cousin right about now, off as he was playing firefighter/cop/mayor/whatever fantasy he was living out rather than doing his duty by his family so that Dante could do as he pleased.

"Prepare yourself," said Sutton, hands out, as if readying to sell him something, "I do believe I have found a way to pay you back for letting me set up a work base here."

"I did not realise that is what I had done."

She waved a hand at him, as if he'd made a great joke. Then hit him with, "What do you say to the Vine and Stein hosting a singles night?"

"A what?"

"A singles night! An event where people who are unattached mingle and meet. Ticketed. Tickets get them entry, nibbles and first drink. Cash bar after that, of which we take a percentage. Or we take ticket sales, you take the booze. All negotiable. We hire a band—"

She seemed to check herself there. "You're not set up for a band. I can source a sound system. We play great music. Make it a Saturday night, seven till eleven. Long enough to pack them in, not so long you have to pay too much overtime."

"Overtime?"

"You'll *have* to put on extra staff."

"Whatever for?"

She looked at him as if wondering if he'd heard a word. "To cater for the customers. Who would come. To the singles night."

"Did you not say, yesterday, that you had not long arrived in the country? And you came up with this idea when?"

"My part in the planning has covered maybe the last hour, or two." Then, "The idea was Laila's—she runs Forbidden Fruits, the local bookstore, and has been thinking about it for some time."

Ah. The R-rated joint that had Nico all het up. The idea suddenly became all the more interesting. "Why?"

"Laila is certain it will drum up business for the entire strip."

"No. Why you?"

Sutton nibbled at the inside of her lip, her cheeks pinking, then she looked away, then down at her hands, then back at him. Gaze beseeching. And it hit him.

"*You* are hoping to meet someone at this...*singles* night?"

"Me?" Her hand flew to her chest, pink blotches now creeping down her neck. "No. I mean, sure. Meeting people is a nice thing, don't you think?"

Dante did not.

"But... That's not *why*. I'm in Vermillion, as it's where my parents met. So maybe I'm trying to find a connection to them here, somehow? I honestly don't know." She wrinkled her nose, as if the whole thing made her feel uncomfortable. Then shook it off and said, "Anyway, if we do this thing, you'd be most welcome to sign up too. To meet *other* people, I mean. Because we've already met. Not that you and I... I mean, if you're even single, that is."

She swallowed, as if waiting for him to confirm or deny. He said nothing. Interested to see where her flusters might lead the conversation.

Then she held out both hands and breathed out hard. "Short answer—*life's* short. When I get the impetus to do something, I don't muck about. So, what do you say? Wanna help us do this thing?"

Having spent the past decade hardening himself to wanting anything more than he already had, having Sutton Mayberry ask him what he wanted felt treacherous. But his duty was to wrestle the Vine and Stein into the black, and Sutton had just offered up a big step toward doing just that.

As if she could sense his defences melting, she smiled warmly, and said, *"Bene?"*

"Sì. Bene."

She clapped her hands, and jumped up and down on the spot. Then, before he felt her move, she took a large step and threw her arms around his neck. Enveloping him in a hug.

As he was leaning against the back of the couch, he reached for her so she'd not topple them both backward; hands landing on her waist, gathering handfuls of soft T-shirt.

Time slowed in an instant—he could feel the shift of her as she breathed, the warmth of her skin through her thin T-shirt. Her hair, soft as silk, tickled his cheek, a soft puff of her breath kissed his ear.

How long had it been since someone had held him this way? Not a welcome kiss from family, or a meaningless night in the bed of a stranger. But held with intent. Such joy.

He drank it in, absorbing her vitality as if it had the power to recharge him for life. Until, in the moment when it would have felt most natural for her to pull away, her arms tightened. Incrementally. Ruinously.

Before he even felt himself move, Dante's hands shifted, sliding around her, gathering her shirt, fingertips tracing the curve of her back, the bumps of her spine, as he pulled her danger close.

While a small voice in the back of his brain tried desperately to get his attention, to warn him to stop, he felt the change in her too. The way she softened against him, her breasts pressing into his chest, the curl of her fingers as they slid up his neck and into his hair—

Then suddenly she leaped away. Ruffling a hand through her hair, tugging at her T-shirt, spinning in a circle.

Dante's hands hovered, midair, reaching for what they'd lost, before he drew them back. His blood thrummed through him, a heavy pulsing beat that made his ears ring, and his chest burn.

"Anyway, I'll go now," she said. "Get the ball rolling. It'll be great. Amazing. Big success. Thank you." She looked up at him then, eyes a swirl of heat and confusion.

Then she held out a fist, begging for a bump. As if that might erase the intimacy of their embrace.

With a soft laugh, he gave her what she needed. When their knuckles knocked, a spark of electricity leaped from her hand to his, or vice versa. Her eyes snapped to his and he knew she felt it too.

Around the couch she bolted, then out the door shouting, "You won't regret this!"

As Dante stood on legs that weren't altogether steady, flooded with thoughts and feelings too frantic to push down deep, he already did.

CHAPTER FOUR

THE AIR WAS cool and fresh, the leaves sparkled with morning dew not yet burned away by the spring sunshine.

Sutton stepped over a lichen-covered log, lamenting her Vans probably weren't the most appropriate footwear for a bush walk, but the Stringybark Loop Hike had been labelled "lightly undulating," and was the shortest trail in Barry's brochures, so it was what it was.

"Why are we doing this?" asked Laila, who was several steps behind, brushing a spiky-leaved bush so it didn't attack her legs.

"Two birds," said Sutton, "one stone."

Laila pressed her heart-shaped sunglasses higher on her nose. "The rare chance your parents walked this path together is not a 'bird.' It's guesswork. Why not call your dad and ask, and next time don't invite me."

Ignoring that perfectly sensible option, Sutton waited for Laila to catch up. "You've lived here, what, a few months now? And you've never done anything on Barry's brochures. If you want to be a part of this community, I think it'll take more than a singles night."

Laila harrumphed. Literally.

"My dad likes walks," said Sutton, as she started up again. "He'd have found these trails for sure."

In fact, Sutton had found him perusing a website about a walking tour in Devon the last time she'd visited. When she'd hinted that maybe Marjorie, his lovely neighbour who gladly checked in on her father when Sutton was away, might enjoy the website too, he'd shut it down and changed the subject entirely.

"And your mother?" Laila asked.

"I actually don't know. Dad's stories are more about that first flush of love, then there's a gap, then it's all about me."

"Hmm. Time to turn around—I only have a half hour till the store opens."

Sutton turned and followed Laila back down the "hill." "A lot of people get the urge to buy Viking romance at eight thirty on a Wednesday morning?"

"It's not about the customers. It's about the books. They miss me."

"Second bird, then," said Sutton. "I spoke to Dante."

Laila caught up faster than a person in wedge heels on a hiking path ought to be able. "And?"

"The Vine and Stein is a go."

"Yes!" said Laila. "How did you convince him? Seduce him with your vixen wiles?"

"I asked. It was that simple."

Though walking in on him sprawled on the small couch like a slain giant had felt anything but simple. The tight purple T-shirt had proved any imaginings she'd had about what he might look like sans flannel shirts and jeans had not done the man justice. Then there was the tattoo—delicate tendrils of what must be grape vines curling out the bottom of the T-shirt sleeve. Working in the indie music scene, she'd seen more tattooed skin than not, yet she'd spent more time than she'd care to admit thinking about Dante's, wondering how far it went—over his shoulder, up his neck, down his back, lower?

"Well, colour me happy," said Laila. "Not only because we have a venue but because I do believe we are at the end of this thing."

Laila all but skipped the final few metres of the trail, patted the sign, and made her way to Sutton's rental car.

On the ten-minute drive back to Vermillion, they talked through ideas for how they could deck out the Vine, what the invitations ought to look like, getting-to-know-you games the attendees could play.

"It's official," Laila declared. "Dante Rossi is officially my favourite Rossi."

"I've not met any others, so have nothing to compare him with."

A quick glance sideways showed Laila's smile was slow and wide. "Oh, honey, you don't need to meet the rest to know he's the one for you."

"I thought we'd established he was off the table."

"Meh. It's a woman's prerogative to change her mind."

When Laila pulled out her phone to start making a music playlist for the night, Sutton wondered what Laila might say if she told her what had happened *after* Dante had said yes.

Music people were touchy-feely—sharing dressing rooms and cramped tour buses, lots of sitting on laps in backs of cars. But hugging Dante, holding Dante, had felt nothing like that.

There was the sound he'd made, a kind of soul-deep murmur. The feel of those big hands on her waist, rough skin catching on her shirt, long fingers spanning her like it was nothing. It was foolish and deeply intimate. And if she'd used it as a form of self-help to get to sleep that night, well that was her own private Idaho.

"Penny for your thoughts," said Laila, radar clearly pinging.

Sutton quickly pointed to the rows of red rose bushes along the outskirts of yet another vineyard, meaning the turnoff to Vermillion was close. "Did you know the roses are an early warning system? They attract aphids and contract diseases, such as black rot, before vines do. Read it in a brochure."

"Look at you being a good little tourist."

"I really am. Drop you at the shop?"

"Perfection. Let's do dinner at the Vine tonight so we can sort out next steps. Say eight?"

"Sure thing." Sutton tapped her fingers on the steering wheel as she pictured walking into the place at night, Dante behind the bar, those hot dark eyes hitting her like a laser beam. "Though we can go somewhere different, if you prefer?"

"And lose traction? Not a chance. Unless there's a very good reason why you'd like to take a breather?"

"Nope! The Vine is fine."

"The 'Vine' is fine indeed."

After Sutton dropped Laila off, she made her way back to the B&B, had a shower, got changed, and listened to a couple of demo playlists she'd been sent. Nearing lunchtime, she grabbed her laptop, and went to head out, only to pause at the door.

Maybe she'd go see a matinee at the local cinema instead.

Was she being a big chicken? Yes.

Could she live with herself? Again, yes.

Throwing herself into Dante's arms in a moment of delight had been one thing, but shoving herself under his nose multiple times a day would absolutely give him the wrong idea.

Best keep some space between. For the way he told it, he was leaving any day now, and the man was the proverbial bear with a thorn in his paw, and she'd not come to Vermillion to get distracted trying to figure out how to remove someone else's ouch, when she had her own stuff to figure out.

And if she kept making excuses *not* to see him, even she'd stop believing she meant it.

For once, Chrissy was early, Kent was in a great mood, and nothing went wrong in the kitchen. The place was even a smidge busier than usual. Yet from just before opening, and all day since, Dante had felt as if his insides were tied in knots.

All because he was waiting for a certain brunette to come walking through his door. To order her horrendous excuse for a coffee, and take her place at the table by the last window, where he'd ordered Kent to place a reserved sign that had stayed there all damn day because she'd never come.

He looked at his watch to see it was a little after eight. Late enough he'd have missed dinner with his aunt, again, and would have to grab a plate of something from the kitchen. After which he'd slink into the guesthouse on the hill, and fall into bed, hopefully exhausted enough to sleep a dreamless sleep.

He'd not seen his aunt since his slip the day before. Or spoken to her since saying Isabella's name. He knew it had provided an opening, and he did not want to have that talk. He'd heard it all. How much they all still missed her. How the tragedy might have been avoided if they'd both been given stronger guidance from their father. How it wasn't Dante's fault.

Leaving Vigna dell'Essenza and turning his back on the family business had been a means of survival. Sorello would never reach the level of Rossi Wines' success, but it was lucrative, and gratifying, and enough to curate his own reputation as a master winemaker.

He'd built a life good enough to sustain him and those who relied on him, but not so much blue sky the guilt of it ate him alive. The balance was finespun, and he would not allow it to become unhinged.

Then, as if the gods had been listening, the door to the Vine opened, bringing with it a wash of cool night air and Sutton Mayberry. A wave of longing rushed over him with such haste, such violence, he had to remind himself to breathe.

Sutton glanced around, as if searching for someone. When her gaze found him, her mouth dropped open, her chest rose and fell. As if she too found herself having to battle that same rogue wave.

"Sutton!" said Kent, moving in beside Dante. So wound up was he, he flinched.

With a deep, fortifying breath, Sutton walked to the bar. "Hey, Kent. Dante."

Dante nodded.

"We were waiting all day for you to come," Kent went on. "We were worried something was wrong." Kent looked to Dante as if assuming he'd back that up.

Dante had no intention of letting Sutton Mayberry know that he'd thought of her at all. The way she felt in his arms. How the scent of her on his skin had lingered for hours.

"I'm great. Spent the day playing tourist. Now I'm meeting someone for dinner. Laila, from the bookstore. We're meeting to talk about singles night."

"It's happening?" Kent asked.

"It's happening."

Kent held out a fist, which Sutton leaned in to bump.

Then her eyes snapped to Dante's, and he knew she was remembering the moment they'd bumped fists the day before. And all that had led to it.

Tucking her hair behind her ear, Sutton said, "Thank Dante. Without the venue, there is no night. In fact, Dante, you're welcome to join us for dinner, if you're free. We're talking logistics and expectations, so…"

"He's free," said Kent, giving Dante a shove.

And Dante found himself wishing that the old Kent was back; the hunched, disengaged Kent who barely looked him in the eye.

"So, yes?" Sutton pointed to her table.

Dante rounded the bar and followed where she led. Gaze on her hair, reminding him it smelled like peaches and sunshine. The sweep of her shoulders reminding him of how she'd thrown her arms around his neck. The sway of her hips had his fingers curling into his palms.

When they reached the table, he was glad to have something to do with his hands. He pulled out her chair.

"Thanks," she said, her voice breathless. Her gaze flickering between his eyes, then dropping to his mouth, then away, before she all but fell into the chair.

He chose the seat across from her, hoping the distance would give him some reprieve. Only the view of her gathering her hair and twirling it over one shoulder, picking up the menu and pretending to read it, nibbling at the inside of her bottom lip, unspooled more longing, only this time inside him.

Then she rolled her eyes, slammed the menu on the table, flattened her hands atop the thing, and looked at him. "So."

"So," he said, leaning back, crossing his arms.

To which her mouth lifted at one corner. "Where's the purple T-shirt?"

"Early retirement."

"Pity."

"Why is that?"

Swirls of darkest blue washed into her eyes. "Could be good for business. Bring in a whole new kind of clientele."

Dante uncrossed his arms, and let his hands fall to the table, his fingertips landing an inch from hers. The knots unravelling in the face of her warmth, the silent conversation happening beneath their words.

"Any other advice?" he asked, shifting his hands forward an inch.

She noticed, her fingers curling, then uncurling. "Kent should be full-time, and front of house at all times."

"Kent costs almost as much in breakages as he does in wages."

"He's faster on POS than you are. And he's a delight."

"Are you suggesting I am not a delight?"

"Not in the least," she said without pause. "Though I'm not sure he'd look quite as good in purple as you do."

Dante shook his head, slowly, side to side. Then pressed his hands forward so that his fingers slid along hers. Her breath hitched, and she curled her hand so the palm faced upward. Vulnerable, trusting. *Hell.*

"Sutton," he said curling a finger around hers—

"Sorry, I'm late!"

The both of them snapped their hands back as Laila the bookstore owner dragged out a chair and sat at their table.

"Well, this is a turn," said Laila, looking from Dante to Sutton, her eyes widening in obvious question.

Sutton's mouth pursed as she shook her head at the other woman, a silent conversation if ever there was one.

"Hey."

All three looked up to find Niccolo standing over the table, his gaze moving over the women, landing on Laila for a long fraught beat, before he said to Dante, "What do we have here?"

"Nothing that concerns you, Constable Goodboy," said Laila, waving a dismissive hand.

Nico bristled.

And Dante, delighted in the turn of events, said, "Care to join us?"

"The more the merrier!" Sutton added. Before wincing, as if she'd been kicked under the table.

Nico slowly moved around the table and took the fourth chair. Then he looked to Sutton, then Laila, then Sutton— realisation dawning in his eyes.

"The brunette," Nico said, clicking his fingers Sutton's way.

"The younger cousin," Sutton clicked back. Then she held out her hand. "Sutton Mayberry."

Nico took it. "Niccolo Rossi."

"Pleasure." She smiled, wide.

And Dante watched his cousin melt. The urge to do some under-table kicking of his own was strong.

"Shall we order?" Dante asked, sliding menus across the table.

"Then to business," Laila grumbled.

Once they'd chosen their meals, Sutton insisting they all save room for donuts for dessert, Dante suggested wines to match. Sutton ordered a lager. Then shot Dante a quick private shrug that had his insides turning over on themselves.

Nico picked up the handwritten "Reserved" sign and waved it at Dante. "Business must have quadrupled overnight for this to be a thing."

Avoiding Sutton's gaze, Dante took it and slid it into his pocket. "Laila and Sutton are going to host an event at the Vine. A singles night."

Sign forgotten, Nico frowned, his gaze going straight to Laila. "What might that entail?"

"Well," Laila said, batting her lashes and curling a finger in her hair. "I'm thinking we black out the windows, add a few red lights, bring in some chaise lounges, a couple of swing sets, hand out handcuffs at the door—"

"It will be a perfectly sensible and sophisticated evening," Sutton jumped in. "The Vine can turn a nice profit while we help the younger locals make new friends."

"Don't bother," said Laila. "Nothing is wholesome enough for Captain Perfect."

Nico, pretending, badly, that he'd not heard her, said to Sutton, "That's actually not a bad idea."

"Right? It won't take much to zhoosh this place up," Sutton said, reaching into her bag for a notebook and a pencil, then sketched out how they might set the space up.

"We have fairy lights in storage at the villa you can use," said Nico.

Sutton clicked her fingers joyfully in his face.

Laila, shaking off her shock, added, "We could do, say, three signature cocktails for the night—you can charge a packet for those."

"As a first-time thing," said Sutton, "I suggest a soft opening. Adjust the space depending on how many tickets we sell. Learn from it. If it works, it could become a regular thing."

"So, when are we doing this?" Nico asked, tagging himself as a part of the crew.

"How about Saturday week?" said Sutton, glancing at Dante. As if checking if he'd still be in town then.

He nodded. She smiled. And the air crackled.

"I can send out word to my mailing list tonight," Laila jumped in. "I already know a bunch of my regulars, book clubbers, who'll be there like a shot. You know everyone else," she said, half looking at Nico. "Spread the word."

"Team Singles!" Sutton put her hand into the middle of the table. Nico went next. Laila's hand hovered over his, as if she feared she might get some boy disease before she placed it atop. The three of them looked to Dante.

With a foreign sense of whimsy, he added his hand to the clump, and the others cheered. After which Dante sat back, tucking his hand under his arm, as if it might help keep that feeling a little longer.

Laila brought out her phone and started penning the invitation email, while Nico and Sutton argued over what they should call the event.

"If there is a hint of wine or grapes or vines in a single suggestion," said Laila, thumbs flying over her screen, "I will scream."

Nico opened his mouth. Laila opened hers. Then Nico held up both hands in surrender.

The wine arrived, and Dante offered to pour. He held the bottle close, caught the notes of berry and cashew and spice, all but tasting the scent on the back of his tongue as he let the liquid—a fine red with a translucent rosy hue, a peachy shine—spill gracefully into each full-bottomed wineglass.

When the bottle reached the wineglass in front of Sutton, she slid a quick hand over the top. "Not for me."

"Won't you even try it?" he asked, his voice low.

Sutton's eyes, such a soft sultry blue, looked between his. And the "try it" suddenly felt a lot like "try me."

As if he'd said the words out loud, her tongue darted out to wet between her lips. His gaze dropped, caught on the sheen. Remembering how her mouth had all but brushed his ear, a puff of happy breath scooting across his cheek.

"I don't think it's a good idea," Sutton said, her voice barely above a whisper.

And when he looked up, saw the tumult in her eyes, he knew they were no longer talking about the wine.

"Can't hurt," he said.

"Oh," she said, with a quick sorry smile, "but it can."

Dante watched her a moment, before he nodded, and drew the wine back to his side of the table.

The lager arrived. Sutton smiled at the waiter, took the drink, and drank straight from the bottle. When she ran her finger over her lips, then let out a big sigh, Dante felt at a loss.

Not that she'd not try his wares. It was the loss of possibility. Something he'd not allowed himself to think about in a truly long time. Only now he'd had a taste of it, he wasn't sure how to go back.

After that night, Dante ramped things up—hiring a book-keeper to tidy up the office and files and internet banking, suggesting Chrissy take on Kent as assistant manager, full-time, and updating Celia in person, by having dinner at the villa most nights.

He'd had to endure a long hug, but Celia had made no mention of mushrooms, or allergies, or Isabella again.

Had he been doing so as it was in the best interests of the Vine? Yes.

Had it also meant he could avoid working the bar floor, thus avoiding a certain customer, one who still had a table reserved every day? Probably.

Not that it made a lick of difference to the direction of his thoughts, anytime they saw a gap.

Can't hurt? Oh, but it can.

The poignancy behind her words haunted him. He knew why he was hesitant, but her story was unknown. Who in her past had hurt her? He wanted names, addresses, almost as much as he wanted to put it out of his head.

All he could do was remind himself that the last thing *she* needed was to get mixed up with the likes of him. Busted, bruised. *More Sasquatch than human,* Nico had called him when he'd landed on their doorstep.

A crash from outside the manager's office, followed by a chorus of voices calling, "Taxi!" snapped him from his reverie. The scent of stale beer and old paper in the office invaded his nostrils with such alacrity, he wondered if it might be damaging his facility for good.

When more raised voices came through the door, he ran both hands over his face, and made his way out into the bar proper.

To find Sutton leaning bodily over the bar. Pressed up onto her toes, loose men's tweed pants hugged her backside, while low on her hips. A fitted T-shirt clung to her in a way that had Dante's mouth turning dry, and a sandal swung lazily from her toes as she lifted a leg to get better purchase on whatever she was reaching for on the other side of the bar.

Dante looked to the gods, begging for forbearance, before he entered the fray. "What was that crash?" he asked.

Sutton's face turned to him, her eyes warming; a smile dashing onto her face, as she shuffled back and her feet dropped to the floor. "Hey! I didn't know you were in."

He kept his smile cool. "The crash?"

"Right. Sorry. I was chatting to the football guys over there, convincing them with great enthusiasm to come to Starry, Starry Singles Night, when I smacked a coffee out of the waiter's hand."

She held up the rag she'd found. And one of the kitchen staff—Dante couldn't remember his name—grabbed it and rushed to clean up the mess.

Dante noted belatedly that the place was busier than usual. Several tables were filled with locals having late lunch, and a few guys in football uniforms had pushed tables together to have post-practice drinks. Nico was up a ladder, being directed by Kent as to where to pin yet more fairy lights.

And Sutton—who'd set up her laptop and papers on the far corner of the bar, near the now half-empty donut cloche—was directing a delivery guy as to where to put boxes of electric candles she'd ordered.

When she turned, face flushed, eyes bright, and skipped over to him, Dante had to press his feet into his shoes so as to keep himself from tipping.

"While I have you," she said, "I've been thinking that it might be fun to build a stage."

Dante leaned against the bar and looked out at how much the space had changed in only a few days. "The event is tomorrow night. I'm not sure even your persuasion skills could make that happen."

"Oh, I could make it happen. I can get a temporary demountable, full lighting, and sound rig organised and set up in two days. But I'm thinking more for the future. This place is solid brick, windows double glazed, you could get a late-night music venue license, no sweat."

When he gave no reaction, certain that if he did, it would give away how impressive he found her, she poked him on the arm. "This place was built for live music, Dante."

"Which will be someone else's problem. When I am long gone."

"Fine," she said, then slunk back to her end of the bar. Where she began tapping furiously at her laptop.

Seeing no coffee at her elbow, Dante moved behind the bar, grabbed an espresso glass, and set to making her a cup. "What are you working on over there?"

When she looked up, her smile told him she'd not been so deeply invested in her work after all. "One of the bands I manage—the Magnolia Blossoms—have been offered a record deal with a reasonably well-known label. I'm working my way through a hundred-odd pages of legalese because chances are there are nasty clauses that will make it harder to say yes than no."

"Might that not be a job for a lawyer?"

"Live and in the flesh," she said, holding out both arms and swinging her torso back and forth, as if presenting herself to him. "I started managing bands for fun while I was in law school. I only take the first pass, then hand it over to a dedicated entertainment lawyer."

"I imagine this band of yours must be seriously good."

"They are spectacular," she gushed. "Finally gaining the notice they deserve, after appearing at Glastonbury last year. Probably time they move to an all-purpose management firm, but were my first band, I was their first manager, and they're stubbornly sticking with me."

"You sound extremely okay with the thought of them leaving you behind."

"Not okay...pragmatic. I'm really good at spotting raw talent, and getting them in front of the audiences who'll love them. The lucky ones will evolve beyond me, requiring hair and makeup teams, PR on retainer. No point getting too attached to something if you know you're going to lose it one day."

She shook her head a little at the last, before getting back to her contract. And while he felt certain there was more going on behind her words than he understood, who was he to pry? He who had walked out on his own family so that people would stop asking if he was okay.

He angled the spoon handle against the inside of the milk jug, and poured a dash of hot milk into the glass. "You sound awfully philosophical."

She shrugged. "I chose a tough industry."

Coffee made the way she liked it, he took it over to her. "You think the music industry is tough, you should try wine-making."

She took the coffee, her finger sliding against his. Dante felt the effect of it far longer than the heat from the glass.

"Please," she said, "from what I saw, 'winemaking' looks to be all wandering through sun-drenched vines and getting tipsy on testing."

"What you *saw*?"

Sutton sipped, paused, swallowed, then said, "So I might have googled your vineyard."

Dante blinked.

Sutton filled the silence. "Sorello. Umbria. You mentioned it that day in your office."

The day she'd thrown herself into his arms.

A few beats slunk by before she said, "I read that you changed its name, when you bought the place a few years back."

Dante wondered what else she'd read. His story would not be hard to find. His family infamous enough for the fallout, and the tragedy behind it, to have made national news. But her expression was merely curious. About him.

"When we were little, my sister..." His heart contracted, as it always did, always would, upon picturing Isabella when they were young. "We would pretend that the southern hillside of the Tuscan vineyard where we grew up belonged to us. We imagined experimenting with varietals, creating genetic wonders that would take the world by storm. We called it Sorello, which, in Italian, means *siblings*."

"Oh," she said. "I love that! It's so...whimsical. Not a word I've imagined relating to your life."

"You've imagined my life?" he asked.

She narrowed her eyes. "I had you pinned as living in some dark castle, all tragic and brooding, frightening local children. Though now, having seen pictures of your place..." She cocked her head. "Dante, it's so beautiful. Honestly. Elysium incarnate."

Dante could not deny how glad he was to hear that's how she felt. "There might yet be skeletons in my attic, you know?"

"Pishposh. Now I'm certain you take in stray kittens, and bake muffins, while your...significant other picks daisies for the kitchen table." She bit back the follow-up question.

And where he'd avoided answering it once before, this time he said, "So close. All bar the significant other."

Her eyelashes fluttered sweetly as a smile flashed across her face. Then she frowned, and looked down at her hands. "Anyway, it's stunning. And the empty hillside leading away from the house—it's the perfect spot for an intimate, day-on-the-green-type music festival."

At that Dante laughed. Rolling pangs of mirth that loosened other feelings in its wake. "Are you ever not on?"

"Hustle, baby. It's what I do."

"Likewise."

Her smile encouraged explanation.

"In between the baking and rescuing of stray kittens—"

"Of course."

"—there is the stress of crop yield, the threat of viruses, of unruly weather patterns, constant battle to find good staff, escalating shipping costs. Then there is the dark-underbelly stories of deliberately damaged barrels, strange accidents, missing bottles. A neighbour of ours woke one morning to find an entire field of vines missing. Torn out overnight."

"You're kidding!"

"I am Italian. We do not kid about wine."

It was her turn to laugh, a gorgeous husky sound that drew glances from tables away. As her laughter faded, her gaze dropped to his shoulder, roved down his arm, all but tracing the tattoo hidden beneath his shirt.

Then she dragged herself back into the moment. Looked at him. And said, "Um, I have to go. Just remembered I'm heading to an art show opening at Corked Creations—a gallery up the road. My dad is a big fan of modern art, so might have visited back then. Though I might be able to drum up a few last-minute Starry, Starry Singles Night ticket sales while there. You?"

"I'll be here, herding monkeys." He gestured to where Kent was holding the bottom of the ladder, admiring the view of Nico above.

Sutton laughed again, then gathered her things. "Then, I guess I'll see you tomorrow. If not tomorrow night, for the big event?"

Dante nodded.

With one last look, tinged with heat, and questions, and loaded unspoken things, she left. And Dante breathed out fully for the first time since he'd seen her by the bar.

CHAPTER FIVE

SO MUCH FOR a soft launch, Sutton thought, watching the line of well-dressed people make their way to the Starry, Starry Single Night registration table at the Vine and Stein's front door.

Once the attendees collected their name tags, and velvet pouches containing takeaway gifts as well as details of some fun games the evening had in store, it was her job to encourage them to head inside, where the place was already pumping.

For the Vine and Stein looked an absolute treat. Nic and Kent had done an amazing job, draping the "sky" with hundreds of fairy lights. The tables had been set up to create spaces to sit, as well as dark corners in which people could chat, leaving the centre of the space a place to mill. To case the crowd. To dance.

The bones really were there—the high ceilings, the gothic architecture—to turn the place into something special. A bit of expense, certainly, and some imagination on part of the owners, but it would be so worth it. Make Vermillion a place not just for those looking for a twee touristy day out, but a destination for wine, beauty, and great music—the holy trinity.

Maybe she'd find a way to meet Nico's mother, plant the seed there. For it wasn't Dante's call. In fact, if this night went well, and the crowds kept improving as they had since she'd first arrived, Dante could soon go home. To his beautiful, halcyon, rural escape, with its golden sunlight, and sweet local village, and his lack of a significant other to pick daisies.

The clock inside her head started to tick double time.

What had she said to him the day before? *No point getting too attached to something you know you're going to lose.* Yep. Good advice. Hang on to that.

"Okay, time for you to go inside," Laila stage-whispered as she hustled past in a sparkling silver catsuit with a deep V and nothing underneath.

The dress Laila had leant Sutton—a.k.a. insisted she wear upon threat of death—felt like something a 1940s movie star would wear to bed. Black, satin, high neck, sleeveless, the fabric shifting over her like a caress, and with a thigh-high split that gaped shockingly every time she took a step. She wondered how soon she could slip out of the heels pinching at her toes and shrug on the Vans she had hiding in a bag in the office.

Sutton checked the others on registration were good to go, and when one slid into her spot, she slipped inside.

Only to stop on a dime when her heart lodged in her throat. *Dante?*

At least she thought it was him. She had to blink to make sure. For in lieu of his usual flannelette shirt and jeans he wore an actual suit. His long hair and scruffy stubble had been trimmed, tamed, making him look less like a bear and more…

The saliva pooling in the back of her mouth made words impossible.

Only he needed to *not* be her focus that night. Things had been so busy, leading up, she'd conveniently let herself forget why she'd agreed to help Laila in the first place. To find a connection to her parents' experience, by opening herself up to meeting someone new.

Maybe someone who liked the kind of music she liked.

Someone who liked to travel. A great conversationalist. Someone who made her feel even a fraction of the spark she felt when looking at the man in the suit casing the edges of the room, like he was ready to grab any troublemakers and haul them out by the collar.

Dante, she thought on a sigh. Only *not* Dante. Anyone *but* Dante.

Dante, who listened to Dean Martin records, was a homebody, grunted more than he spoke, and was clearly not open to anything happening between them. Despite the fact that they sparked, and flirted, and somehow found ways to be together more than was necessary.

Time was ticking. It was only a couple of weeks till her birthday; till she was the age her mother was when she'd been given no more chances. This was not the time to prevaricate. Love lightning was a stretch, but this night was opportunity, at the very least.

She gave her dress one last tug, so as to maintain some sense of propriety, then readied herself to meet as many single men as the night allowed. But first she needed a drink.

The fact that Dante had moved behind the bar was by the by.

Sure, a voice in the back of her head scoffed. *You tell yourself that.*

Sutton felt flickers of interest as she moved across the floor, but only peripherally. For her attention was on Dante, who had quickly gathered himself a fan club, a veritable plethora vying for his attention.

"I'm as flabbergasted as you are."

Sutton looked up to find Nico standing beside her. Wearing a suit, no tie, he'd scrubbed up mighty well himself. Yet she felt none of the same visceral turmoil as she did at the sight of Dante.

"Did he get a *haircut*?" Sutton asked.

"Looks that way."

Still long, his hair no longer hid the deep warm brown of his beautiful eyes, the cut of his cheekbones, the newly tamed stubble, the hard angles of the jaw beneath.

He leaned forward as one of the singles crooked a finger his way, asking for a drink. Or maybe his phone number. Or firstborn child.

His frown as he leaned back made Sutton's tension ease. *There he is*, she thought. *There's Dante.*

And like rocks atop a mountain tipping into an avalanche, heat spread through her, turning her knees to liquid.

"Huh," said Nico.

Sutton looked his way to find him watching her with a small smile on his face. "What?"

"Nothing." Nico lifted both hands in surrender. "Wine? Signature cocktail?"

"Gin gimlet. Lime. No garnish."

Nico grinned. "Coming right up."

As Nico moved behind the bar, half the crowd seemed to roll in his direction. Dante, sensing the shift, looked up, his gaze going straight to her. There it stayed. Caught. Locked onto her for several long, hot moments.

Then, as if coming from a trance, he shook his head, lips pursed into a long silent whistle.

Sutton, feeling the full force of his blatant approval, cocked her head. *Right back at you.*

Something shifted in his eyes; something deep, rich, heady, and unstoppable.

Then someone walked between them; Chrissy, moving the crowd aside so she could ask the Rossi men a question.

Spell broken, Sutton spun away. Hand to her heart, to find it racing, she gave herself a few moments to catch her breath.

"Gimlet on lime. No garnish," Nico said, from behind her, his voice coming to Sutton as if from underwater.

Sutton murmured her thanks, turned long enough to grab the drink, lifted it, drank it in one go, placed the glass on the bar with vigour, then headed out into the throng.

"It's game time!" Laila called over the speakers. "If you haven't already, check your pouch for the name of a famous romantic literary character. Then go forth and find your match."

Sutton opened her velvet pouch to find a slip of paper with a name on it, and laughed out loud.

She'd helped Laila put together the goodies each attendee would receive—a box of chocolate hearts, a small bottle of lube, scented condoms, a little black notebook and pen with Forbidden Fruits branding, a ten-percent-off voucher for Forbidden Fruits, and one half of a famous romantic literary couple.

"Sophia Stanton-Lacy and Charles Rivenhall?" Sutton had asked as she'd snipped the laminated names apart.

Laila had shot her a look that was most unimpressed. "*The Grand Sophy?* By Georgette Heyer?"

Sutton had shrugged and moved on to the next. "Georgie and… Vektal?"

"Are you seriously telling me you've not read *Ice Planet Barbarians*?"

Sutton shrugged. "You're a book girl, I'm a music girl, get over it. Ooh, Edward Cullen and Bella Swan. I know them! I think. Maybe not. Who are they again?"

"Heathen," Laila muttered under her breath.

Now Sutton found herself looking at a piece of paper that read Miss Piggy. "If I'm not looking for Kermit the Frog, I'm giving up now," she muttered.

For while she'd mixed and mingled, and convinced a whole lot of people to check out her bands, there had been no sparks. Much less lightning. But the night was young, and her mind was open, and if a person couldn't find even a flutter of romance on a night like this they might as well not bother with it all.

She looked up, hoping to catch someone's eye so she could compare literary names, and as seemed to be her doom, her gaze instead found Dante.

He was out from behind the bar, leaning against one of the high tables at the edge of the room, talking to a really sweet redhead Sutton had met earlier that night. Dahlia? Dahlia— who was smiling and laughing at something he'd said.

And he looked…if not relaxed, then as if he wasn't having a terrible time. Which, for him, was huge. Or was she reading more into it than was there, because the idea of him coming out of that impressive shell of his with anyone but her made her heart hurt.

"You don't happen to be looking for Rhysand?" a deep voice asked.

Sutton looked up to find a tall, ostensibly handsome man with thick sandy hair, perfect teeth, and a dimple smiling down at her. "Sorry?"

He looked at a piece of paper. "Rhysand. I hope I'm pronouncing that right."

When she blinked up at him, he reached for her hand, turned it gently over, and found *Miss Piggy* written on her piece of paper. He laughed. Then leaned in, not too much, but enough to make it clear he was happy to remain right where he was. "Is it wrong to admit I've not recognised a single literary name I've heard thus far?"

Sutton, having finally collected herself, said, "I think he's some kind of fairy? But I'm honestly as clueless as you are."

"Shall we call it even?"

After a beat in which she pictured Dante, smiling and talking to a really nice woman, who was not her, which he was absolutely within his rights to do, she held out her hand.

"I'm Sutton."

* * *

It was nearing midnight and the sky was soft and sparkling. Main Street, Vermillion, with its fairy-light-bedecked avenue of trees, and warmly lit shop fronts, was built for a night like this.

Sutton grabbed the folding table by the front door and took it inside, leaving Nico to look after the last of the stragglers. He seemed to have it under control—taking his job of marshalling everyone onto the footpath as they waited for the courtesy bus, or taxis, or lifts home terribly seriously.

Inside the Vine, the lights of the bar were on low. Chairs scraped through the sticky confetti covering the floor as the staff upended them onto tables, leaving room for the cleanup crew they'd hired to come in the predawn to put the place back to rights.

"Wondered where you'd got to."

Sutton's overwrought nerves sparked merrily at hearing Dante's voice, despite the workload they'd carried all night.

"Just cleaning up, as much as I can," she said, turning to find his hands resting in the pockets of his suit pants, doing things to the shape of him that had her mind reeling.

He'd lost his jacket. His pale button-down shirt was slimmer fit than usual, meaning it pulled just so against his broad chest, hinting at the impressive shape beneath. The slight shadow of his tattoo could be seen through the fabric, curling up and over his shoulder.

Thankfully Dante missed her hungry gaze as his was on the dance floor.

Kent and Chrissy slow danced, a good metre apart, and as if they were on the moon, while "Creep" crooned moodily from the sound system. While Laila was holding a couple of kitchen staff hostage, telling them about some spicy fantasy book they had to read, if their slack-jawed attention was anything to go by.

"How was your night?" he asked, his voice low, rough, as if he'd used his daily allocation of words.

"Tiring," said Sutton. "Mostly."

"Hmm," Dante seemed to agree. Then, "I thought that was your thing—packed bars, loud music, happy people."

"It is. It's just, I'm not usually—" She stopped, not quite sure how to word it.

"The one on show?"

She'd been going to say *I'm not usually one to compare.* But all night that was all she'd done; comparing the dashing ginger-haired gent with the expansive indie music knowledge, and the charming guy who'd been her Kermit the Frog, or any number of others she'd found herself paired with in Laila's litany of games, with the man beside her now.

Glancing up she found Dante watching her, with that warm dark inscrutable gaze. The jaw beneath his trimmed stubble such a perfect sweep from ear to chin she felt an urge to trace it with her touch.

"Something like that," she managed. "How about you? Nice night?"

"It was, surprisingly." A smile hovering on those beautifully shaped lips.

Sutton's belly tightened. But she said, "I'm glad."

They were shoulder to shoulder, but not touching. There was more than enough physical distance between them to feel perfectly civilised, yet Sutton's skin felt aflame, the urge to lean into him so strong she had to press her toes into her shoes. Hard.

Then she made the mistake of breathing in through her nose. Even after a long night in the bar, he smelled amazing. Like clean skin, and freshly washed cotton sheets, and some rich earthy something that was purely him.

Some fresh ache began to build inside her. It felt a lot like disappointment. As if she'd actually held out some small hope that she'd look across the crowded room and *boom*! The way it had happened for her parents.

Only she'd never had a chance, and it was entirely her fault. She'd spent the entire night wondering where Dante was, what he was doing, whom he was talking to. Because somehow, she'd become stuck on *this* guy. This big, elusive, closed-off, grouch of a man.

What an unholy waste.

"Sutton! Dante! Get the hell over here!"

As one they looked over to find Kent waving while the wait crew, kitchen staff, and temp bar staff had now all spilled into the big empty space, joining Kent and Chrissy in their slow-mo dance.

Prepared to wave them away, Sutton baulked when Dante's hand appeared in her vision.

"You're kidding," she said, looking up to find him smiling down at her. Smiling! Her poor foolish heart. "You *dance*?"

"I'm Italian, we do not kid about dancing." His eyebrows waggled, and the joy that spilled through her was something else.

"Come on!" Chrissy shouted.

"Okay, then." Sutton placed her hand in Dante's, and when his longer fingers closed around hers, it felt so lovely, so true.

Without hesitation, he strode out onto the makeshift dance floor and she had no choice but to follow.

The crowd quickly moved in around them. Then someone started a slow-motion conga line. Rather than joining in, Dante pulled her gently into his hold, one hand holding hers, the other warm and sure on her lower back. And together they swayed.

"Creep" finished, "Unchained Melody" began, Norah Jones's voice a plaintive sigh echoing through the space.

Someone dimmed the lights to a flicker of starlight and little more, and a conga line dispersed into a moonscape slow dance once more.

Dante curled his hand around hers, spun her out to the end of his arm and back again.

She let out a huff of laughter, her hair falling about her face, as her hand landed on his chest. He curled his around it, holding it there. His other arm sliding farther around her back until they were as close as two people could be without public indecency.

Then he breathed out a long-suffering sigh, as his gaze dropped, landing on her mouth. Watching as if waiting to see what she might say next. Or wondering what she might taste like. For real.

Her fingers curled tighter around his and his gaze lifted. Pure smoke, not a hint of a smile. And her heart began to beat double time.

Dante shook his head. A lament. A curse she understood far too well, but had neither the experience nor the courage to break. She wished she could just lift up onto her toes and press her lips to his. She wanted it more than she wanted to breathe.

Instead, she turned her head away, leaned her cheek against his chest. The steady beat of his heart made her feel like crying.

When they turned, a gentle move, the music guiding them, Sutton saw Laila now sitting on one end of the bar.

Sutton lifted her head, mouthed, *You okay?*

Laila lifted her shoulders, gave them a happy wiggle, then grinned as she raised her drink in salute. Then mouthed, *Are you okay?*

Sutton opened her mouth, closed it, and shrugged.

Dante, feeling it, pulled her closer still. Till she felt as safe and secure as if she was wrapped in the world's most luxurious blanket.

Then "Lickety Split" by the Magnolia Blossoms rent the air, all cacophonous vocals and mad drums. And Sutton's head snapped up.

It was enough for Dante to lose his rhythm. The both of them coming to from whatever place had made them think they could dance so close, and get away with it.

"I love these guys!" Kent shouted, grabbing the remote and turning it up.

"They're mine," Sutton shouted back.

"Yours?" Kent asked.

"The Magnolia Blossoms. I manage them."

"Get out of here!" Kent gawped.

Sutton gawped back, spinning in Dante's arms. Only he gently pulled her back against his chest as his hand rested around her waist. She felt the heat of him all over her now. Evidence that she wasn't the only one existing in this strange place between reality and desire, pressed against her backside.

It was so wild, so overt, she laughed, and hiccupped. Then she couldn't stop.

"Who else?" asked Kent.

"Currently?" *Hiccup.* "The Sweety Pies. Candy Carter... I managed Crochet for a bit, before they took off."

Kent glared at Sutton. "If you tell me you've met the Floss Babies, I will literally throw myself off the nearest bridge."

Hiccup. "Does an ironic B&B crawl holiday through the Cotswolds one spring count?"

Kent threw his hands in the air in mock disgust, before grabbing the hands of those nearest and jumping up and down till the floor shook.

Sutton spun back into Dante's arms. And at the sight of his beautiful face, her hiccups just went away.

This, she thought, *this is the very best part of the night.* And that was okay.

"What do you think?" she asked, motioning to the music blasting around them. "They're amazing, right?"

Dante smiled as he shook his head. As if he knew as much about folk punk as she did about wine. Which felt just about right.

Sutton took him by the hand, encouraging him to twirl her out to the end of his arm, only this time she let him go. She laughed at the indulgent look on his face. Her laugh turned into something bigger. Freer. And below a canopy of pretend stars, her favourite band filling the night with music, Sutton finally kicked off her shoes and danced.

CHAPTER SIX

SUTTON SAT IN the jewel-green velvet couch in the front window of Forbidden Fruits as Laila brought over two glasses and a bottle of Vermillion Hill bubbly.

She held it up and Sutton shook her head no, cradling the coffee she'd picked up from the bakery, as the Vine wasn't open for another hour. The coffee was too milky, and not hot enough, but she hoped it might still work some magic. After very few hours of restless, dream-filled sleep, she needed it.

"You do realise Nico Rossi had something to do with the making of that wine," Sutton niggled as Laila poured herself a glass.

Laila shrugged as she sat in a gilt chair with pink velvet seat. "What that man doesn't know won't kill me. Now, let's break down how last night went."

"A success?"

Laila lifted her bubbly in salute. "Okay, now that's done, did you have fun?"

"I really did." What she didn't say was that the after-party was her favourite part, a million times over. "How do you think everyone else has come up this morning?"

"Not my problem," said Laila.

While by "everyone" Sutton actually meant Dante. It was a Sunday. Would he be at the Vine? She had work to catch up on. Should she head in, reclaim her table? Would things be strange between them, after their dance? If they *weren't* strange, would she be disappointed?

"Now," said Laila, cutting into her reverie, "we have to follow up ASAP with the results from the compatibility tests."

Laila grabbed her tablet from the coffee table and swiped madly over the screen, no doubt bringing up the app she'd sent to all attendees when they bought their tickets, requesting they fill it in. Questions included whether a person preferred bubble baths or showerheads with alternating spray options, so Sutton had limited hopes regards its veracity.

"Anyone in particular you want me to check against your profile?" Laila asked.

Dante's face was the first, and only, that popped into her mind. She blinked it away. "I met lots of nice people, but—"

"No love lightning?" Laila guessed.

Sutton *had* been about to blurt that she'd been having second, third, and fourth thoughts about a certain Grumpy Bartender after holding his hand had felt like a literal highlight of her pretty darned fabulous life.

Then a frown creased Laila's face. "Huh."

"What's wrong?"

Laila looked up, face pure guile. "Nothing. Not a thing."

Sutton clicked her fingers Laila's way. With a grimace, Laila turned her tablet around to show Sutton's profile beside...

"Dante?" Heck, even saying his name now made her feel weak all over. "When did *he* fill out the questionnaire?"

"He was my guinea pig. I made him fill it out a few days ago to check that it worked."

Saving questions as to how on earth Laila convinced Dante to say whether he preferred snuggling up with his special someone beneath a blanket by a fireplace in winter, or skinny-dipping together in a pool at the height of summer, Sutton asked, more than a little breathlessly, "Are you telling me Dante and I...*matched*?"

"Um..." said Laila, as she scrolled down the screen to where *Eight percent compatibility* glared back at them in unhappy, tomato red.

"Eight percent," she muttered. *Eight percent!* Yes, she'd just been thinking it was probably a load of bunkum, but even so, eight percent was pretty damning.

"Ignore it," said Laila. "It was a silly idea. Just one more way to keep customers on the hook." Then, "Unless... Were you hoping you had matched with Dante?"

Sutton opened her mouth. Then closed it. What to say? No? Yes? Gods, yes, pretty please, with sugar on top?

Laila put a hand on her knee. "Whatever you are thinking, stop. You look like you're about to burst a vein! You like him, he likes you. That much is obvious to everyone."

"Who's everyone?"

Laila waved a hush-up hand between them. "The thing is though, in my experience, sexual chemistry isn't everything. In fact, it can blind you to the important stuff."

Trying her best to get past the fact that "everyone" thought she and Dante had "sexual chemistry," Sutton asked, "Which is?"

"Location, ethics, lifestyle, family, hopes and dreams, whether you're a *Star Wars* or *Star Trek* fan? Who knows? I spend my days surrounded by men who aren't even human, or real. I'm clearly not the one to ask."

Sutton made a sound that sounded like a laugh but felt like a choke. And Laila's smile was far too understanding for comfort.

"Okay," Laila said, "considering the eight percent, let's count Dante out, for now, and see if there are any guys with whom you did match. In case there is someone perfect for you who you didn't get the chance to meet last night."

Count Dante out. Wasn't that what she'd been telling herself to do from day one. Some instinct assuring her she wasn't up for the likes of him. The quiz might be made up, but what if it was also a sign from the universe that holding hands with Dante, dreaming of Dante, dancing with Dante was setting her up for a huge fall.

"Sure," Sutton said, curling her feelings for the man deep down inside her, tucking them into a safe little box where they would hopefully stay this time. "Why not?"

She'd travelled halfway across the world looking for *something*.

The best thing she could do for herself was to keep trying to find it, till she figured out just what it was.

Dante crouched before a Chardonnay and Pinot Blanc hybrid vine, running his hands over the graft, tracing the petals of small white buds flowering at the tips.

It was the first time he'd stepped foot among the vines since arriving in Vermillion. Helping Zia Celia with real estate concerns he could handle, helping Rossi family wines had been an absolute no. Meaning Celia had saved telling him about their new graft until he was primed. Distracted. In a good mood.

That morning, even after very little in the way of restorative sleep, he'd woken feeling invigorated. Enlivened. As if the colours of the world had changed overnight. The need to walk among the vines, any vines, had been impossible to resist.

His phone buzzed. He considered ignoring it—the cleanup crew would have done their job, the staff would all arrive on time; he was sure of it in a way he'd not imagined he could be when he'd first arrived.

But his sense of duty had him wiping the dirt from his hands, before answering. *"Pronto?"*

"Dante? It's Sutton."

"Sutton," he said. His heart slammed into his throat and he stood so quickly he felt lightheaded. They'd shared numbers in preparation for the singles night, but she'd never called him before. "What is wrong?"

"Wrong? Nothing." Then, after a pause, "Took some time to come down after last night, but other than that, I'm great. You?"

Dante, realising he was pacing, stopped and gripped the back of his neck, pressing into the tension that had strangled him the moment his imagination had run away from him. "I slept fine. Thank you."

Though it had been well after three by the time he'd made it back to his bed, for he'd stayed after everyone else had left. To count the night's takings, to restock the bar, to lock up. To think, to reset, reassess.

For while the entire night had been a study in what passion and purpose could accomplish in a wildly short amount of time, the after-party had been something else entirely. Specifically, the dance, with Sutton.

It had lasted less than half a song, yet he'd walked out onto the dance floor with rigid purpose, and left it feeling as if his foundations had been whipped away.

"Where are you?" Sutton asked.

"Vermillion Hill," he said, his voice gruff, throat clutching around all the things he felt he wanted to say to her, but could not. *Should not.* Should he? "You?"

"At the Vine. I thought you might be here."

"I gave myself the day off."

"Totally fair." A beat, then, "You should see the place, though, Dante. There is not a table spare. Even the barstools are full. And there's a line at the door. There are a number of familiar faces from last night—city folk who stayed over, locals, and tourists swept up in the crowd. Chrissy found a lectern and she's set up a booking station at the front door. It's madness!"

Dante blinked into the middle distance. "You are serious."

"As a heart attack." Sutton laughed, the sound turning up the sunshine. "But that's not why I was calling."

Dante's focus contracted like the crack of a whip as every sense went on high alert. Sutton had *called* him. Sutton who had melted against his chest, her hand playing with his hair, before looking up at him as if it was taking everything in her not to lift onto her toes and kiss him.

"So, this might sound out of left field," she said, stopping to clear her throat. "And if you're not up for it I totally understand."

Dante's heart thundered against his ribs at the possibilities of what she might say. None of which was:

"So, you know the compatibility test?"

"The—?"

"The questionnaire, on the app, that Laila forced us all to fill out."

Ah. Dante could hardly remember how Laila had convinced him to do so. Witchcraft was not outside the realm of possibility. But what did that have to do with the dance?

Then Sutton went on. "Turns out I got quite a few hits. With men. With whom I might be compatible." She went on quickly. "And while it really was a silly quiz, I kind of feel as if I have to let it play out. What if it's the reason I came here? I don't know. Either way, I plan to set up as many dates as I can in the next couple of weeks. And since I don't know these guys, I thought it best to do so someplace safe. The Vine is my safe place. And it would be great to know there was someone, a kind of wingman, on my side, to move them on if needs be."

Dante, who had finally caught up with how the conver-

sation had turned, knew what was coming before she even
said the words.

"I was hoping that you might be that person. For me?"

The desire to laugh, and throw his phone across the field,
came at him in equal measure. Instead, he pressed finger and
thumb to his temple and rubbed.

"I could ask someone else," she said, when he said nothing, "if it feels weird. It is weird right? In fact, I'll try Kent.
Or Nico. Though what with the winery and his volunteer
work he might not have the time—"

"I'll do it," Dante growled.

She needed him, he'd be there, it was that simple. No matter how deep the cut.

A beat, then, "Thank you, Dante. Just…thank you."

Sutton's hands were shaking as she hung up the phone. She
threw the thing on her bed and lay back on the feather-soft
mattress with a thud.

Looking up at the lacy canopy, she let out a great big sigh.
Then a growl. Then, grabbing a pillow to put over her face,
a yell.

For a second there, longer, a deep soul-clutching breath,
she'd considered saying something else entirely. Considered
telling him how lovely it had been dancing with him. Asking if it had felt special to him too.

But then she'd pictured her dad, sitting in his wing chair
every night, listening to her mother's favourite records, glass
of wine in hand, heartbroken even today, and such words had
felt impossible.

Yes, she wanted to be braver when it came to affairs of the
heart. Wanted to open herself up to all of life's big moves before her twenty-eighth birthday. But she wanted to be careful,
to ease her way in. And Dante Rossi was anything but easy.

"Good decision," she said to the ceiling.

Then again, and again, until she started to almost believe it.

A couple of nights later, Sutton stood outside the Vine and Stein, her hand reaching for the door, then pulling away. Reaching, and falling back. It felt like her first day all over again, only this time she knew what she was walking into.

"What are you doing?" Laila asked.

"Prevaricating."

"We went through this. You are to get in there early, choose the spot with the best lighting, have a schooner to loosen up, and prepare to fall madly in love. Right?"

"Right." Sutton had agreed to all of it, in theory. "Is this really a smart move?"

"I'm not sure about smart, but it's worth a shot. Now go, get in there. Message me as soon as you're done."

"You're not coming in?"

"Yikes no. You already have one too many people watching over you, in my opinion. You do not need a whole audience. Go get 'em!"

Laila backed away, while Sutton opened the door.

Remembering the chill wind that had rushed through her all those weeks ago, as if a sign that change was coming, she told herself that change didn't always happen *to* a person, sometimes it happened because a person decided it was time.

Five minutes later Sutton sat at her usual table, deciding on comfort over "best lighting."

Someone had set it with a linen tablecloth, and an old Chianti bottle with a real lit candle inside, while Dean Martin crooned from a speaker hidden somewhere nearby. Meaning either "someone" had kindly looked up "classic romantic first date" decor, or they were messing with her.

That "someone" had to be Dante. Dean Martin? And no one else bar Laila knew her plan.

Though the man hadn't even looked up once since she'd arrived. He seemed to be going through paperwork behind the bar, which he could be doing in the office. Meaning he was doing as she asked, and looking out for her, as requested. Right? Not being there, all gorgeous, and grumpy and—

"Sutton?"

Sutton flinched, then looked up to find a man standing by her table.

When she said nothing, he scratched his chest. "I'm Mando. From singles night."

"Mando!" She pushed back her chair, the thing catching on a knot in the wood floor as she stood, so that she nearly chopped herself in half against the edge of the table.

Mando laughed. A nice deep laugh. That was a good thing. Right? A good start?

Once she extricated herself from the table, she took his hand and he pulled her in to lay a kiss on her cheek. He smelled nice. He was good-looking. Yet as he sat in the proffered chair across from her, the urge to look past him, to the man at the bar, was so strong it took physical effort to keep her gaze where it ought to be.

She looked to… Mando? Mando. With an encouraging smile. "So, singles club. What a night, right?"

Sutton had been right about one thing—the Vine was getting busier every single shift. If it kept going this way, they might break even that week.

While Dante should be feeling over the moon, by the third night of their blind date deal, he wished he was hitting a boxing bag at the gym, or chopping down a tree, for he had a sudden surfeit of energy he could not deplete.

He glanced up at Sutton's table, where that night she was

chatting with a giant of a man with curly blond hair. Night
before had been a dark-haired guy with a ponytail. Night before that a ginger-haired guy with dimples.

"Is that one of Sutton's bands playing over the sound system?" said Laila, who had snuck in after the bookshop closed.

"It is," Dante said.

The first night, once her date had left, Sutton had stalked
up to the bar, all riled up as if he'd done something wrong.
He who had danced with her, held her in his arms, begun to
believe that maybe there was something between them that
could no longer be denied, then been asked to be her *assistant* on a series of blind dates.

She'd clicked her fingers at him when he'd not deigned
look up the moment she appeared.

"Something I can help you with?" he'd drawled.

"Whatever device is playing the music next to my table—
give it to me."

He placed down his pen and looked into her eyes. "And I
thought you were a music lover."

The way her lashes had batted against her cheek, the
way her tongue had slipped over her bottom lip before she'd
dragged it into her mouth... He felt it like a living thing, roil-
ing inside him.

She'd said, "Dean Martin singing 'Memories Are Made
of This' over and over again for an hour and a half is not
'music.'"

Dante pulled out his phone, typed in his passcode, and
handed it over. "Was your date a success at least?"

"It was fine," she gritted out as she swiped through his
playlist.

"As far as I know the Vine has never hosted a wedding
reception, but we are all about trying new things here now."

Her eyes were sharp, her smile fake, as she handed back

her phone. "Great. I'll keep it in mind." With a dark look, she'd grabbed her stuff and left.

Not five minutes later she'd texted him an apology for being so abrupt, thanked him for his help, signed off with Sutton x and made him feel like a bad friend. And like more than a friend as he took that *X* and imagined meanings that were simply not there.

"Ooh, I remember this one," said Laila, dragging Dante back into the present to find Laila watching Sutton and her date laugh together. "Hot. Big muscles."

Dante grabbed a bar towel and wrapped it tight around his hand till his fingertips turned numb.

Nico—who had been sitting at the other end of the bar, pretending to ignore Laila—sauntered to sit at the seat beside hers, and said, "She's smiling. That has to be a good sign."

"It's not reaching her eyes," said Dante, as he wiped down the bench hard enough to take off a layer of shellac. "Not the way it does when she really smiles."

After a pregnant pause, Laila and Nico spun on their barstools to stare at him.

"Not a word," Dante growled, as he stalked into the office. "Not a single word."

After a late-afternoon tour of a local historical house, Sutton hustled up Main Street, on her way to her next date with a guy named… Greg? Or was it Craig? After a week of blind dates, they were starting to blur.

At least she knew if it was worth extending the dates past a single drink quickly now. The night prior she'd given Dante the signal, shaking a hand through her hair, to let him know to come to the table with a "phone call" after less than ten minutes.

Her phone rang with a real call as she neared the Vine. When she saw it was her dad, her heart leaped into her throat.

They'd been in touch—sending funny cat memes, and checking in with their daily Wordle scores. She'd called a couple of times too. Sure, she'd known he'd be at work, but she'd left long messages, asking after his shifts at the local grocery store.

But it had been long enough. The time had come to tell him the truth. Spotting a bench beneath a cheery blossom, she sat, and picked up the call.

"Dad!"

"Honeybun! I'm so glad I caught you. You've been busy?"

"Good busy."

"Glad to hear it. You know I've been hoping it's because you've met someone nice."

She laughed, as was expected, only for the first time in her life she wished she could tell him that she had. "I meet nice people every day, Dad. You know that. Now how about you? Booked that Devon walking holiday yet? The scenery looks gorgeous. All that fresh air. Did you show Marjorie?"

A pause, then, "It sure looked wonderful, honeybun."

Sutton bit her lip as even she could hear she was being far pushier than usual. But the fact he spent his nights alone, when he was still young enough to carve out a different life, it pained her.

When her dad made no further comment, she braced herself and said, "So I have some fun news. You won't believe where I am right now."

"Where's that?"

"Sitting on a bench on the Main Street of Vermillion." The silence that met her was heavy. Heavy enough she said, "Dad? Are you still there?"

"By Vermillion you mean…?"

"South Australia. Where you met Mum!"

A strangled noise came from the other end of the line.

Heart in her throat, Sutton shifted to the edge of the seat. "Dad, are you okay?"

"But why?" he said. "Why would you do that? Why would you not tell me you were going, so I could… I could…"

Sutton held her tongue. The same protective instinct that had stopped her from telling him where she was, was now telling her to give him grace.

"So you could tell me your favourite haunts?" she allowed. "I would love that, actually. I keep wondering if I've visited the same places you guys did."

When he said nothing, she put the back of her hand over her eyes. "I've upset you, haven't I? This is why I didn't want to tell you. But it's a *nice* thing, Dad. I'm twenty-eight in a few days, the same age Mum was when she died. And coming here felt like something I had to do."

"Of course," he said, after another long silence. "Of course, my love."

"Are you sure?"

"Its fine, honey," he said. "I understand. Enjoy yourself, and when you come home, tell me all about it."

"Okay. Love you, Dad."

"Love you, honey."

Sutton rang off. Then sat there for goodness knew how long, cradling her phone, and feeling more confused than ever.

Sutton looked miserably into her drink. It was her third. Or fourth. She'd needed something to distract her from the conversation with her dad.

Her sweet, loving dad who'd been nothing but wonderful to her. She'd not wanted to hurt his feelings, and now she was all but certain she had. Yet there was more going on, something behind his reaction, she was sure of it.

And instead of finding out what that was, she was on a

stupid date. With a stranger. Because she was too much of a scaredy-cat to ask out the one person who actually floated her boat.

"Sutton?"

Sutton looked up to find Craig, or Greg, sitting across the table, looking at her with concern. She lifted her hand straight up in the air.

His gaze followed the move. "Are you okay?"

"Yep, just signalling my wingman so he can come rescue me."

"Your... *Seriously?*"

Realising she's just said that out loud, she winced. "It's not you, it's me."

Greg, who was gathering his things, said, "Yeah, you've got that right." He grabbed his glass of wine—a delightfully plummy Vermillion Hill red he'd spent their entire date orgasming over—downed the dregs, then left.

Sutton slowly slid down deep in her chair. Footsteps neared, then stopped. She lifted her head to find Dante standing by her table: "Oh, hi."

He glanced at her arm, which was still raised in the air.

Sutton dropped her hand and patted the seat beside hers. "Sit."

"I'm working."

"No, you're not. You've done all you came here to do. Now you're just pretending to work so that you can stay here and spend time with your family who you miss terribly. You're all just too stubborn to admit it."

Dante's jaw worked. Yet, for whatever reason, he sat. "I think you need some water."

"Water-schmater. And wine-schmine for that matter." She flicked her date's wineglass a *ting*. "What's so good about it anyway? A grape is a grape is a grape."

Dante, mouth twitching, said, "I have offered to show you

why that is simply not true. But you have refused me. More than once."

She looked at him, sensing a hidden message between his words too. Men and their secrets! *Pfft*.

"Fine," she said. "Show me now."

Dante shook his head. "Not now."

"Why?"

"Because I'm not sure you'd remember it afterward."

Sutton swallowed, certain she was missing something now. Certain her lucid self would kick her for not knowing what it was. So instead, she frowned down at her cocktail, the colour lost to the silvery sheen of melting ice.

"Are you okay?" Dante asked.

"I'm not sure that I am." When she looked up, her beautiful grumpy bartender was watching her with a level of tenderness she did not know how to deal with.

"Tell me something in Italian," she blurted.

Dante, seeing her change of subject for the distraction that it was, leaned back in his chair, and looked at her from under his dark brows. "Such as?"

She leaned forward, and reached across the table. "Anything you like. Let that ridiculously sexy voice of yours go for broke."

After a long, loaded beat, in which she saw Dante's pulse leap in his throat, the man crossed impressive arms over his impressive chest and said, *"Cos'è rosso e si muove su e giù?"*

"Hmm?" was about as eloquent a response as she could come up with, for she was only half paying attention to his words. That face, those eyes, his body language were all so damned compelling it was hard to think of anything else.

A smile kicking up the corner of his mouth, he added, *"Un pomodoro in un ascensore."*

"But what does it mean?" she asked.

"It means," said Dante, "what's red and moves up and down?"

Chrissy, who was passing by with a drink order, said, "A tomato in an elevator."

"Si, bene."

Dante smiled, Chrissy smiled, Sutton frowned.

Then, expression turning serious, Dante said, "Chrissy, I'm going to take Sutton home."

"Nice," she said with a grin.

Dante's smile disappeared. "Not like that. She's...under the weather."

"Oh. Right. You go, we've got this. Take your girl home."

"Home?" Sutton called after her. "I have no home!"

"The B&B," Dante offered gently, now standing by her chair, holding out a hand. "What was it called? Grape Expectations?"

"If you say so," Sutton said, then, with only a moment's hesitation, put her hand in Dante's, wondering why it had taken her so long to do just that.

Sutton leaned her head against Dante's car window, her breath creating small patches of fog on the glass. Dante wondered if she'd fallen asleep.

If so, what ought he do once they arrived at the B&B? Rouse her? Walk her to her room? Carry her? The thought of having her warm body tucked up against his chest again, her head tucked under his chin, her hands wrapped trustingly about his neck again, was enough for him to grip the steering wheel hard.

"Sutton," he said, when they turned up the pretty driveway leading to the B&B.

"Hmm?" she said, her voice forlorn.

"We're here."

"Here," she repeated. "My mum and dad fell in love *here*, did you know that?"

"I did know that."

"And I can't even meet someone who'll stick around longer than one drink. What's wrong with me?"

Not a damn thing, he thought as he bumped up the driveway and pulled into a visitor spot in front of a three-story inn.

He turned to face her. "You are discerning."

"I'm broken," she said. And a single tear slid slowly down her cheek.

Dante cut the car engine, so that the only sounds were the tick-tick-tick of cooling metal, the haunting calls of night birds outside, and the myriad thoughts spiralling through his head.

He was the broken one. Sutton was vitality personified. The more he knew her, the more he believed that she was light, and life and... She needed to talk to someone, this was clear. In that moment, busted or not, he was all she had.

He turned more fully on the seat, his knee an inch from hers.

"You're not broken, Sutton," he said. "At least no more than the rest of us. But something has clearly happened to upset you tonight."

Sutton tipped her head to face him, more tears pooling against her lower lashes. "I was a maniac back there. I should have postponed the date. Or cut myself off. Instead, I made that poor man sit with me and bear the brunt of my self-immolation."

She closed her eyes and sank deeper into the seat. "I can't keep going like this. Living in the moment, going with the flow, sleeping where I land, or one day I'll wake up and I'll be sixty and alone and unable to see a way out."

"How old are you?"

"Twenty-eight next week."

"So not quite sixty, just yet."

She sniffed, a smile kicking at the corner of her mouth before disappearing again.

"Meaning," Dante went on, "you have a little time to sort yourself out." Then, well aware he was talking to himself now as much as he was to her, "If you admit to your own foibles and limits, as well as the things you truly want, only then do you have the chance to improve your situation. Right now, here, think of this as a good start."

"I guess that makes sense," she said, then after looking at him for a few long beats, she curled herself to face him. Her gaze roving over his cheek, his jaw, his neck, before moving back to his mouth. Where it stayed. While she sighed a hearty sigh.

Dante's gaze took in her determined chin, her shoulders lifting as she sniffed, collecting herself. Before being inexorably drawn to her mouth too. To the slide of her tongue over her lower lip, the catch of it between her teeth.

Before he felt himself move, Dante reached up, his fingers cupping her jaw, his thumb tugging at her lip, setting it free.

Her breath hitched, and she swallowed hard. Before her lips pursed, and kissed the end of his thumb.

Gaze fogging, desire swarming over him, Dante ran his thumb over her lip again. The soft, plump give was like everything he'd imagined it to be, and so much more.

When she leaned in, her teeth scraping over the end of his thumb, he felt so many feelings at once he feared he might expire on the spot.

Then, remembering how many drinks she'd had, he gently curled his hand away. When her eyes lifted to his, confused, he smiled, not wanting her to feel she'd done a single thing wrong.

Then her eyes looked past him out the car window. And she screamed.

Dante spun to find a tall thin balding man in a cardigan and tiny glasses barrelling toward them.

"Sutton," the man called, his voice muffled by the glass, "is that you?"

Dante opened the car window. "Barry?" He'd called the man before coming, hoping he'd have a spare key to Sutton's room.

Barry leaned into Dante's window. "Dante, I assume? And how is my little pepper pot?"

"Rubbish," Sutton said. "Sorry I screamed."

Barry waved it off. "Happens more than you'd think. I have snacks. A bucket of water for you to drink. Your bed is turned down for the night."

"Thank you." She gave Barry a huge, grateful smile.

Then turned that smile on Dante. His heart twisted in such a way he wasn't sure it would ever be right again. "Thank you for being my wingman."

"Anytime."

A million thoughts seem to scurry across her eyes. She opened her mouth as if about to say something, then snapped it shut. With one more tight-lipped smile, she hopped out of the car.

Dante waited till she was in the front door, Barry bouncing around protectively behind her, before he gunned the engine and drove away.

CHAPTER SEVEN

THERE WAS ONLY one other car in the staff parking lot when Sutton pressed the buzzer at the back door of the Vine and Stein—the Range Rover Dante had driven her to the B&B in over twenty-four hours before.

She'd woken twelve hours later feeling sober and sobered by the choices she had made.

Forcing herself to go on blind dates? That wasn't her. Not telling her father her plan before she left? That hadn't been sensitive, or fair. As for Dante, and the walls she kept building between them, when all he'd done was be generous and supportive the entire time?

It was now three days till her twenty-eighth birthday and the near constant *tick-tock*, *tick-tock* in the back of her head had clearly sent her around the bend.

There were so many sensible reasons why leaning into her feelings for Dante wasn't the savvy thing to do. Yet, there was no escaping the fact that from the moment she'd first set eyes on him, felt that restrained bear energy, she'd honestly *liked* the guy. The very least she could do was make it clear to him he wasn't merely her wingman, chauffeur, or barista. She was truly grateful he was in her life.

She lifted her hand to knock again when she heard footsteps behind the door. It wasn't a cool night, yet an anticipatory shiver rocked through her. And when the door opened, Dante on the other side, the light of the single bulb over the

back door making him look as beastly as ever all she felt
was relief.

"Hey," she said.

"Hey." He leaned in the doorway. "How are you feeling?"

"Fine," she said, then, "better. Thank you." Then, "Can
I come in?"

Dante hesitated; hesitation being his prime mode of com-
munication where she was concerned. The both of them as
bad as each other.

"Let me in, Dante."

After a hard breath out, he opened the door wider. She
slipped through her gap, the brush of her arm against his
chest sending shivers of awareness through her.

Door shut behind them, he led her via the kitchen, into
the bar. Only the emergency lights, and the desk lamp in the
office, were on.

The look of the place was reminiscent of that first morning, but every other thing about it was significantly different.
She now knew this man—more than he probably wanted, and
less than she'd like. And the energy that crackled between
them as he turned to face her was filled with a history of
days, weeks of building tension.

"So," she said, hitching her backpack, "I came here tonight to thank you for—"

"No need."

"Let me finish, please."

He held out both hands. "Of course."

"Thank you for driving me. I honestly can't remember
if I said so last night, so thank you." Noting a mark on the
bar, she rubbed at it with her thumb as she said, "On top of
that I want to apologise for putting you in that position in
the first place."

When she looked up, Dante had his arms crossed. Barriers
up, yet watching intently, listening fully, as always.

"You've been so generous, letting me work here, allowing us to take over the place for an event that was a complete Hail Mary, not rolling your eyes every time I sprout some idea on how you could improve the Vine—"

"Sutton," Dante said, his voice low, quiet in the semidarkness, but carrying to her all the same.

"Not finished," she said, unable to meet his eyes for this last part. "Asking you to watch over me while I met other men, when you and I... I mean, I don't know what we are. To each other. But we're enough of a something, I think, that asking that of you was a crummy thing to do."

Her heart was thudding so hard by that point her ears rang. Yet she forced her gaze to his as she said, "Okay, now you can talk."

Dante's dark gaze was impossible to read.

"Did I blow it?" she asked. "Tell me what I need to do to make you like me again."

"Sutton," he said, voice pained. He took a step forward, then stopped. *Always* stopping.

While she'd lived by the mantra of throwing herself at every opportunity life put in her way, in every part of her life bar this one. She let her backpack fall to the floor with a slump. Then took a step toward him. And another. And another.

Dante's chest rose and fell, but he did not move.

One more step and the tips of her Vans kissed the tips of his boots. Then she lifted her hands and laid them against his jaw. "Talk to me," she said. "Please."

His stubble was softer than expected against her palm. She ran her thumbs over the skin above his stubble and could feel him vibrating. She looked up into eyes that were dark pools of swirling smoke and said, "If you want me to leave, I will. If you want me to stay, I will. I'm sick of questioning myself where you're concerned. Tell me what you want instead."

Her hands slid away from his face, and dropped to his chest. Beneath her touch, his heart was as erratic as her own. It was enough for her to curl her hands into the cotton of his shirt and give him a frustrated little yank.

He went with it, swaying to her as if she had control of him, of his breath, his body, his next move.

So, she did it again. Pulling him closer, only this time not allowing him to sway away.

Then a sound came out of him, like something that had been kept locked away for centuries, and his arms swept around her, lifting her off her feet, as his mouth came down on hers.

And oh, it was a kiss that had been a long time coming. Building. Hovering on the edges of their interactions until they were stupid from wanting.

After a few long moments, in which time felt suspended, his lips began to move over hers. Hot and slow, the bristles of his stubble tickling at her skin. His arms slid farther around her, holding her as close as he was able.

The emotion that swelled inside her as this man held her was like nothing she'd ever felt. Gentle and wild, soft and deep all at once. When he found a way to hold her tighter still, she moaned against his mouth.

With a growl, he deepened the kiss. Sweeping his tongue into her mouth, as if she was his breath, his very life force. The pressure sending her backward, till she bumped against the bar. It was so glorious, she huffed out a puff of laughter, of pure joy.

It was enough for Dante to snap back into his body—she felt it happen. He pulled back, flinching away from her, as if he'd been shocked.

She grabbed at him, hauling him back, wrapping a leg around his calf so he couldn't get away. And he didn't, not yet. But neither did he kiss her again. Breathing hard, he let his forehead drop to hers. And swore, softly, in his native language, while the hand at her waist gripped her, as if he was loath to let her go.

"I tried so hard not to let that happen," he said.

"Tell me about it," Sutton said on another huff of laughter.

He slowly shook his head, his hair catching on hers. "I had good reason. Without it I'd have given in to this, to you, weeks ago."

"Are you sure about that?" she asked, having recently pulled her own "reasons" apart as easily as dandelion fluff.

He lifted his head. Her heart hitched at the hardness of his gaze. "I am sure," he said. "Even now. I cannot give you what you need, *tesoro*."

Something inside her threatened to crack. But she braved up and said, "I think I know what I need better than you do."

Dante lifted his hand to cup her jaw, thumb tracing her cheekbone, the edge of her brow, the movement so sweet, so tender, especially when contrasted against his next words. "I am not the man you think I am."

"And what kind of man do you think I think you are?"

"A man who can treat you with casual regard and live with himself."

Sutton winced. For this moment, this man, had felt anything but casual. Not that she could tell him so; her bravery only went so far.

"Then you know what you can do?" she said, with what she hoped was a sassy smile. "Treat me with thorough regard, instead."

He laughed, a deep rumbling sound that all but took her knees out from under her. Then, eyes almost black with desire, he placed a finger under her chin and lifted her face, pulled her close, and kissed her.

A kiss so gentle, and so sweet, he might as well have

yanked her heart off its leash. Leaving her unprepared when Dante pulled away again.

The hand at her side gone, the man moving away so that she could not reach for him again, she had to grip the edge of the bar so as not to collapse in a molten heap.

"Dante?"

"Scusata," he said, shooting her a look that made her heart tremble. "I'm sorry. I can't. I just… Do you need me to drop you home?"

Sutton blinked. Barely able to remember where she was, much less how she'd got there. "I… I drove."

He nodded. "Then I will see you out."

"I…sure. If that's what you want?"

A beat later, so many emotions washing over his face she had no hope of keeping up, he said, "It is."

She reached down for her bag, lifted it listlessly onto her shoulder, and led him back through the kitchen and out the back door.

He waited for her to get safely to her car, before he lifted his hand in a wave, and closed himself inside the Vine.

Sutton coughed out a laugh, though there was no humour in it at all. "Good. Great," she said to the empty night. "Glad we cleared that up!"

A flicker of lamplight through the frosted glass of the back door told her Dante was at the door, pacing. That she wasn't the only one left feeling askew.

When the kitchen light switched off, with a loud, Dante-esque growl, Sutton gunned the engine and left.

"Happy birthday!" Laila sang, as she leaped out at Sutton as she trudged through the foyer of the Grape Escape on her way back from breakfast.

Sutton, still in her pyjamas, found herself holding a bunch

of helium balloons with a mix of baby paraphernalia and Disney characters on them.

"It's all they had left at late notice," Laila apologised. "Anyway, go get changed, I have a day planned."

Sutton looked longingly up the stairs. She was finally twenty-eight. Her plan had been to mope under the blanket in her room and let this day of all days pass her by with a whimper. Especially after the disaster with Dante the other night. All her impetus to explore the town, connect with her parents, open herself up to lovey-dovey stuff had felt flat after that. Enough she'd even begun thinking maybe it was time to leave.

Laila turned her around and shoved her toward the stairs. "I'm taking you somewhere fabulous. A Vermillion mustsee. You'll love it, I promise!"

"Okay," said Sutton, shaking off the doldrums and deciding what the heck. Birthday spirit, it was. "Dress code?"

"You do you, Boo. Just make it quick. Because…yep! Our bus is here."

"Bus?"

Laila pointed through the front window to where a small bus, filled with a dozen or so other people, awaited them. Vermillion Hill Cellar Door Tours written in bold red font on the side.

Sutton stood at the back of the small tour group, listening with half an ear as the guide talked about the history of the vineyard. Delighting as she was in the gorgeous old stone buildings, trees growing up against their rooves, the cobbled paths with horse and cart tracks worn into grooves over a century before, and the gentle hill covered in squat grey grape vines rising up to what the tour guide called "the family house."

"Are the Rossi family in residence today?" Laila asked.

"I believe so," the tour guide said, solemnly. "We see them on occasion. You might be lucky today!"

Laila nudged Sutton in the ribs. "Hear that? You might get lucky with a Rossi on your birthday!"

Sutton, who had *not* told Laila about the events of the other night, coughed, choked on the cough, and was given first entry into the cellar door space, so she could grab a glass of water before the tasting.

The cellar door was tiny, smaller even than Sutton's B&B room. No windows, ancient grey stone walls, uneven slate floors, massive wood beams crisscrossing overhead.

Behind a rustic wooden counter stood a man in his early twenties, neatly trimmed facial hair, red flannelette shirt over dark jeans. "Hey, I'm Josh. I'll be hosting your tasting today. First time at Vermillion Hill?"

"We're Vermillion Hill virgins," said Laila. "And it's this one's birthday!"

Josh's smile never faltered. "Happy birthday. How this works—I'll pour a taste of each of the six wines on the menu, you drink, and hopefully we can find you a new favourite drop."

He passed each of them a list of the wines they were set to try, a mix of red, white, and fortified vintages, awards and plaudits attached. He then set up a pair of fresh wineglasses, and spoke of organic certification, biodynamic systems, malolactic fermentation as he poured. While Sutton's gaze kept straying to the open doorway in case a certain Rossi might stride past.

"Nice legs," said Laila, swirling her glass dramatically, before downing the lot in one go.

Sutton spun, saw Josh leaning over to put a bottle away, and pinched Laila on the arm. She whispered, "You can't say that!"

"Legs is the lay term for the grip and drip of the wine as it slips down the inside of the glass."

Warmth slipped down *her* insides as Sutton spun to find Dante strolling through the door. Backlit by golden sunshine, he was all broad shoulders and sexily mussed hair, and the longing that rose in her was overwhelming.

"It speaks to the viscosity of the blend," Dante continued as he moved in beside her, easy as you please, and motioned for Josh to lay out a third glass, "but has no relation to the quality. Yes?"

Josh smiled. "Quite right."

Sutton looked to Laila, asking all the questions with her eyes.

Laila batted her lashes innocently, then leaned back to catch Dante's eye. "Hey, Dante, fancy meeting you here. Do you know Josh?"

Dante held out a hand to the man behind the counter. "Josh. Dante Rossi."

"Signor Rossi, it's an honour," Josh fawned. "Are you happy for us to follow the menu, or would you prefer to choose for our guests?"

Dante waved a hand, as if just happy to be there. The man who famously never looked happy to be anywhere.

"Next up, the Red Velvet," said Josh, holding up a bottle. "We grow many varietals here at Vermillion Hill—Riesling, Semillon, Chardonnay, Grenache. But the Barossa is best known for Shiraz."

Once the wine was poured, Dante picked up his glass using the stem, held it at eye level, and swirled it in a way that made the liquid swish up the sides of the glass without tipping over the edge. He lifted the glass to his nose, breathed deep, then sipped. Eyes closed, strong throat working, expression solemn.

Sutton wanted to kiss him, right there, where his throat

bobbed. She bit her lip to stop herself from whimpering at the effort of not doing so.

After placing the glass on the bench, Dante turned to her, expression quizzical, then looked at her hand, which was gripping the bowl of her delicate glass with all her might.

He laughed through his nose, the smile hitting his eyes, and her heart quickened. What was happening right now? Where was the usual grouchy Dante mask? It usually did a pretty good job of hiding his thoughts, but now she could see pleasure in his gaze. Pleasure that flowed through *her* like a waterfall.

Leaning in, voice low, he said, "The point of a wine tasting is to taste the wine."

"Told you," Sutton managed to say, "I'm not a wine drinker." Her father was the wine drinker. Every night, listening to those records, as if the sense memory might bring him back to this place.

"Then why are you here?"

"Laila's idea."

Laila and Josh chatted nearby, voices muted, as if they'd moved to the other end of the small bar to give Sutton and Dante some privacy. If he thought that was her doing...

"I didn't come here, in the hopes of—"

"I know," he said, eyes crinkling. "I know."

Then his eyes dropped to her mouth, as he slowly breathed out, and the memory of their kiss, the way he'd held her as if she was something precious but also something he wanted to ravish with every fibre of his being, made her body hum.

Yes, he'd put a stop to it, which had shaken her. But while it had felt like a rejection, he'd actually rejected *himself* on her behalf. And she'd never know why if she hid from him, or kept pushing him away.

She swallowed, and said, "A while back you said you thought you could change my mind."

Dante cocked his head.

"About wine."

"Ah."

"I'm willing to try now, if you are."

Dante's gaze was potent. Focused. Then with a nod he looked to Josh, at the row of wines on a shelf behind his head, and said, "Is there a Sangiovese Grosso 2003 Vigna dell'Essenza nearabout?"

Josh's eyes widened, then he disappeared through a small door, footsteps leading down to what must have been an underground cellar, and came back a couple of minutes later with an older-looking bottle. Sutton recognised the sketch on the label as the house from the large photograph on the wall of the Vine and Stein office.

Only once Dante nodded did Josh slip the cork free with a soft pop. He sourced two fresh glasses, and poured a very small amount into each.

This time Dante simply drank the proffered wine and the sound that came from him—throaty, appreciative—traced Sutton's spine like a slow, deliberate finger. When he looked to her, she had to press her knees back hard so as to keep them from giving way.

"Do *I* just drink?" she asked. "Or ought I do the whole swirl, sniff, sip thing?"

"Just drink," Dante said.

Hands trembling a little, for it was clear this wasn't just any bottle of wine, Sutton lifted the glass to her mouth, took a swig, and swallowed it down.

"Then tell me what you think," said Dante.

"It's…strong," she said, on a little cough. "Spicy." The aftertaste kept changing depending on which part of her mouth she focused on.

"Good," he said. "Now try it again."

He nodded and Josh poured for them both again.

Dante dismissed him with a polite movement of his head before turning to Sutton. "Only this time, swirl the glass like this, to let oxygen play its part. Then close your eyes, let the scent fill your nose. Then take another sip, and allow *all* your senses to take part. Wine is not a drink so much as it is a sensory experience. A memory, a tradition, a connection to the earth, the sky, the past."

Sutton, feeling as if she was about to take a test for a subject she'd not studied, went through Dante's instructions, one by one, finally allowing the wine to coat her tongue, the sides of her teeth, the back of her throat.

Dante's voice crooned, "The Sangiovese is a grape well known to Siena. High acid, vibrant, fresh. A grip that softens with age. The Vigna dell'Essenza brings flavours of dark cheery, leather, spice. It was a dry year, low rainfall, resulting in a complex, full-bodied vintage."

Sutton had always thought the language surrounding wine sounded so unapologetically pretentious. With Dante weaving a story in her mind as the liquid moved over her taste buds, she felt a ripening, sensed latent sweetness, imagined electric storms with no rain.

"How do you know so much about a single bottle?"

"As children Nico and I, and my sister, Isabella, helped pick the crop you are enjoying now."

Sutton slowly opened her eyes to find Dante watching her. His expression serious. She swallowed again, and as the wine hit her belly, it seemed to catch on the thread of heat she could see in his eyes.

"What do you think?" Dante asked.

"It...tastes like grape?"

Dante blinked, his eyes moving to the bottle, to her glass, to her face, then he burst into laughter. A rough, raw, sound so deep and inviting she felt a heated smile warm her face.

Then his hand landed on her back—a warm, solid touch

that had her wanting to lean into him. To turn and bury her face in his neck. And wrap her arms around him and climb into his arms and not let go.

It also made her wish they'd never met.

For try as she might, she could not see this ending the way her relationships usually did. Like a crew at the end of a fun tour—hug, shake hands, and move on. Despite all the effort she'd put into not letting her crush on the guy move beyond that, she'd already failed.

Then Dante raised his glass to her. "Happy birthday, Sutton," he said.

She lifted hers, clinked, then they took their final sips together.

Josh cleared his throat and said, "What would you like me to do with the bottle?"

"Enjoy it," Dante said, not taking his eyes from hers.

"Seriously? Thank you."

"No time like the present," said Laila.

"It's a thousand-dollar bottle of wine," Josh murmured.

"Then earn your keep, Joshy-boy. Convince me this thing is as good as those two made it look."

Sutton, feeling a little as if she wasn't entirely in her own body anymore, said, "I think I need some air."

She put down the glass, turned, and all but bolted outside, where she found a bench seat carved from a fallen tree. She sat; fingers curled around the wood, sun dappling her skin through the branches of a tree swaying overhead.

She wasn't surprised when Dante sat beside her.

Out of the corner of her eye she saw him lean back, arms crossed, legs stretched out before him. In the sunshine she noticed his jeans were old, boots scuffed, skin was swarthier than usual—all signs he'd been working at the vineyard all day.

He breathed out a long slow breath, as if he felt...*at ease*.

Something she had never seen at the Vine. There he was all clenched jaw, hard eyes, a constant growl beneath his words. Here, under a wide-open sky, the scent of dirt and flowers in the air, near the thing that gave him purpose, it hit her that she was seeing Dante, in his natural environment, for the first time.

While grumpy Dante tied her in knots, this Dante might just be her undoing.

Giving up on finding her feet anytime soon, she slid down in the seat, crossed her arms, crossed her feet at the ankle, and let her head fall back against the back of the bench.

They stayed like that for several long moments, before Dante said, "Tastes like grape." Then he laughed again.

And this time Sutton laughed with him.

"I'm so sorry," she said, covering her face, before looking at him through one eye. "I like grapes, if that helps."

He laughed again; this time his gaze stayed on her. Then, with a hard outshot of breath, he said, "You've not been around the past few days."

"No," she agreed.

"Might that have something to do with the other night?"

She looked up at the tree swaying overhead. She *could* talk about it—she wasn't afraid of tough conversations, unless they involved her dad, clearly. She just didn't want to hear Dante tell her he liked her, only not that way. Not the way her father had seen her mother and just known. Not today.

"It's my birthday," she said. "That means I get to decide what we talk about and what we don't."

"Fair," he said, then pulled himself upright. "So, what would you like to talk about?"

"The weather? It's a pretty nice day for a birthday."

"So it is," he said, not taking his eyes off her.

She pulled herself upright as well, taking the chance to put an inch of space between them. Only when her hand landed on the bench, her little finger brushed his. A moment later his hand moved over hers. Warm, rough, steady.

"There you are!" Laila cried as she burst out of the cellar door, as the next group went inside for their turn.

Sutton gently moved her hand to her lap.

"What did I miss?" Laila asked. "What were you guys talking about?"

"My birthday."

"On that," said Dante, pressing himself to standing, "if you're free, how does lunch at the villa and a proper tour of the place sound?"

When Sutton looked to him, he raised a single eyebrow in what looked very much like a dare. Who was this man and what had he done with Dante? Then it hit her—maybe it wasn't simply the location. What if by fronting up, grabbing the guy by the shirt and kissing him, she had changed things between them after all?

"Sounds fabulous to me," said Laila, checking her bag for her sunglasses, before moving in to give Sutton a one-armed hug. "You two have fun."

"You're most welcome to join us," Dante said.

"And if you're leaving, I'll come with you," said Sutton.

"Stay," said Laila. "I'll go talk Joshy into another glass of that spectacular wine, then go back on the bus with the others. I have plenty of boxes of books to unpack, anyway. Better now than late tonight," Laila said. She pointed a finger at Dante. "Make sure she gets home safe."

"Will do."

"Happy birthday, my love!" Laila called, then disappeared back into the cellar door.

"Shall we?" Dante asked, holding out a hand.

Sutton, wondering how the universe had put her there again, took it.

CHAPTER EIGHT

WHEN THEY REACHED the eastern vineyard of Vermillion Hill,
Dante stepped into the field only to find Sutton had stopped
short.

"Are you sure I can go in there?"

"Why would you not?"

"It feels like a sacred space. Out of bounds. What if I have
one of those diseases on my shoes the tour guide was talking
about, or a bug on my clothes. What if I poison them with
my perilous lack of wine knowledge?" Then she whispered,
"What if they know?"

He placed a hand at her back and gave her a light push, enjoying having her there beside him more than he'd have ever
imagined. The soft quiet of the vineyard, so different from
the dark, the noise of the Vine, along with the sunshine and
dust motes, made time stretch out before him.

Soon Sutton walked ahead, turning back to ask questions
every now and then—about the crop, or the process, or what
it was like back home—or simply running a hand over the
vine leaves once assured it was okay to do so.

While Dante spent every second in between remembering how it had felt to hold her, to pull her close, to kiss her.
How hard it had been to let her go.

In the moment it felt like the right thing to do.

It wasn't as if he'd denied himself pleasure in his life. Or companionship. He ate well, drank well, had work that gave him immense satisfaction. It was just that it already felt like far more than he deserved. For if Isabella was unable to enjoy such an abundance of delights, why on earth should he?

Sutton Mayberry was, quite simply, more than he could ever accept. Her vitality, her bumptiousness, her...*amore per la vita*, the way she gathered people close, and threw herself at life with such abandon.

He'd spent weeks telling himself she was not his to want.

Now, watching her stroll his family's land, in the hazy stillness of a warm afternoon, he felt his self-denial slipping. For how could being with her, laughing with her, watching her enjoy the world be wrong?

It was a slippery slope. One that would take vigilance, if he was to get out of this place without doing something for which he'd truly never forgive himself.

She stopped at the edge of the vineyard, where a single-lane dirt track cut up the hill toward the house. "Question."

Bring it, he thought.

"The vines on that side of the path," she said, pointing to the left, then pointing to the right, "and these—why are they so different?"

Dante moved up beside her, his skin twitching from how near she was. And gave her a lesson on the differences between the thick, squat, twisted, Grenache bush vines and the daintier, trellised Pinot Noir. Which led him to tell her about his Sagrantino vines back home.

"Comparatively, the leaves of the Sagrantino are a vibrant orange this time of year—the local hills look like fire in the autumn light. Come winter, the vines are bare. Spring hits, the buds appear, new wines are released. We pick in summer. And it starts all over again."

He looked to her when he was done to find her smiling up at him. Hands on hips, cheeks pink from exercise.

"Look at you," she said, "all puffed up and proud. You're practically giddy."

"I am not giddy."

"You are so giddy," she said, moving to knock her shoulder against his. "We are lucky, you and I. To do something we feel passionate about. Not everyone finds that in life."

On that they were in agreement.

He motioned they head up toward the house.

"How does this place compare to Sorello?" she asked, falling into step beside him,

"Land-wise, Vermillion Hill is probably three times bigger. We would be considered a boutique label in comparison. But the latitude and climate are similar."

"Do you miss it?" Sutton asked.

"Enormously," he admitted. "But I have a good team running the place in my absence. We check in once, twice daily. All, I am assured, is well."

"I'm sure they'll be glad to see you return. Soon."

He felt the question hovering between them: *When might that be?* The Vine was much improved, only he could not seem to pull the pin just yet.

"How about you?" he asked. "Are you missing home?"

"I tour a lot, so I don't really have a place that feels like home. Not in the way you do." She swallowed. "Though my dad and I are very close. Only we argued, the other day, just before my disastrous final blind date, which we never do."

"Have you spoken to him since?"

"We've messaged, but no. No calls. And no mention of the argument. He'll call me later today, for my birthday, no doubt. Maybe I'll bring it up then. Maybe not." She shook her head. "You've mentioned a sister. Is she in the family business too?"

They were near enough the house, he knew he could change the subject easily enough. Only with her looking up at him, her genuine interest in what made him *him* clear as day, he found himself saying, "Isabella passed away quite a number of years ago."

Sutton stopped. Reached for his arm when he kept walking. "Dante? What happened? Or... Don't tell me, if you don't want to."

He took the hand on his arm and tucked it into his side once more, forcing her to continue walking toward the house. "She was several years younger than me, making her terribly young when our mother died. My father made it clear he preferred me. He found me easier, I think. She was bright, creative, completely uninterested in the family business. They knocked heads, constantly."

"That must have been hard," said Sutton, sliding her hand a little farther up the side of his arm so that their bodies brushed as they walked.

"Hmm. We were close, so that gave her some protection. Only as she hit her teens, and their relationship became more combative, she fell in with friends who were not good for her. It was around the same time that I was becoming more involved with Rossi Vignaioli Internazionali, firstborn son, bred to take over one day. It got to the point where she wouldn't even talk to me."

Step, brush, a gentle squeeze of his arm. It kept him tethered, even as his mind went to events he'd done as much as possible to distance himself from. Fearful that if he ever leaned into them again, this time he might never lean out.

"One night, I had planned to be home for dinner, but having spent all day trialling a new fermentation process on a small batch of grapes I had grown on my own, I was late. All we can figure is that she had been drinking, went for a swim in the southern dam..." He swallowed. "I found her late the next day, unaware she'd even been missing."

Sutton tugged so hard on his arm then, he had no choice

but to stop. Then she turned him so that he faced her. Her spare hand slid up to his shoulder, then when he refused to meet her eyes, she cradled his cheek, lifting his face so he had no choice.

"I'm so sorry. The way you spoke of her, of your plans when you were younger, I had no idea."

"Of course you didn't. I never talk of her," he admitted.

"Why?" Then, with a frown, "Don't tell me you think it is *your* fault."

Dante shook his head. He *had*. But over time he'd come to see the cogs and spokes and moments that had led to what was a horrific accident. "My father did not feel the same, unable to see his part in her self-destruction. When he began telling everyone in the family what I had, and had not done, to help, I could not take it anymore."

Sutton's eyes blazed in fury. Then she moved her hand, as if about to run it through his hair, in comfort. In care. Only at the last second, she stopped herself. Brow furrowing as if she remembered what had happened the last time she'd touched him.

When she made to take her hand away, Dante's hand caught hers, and after a pause, slowly placed it back against his cheek.

Her eyes grew dark. Her chest rose and fell. Then her thumb traced a slow arc over his cheek. The hand still curled around his arm pulled him close and she leaned her cheek against his chest and held him. Pure comfort, and kindness— her way of showing him that she was on his side.

Then her phone rang, and he felt her flinch against him.

"I'm so sorry," she said, slowly uncurling herself from around him. "That's my dad's ringtone. He'll be calling to wish me happy birthday."

"Answer it," he insisted, bringing the hand that had been at his cheek to his lips so that he might kiss her palm. Then he let her go.

Looking as if emotion and sense were warring inside her, she stepped back, and answered. Her voice sweet and kind, as she said, "Dad, hey."

Dante moved a little farther way, giving her privacy as she paced back and forth. He heard the occasional *mmm-hmm*, and *thank you*, and *love you, Dad*. The rest he only picked up by way of her body language.

Something wasn't right. Most people wouldn't see it, but he did. He recognised in her a need to wear a mask at times, to keep people at arm's length. While his was cantankerous, hers was a show of strength.

And it hit him, for all the ways they were dissimilar—beer versus wine, travel versus home, preference for noise versus quiet—in the deepest, most personal ways, they might actually be very much the same.

When she hung up the phone, she shot him a quick smile, the slight wobble making a protective instinct rise up like a roar inside him.

"You okay?"

"Sure. He'd love to have seen me today, of all days."

"Is it tradition to spend your birthdays together?"

"It's not that. It's just… My mother died when she was twenty-eight. Today I'm twenty-eight. He adored my mother. When she died it all but destroyed him. It's a big part of why I came here."

Dante wished he could give her the solace she had just given him, but she was coursing with an excess of energy, where in such moments he tended to shut down.

She shook her head, and pocketed her phone. "I'm probably making something out of nothing. Either way, I've taken up enough of your day. I should probably let you be."

"Stay," said Dante before he felt the word leave his mouth. "Please."

Her gaze moved over his as she made her decision. He

did not blame her for taking her time. Until now he'd done his utmost to find reasons not to spend time with her. A kiss had changed it all. Changed him. Now he was flying without a map.

"Stay," he said, moving in, cupping her elbows, "have lunch with me. A birthday celebration. My aunt Celia will be there. Chances are Niccolo will join us, which will give you the chance to watch him be taken down by his mother."

"Bonus," she said, leaning into his touch. He wasn't sure she even knew she was doing so.

"Is that a yes?"

She looked out over the vineyard, then down to her phone, then with a smile that would forever more be burned onto the backs of his retinas, she said, "That's a yes."

Where the cellar door was quaint, the private grounds of Vermillion Hill were pure elegance. A sweeping stone home perched atop the hill, tennis court, indoor pool, wings seemingly added over the years. All of which Sutton would have gushed over, if her mind wasn't still so snagged on her father's call.

Unlike the last time they'd spoken—when he'd stuttered, and seemed not himself—not only had he informed her he'd looked into the walking tour, he had asked Marjorie, the neighbour, to come over with her laptop so they could look at more pictures online together.

Which was good. Great, even. Only the timing felt too fortuitous to be a coincidence.

"Sutton! What a delight!"

Sutton turned to find Nico walking toward them, wearing what looked like a firefighter uniform. "Ah, what's happening?" she muttered to Dante.

Dante leaned in, murmuring, "My cousin likes playing hero in his spare time."

Sutton thought to the way he tried to keep Laila in line. "Only in his spare time?"

Dante's laugh shifted against her hair.

"Hey, Nico," she said as he neared. "You didn't have to dress up for my birthday. Unless… Oh, my gosh, are you a strip-o-gram? If so, go ahead."

Nico blushed. Blushed! Glared at Dante, then leaned in for a double-cheek kiss. "Happy birthday, Sutton."

When he moved back, Sutton felt Dante move in closer. Proprietarily.

"What are your plans?" Nico asked.

"Dante asked me to stay for lunch."

Nico looked over Sutton's shoulder. "Did he, now?"

"He did," said Dante, his voice deep with warning.

"So long as that's all right with your mother," Sutton added.

"Are you kidding?" Walking backward toward the door of the house, a dimpled grin on his handsome face, Nico said, "Wait till my mother gets a load of you."

Sutton had never found cause to use the word *insouciant* till she met Celia Rossi.

Niccolo's mother—a.k.a. Dante's aunt, who had begged and pleaded and guilted him into coming over to "save the Vine"—was the epitome of casual elegance.

Celia whipped her large sunglasses from her face as she went first to Dante. *"Caro!"* she intoned, drawing her nephew in for a double-cheek kiss.

Nico, looking most put out, said, "Firstborn son, here."

His mother tutted, before pulling him into her embrace. "You get plenty of hugs. This one has been in deficit for far too long."

She patted Dante's cheek, then her gaze swung in a wild double take as she saw Sutton. "What have we here?"

"Zia," said Dante, "*questa è* Sutton Mayberry. She co-hosted the recent singles night at the Vine that was such a success. Sutton, my aunt Celia Rossi."

Celia's eyes narrowed in a way that had Sutton wanting to tug at the waistline of her low-slung jeans and put on pearls. "Are you the bookstore owner giving my Niccolo such troubles?"

Sutton smiled. "I'm the tourist who found herself swept up in the bookstore owner's madcap, but ultimately successful, plan."

Celia, clearly appreciating the light sting in the tail of Sutton's words, held out a hand. "Then I am very pleased to meet you, Sutton. You are staying for lunch, no?"

"Yes? If that's all right with you."

Celia slid a hand through Sutton's arm and led her toward the house proper.

"It's Sutton's birthday," Dante warned. "So be nice."

"*Buon compleanno.* And shush, I am always nice."

Sutton let out a sigh as she leaned back in the plush outdoor chair, having enjoyed an astonishing assortment of cheeses, cured meats, olive oil, and breads over the past few hours. For lunch had come late, morphing into early dinner, and while Celia flitted in and out, Dante and Nico had chatted, laughed, and told stories of their childhood together.

She'd even made her way through a half glass of wine—too scared to offend Celia to say no.

Did it taste like grape? Yes.

Would she try some again, off her own bat? Undecided.

Considering the long lead-in to this day, and the deep reverence she'd attached to it, it had turned out pretty darned wonderfully. Much of that thanks to the man sitting across the table, watching her in a way that had her feeling as if her blood was filled with bubbles.

Nico grabbed the closest bottle, filled a glass for himself. Dante shook his head, done. While Sutton had to wave him away again, even after she'd done so several times. They were wine pushers, the lot of them.

"Tell me about yourself, *mia cara*," said Celia as she settled into a chair, curling her feet up, glass of wine in hand. "What is your story?"

Having told more people "her story" than she'd ever imagined she might over the past few weeks, Sutton gave Celia the CliffsNotes, touching briefly on why this birthday was bittersweet. Concluding with, "I wonder if you ever met my father. Gerard Mayberry? He was a backpacker, working around here when I was born."

"Alas, we've only been here the past twenty-some years. The children were primary school-aged when Rossi Vignaioli Internazionali bought the Vermillion Hill estate. Yes?"

Nico nodded.

"Was it your choice to move so far away?" Sutton asked, feeling a pang at living permanently far away from her dad.

"A little distance from family is never a bad thing," said Nico, as if parroting a line he'd heard many times before.

Dante's, "Mmm-hmm," had Sutton turning her head, in time to watch the movement of his throat as he swallowed a mouthful of wine. She remembered the graze of that stubble on her own skin, the way those lips felt on hers—

"And your mother?" Celia asked. "Was she from around here?"

Dante's gaze rocked to hers, his big body curling forward on his seat, as if readying to swat the question back if need be. Sutton shook her head, and he backed down.

"They met here," Sutton said, "lived here for a while. But she passed away when I was young."

"Ah. I am sorry to hear that." Then, "Her name?"

"Mya. Mya Hawthorn."

Celia blinked. And turned to her son. "Nico, *ho sentito bene*? *Ha appena detto* Mya Hawthorn?"

Nico, who had been only half paying attention, looked to Sutton and said, "Mya Hawthorn was your mother?"

Sutton nodded. And swallowed, hard. Her gaze flicking between Celia and Nico. For something in both of their expressions had lifted the hairs on the back of her neck.

Then Celia smiled and said, "What a lovely name! Now, Dante, tell me, how are you and that little pub of mine getting on?"

And the hook in Sutton's belly let go.

"The Vine is a changed place. The staff have stepped up, taking ownership, coming up with new ideas to keep it in the public eye, in order to help it stay that way."

"Well, that's nice."

"Nice?" Dante repeated, after a beat. "I came all this way as you assured me the entire Vermillion Hill business would be on the verge of collapse if I did not."

"Well," Celia said, lifting her wineglass between the tips of her fingers, "I may have exaggerated."

Sutton looked from Dante, to Nico, then to Celia.

Holding out her glass for a refill, which Nico promptly afforded her, Celia added, "It has been a loss leader for a decade, now. We've had offers to sell, but we feared the new owners might stock it with non-Rossi wine, so we kept it. I may yet knock it down and build rentable shop fronts."

"No!" said Sutton, imagining the Vine crumbling. All that potential going to waste.

Thankfully, at the same time Dante, chastised, *"Zia!"*

"Do not *Zia* me, *ragazzo*. I am an old woman. The benefit of which is that I may say and do as I please. Including inventing a reason to bring you out here, in the hopes of shaking you out of your silly doldrums."

Sutton grabbed a piece of capsicum and nibbled, in order

to stop herself from calling out again. Considering the storm clouds gathering over Dante's head, she wondered just how much of the thorn in his paw had to do with his family situation. Quite a bit, she guessed.

"La mia stasi era tutt'altro che scioccaas," Dante shot back, no doubt explaining that his doldrums were anything but silly.

"Si. But everything, good and bad, has its time. Your banishment, self or otherwise, should never have gone on as long as it did. It's time we all let that go."

"Let that go," Dante growled, sounding very much the Dante of old. "By that do you mean I am to let Isabella go?"

Celia's fraught gaze slid to Sutton, who paused mid-chew.

"She knows about Isabella," Dante said.

And his aunt flinched. *"Caro,"* she said, "I was speaking of my brother-in-law. Your father. His challenges. His choices. It is time we each stop letting that shape our lives, now that he is long gone."

Dane's nostrils flared, before he let his head fall into his hands.

Nico muttered, *"Mamma Mia,"* under his breath, as if he'd heard it all before.

Celia held up both her hands in surrender. *"Scusa.* Everything I do I do in love." Then, turning to Sutton, reaching out and taking her hand. "Forgive us for making such a row on your birthday. We are an emotional family."

"Nothing to forgive," said Sutton, "when everything you do you do in love."

At that Nico snorted. Then began to laugh. So loudly he rocked back in his chair and held a hand to his belly. Soon Dante's shoulders were shaking, his own laughter close behind.

Celia's smile was slower, as she took in her nephew with wide eyes. When Dante lifted his head and looked to Sutton, smiling as he shook his head, Celia's gaze moved on Sutton once more. This time it stayed, as if seeing her for the first time.

Sutton didn't realise the older woman was still holding her hand until she felt the grateful squeeze.

As Dante led Sutton out to the Land Rover, she shivered, for night had fallen fast. It tended to, when his family got to talking. He didn't realise how much he missed the rubbish, the ribbing, the reminiscing, till that night.

"Are you cold?" he asked.

"A little."

Dante took his jacket from his back, and draped it over her shoulders. She instantly slid her arms into the sleeves with a low hum of appreciation that he knew he'd be replaying in his head for some time.

The trip back to the B&B was mostly silent, both talked out, both lost in thought. Dante's thoughts swirling around the fact that this birthday of hers had seemed to be some sort of full stop for her. While for him the Vine was clearly no longer an excuse to stay.

Time was truly ticking down now. He could feel it in his bones, in the thrum of his blood. The circumstances that had brought them together in this space, this time, would soon no longer be in play.

When he pulled up to the front of the Grape Escape, and Sutton didn't immediately get out of the car, instead leaning her head against the headrest and letting out a great sigh, Dante turned off the engine.

"I have something for you," he said.

Her smile was soft, her voice little above a whisper. "You do?"

"In case I saw you at some point today." He leaned into the

back of the car, took the donut out of the container he'd put it into that morning. Then he stuck a single candle into the top.

She laughed, all delight, when he placed it on her up-turned palm.

"Shh," he hushed her, pulling out a lighter. He cradled her hand in his, steadying her, and lit the wick.

Over the glow of the flickering flame, her soft blue eyes were glossy, her smile radiant. "*Buon compleanno*, Sutton. Happy birthday."

"Dante, this is… I can't even…" But she could, and she did. Telling him how delighted, how touched, with every spark in her eyes, with the shape of her smile.

"Make a wish," he said.

She nodded, her face turning solemn as she closed her eyes, then blew out the flame in a short sharp puff. A sliver of smoke rose between them, a puff of white disappearing into the darkness.

The front porch light of the B&B was but a soft distant glow.

And Celia's words—*time to let go*—rang in his head. Not because they had been difficult to hear—although they were—but because they echoed what had become an insistent voice in the back of his head urging him to give himself grace for some time now.

Not to move on, but to move forward.

"To my mind," he said, his voice like gravel against the emotion pressing tight against his throat as his gaze roved over Sutton's lovely face, "that thing looks far too big for one person to eat."

Her gaze lifted to his, and she let out a huff of breath through her nose. As if she too was battling more emotion than she could contain.

Dante shifted, and leaned toward her, his hand sliding into the hair at the back of her head. "May I come up?"

"Dante," she said, eyes wide, lips parted, a thousand thoughts flittering across her face.

His thumb traced the curl of her ear. "May I come up?"

She nodded. Then said, "Yes. Please. Do."

He smiled, even while he felt like laughing. As if a simple yes from this woman was enough to unleash more joy than one simple man could possibly know what to do with.

Dante followed Sutton up the stairs of the sleeping inn.

He counted the places he wanted to kiss her—the jut of her shoulder bone, the dip of her neck. He watched the clip keeping her hair in a messy twirl atop her head, imagined removing it, feeling the cool silky weight of her hair in his hands.

When they reached the first landing, he took an extra step and rested a hand on her hip. She stopped as his thumb slid beneath the hem of her top. A heady sigh escaping her mouth.

He took it as a good sign and slid his hand around her front, grazing the dip of her navel, feeling her skin twitch beneath his touch.

"Hurry," she whispered, her hand over his as she guided him up the next lot of stairs.

Then a stair creaked, the light in the sconce flickering, and Sutton stopped, swearing lightly beneath her breath.

"Why are we tiptoeing?" Dante asked, loving the way she shivered as his breath brushed over her neck.

"I'm worried about Barry."

He stopped her then, spinning her, two steps above him, to face him. "I'm sorry?"

"No!" she said, eyes bright as they roved over his eyes, his cheeks, before settling on his mouth. "Not in that way. If he knew you were here, he might insist on sitting you down and asking your intentions."

Dante moved up a step till they were flush against one another. His hand curving around her back, skin on skin.

"I'm happy to explain my intentions," he said, "to you."

"You have intentions?"

"I've had intentions for weeks now. Specific, well-thought-out, richly detailed intentions. I can share them with you now, in English and Italian, if that was your wish."

She held the donut in both hands, between them, like a chastity belt. "It wasn't my wish. Though it might be nice. Then again, I do like surprises."

His voice was a growl as he said, "Let's get a move on, then, shall we?"

With that he spun her, and hands spanning her hips, encouraged her up the stairs. She laughed as she found herself taking them two at a time. Then bit her lip, trying to keep her laughter in check, lest Barry show up and get in their way.

Naturally, her room was right at the top. A converted attic, no less. Once there, she passed him the donut, her fingers fumbling with the key. When she finally slid it into place, the opening of the door was like a flint to a stone.

Sutton's arms were around Dante's neck, donut and all, as he walked her backward, kissing her for all he was worth.

"Duck," she breathed, leaning back so he'd not hit his head. Then she tore his jacket from her shoulders, one arm at a time, and tossed it across the room while keeping the donut safe.

While Dante reached out with a foot and slammed the door closed. Barry be damned.

Then they had their arms around one another again, all hot breath and lush kisses. The room so small, the back of Sutton's knees hit the bed seconds later, and together they fell. Dante shifted at the last so as not to land on her, or the donut, and they hit the mattress in a twist of limbs, puffing breaths.

He lifted his hand, swept her hair from her eyes. To think, all those weeks of flirtation, finding excuses to spend time together, finding reasons why they should not, had led them to this moment.

"Tell me what you want, Sutton."

Her voice was a smidge above a whisper as she said, "I can't."

"Trust me, you can," he assured her, pressing a kiss to the tip of her nose.

"I don't mean I *can't* can't. I can't because it might ruin my birthday wish." She glanced quickly at the donut, as if hoping it wasn't listening.

If Dante's heart hadn't been hammering in his chest by then, it was now.

"And even though you're here," she went on, "considering we are us, I'm quietly terrified it still might not come true."

There was one sure way to prove to her she had nothing to worry about.

He shifted so he was up on one elbow, held out a hand. "Donut, *per favor.*"

She passed it to him, a miracle it had survived the trip. He reached out to place it carefully on the bedside table, where a lit lamp sent a soft arc of light over the bed, bar a shadow from whatever creature was leaning in its base.

"The bedside drawer," she said.

After a pause, Dante opened it to find empty lolly wrappers, brochures for Vermillion sights to see, and a box of condoms. Unopened.

He placed the box on the bed, and closed the drawer, then turned back to find she'd rolled onto her back, her hands over her head, her dark hair splayed out around her, having lost her hair clip along the way.

She glanced at the box, her tank top lifting at her waist as she moved, and staying there, revealing a sliver of pale skin above the low rise of her jeans. "Wishful thinking?"

"Not anymore," he assured her.

And when she smiled, his hammering heart swelled to fill his entire chest.

"Bellissima," he said as he looked at her. Then, *"Splendido, adorabile, dolce, spettacolare, affascinante."* And any number of endearments. None of which came close to touching on how seeing her there, wanting him, made him feel.

He ran a hand down the edge of her jaw, scooting past the edge of her lush mouth, which dropped open on a sigh. He traced the side of her neck, the ridge of her collarbone, the neckline of her top.

She writhed up into his touch, and his finger slipped beneath the fabric, tracing the swell of her breast. Then he hooked his fingers under the strap of her top and pulled it over her shoulder, revealing a soft pink bra strap. He leaned in, took it in his teeth and gave it a short twang, before he slipped it off her shoulder.

"Dante," she said, pulling his face into her neck. Her hands in his hair, tugging and holding him close as his tongue traced the swell of her breast, then the dark pink smudge at the edge of her nipple.

When he pushed the last of the fabric aside with his nose, she whimpered, and hooked her leg around his. Whispering his name, like an incantation. *"Dante, Dante, Dante..."*

With a growl that came from some deeply primal place inside him, he took her nipple in his mouth, sucking, licking, nipping. She cried out, and he took more, cupping her breast in his hand, the skin warm and velvet soft, as he opened his mouth to her, his tongue lapping at her in an age-old rhythm that had her arcing into him. Crying out. Telling him what she wanted in every way bar words.

Constricted, needing skin on skin, he moved onto his knees and whipped his shirt over his head. Her eyes were dark, unseeing, as she reached for him, running her hands down his chest, tracing the lower half of the vine tattoo that swept over his shoulder, scraping her nails over the ridges of his muscles, before curling her fingers into his jeans, yanking open the first two buttons and pulling him to her.

He fell forward, bracing himself once more. Then made it his mission to kiss every inch of her.

Her left breast, the skin now pink from the abrasion of his beard. The pair of moles beneath her right breast. The small appendix scar low on her belly. Rolling his tongue around her navel, catching on scars left by a once-upon-a-time belly ring, he hooked the button of her jeans through the buttonhole, and tugged at her fly.

Half-gone, lost to pleasure, even more of a sensualist than he'd imagined she would be, she lifted her hips helpfully as he tugged at her jeans, and slipped them over her feet.

Her underwear, white cotton, with a small bow at the top, was twisted from the fact she could not keep still. The apex damp. The scent of her desire, the way her legs rubbed against one another as if she was lost to pleasure already, had him cupping himself for a moment, breathing through a wave of need so strong he feared, for him, it might be over before it began.

"Dante," she said, as if it was the only word keeping her tethered.

"I'm here, *tesoro*," he whispered, running his hands down both legs, from hip to knee, pressing them apart. She lifted off the bed, her eyes smoky, then falling back spilled open for him.

Unable to wait another second to taste her, to own her, to make her birthday wish come true, he swept her underwear to one side, traced his finger down her centre, before following with a long, slow, flat sweep of his tongue. He took his time, dipping the tip of his tongue inside her, circling the bud above, and when she began to whimper, he took it between his lips and sucked. Lathed, and sucked. Lathed and sucked.

Till she bowed off the bed, her breath held, and he pressed her legs apart with his shoulders and took her centre in his mouth and held her there, tongue sweeping over her as she cried out. And cried out. And cried out.

When he felt her shuddering, he eased back. Only to realise she was laughing. Spent, her taut body flopping to the bed, her head fell back as she laughed and laughed and laughed.

He moved over her, to lay his length alongside hers, brushing aside the soft wisps of damp hair curling about her temples. Her eyes still dark with desire. Her face a picture of pure joy. And relief.

As her laughter eased, and their gazes caught, her body warm and syrupy soft, his suspended on the edge of need, it felt as if time stretched once again. As if the universe granted them extra, when they needed it most.

There was no rush. Certain when his time came it would be worth the wait.

A while later, after she'd told him stories of birthdays past, comparing them all with this one, Sutton sat on the edge of the bed with a sheet wrapped around her, donut in hand.

She tore it in half, as promised, and offered him the smallest portion.

"It's my birthday donut," she said with a shrug, before biting down on the thing, her eyes rolling back in her head in pleasure.

And Dante saw a future unspool before him. Rough-edged and out of focus, but filled with laughter, and time spent learning one another's desires, and pasts, and intimate moments such as this.

Tossing the donut over his shoulder, he grabbed her, sheet and all, and pulled her onto his lap. His feet found the floor, at the end of the bed. She shifted till she straddled him, and wrapped the sheet around them both.

Then slid her hand between them, to unhook the last button of his jeans, slide her hand into his underwear, and free him with zero compunction.

Then, after swallowing the donut, and licking her fingers, she leaned in, wrapped her arms around his head, and kissed him hard, deep, wet. Rolling against him, till he could barely see straight.

When he felt himself teeter close to the edge, he lifted her to her knees, shucked off his jeans, and grabbed one of the rows of condoms from the box they'd moved to the middle of the bed.

There he made her wait, hovering so close, as he sheathed himself. When he nodded, she sank down over him, taking him in one go.

Her smile was impudent, confident. He rocked up into her, and her mouth opened on a gasp. Laughing, he slid a hand around her back, and rocked up into her again.

This time she was ready. And together they moved, slowly, incrementally, feeling every sensation, face-to-face. His hands sweeping her hair from her cheeks, holding her as he kissed her gently. Then more deeply. Her hands running through his hair, kneading his back, holding her to him when he changed the angle.

Till Dante felt Sutton clutch around him, her hands gripping his hair, her thighs quivering against his. Holding her through it, watching her face—eyes closed, skin pink—she teetered on the very edge of release, for an eternity, before collapsing against him with a whimper and a cry.

Holding her tight, he thrust once, twice. She shifted, one hand clutching his shoulder, the other braced against his knee, as she leaned back, taking him deeper than he'd imagined she could. Holding her there, taking her breast in his mouth, he came like a rocket. All power and heat, his vision nothing but stars.

Later, Sutton told him he was welcome to stay, then fell

asleep the moment her head hit the pillow. Dante hadn't planned on going anywhere.

When he woke in the night, he found Sutton curled up into his chest.

He waited for the usual rolling litany of recriminations to pervade his mind—the long-held, deeply embedded voice telling him he did not deserve this much good. But wait as he might, none came.

Then, as if his stillness unsettled her, Sutton shifted. Her hand uncurling to lie gently over his heart. And from one beat of that heart to the next, he knew he'd never be the same again.

CHAPTER NINE

IT WAS A good couple of hours before the Vine would open, yet she sat at the bar, drinking a milkshake and mooning over Dante while he made notes in the margin of an ancient occupational health and safety manual.

She knew it wasn't something he needed to do, just as she knew sitting around drinking milkshakes while mooning over the man wasn't sustainable as a lifestyle choice.

Sure, it had more than sustained the past week, to the point she'd had to make another trip to the chemist for a second box of condoms. But this man had not been on her "to-do list" when she'd bought the ticket and jumped on that plane. Or had he? Did it matter, when, in the long run, they both had real lives to get back to?

"This cannot be interesting," Dante said, in that gruff voice that she adored so very much. Especially when it was whispering sweet nothings in her ear as she fell apart in his arms.

Gaze tracing the column of his neck, she could all but taste the salty tang, feel the delicious give of his skin when she scraped her teeth over the tendons. "You have no idea."

He looked up, his eyes dark, filled with smoke and memory, an aura of contentment for which she took complete ownership. *"Tesoro,"* he said, "I have every idea."

Kent, who had been walking behind Dante at the time, looked at Sutton with wide eyes, and mouthed, "Oh, my God!"

Sutton laughed into her milkshake and motioned for Dante to get back to work.

Then she tried her best to do the same; answering the slew of emails and messages she'd let slide the last few days. Something she never did. Even when touring, or unwell, she was a manic checker-inner with the bands she managed. The best, most connected, most present partner they could ever hope for.

Now she wondered if it had been less innate conscientiousness, and more due to the metaphorical hand of time that had been pressing her onward all these years. As such, for the past few days she'd put the living of her own life ahead of worrying about anyone else's first for a change. Living in the moment with Dante, knowing how special it was. That *he* was.

"You're watching me," Dante said, watching *her*. His chin in his hand, knuckles curled against his cheek. All dark eyes and ruggedly elegant beauty. "I can feel it."

"Lies. All lies," she said, picking up her phone, and finding a message she'd drafted to send to Bianca. "I am an independent woman, with hobbies and interests and obligations outside of this."

She flapped a hand at him, edited the message, and pressed Send.

Then, proving her words, she pulled up her socials, scrolled through posts about music festivals, images from live shows. She saved one post into her "photography" folder, thinking the imagery would really suit the Magnolia Blossoms.

The next post in line had a chill coming over her.

The headline read: "The Sweety Pies Cut Record New Record Deal under New Management."

Thing was, she'd been their manager for years.

Swiping to her contacts, she tried calling Landry, the lead singer. Nothing. She texted them a screenshot of the post, and a text shot straight back.

Ack. Sorry you had to see that.

So it's true?

We wanted to tell you in person but you've been hard to
get a hold of of late.

Ouch.

Sutton went to type something else, to explain, or to ask
them to explain, considering she'd discovered them, nurtured
them, guided them through so many near breakups. But her
hands were shaking.

She closed her eyes for a moment, and centred her
thoughts. She'd lost bands before, it was par for the course.
So why did this change make her feel so adrift?

Because it was *them*? The shock of not being given the
courtesy of a heads-up? Or because of who she had morphed
into since coming to this place. The fierce, independent, go-
getter now sensitive, unguarded, soft.

Another text hit her phone before she'd had the chance to
come up with a response:

We're good, though, right? You always said you'd be fine
if the time came we needed more.

Sutton let her phone drop slowly to the bar. She had said
those words, more often than she could remember. In fact,
she'd made a life out of walking away and not looking back.
Thinking it made her tough, inured to personal pain. Never
putting herself in a position to break, unlike like her dad. In
love, or life.

But seeing it written that way—made her feel lonely, disappointed, and sad. And she didn't like it one single bit.

"Everything all right?" Dante asked, no doubt sensing her discomfort.

"Peachy," she said, blinking furiously to hold back the sting in the back of her eyes. "I'm just going outside to make a quick call."

She sent a quick screenshot to the Magnolia Blossom group chat, only for her phone to ring just as she hit the footpath.

"Wild, right?" Sutton asked, rubbing at her temples.

"Did you know?" Bianca asked. "I feel you'd have told us if you'd known."

Sutton shook her head, and all three Blossoms made it clear what they thought of how it had gone down.

Francie pushed Zhou and Bianca out of the frame. "Next time I see them, I'm going to…steal their mike stands."

Sutton laughed, then turned the phone away as she swiped at the stupid tear that had spilled from nowhere.

"You okay?" Bianca asked.

"Yeah. Of course. Just in shock, I guess. But it's fine. It will be fine. I mean, you guys know that I support whatever decisions you believe you have to make for yourselves. I've always been up-front about that. I just hope, if you ever feel it's time, that you'd say so—"

"Never!" said Bianca, holding the phone close to her face. "You are our ride or die. We'd not be here without you and we love you. And that's the end of that."

"Okay," said Sutton, the emotions rushing through her strange, and disconcerting in their enormousness. As if the past few days spent with Dante had turned on some tap she didn't know how to turn off. "If you're about to suggest we get matching tattoos, I get final say on the design."

"Boo," said Bianca. Then, "Oh, and while I have you, your dad messaged me. He asked if I knew of any walking tours in my neck of the woods."

Sutton blinked. "In *the Netherlands*?"

"Yep! He said he and a friend were out to lunch, talking about walking holidays, and were 'collating a list of possible future adventures.' How cool is that?"

Out to lunch, with a friend. This from a man who'd not dated, as far as Sutton knew, since the day she was born. How much more of her world would be upside down when she got back? If she waited much longer, it might not be recognisable at all.

"So cool," Sutton managed. "Now don't forget to send through any photos, video, et cetera of the Liefdescafé shows, okay? Hope they go brilliantly!"

Zhou said. "Will do!"

"We miss you!" Bianca added.

"Next time we expect real tea!" Francie insisted. "The dirty stuff!"

With that they rang off, and Sutton gripped her phone for a few long seconds as the news upon news upon news swirled and settled inside her.

When she glanced up through the windows of the Vine and Stein, she could just make out Dante talking on the phone. His expression was cool, his movements spare and strong, his brow furrowed in that gorgeously Dante way as he listened without interrupting.

And just like that all feelings of sadness, and loneliness, dissolved away.

While that should have felt like a good thing, the best thing, she felt herself begin to tremble. All over. Knowing that when the time came to walk away from that man, *not* looking back would be an impossibility.

Dante hung up the call from his aunt. His blood felt cool, thick, as he held his phone for a long moment, then ran a hand over his mouth as he looked up to see Sutton was once again pacing, as she took another call, through the glass.

The way she curled her hair around a finger, kicked at the ground, looked up, and smiled as a stranger passed her by—he knew he'd never be able to see such movement from another person and not think of her.

How soon that time came did not feel up to him. Not anymore. For the moment he'd gotten over himself enough to let her into his heart, he was done. And he knew, in that same heart, that she felt the same way.

The problem was, there were more than two of them in this relationship, and always had been. His aunt and cousins, her father, the Vine staff, their new friends in Vermillion, his people back at Sorello, the bands who relied on her—they all tugged, and begged for attention, and got in the way.

And now...

He looked once more at his phone, as he heard the snick of the front door.

"Hey!" she said, her hair lifting and falling as she strode his way and pulled herself back onto her stool. Then, "You okay? You look as if you've seen a ghost."

"It is. I think. I..." He put his phone into his pocket and rounded the bar. Pulling up the stool beside hers. "My aunt just called. Apparently, she has been mulling over your conversation, from the night you came for dinner. Specifically, your mother's name."

Sutton stilled, the blood rushing from her face. "Oh?"

Dante reached out and took her hand, gently rubbing warmth into her fingers as they lay limply in his hold. "Apparently her name rang a bell, the other night. Turns out there is a Mya Hawthorn—an artist, a potter—who lives in the next town."

Sutton shook her head. "Did you say 'lives'? As in...present tense?"

Dante nodded.

"Wow," said Sutton, eyes wide. "I mean, it could be a relative, right?"

Dante breathed out. "Celia has met her. At a fundraiser a few years ago. She said she would be the right age...to be your mother."

Sutton pulled her hand back, curling it against her chest. Swallowing hard, she shook her head. "That might be, but... I mean, she wasn't intimating that this Mya could be my actual mother?" She shook her head, hard. "My mother died. When she was twenty-eight. Sending my father in a spiral of romantic despair, that he apparently is only just now coming out of."

Her gaze slid over his shoulder, far away, as she whispered, "Now that he knows that I am here."

"Sutton—"

Shaking her head, she slid from the chair, looked around, grabbed her backpack from under her stool, and slung it over her shoulder.

"Sutton—" He tried again.

She held up a hand; gaze hard, shining like glass holding back a wash of tears. "Your aunt is wrong. Or lying. Or... I don't know." Her hand balled in a fist at her belly. "Oh. This just feels too cruel."

Dante's hands clenched and unclenched at his sides, uncertain how to help her. "My aunt is a lot of things," he said, "but she is not cruel."

Sutton shook her head, then turned and strode toward the front door.

"Where are you going?" Dante called. "Let me drive you. Or I can find this woman. Talk to her for you—"

Sutton stopped at the door. "Don't, please. Just give me some space, to figure this out."

"So long as you know you don't have to do it alone." Dante

waited for her to turn, to change her mind. To need him, as he'd come to need her.

Only she swept out the door and didn't look back.

An hour later, Sutton stood outside Artisan Row, a creative collective in Griffin, about ten minutes down the road from Vermillion.

The hand gripping the strap of her backpack felt about as damp as her mouth felt dry, and her insides twisted over on themselves as she turned that last conversation with Dante over and over in her head.

Should she have let him come with her? Had she been too dismissive? The thing was, he wasn't her partner, or even her boyfriend. He was a crush she was sleeping with a thousand miles from home.

Okay, so Dante was more than that. Much more. But that was the problem! He was some magical, unicorn, fairy-tale, grumpy, gorgeous winemaker from some halcyon pocket of delight in the heart of Italy, for Pete's sake!

While this—this *mess*, this possibility, this thread of discomfort in her belly—was her real life. And she'd come to Vermillion looking for connection to her past, not some mythical magical future.

Careful what you ask for, she thought as she sucked in a deep breath and forced herself to walk through a twisty series of stone paths, and cute hedgerows, and garden statues, and caravans filled with handmade art.

Bracing herself against whatever was to come, calling on whatever inner steel she had at her disposal, she turned a corner to find a garden filled with hundreds of pots. All kinds of pots. And a hand-burned wooden sign reading Pots by Mya Hawthorn.

Her stomach tumbled, knotting in on itself as dread and

hope intermingled inside her. She took every effort to haul herself in.

Was it possible, actually possible, that she was about to meet her mother? *Her mother!* Alive. If so, her life's philosophy, all those years spent racing against time, were based on a myth. Which, ironically, the past week she'd let go—being still, living in the moment, finding contentment in doing not much at all. And it had been wonderful.

Then, *Bam!* Fate stepped in and smacked her across the back of the head.

Stairs led to a small cottage with a front porch covered in ivy, and laden with pots hanging in crocheted baskets. Only way to know for sure was to go inside, only her feet wouldn't move.

Couldn't.

Until Dante's words came back to her, his voice strong with understanding, as if he was used to taking the big emotional hits so that others didn't have to. *"So long as you know you don't have to do it alone."*

It was enough for her to take the first step.

A bell tinkled as she walked through the door. The space was overflowing with baskets filled with wool, shelves stacked with crockery, vases, plant pots of all shapes and sizes. She could barely get her bearings before a woman walked through a door behind the small counter, wringing a towel around her hands.

She wore a yellow, paint-splattered apron over a knotty knitted jumper, denim overalls, and khaki gumboots. She'd used a paintbrush to twirl her long wavy hair—once dark, now salt-and-pepper—into a loose bun.

Sutton's father had no photos of her mother, his memory of her "strong enough." His descriptions, when Sutton had pressed, ran to "dramatic, ethereal and gifted." Nothing ethereal about this woman—she was real. Right there. Flesh and blood.

And when she looked up, and spotted Sutton, it was like looking into her own eyes.

"Hey, honeybun," the woman said, her face creasing as she smiled. "What you looking for?"

Sutton nearly choked, hearing her father's endearment in this stranger's voice. She opened her mouth, but nothing came out. Some huge writhing thing inside her stopping her from speaking. Waiting for this woman Mya Hawthorn to put two and two together on her own.

See me. Recognise me. Make me believe that you are why I came here. Give me the connection, the foundation, the feeling that I'm home I've probably been searching for my whole life.

But the woman only cocked her head, and waited.

Sutton licked her lips, lifted her chin, and said, "I'm… Are you Mya Hawthorn?"

"That's me," the woman said, giving an empty shelf beside her a quick wipe so she could then fill it with knitted knickknacks.

"My name is Sutton. Sutton Mayberry. I think… I think perhaps you once knew my father."

The woman's hands stopped fussing. Her eyes widening imperceptibly, before she turned and looked deep into Sutton's eyes. Then cool as you please, she said, "How is Gerard these days?"

"He's well," Sutton found herself saying, even as tears welled inside her, as if filling her from her toes all the way to her chest.

And where she wanted to say to this woman, *Did he leave you? Did you leave him? Does he even know you're alive? He's lonely. He misses you. He mourns you. I mourn you*, Sutton thought, voicing something that had never explicitly occurred to her. But it was true. Not having known her mother, she'd spent a lifetime chasing her down.

Instead, she found herself saying, "He's planning a walking tour, through the Netherlands, with his friend. Marjorie."

"That sounds like something he'd enjoy," said Mya, not unkindly. "And you? What brings you here?"

"I'm sorry," said Sutton, closing her eyes, holding out her hand as she attempted to get her bearings. "I'm sure you can imagine this is all rather a lot for me to take in. I... I was led to believe that you were dead."

Mya let out a long breath. Then, moving a roll of brown butcher paper from a chair, motioned for Sutton to sit down. Sutton did, her legs giving way as soon as they had permission to do so.

"I'm going to make us a cuppa. Vanilla? Caffeine-free suit?"

About as much as a glass of wine, Sutton thought, holding back a slightly hysterical laugh. "Sounds fine."

Tea served, Mya sat on the chair opposite Sutton's, curling a foot up beneath her. While Sutton absorbed everything about her that she could—looking for signs, for similarities, while waiting for a torrent of anger, of futility, of sorrow to whip up inside her.

But she felt nothing. Perhaps she was numb, in some deep self-protect mode. Or it was all backing up inside her, waiting for the right moment to break loose.

"Sutton. I always thought that was such a pretty name. Your father chose it, you know? What did you come here looking for today?"

"I'm not sure. Maybe the truth."

Mya looked at her then, for quite a long beat. Gaze raking over her hair, her face, her clothes. Was *she* searching for similarities? Imagining herself the same age? The age at which this woman had died in Sutton's mind.

Because her father…

No, she couldn't go there. Couldn't think about his complicity in the falsehood. Not now. Not yet.

"Truth is a slippery thing," said Mya with a soft smile. "Altered by time, memory, repetition, the needs of the players involved. All I can safely say is that your father wanted more from me than I had to give."

Sutton flinched. Not because Mya's words were harsh, for they were gently offered. They were so close to the words Dante had said to her the night she'd first kissed him. The night he'd tried to stop things going further. As if he knew the day was already nearing when it had to end.

"So you *left* him?" Sutton asked.

And me, she thought. *You also left me.* Which was an awful thing. Wasn't it? This woman certainly didn't seem torn up about it.

"No," Mya said, her voice gentle yet assured, "I suggested it would be better for him, and for you, if he left. This was my home. *Is* my home. I needed for it to remain that way."

Sutton shook her head, slowly, back and forth. Trying to make sense of this woman's absolute certainty that she'd made the right choice. Her peace of mind—even in the face of seeing the daughter she'd abandoned.

Maybe that would take another twenty-eight years to understand.

Sutton felt a kind of numbness come over her at the thought. Really? Was she willing to do that all over again? Chase understanding of someone else's choices rather than make her own?

Again, she found her mind tipping to Dante. To the choices ahead of them both. Her tongue felt thick in her mouth, as she asked, "What did that mean—that my father wanted more than you had to give?"

Mya leaned forward. "I never wanted to be a wife, or

a mother, I just wanted to live a life that filled me with a sense of purpose. While your father wanted security, assurances, promises I had no hope of keeping. Does that make any sense?"

More than Sutton cared to admit.

Mya and her father were complete opposites. Had different energies, different visions, different post codes, different goals. Neither love, nor a child, had been enough to combat that.

"Do you have any regrets?" Sutton asked, knowing it was the one truth that she needed to know.

Mya reached out, and wrapped a cool hand around Sutton's wrist. "I regret none of it," said Mya. "Not the relationship, not you, nor the fact that we went our separate ways. Not for a moment."

Sutton nodded, believing her, and sipped her tea.

Dante paced the office of the Vine, wearing a path into the floor.

It had been hours since Sutton had left. He could wait outside the B&B, or drive the streets until he found her, only he had no idea if she'd gone looking for Mya Hawthorn, gone for a drive to clear her head, or if she'd *gone*...period.

And it was his fault.

Not directly, he knew that. But partly, certainly. He could have shared Celia's news in a different way, a different place. Instead, he'd charged in like a wounded bear, without nuance or sensitivity, only certain it was too important to keep it from her.

Now she was out there somewhere, hurting, confused, alone.

Not that he thought she'd do anything foolish. Or put herself in harm's way. But then he'd never imagined Isabella going that far either.

Dante rubbed both hands over his face and growled, hating this feeling of utter helplessness.

It was not the same. He *knew* it was *not the same*. Try telling his heart that—caught as it was in a loop of flight or fright, spinning him back in time to how it felt as his feet sank into the mud, sucking at him, making it near impossible to get to her. To *Isabella*. Face down in the dam.

Sutton was a grown woman; strong, resilient. She faced down dragons every day of her career, and woke the next ready to face more. He'd never known anyone who could ride the waves of life's ups and downs with more grace, humour, and delight than she.

Yet when his phone rang, and he saw Sutton's number on the screen, his relief was so strong he moaned. "Sutton."

"Hey." Her voice was soft. Tired.

"Where are you?"

"In the car. Pulled over halfway between Griffin and home."

Home. Dante knew she had a complicated relationship with that word. The fact that she'd used it now cut deep. Home for her was not about place, but people. Home, in that moment, meant him.

"Can I come get you?" he asked, hand tugging at his hair.

"I'm okay. I just needed to hear a friendly voice."

Feeling anything but friendly, Dante pressed his hand over his mouth.

"I found her," she said, into the silence. "Mya Hawthorn. My mother."

Dante twisted and sat on the arm of the couch. *Hell. Just... hell.* "Have you spoken to your father?"

"It's four in the morning over there."

"Still, I'm sure he'd understand."

"I'll wait till morning."

Morning meant several hours of being alone with this

news. Of feeling in limbo. A terribly lonely place to be. And even while he knew he should be facilitating her needs, he needed to see her. To be sure she was all right. To know she was safe.

"Can I see you tonight?" he asked. "To listen, or hold you, or just be there."

The phone stayed silent for several long beats before he heard her sob. "Actually, can you come? Can you come get me?"

Dante had his car keys in hand before she finished the request.

CHAPTER TEN

EYES CLOSED, Sutton heard the crunch of tyres on gravel, then the slam of Dante's car door.

When without preamble he opened her door, and held out a hand, she took it, stepping into his big, strong arms. She pressed her face to his chest, drinking in the dry, earthy scent of him. Hands catching on the warm, familiar weave of his flannelette shirt. And as his coarse palms caught on her hair as he stroked her, and he murmured comforting words in a language she barely understood, she felt so much. Too much. Especially when compared with all the *nothing* she'd been feeling the past few hours.

It was enough for her to pull back.

Placing her hands flat against his chest, she gently pushed him away. Giving herself space to breathe. To think. To consider for once, rather than going with the flow.

"Thank you for coming," she said, then, "I'm not even sure why I called—"

"I'm glad you did."

She ran a hand through her hair and took another step back. It was a moment before he slid his hands into the pockets of his jeans, when he clearly wanted to be holding her still.

"I think I'm okay to drive now. If you follow?"

"Are you sure? I can organise for someone else to pick up your car."

She breathed out, the tumult inside her slowly settling. "I'm sure."

"And where do you wish to go?"

"Back to the B&B, I think. I should eat. Hunker in for a bit to get my head around all of this." Then, after a beat, she added, "Would you... Could you come with me?"

His eyes, those deep dark chocolate penetrating depths, filled with such raw emotion she felt the hit of it right in the centre of her chest. An explosion of warmth, of feeling, of happiness and heart pain. As if he alone knew how to unlock the more vulnerable places inside her, the ones she'd been all too happy to keep hidden, keep safe.

If she'd taken one thing from finding her mother, from Mya Hawthorn's calm certainty that things were exactly as they ought to be, was that giving someone the key to loving you meant they had the key to hurt you.

Still, when Dante caught her eye, and smiled at her, waiting patiently for what she needed, she said, "Come. And stay."

Dante reached for her, hauled her close once more, kissed her atop her head, then helped her back into the car.

Later that night, Sutton lay curled up in Dante's arms, her leg resting over his, his meaty bicep a pillow beneath her head.

While Dante had been breathing softly, rhythmically, for some time, she was a million miles from sleep. Her brain was all knots, and electric sparks, and rabbit holes, determined to fix every problem on her plate before it could shut down.

The Magnolia Blossoms were off having fun without her, while the Sweety Pies had left her. Her dad was making big plans in his life, for the first time ever, and she wasn't there to help. Her dad, the one person she trusted above all others, had been lying to her for all these years. Her mother was alive, and unrepentant.

It was a lot. And Sutton had spent her adult life avoiding "a lot." Taking on just enough work to enjoy it without ever really stretching herself. Keeping lovers at arm's length— friendly, never serious, as off she went to the next city, the next adventure, with a smile and a wave. Telling herself it was so she had time to experience as many facets of life as she could in her time on earth.

Dante shifted, a growl rising from his chest even in sleep.

Could she really do the same to him? Smile, and wave, and leave.

She tipped her head the smallest amount to press a gentle kiss to his warm, bronzed skin, and could feel the Italian sunshine that had made him that way. Smell the soil, the leaves, the tannin of the grapes that had given him calluses on his hands, and built up the muscles on his bones.

She slowly moved the sheet, tracing the edge of his beautiful tattoo, tenderly, so as not to wake him. She flattened her hands over the slabs of his large pecs. Fingers catching in the light smattering dark curling hair that arrowed over his rib cage. Lower.

When his skin retracted from her touch, a slight hiss dragging between his teeth, she lifted her head, but his eyes remained closed.

She laid her hand on his chest, and rested her chin on her hand, and looked at him. The dark lashes creating a smudge against his cheeks. The dark stubble, throwing auburn and flecks of silver in the low glow of the Minotaur lamp.

She could think in circles all she wanted, but the truth was she had to go back to her real life soon. As did he. And they'd both be okay. Surely. Like any holiday romance, it couldn't possibly feel as big, as acute, as important later on as it did while in the midst of it.

"What is going on in that head of yours?" Dante asked,

lifting his head and placing his spare arm beneath. "I can *feel* you thinking dire thoughts."

"I'm thinking about my mother," Sutton said. Which was, at least, partly true.

"What about her?"

"She was so unruffled by my appearance. So settled in her decision to let us go. I should be a mess, right now, right?" *Angry, desolate, hurt—something.* "Instead, I feel as if she could have been a woman who ran a pot shop, and nothing more." Her eyes swung back to his. "Is that healthy? Or a sign that I'm missing some basic human ingredient?"

Dante rolled so that they faced one another, nose to nose, limbs wrapped loosely over one another. The hand on her chest, dropped and curled backward, against his heart.

"Self-protection is a pretty powerful human ingredient. Yes, it can keep people from getting too close, but it also stops them from having the capacity to hurt us. Something we are both rather adept at, I believe. Or at least I was. And then I met you."

Sutton swallowed, her throat tightening, the backs of her eyes hot and scratchy.

Smiling and frowning, all at once, Dante lifted a hand to brush her hair from her face. His fingers traced down her cheek, his thumb tugging at her lower lip before he leaned in and kissed her. Softly. As if marking his place. Marking her.

"You know the Vine does not need my help anymore, yet I am still here. Just as I know there will be no *second* dates for you, yet you are still here."

Knowing where he was going, and unable to control the rush of feeling rising inside her—so much everything compared with all the nothing—she shook her head, just the once. One final flash of self-protection before it burned to ash.

"You care for me, Sutton."

"I don't." Then, "I mean, I *do*. Of course I do. Just not…
Not in the way I think you are intimating. I mean, I can't…
I don't think I'm able." Her voice broke at the last. How was
that for a truth that had been living inside her for as long as
she could remember?

Dante's smile only grew.

"You care for me," he said, again, his fingers now sliding into her hair, sending ribbons of pleasure from her scalp
to her centre. "You care for me, and I care for you. We both
fought it, to no avail."

He moved so that her leg was tucked around his hip.
Moved so that her chest was flush against his. Moved so
that pleasure shot up in a thousand places on her body in
such a visceral rush she began to tremble.

"Soon I'll be heading back to my vineyard, on a hill, near
a small town, in the heart of my country, and you'll be back
whizzing all over the world with your music, but that does
not mean—"

"Stop," she said, lifting a hand to his mouth when the
burning in the back of her eyes threatened to give way to
actual tears.

He took her literally. His hand softening in her hair, the
slow undulation of his hips ceasing on a breath. And the world
seemed to teeter in that moment.

On one side, she could rest her head against this chest and
tell him all her wild and frantic fears, and he would listen, and
everything from that moment would be new and unknown
and out of her control.

On the other side, it was time to say goodbye to the beautiful oblivion that was Vermillion, and step back into the life
she'd known till now.

She moved her hand from his lips, and held his cheek.
"Stop talking," she said, "and kiss me."

A beat slunk by, a beat in which she knew he knew the

tumult inside her. Then he rolled over her, bracing himself so as not to crush her.

Brushing her hair off her face, he looked deep into her eyes. Then he kissed her; gently, on the tip of her nose, the curve of her cheek, on one closed eyelid, then the other. Then, while she hovered on the verge of sweet luxuriation, he kissed her. His tongue tracing the seam of her lips, before sweeping deep into her mouth.

Her arms slid around his neck as she pulled him close. Curling into his big, hard body, needing as much of him as she could get. For he knew what he was doing, conjuring delicious warmth in her limbs, waves of pleasure that lapped at her doubts, wearing them down.

Only he had no idea how deep her self-protection went.

Even as they moved and sighed in one another's arms, as her feeling for him swelled and grew, her mind wheeling with adoration and desire, falling into the picture he'd been offering her, all she could think was:

So much. Too much.

Even as all thought and feeling coalesced into a declivous ball of heat and joy and maybe even love, spilling out to her extremities and back again in waves of the purest of pleasure, some small part of herself baulked. Held back. Hunkered down. Tried with all its might to hold tight.

As Dante slept, a deep, unfettered sleep, Sutton lay staring at the ceiling and let the tears fall. The streams pooled in her ears before spilling to the damp pillow at her back. For finally the disparate threads in her mind had twirled into one perfect string.

She'd thought the inconsistency of the music industry suited her so well because she was able to cope with change.

She'd thought the fact she'd come out of meeting her mother feeling so little pain was down to that willful self-control.

She'd thought her romantic relationships never amounted to anything serious because she had *decided* she would never put herself in a position to end up like her beloved dad. Broken by love, lost to the past.

She'd thought it had all been by choice.

What if it wasn't? What if it was innate? What if she held back, because she did not have it in her to let go? To be open to more. To love deeply. Truly. In a forever kind of way.

Something cracked inside her as it all came together in a bright burning truth. And where moments earlier she'd felt such comfort, such safety, such warmth in the arms of the beautiful man sleeping beside her, cold rushed in.

Maybe her choices had *never* been about avoiding her father's experiences. Maybe she'd been her mother's daughter all along.

Dante woke to find Sutton packing her bags.

His first thought was that maybe she was simply tidying up. She was a "clothes piled up on the chair in the corner are clean" kind of person. Not that he minded—he was a buy-five-of-the-same-shirt-and-two-of-the-same-jeans kind of guy.

Till he stretched, made a sound to go with it, and saw her gaze when it snapped his way. Shrouded. Dusty. As if her mind was only half in the room.

It had been a big twenty-four hours. Meeting her mother, processing the seed he'd hoped he'd planted in her mind—finding a way for this not to end when they went back to their real lives. Finding a way to make it last. Forever if she'd have him.

"Tesoro," he said, his morning voice gruff, as he leaned up on an elbow and ran a hand through his hair.

She narrowed her eyes at him, her lips thin.

"What?" he asked, laughter in his voice. In his soul. Something he'd never have expected, or asked for. Now he knew he did not want to live without it.

Her hand flapped at him, violently. "Why do you have to look like that?"

"Like what?" he asked, glancing down at his bare torso. He scratched at the edge of his tattoo.

She made a sound halfway between a groan and a growl. "All warm, and big, and hot…and you."

"I apologise," he said. "I will do my best not to be any of those things in future."

On the word *future*, she flinched. Which was his first sign that something might be seriously amiss. He lifted the sheet, his legs swinging to the floor, when she held up a hand.

"Stay. Please. I can't do this otherwise."

He let the sheet drop over his lap, and curled his fingers around the edge of the mattress. "Sutton," he said, "would you like to tell me what is going on?"

"I'm leaving."

He looked once more to her now frantic packing, and felt a tug of something slippery inside him. Like he was reaching for a ribbon, only for it to keep fluttering out of his grip. "By leaving you mean…"

"*Leaving* leaving. Going back to the UK. I should see my dad, to talk to him in person."

"You could call him—"

She shook her head. "No. It has to be in person. Then I have to go to the Netherlands to meet up with the Magnolia Blossoms, make sure they're being treated right by the manager of the place they're playing. I should rightly have been there all along anyway. Then I should go to Dublin to see the Sweety Pies. Beg them to take me back. Either way, it's past time I got back to real life. You should too."

"You're right," he said. "In fact, I was hoping we might be able to leave together. That you might wish to return by way of Umbria. So that I can show you Sorello. It's then only a two-and-a-half-hour flight from Perugia to London."

Dragging at a zip that was clearly caught on something, she barely seemed to hear him, so he added, "I looked it up. Some time ago, actually."

Her eyes drifted closed, and her fingers gripped the edge of her bag. "Dante," she said, "can we just not? Can we just agree that this was fun? A lovely, unexpected side benefit for the both of us. A holiday fling, if you will. We can then go our separate ways grateful to have met."

Grateful to have *met*?

Dante reached out, grabbed his jeans from the floor by the bed. Forgoing underwear, he slid them on and went to her. Taking her by the elbows, and turning her to face him. "Can you slow, for just a moment? Tell me what has happened to send you into such a spin."

"This is not a spin," she said. "This is me finally snapping out of whatever whim brought me here. Leaving my life back home to fall apart without me."

She lifted her elbows from his grip and he let her. Then he placed a finger under her chin and tipped her face back to meet his. Her eyes blazed as she looked up at him, but he could feel her trembling all over.

While all kinds of words, and questions, and negations spilled onto the back of his tongue, he knew that she wasn't in any state to hear them. So, he took her hand and led her to the bed, where she slumped at the end, shoulders hunched, hands in her face.

Dante crouched down before her. His hand on her knee to keep her tethered. Connected to him. As he felt, deep in his bones, that if he did not, she would fly away, and he would lose her forever.

"Can we slow down for a moment?"

"Slow down? Dante, in my entire life, I've never been as

slow as I have been the past few weeks. And maybe that's the problem," she said, her hand flinging out dramatically, her knees now juddering as if she had a surfeit of energy she couldn't contain. "Way too much thinking time."

He lifted a hand, pressed his thumb to the middle of her forehead, and gave it a gentle push. She rocked back an inch, and stopped jiggling.

"What was that for?"

"My attempt to help you focus on one thing at a time." *Me*, he thought, holding her gaze. *Focus on me.* "Whatever has you spooked, *tesoro*, it will pass. All burdens do, eventually." Leaving space in the cracks for hope and happiness to flourish and grow.

Only Sutton seemed to be fracturing before his eyes. All cracks, no sunshine.

"Talk to me," he said. "Tell me what's wrong."

"What's *wrong*? Me! Clearly I am. Look at you."

She held out her hands, as if about to cradle his face, only to curl her fingers into her palms and shake them at the sky. As if touching him would undo her completely.

"You are so wonderful, Dante, and generous. Look at what you have done for your aunt. For the staff at the Vine. Because you are an exceptional human. So diligent, and…and responsible. You are a homeowner! While I'm so terrified of wanting stability, I sleep on strangers' couches more often than any twenty-seven…no twenty-eight-year-old should."

Dante would not have imagined being called a homeowner could feel like an insult, yet he was well aware she had flung it at him like a grenade. Even as he felt parts of himself begin closing up, like shutters against a storm, he dredged up a smile. "I think you'll find that Sorello is more of an estate, than a mere home. If that helps."

Sutton, who had been lost inside what maelstrom was inside her head, blinked. Then coughed out a laugh. Then a tear slid from her right eye.

Dante winced at the sight. Emotion now battering him from all sides. Emotion he was not equipped to handle. To abate. To fix. So much pressure, being the one upon whom another person's spirit depended. What if he was getting it wrong? The outcome could be catastrophic.

He felt himself sway away. And saw the moment she noticed.

She blinked against the glistening in her eyes, and took in a deep breath. When he opened his mouth to speak, she curled herself away from the bed, managing not to touch him as she moved back to her bags and kept on packing.

And for the first time in an awfully long time, Dante knew what true fear felt like.

Dante stood from his crouch, his knees groaning, bones protesting. Even his blood felt pained, as if tainted with acid. While his mind felt as scattered as his clothes, strewn about the room. Needing to feel something concrete, something real he could count on, he gathered them, put them on.

Then stood, tugging at his hair. "So, this is it?" he asked.

"I think it has to be. For both our sakes."

He breathed out hard, nodded, then made his way to Sutton's bedroom door.

"Dante?"

He stopped, and turned to find her watching him, her eyes wide, mouth downturned. "You'll thank me for this," she said. "I'm sure of it. I've spent my life avoiding tangles, while you've held on to your thorns like lifelines. Neither of us came here in any way prepared for this. For us."

Then, lovely face solemn, Sutton walked to him, placed a soft hand over his heart, lifted onto her tiptoes, and pressed a kiss to his cheek. "Thank you."

"For what?" he asked, feeling like his vision was filled with dust.

"For holding my hand through this most ill-thought-out of pilgrimages. I'm certain it wouldn't have been half as fun, half as satisfying, half as meaningful without you in it."

He offered a nod, then let himself out of her room, and out of her life.

Only half-aware of his surroundings as he jogged down the stairs of the B&B—trying not to remember kissing her on one landing, carrying her over another—then out the front door, and into the early morning light, his thoughts stray shrapnel in his head.

Once upon a time he'd retreated to a hillside lair, hiding away from all who knew him best, all who might look to him with regret or blame in their eyes. He'd cut himself off from family, from kinship, from partnership. As punishment.

Now, as he walked away from Sutton Mayberry, and all the delight, and humour, and warmth, and companionship that being with her had promised, he knew that solitude had been the easy way out.

CHAPTER ELEVEN

As soon as Dante shut her bedroom door, Sutton hunched over her bag. Her hands cramped, her entire body shook, as she did her all not to cry. Or hyperventilate.

She'd done the right thing, not letting it get any more serious than it already had. If she'd been a *better* person she'd not have let it get this far.

She'd spent so long finding ways not to get hurt, it had never occurred to her she had the ability to hurt someone else. Now all she could hope was that his feelings weren't as far down the track as hers had gone. Which, now he was gone, she could admit to herself was all the way.

Her phone pinged. Then pinged again.

While Dante had slept, spread out over her big soft bed, looking like some heavenly giant, she'd messaged everyone to let them know she was coming back. As if she knew she wouldn't be strong enough to do so without backup.

She picked up her phone, and with thumbnail lodged between her teeth, she started with Laila.

You can't leave, friend!

Then...

At least not without one final blowout at the Vine. Some grand, banger of a night filled with cocktails, and, naturally, some kind of means to collect email addresses for my mailing list.

Next message was from her dad.

She'd told Dante she wanted to see him in person, but the honest truth was she was terrified. Terrified she'd never forgive him. Terrified he'd solidify the fear she was just like her mother.

Only now, having sent Dante away, she felt flayed. As if she'd torn Band-Aids off every inch of skin. Calling her dad couldn't possibly make her feel worse.

She pressed the call icon, sat on the corner of the bed, and waited.

"Honeybun," said her dad, with his lovely accent, and smiley kindness. "It's been too long."

"Dad," she said, clutching her arm to her belly.

And while she'd spent the past twenty-four hours in such turmoil, hearing his voice she only felt love, and certainty that whatever his explanation was it would all be okay. For while her mother had sent them away, this man had cared for her with all his might.

"Are you at home?"

"Of course, love."

"Are you sitting down?"

Her father's silence was telling. As if he knew what was coming.

"I met someone yesterday," she said. "I met Mya Hawthorn."

She heard her father sigh. "Oh, love. I hoped… Well, I'm sure you know what I hoped. I can't even begin to apologise for how confronting that must have been. Oh, the thoughts you must have had about me. How upset with me you must be."

"No!" Then, swiping a finger under her eyes. "I mean, I was surprised. And hurt. And confused? Can you explain your side—why you chose not to tell me the truth?"

"You've met her," he clarified, his voice deadpan.

And, unexpectedly, Sutton felt laughter bubble in her belly. "She was rather open about her lack of interest, in either of us."

"Hmm. Something that became obvious over the months we were together. I tried to change her mind. For your sake, as much as mine. I did love her. Do still, I fear."

"I know."

"I never wanted you to think that you were not the most loved and lovable child that has ever been."

Sutton breathed out hard. "You certainly did that." Then, "Am I like her, do you think?"

"Are you *like* her? In what way?"

"I've never settled. With anyone. I expect people to move on, and I do the same, super-fast, when they do. Do you think I even have it in me…to love?"

"My girl! You are love. You are fiercely protective, loyal, selfless, devoted. You have dedicated your life to standing up for those under your care. To your own detriment at times. I feel as if this is the right moment to point that out. Your mother kept her life to herself, and herself alone. You're as similar to *her* as I am to a pot plant."

Sutton laughed, as she was meant to do. And in someplace deep down inside, she felt a flicker of a flame come back to life. A kind of screw you, to anyone telling her she was insufficient in some way. Including herself.

"Is it wrong to say here that I think you are rather like me? You don't suffer fools, won't waste your precious time on anything you don't see as worthy of it. One day you'll meet someone, the right someone, someone strong, and joyous, who adores you and keeps you close. Someone who makes your heart grow three sizes bigger. Then you'll know how different you and your mother truly are."

Sutton wiped her nose, and blinked to clear the tears from her eyes.

How could she tell him she'd already met someone just like that? That she'd walked into a bar in Vermillion, spied a gorgeous, dark-haired Roman god of a man, a big hot bear with a thorn in his paw who looked at her as if she was the sunshine in his life, and turned her blood to fizz. And despite all that she'd already pushed him out the door?

Sutton ran a hand over her face, and gave her head a big shake. "On that," she said, "how is Marjorie?"

Her father's laugh was gentle, and warm. "When you told me where you were, it was a wake-up call. How small I have made my life, out of fear of having my heart broken again. And so, in an effort at being brave, like my daughter, I have booked that walking tour you told me about it."

"Oh, Dad. That's wonderful."

"So, if you were thinking of coming to visit over the next couple of weeks, I'm sorry, but I won't be here."

She laughed louder now. "Fair enough."

"Are we okay, you and me?" her dad asked, his voice unsteady, as if he knew things had changed a little between them, as they had changed in himself.

"Always."

After promising to call again the next day, with concrete plans, she rang off. Only to accidentally answer Bianca's call.

"Hey," said Sutton, putting it on speaker so she could pace.

"Hey! So you're coming back?"

"I am," she said, ferreting around till she found a tissue box, and carefully wiping her nose. "Excited to be up close and personal once more."

"Are you?" Bianca asked. "Because you sound kind of floopy."

"Probably just the phone line," she lied. "How are the new songs coming along? Any crowd favourites rising to the top?"

There was a beat before Bianca said, "Sure! Plenty."

"She's lying!" Sutton heard Francie call out in the background.

"Shush," Bianca hissed, the blur of her voice making Sutton picture her turning away from the phone. "This isn't about us—I think she's having an existential crisis over there."

"About time," Francie called out.

"Bianca?" Sutton called. "What's going on?" Doing some band manager magic would be the very best thing for her right now.

"So last night Francie tripped over a stray cord, not ours, fell and hurt her wrist."

"I'm fine!" Francie insisted.

"And yet we cancelled tonight so she can ice and elevate. Now Gustav is refusing to pay for Francie's hospital visit, even though the fault was theirs, refusing to pay us for our gigs to date, and threatening to sue over the lost earnings for any future dates we miss."

As Francie and Bianca argued, Sutton began making plans in her head. Using the band, and their worries, to push out all thoughts of Dante, and her parents, and leaving this sweet place behind. Who had time to think about one's future when one's present was a constant tightrope?

Sutton stopped rubbing at her temple. Opened her eyes. And repeated her thought out loud.

"Who had time to think about one's future when one's present was a constant tightrope?"

Before her trip she'd have gladly trotted that line out with pride. Now, sitting on a bedspread covered in cabbage roses, a Minotaur lamp looking solemnly back at her, the scent of a gorgeous giant lingering in the air…

Dante.

Just thinking his name made her heart press hard against her ribs. *Grow three sizes*, she thought, her father's words coming back to her.

She looked to the door. Pictured him standing there, hand in his hair. Doing as she asked and leaving. Not because he agreed, but because he'd want to make sure she was happy before looking after himself.

Dante, she thought, a sigh sticking in her throat as she tried to imagine a future in which she never saw him again.

Only it was impossible. No matter how hard she tried. Making her wonder why the hell she was trying so hard.

For him, a small voice in the back of her head reminded her. She was doing this for him—sending him away before she really hurt him.

What a fool, she thought. *What a reckless, misguided thing to do.*

Then she kicked the bed. Then kicked at it some more. Before letting out a great rage-filled roar.

"All better?" Bianca asked through the speaker on her phone.

Sutton flinched, having forgotten they were even there.

"No, actually," she said.

"Give it another go," Francie shouted back. "Let it all out!"

Let it all out.

Sutton took in a long slow breath, and on her next breath out did just that.

She let out the worry she'd end up like her dad. Let out the fear she might be more like her mum. Let out whatever remained of the ticking clock that had had such a hold over her life. Let out her need to be all things to all people so they'd like her, love her, and maybe, this time, never let her go.

And something inside her shifted. Something huge. As if she'd been looking at her life through a particular lens, and that lens had been whipped away.

"Bianca?"

"Yep."

"You know how I've always made it clear that if you ever

felt as if you'd outgrown me, I would be happy to pass you on to a bigger agency. I take it back. If you try to leave me, I will follow."

"Hell yeah, you will!"

Sutton nodded, and began bouncing from foot to foot.

"In fact, I'm going to get the Sweety Pies back too."

"Hell yeah, you are!"

"And it's past time I hire an assistant. And maybe get a budgie. Or a goldfish. Whatever my neighbour will happily look after when I'm away."

"Your neighbour?"

"In the new flat I'm going to buy."

"Okay, you've lost me now."

Sutton fell back on the bed, arms out, total starfish. And she started to laugh. And laugh. And laugh.

"Definite existential crisis," Zhou muttered, before Sutton told them all she adored them, and would call again soon with news on how she planned to get them out of the Liefd-escafé contract, but not before making the horrid manager pay through the nose.

Phone now silent, she glanced sideways, at her suitcase—half packed, for she'd done a half-assed job. As if the whole thing had been performative, only she'd honestly had no clue. Faking it, till she was certain leaving was the *only* choice.

Which she was—mostly. For both their sakes.

And yet, she let her next thoughts move inside her head with grace. Thought about planes and plans and amazing venues that would kill for a band like the Magnolia Blossoms to headline.

A few days later, as Dante stalked through the Vine kitchen—the staff scattering, aware that their temporary boss had been in a thunderous mood—he banged into Niccolo before he even saw him.

It took him a minute to recognise his cousin in his suit and tie, rather than the usual volunteer gear.

"Whoa," said his cousin on a laugh. "What's the rush, big guy?"

"No rush." Dante glared at Niccolo. "Some of us work around here."

"Some of us. But not you, right? Not anymore?"

He was right. Dante had "given his notice." Yet Nico's smile as Dante glared at him made Dante want to wrestle him to the ground as they had as kids.

"I get it," said Nico, slapping him on the arm. "My mother can drive the sanest person crazy. Piece of advice, try not walking around, all hunched and cantankerous, looking as if secretly imagining how you might burn the place down. You've done such a good job building the place up."

Dante, feeling the pinch in his shoulders, the sneer on his lips, sucked in a breath and slowly rolled his shoulders, putting him an inch over his cousin's height. His cousin was right—he could feel as rotten as he liked, the staff and customers at the Vine did not need to bear the brunt of it.

His mood was not their fault. It was entirely his own. For he'd left, giving Sutton what she'd told him she wanted. He'd left, *knowing* she was dead wrong.

"Better," said Nico, grinning wider and whistling as he strode into the Vine proper, where he happily chatted up the bustling clientele.

Dante took a second to centre himself before he pushed through the swinging door. And what had started out as a quiet spot for stray tourists, and happy-hour locals, was now a thriving concern. Filled with ambient music, lit with a canopy of stars, left over from the singles night.

Something new was happening at the far end of the space, where they usually kept spare tables and chairs. Storage? Construction? Lots of wires and wood seemed to be involved?

Something Chrissy and Kent had assured him they were on top of as it was no longer his concern.

After walking out of Sutton's bedroom, he'd driven straight to Vermillion Hill and told Zia Celia he was leaving. He offered three days to tie off loose ends. She'd not asked why, not asked how Sutton felt about that. She looked at him, and negotiated a week.

That date had passed two days earlier, and he was still hanging around. Because as far as he knew, Sutton was still in town. He did not know why—could only assume it had something to do with discharging the reason she'd come to Vermillion in the first place.

He'd not seen her, not once. Though he could feel her everywhere. Walking down Main Street, at the local grocer who stocked the raspberries she loved, at the vineyard, since he'd taken her on a tour of the entire place.

Yet knowing she was near meant he could not leave. Despite all that called him home, the invisible string tying him to her still pulled tight. Until he was sure she had left the country? Once he was certain she was safely back in the arms of those who loved her?

He knew he wasn't the only one. Despite her lauded independence, her support system was clearly wider and deeper than she realised.

Leaning against the edge of the bar, nearest the espresso machine, breathing in the scent of burned coffee beans, he knew what he'd just admitted to himself.

He loved her. Only it did not feel like news to him. It simply was. As if it had always been. Always would be. What a man did with that was beyond his expertise.

"Dante?"

Dante turned to find his aunt walking through the Vine's front door for the first time since he'd come to town. Her face lit up at the noise, the laughter, the electricity in the place.

"Zia Celia," he said, kissing her cheeks as she neared.

"Dante, this is more than I even expected. I can't believe the change that has come over this place. What's your secret?"

"Life," said Dante, "finding a way."

She must have heard some burr, some pain, in his words, for she turned to him, her expression concerned. "Life does that, you know. All you need to offer up is the smallest opening, and *la vita ritorna*."

Dante, well aware, having lived it over the past months, pressed a closed fist to his chest. To the place where his heart still beat stronger, even now, since letting Sutton Mayberry in.

Celia patted him on the cheek. "Now, might there be a table free, so an old lady can grab a light bite?"

Dante looked to Chrissy, who had been behind the bar, listening. She shrugged—no free tables.

"I believe there is one," said Dante, motioning with his head to the only table at which no customers sat.

Chrissy, nodding, hopped to it, grabbed a menu, and led Celia to the table by the last window. The one that still held a reserved sign. Even now.

Just as Dante's heart would forever be—reserved for the bolshie British brunette who had given it life again.

Sutton stood outside the Vine and Stein, looking up at the metal sign swinging from the horizontal pole over the door. The first time she'd seen it, her belly had been filled with anticipation. This time her emotions were far too fraught and too many to pin down.

Either way, something had sent her into *this* bar all those weeks before. The universe, fate, need for Wi-Fi—whatever it was, she'd had no idea that that moment was the true hinge on which her life would turn. For there was *before* she'd walked inside the Vine and Stein, and there was *after*.

She pushed open the door and was hit with a wall of white noise. Voices raised in conversation and laughter, from the group of people lined up before a lectern and the crowd filling the venue to near capacity. Kent, who was checking names against a booking calendar, looked up, saw her, and motioned for her to slip past.

Which she did, only to find the place looked like an absolute dream. The fairy lights in the ceiling had tripled since last she was there, the chandeliers had been dropped, hanging low over the crowd, and hidden fluoro rods she'd had Nico order and install added a pinkish dreamscape quality.

While at the far end of the space stood a purpose-built stage and small but effective light and sound rig. Dark purple velvet curtains swept from a centre point high above, curving to the edges of the stage, making it look fancier than it was.

It was just as she'd described it to Laila and Nico, Chrissy and Kent, who had all pitched in to make it happen, after she'd rung and explained her near-impossible idea. Which filled her with such poignancy, such honest joy, her heart hiccupped.

She apologised as she stood aside for staff she didn't recognise, moving through bussing glasses, then she slipped down the outer edge of the room, past her window, not looking to her table, in case someone else was using it.

All the while searching the crowd for a certain big, gruff Italian import. For if he wasn't there to see it, did it really exist?

Her spies had told her he was still around; still tying up loose ends, before he moved on. Some small part of her wondered if it was because he knew she'd not yet absconded, but that was the most wishful of thinking.

Either way, she wanted to give him this, this last hurrah to really set up the Vine for the future. To show Dante how much he meant to her, how much he meant to them all. Then maybe she could live with all the mistakes she'd made along the way.

And he could go home, to his beloved vineyard, and no longer feel beholden to anyone else's pull on his time. He could live his life, his passions, forevermore.

Dante, who'd been stuck at the vineyard the past couple of days—helping Celia train a handful of new sommelier recruits, something Nico could have done with his hands tied behind his back—went by the Vine to search for a "very important purse" Celia had left behind the other day.

While telling himself this was the very last thing he would do for the family. Underlined. Full stop. Then, once assured Sutton had left, he'd be on the next plane home.

Only the staff car park was full. Main Street the same. He had to park way down the road, and had built up a fair head of steam by the time he reached the Vine. Only to find the sounds coming from inside its walls none he'd heard before.

Pressing his way through the front door for the first time in days, he stopped, looked up at the sign, wondering if he'd walked into the wrong place. For it looked like a completely new place. Lights that he'd thought busted glowed gold and pink behind the mirrored wall behind the bar. The floor, having clearly had a polish, shone. And that was the least of it.

Pressing inside, he caught Kent's eye over the crowd.

"Mad, right?" Kent shouted from his spot behind the bar, slinging cocktails like he was born to it. "Can't believe she actually pulled this off."

She? Dante went to ask, only to realise he knew. There was only one person with the eye, the desire, and the tenacity to make such an event happen.

"Sutton." He realised he'd said it out loud, when Kent waggled a hand toward the back of the room.

The construction the others had waved off as a little upkeep turned out to be a stage. Speakers. Lights. Curtains. Then bodies walked out onto the stage, taking place behind drums, mike stands. Spotlights lit up and followed them, and the crowd pressed forward. The noise went through the roof.

"Dante! So glad you could make it!"

Dante turned to find Laila swishing past, cocktail in hand.

"Classic, cuz. Late to the party," said Nico, from his other side.

"Who is that?" Dante asked as the lead singer shouted something unintelligible into the mike before playing some raucous cacophony that sent the crowd wild.

"That would be the Magnolia Blossoms."

Dante looked to his left to find Sutton where Laila had been. Her hair tied back in a loose ribbon at her nape, small curls escaping at her cheeks. Looking mouthwatering in a black leather dress that dipped low in front, hugged her tight and stopped at her knees. She swayed in time with the music for a few beats, before her gaze lifted to his. *"Ciao."*

"Ciao," he managed, shaking his head. Mesmerised. Confused. Bursting with a life force that had flourished inside without him even knowing. "I thought… I thought you were leaving."

"Well," she said, leaning in closer so she didn't have to shout. Or so that she could lean in closer. Gods, how he hoped it was the latter.

"Turned out the Magnolia Blossoms were not being treated as they deserved by their last venue so I told them to come out here, and play a week of nights at this fabulous venue in the small winery town of Vermillion, South Australia." She shrugged. "I figured I'd better stay, at least until they arrived."

"How did you pull this off?" he asked.

"Told you once before, when I decide to do something, it gets done. Also, it turns out Kent's uncle works in immigration so put us onto the right people to get escalated visas. And if you give Laila a budget, not using her own money, she's a whiz with decor. Nico knows everyone, so staffing was a cinch."

Dante turned to find Nico now by the bar. He lifted a drink in salute, then flapped his hands, encouraging Dante to turn back around.

When he did, it was to find Sutton watching him. The band, the crowd, it all faded into insignificance as her eyes caught on his; hopeful, and wary, and bright. The crowd pressed in, knocking them toward one another. When their arms touched, she didn't pull away.

"Don't you want to know why?" she asked.

Dante was fairly sure he knew the why, but was happy to hear her say the words.

"It's time for you to go home, Dante. Stop looking after everyone here. That's what you want, isn't it?"

"Si," he said. "At least that was what I wanted."

"Oh?" she said, her throat rising and falling.

He put a hand at her back when the crowd jostled them again. Ran his knuckles along her hips when he let her go. She rolled into his touch, heat sweeping into her eyes. And it was enough to help him say:

"I've been trying to pinpoint when that changed."

She swallowed, watching his mouth, waiting for his next words as if they were the air she needed to breathe.

"Was it the night you banged on the back door of the Vine, demanding to be let in? Or was it the day in the office, the delight on your face as you took in the picture of my family's vineyard? Perhaps it was that first morning, when despite how hard I tried to get you to leave, you refused me."

"Dante," she said, then licked her lips.

He lifted his hand to hold her chin, then dipped his mouth to hers. Tasting her glistening mouth. "I couldn't go, not yet, knowing you were still here."

"I stayed," she said, "because you stayed."

Dante pulled her to his chest, the music reverberating through his shoes and into his bones. The beat of her heart against his drowning it out.

"Is it too late?" Her voice was light, but carrying to his ears anyway.

"Too late?" he asked. Knowing that for him, where she was concerned, time and place had no meaning.

"Is it too late to take back all the things I said the other day? I was overwhelmed, my head was a mess. And I think I took it out on you because you were the one thing I could trust."

She paused to take a breath, but Dante, hearing the words beneath her words, knew it was his turn to speak his truth.

"I love you, Sutton."

She breathed out hard. Her lashes fluttering wildly against her cheeks.

"I am in love with you," he said, leaning in to press his forehead to hers. "You took my heart the moment I laid eyes on you, and never gave it back. And if all this—" he motioned to the lights and the music and the crowd dancing around them "—means I have even the slightest hope that one day you might be able to return those feelings—"

Sutton threw herself into his arms, her head buried against his neck, words muffled. While he could have kept her there, his arms wrapped tight about her forever, he had a feeling those words might be worth hearing. He eased her back and said, "Could you say that again?"

"I love you so much, Dante. So much it scares me. In a good way. I thought it was a bad way. As in too much for me to handle. That if you didn't love me back, I might never recover. But then when you walked out my door, I realised that loving you *too much* is way better than any other life I might have. If I'm not too late, if I didn't screw everything up royally, I'm here now. Ready and willing. If you'll have me."

"I will have you, Sutton Mayberry, if you will have me. A humble, solitary, gruff, grape farmer."

She laughed, her head thrown back, and he pulled her closer.

"Are you sure you know what you're in for? Your life is dictated by sunshine, mine by moonlight. It's a mercurial existence."

"It's exciting," he amended, sliding a hand up her back, the other over the top curve of her backside.

"I'm impulsive."

"You're enthusiastic."

"I'm chaos."

"You're *vital*," he said, stressing the final word with so much passion, Sutton stopped coming up with reasons why they might not work. And hit on the one reason they would.

She gripped him tight, and lifted up onto her toes to whisper against his ear, "You are vital to me."

"Lucky then, for it seems we are vital to one another. From the moment I first saw your face, heard your voice, felt your stubbornness coming at me like a weapon, it was like the tolling of a bell. As if I'd been hit by... By..."

"Love lightning?" she asked, a small smile curving at the edge of her lovely mouth.

Dante took a moment, thought about the angle his life had taken. The colour, the light, the possibility that bled into every crack in his well-tended armour since coming to this place. And he said, "Love lightning."

Then noise rose as the crowd around them cheered. For a moment Dante thought it was for them, then he realised the band had stopped one song, pausing before the next.

She looked to the stage, to her band, and held up both arms and cheered. When her arms came back around his neck, Dante brushed his lips over her jaw, her ear, the edge of her mouth, and finally closed over hers.

More cheers went up around them, and most definitely *for* them.

When they pulled apart, she laughed, happy as he'd ever seen her, then turned so that she was watching her band, holding his arms around her.

Sutton, her head leaning on Dante's shoulder, said, "So I'd class tonight as yet another success."

"You would, would you?"

"We saved the bar. The girl got her guy." She tilted her head back and smiled. "If only I'd worn heels, so I could see better, then it would be perfect."

Dante sank down onto his knee, and pointed to his shoulders. "Get up," he said.

"What?" she called.

"Have you not been to a music festival before?"

Laughing, she took about half a second to agree, tucking her dress up to her thighs, she slung a leg over his shoulders, and whooped as he lifted her in the air.

She stayed up there for the whole song, singing at the top of her lungs, before she tapped out. Once on the floor, she thanked everyone around them. Explained they were her band. Promised them all a meet and greet with the band afterward.

After which Dante pulled her back in front of him, gathering her close, swaying with the crowd as the music, her band, cacophonous as they might be, became the soundtrack to what might be the best night of his life.

Best night so far, he thought, kissing the top of Sutton's head as she pressed back into him. *So far*.

EPILOGUE

SUTTON SAT AT the long table on the east lawn of Villa Sorello, her laptop open, papers spread out, as she ticked off the final checklists for all that had to be in place for the big weekend ahead.

Francie came out carrying a plate of prawns. "No truly," she was saying to Celia, who carried a plate of eggplant parmigiana. "The sauce is a family recipe. We are famous for our seafood in Positano."

"Pfft," Celia scoffed. "No one is actually *from* Positano."

When Francie went to object, Sutton caught her eye, and shook her head. Francie, for once, in the face of Celia's Celia-ness, backed down.

A happy sigh on the tip of her tongue pretty much at all times these days, Sutton looked around, taking in the soft sunshine, the plates upon plates of wonderful food, the earthy scents making the place feel like some hazy dream.

But this was no dream. This was her life now.

Splitting her time between London—visiting her dad as often as she could, when he was home—and traveling with her bands. But most of her time, more and more as the months went on, she spent here, in this most beautiful of places, with the man that she loved.

Bianca came bustling out of the side entrance, carrying her famous *bitterballen*, Dutch meatballs. Zhou had made cranachan, a creamy raspberry dessert. And Dante's cook had put on the usual antipasto and pastas, along with several bottles of local wine, decanted and ready for the enjoying.

They'd all wanted to contribute, knowing how busy Dante was, on the verge of launching his first cellared release—a ten-year-old Sagrantino he'd bottled the year he'd bought the vineyard. Sutton was busy too, as organiser of the Note di Vino music festival, due to take place on the gently sloping lawn to the south of the Sorello estate that weekend.

"I do believe that is everything," said Celia.

And Sutton quickly checked a couple of more emails before closing her laptop.

"Was that from Nico?" Dante asked, as he appeared at Sutton's side.

"It was. He still thinks we should have called the festival Grapestock."

Dante, grinning, passed her a bottle of lager, chilled to the touch. He kissed the top of her head as she took it, murmuring, "I must really love you if I can handle watching you drink that swill."

"You love watching me do just about anything, I've found."

"True," he said, nipping at her neck, before he took the seat beside hers.

The Magnolia Blossoms, Crochet, and the Sweety Pies—still under new management, yet attending as headline guests—were all staying in the village, in preparation for the weekend. Her dad and Marjorie were coming the next day. Nico had stayed in Vermillion to "keep an eye on things," though Laila, also in Vermillion, running her beloved bookstore, kept messaging, saying she was certain Nico hadn't come as he was still pouting that his name wasn't chosen.

Once everyone was seated, food piling up onto plates, conversation flying, Dante's hand landed gently on Sutton's neck, his calloused fingers caressing her hair out of the way so he could touch her skin.

Her hand landed on his thigh, tracing circles that were just shy of risqué in such company.

Dante looked her way, leaned in for a kiss, mouthed, *"Ti amo,"* then drank his beloved wine.

Sutton listened for a tick, or a tock, and heard neither. Only the gentle hum of bees, the rustle of pencil pines, and the quiet, steady thud of her happy, happy heart.

* * * * *

If you enjoyed this story,
check out these other great reads
from Ally Blake

Always the Bridesmaid
Secretly Married to a Prince
Cinderella Assistant to Boss's Bride
Fake Engagement with the Billionaire

All available now!

BEST MAN'S SECOND CHANCE

SUZANNE MERCHANT

MILLS & BOON

PROLOGUE

Two and a half years ago

BY THE TIME Isabella boarded the train to Edinburgh she was running on empty. Work had consumed her for weeks on end, with exhaustion the only payback. She couldn't remember when she'd last taken a day off, and that included weekends.

The boyfriend she'd been with since college had ended their relationship, pointing out that he hadn't seen her for three weeks and he felt her loyalties lay elsewhere. She'd hardly had time to feel sad. After all, how could she miss someone she had seen so little of lately?

If determination and sheer hard work could save the company which had been in her family for several generations, then she'd be the superhero who accomplished that seemingly impossible task.

Months of trying to persuade her aging father that they needed to embrace new methods, follow up-and-coming trends and allow several elderly members of staff to retire gracefully, if their woollen spinning and weaving business was to survive fierce competition from abroad, had culminated in a fiery disagreement over dinner the previous evening. He'd refused to listen, countering her arguments with his own, and eventually she'd pushed her bowl of apple crumble away. The meal, as always, had been delicious, prepared with care by her father's housekeeper, Beryl, but Isabella couldn't stomach another mouthful.

She'd left her father at the table and walked out, reminding him she'd be away for the weekend. It was the only serious argument she could ever remember having with him and it had upset and unsettled her.

Sleep, lately elusive, had proved completely impossible after that. Now, her eyes burning and her head throbbing, she stowed her carry-on bag in the luggage rack, flung herself into the seat she'd reserved in the designated quiet coach and made a decision.

This weekend in Scotland, being bridesmaid to her friend Hannah, was going to be her timeout. Work problems would not intrude on her at the Castle of Muir, on Hannah and her twin Emma's Highland family estate. She was going to throw herself into the wedding celebrations and enjoy herself. The argument with her father had been horrible and had left her feeling miserable, but she'd message him later and suggest that they could take up the discussion again next week, when they'd both had time to cool off and reflect.

She leaned her head back against the seat and turned to watch the suburbs of north London slide past the window. Exhaling a deep sigh, she closed her eyes and willed the pent-up tension to leave her body.

What she needed was a distraction to short-circuit the constant stream of anxiety about the business, which played on a relentless loop in her brain.

Who knew, perhaps there'd even be a hot best man to provide it.

Apparently, discovering whether the best man was hot or not would have to wait until the ceremony, because he hadn't turned up the night before for the rehearsal or the dinner.

Hannah had rolled her eyes. 'Let's hope he pitches up in the morning, otherwise…'

But Robert, her husband-to-be, had been reassuring. 'He will. He may be wild, but he won't let us down.' He'd dropped an arm around Hannah's shoulders. 'He's on the early flight tomorrow. It'll be fine.'

Isabella glanced between them, seeing the look of worry on Hannah's face. 'I know this is going to be hard for him. And with his current reputation, perhaps…'

'You'll see,' Robert had replied firmly. 'He'll be here and he'll charm the socks off everyone.'

'As long as it's only the *socks*.'

The hours before the wedding unfolded according to a carefully orchestrated plan. Isabella and Emma helped Hannah into her cream brocade silk dress, handed her the bouquet of perfect pale pink roses, picked in the rose garden that summer's morning, and walked with her through the castle, across the courtyard to the chapel, where their father waited.

It was all a world away from the problems Bella had left behind in London, and she breathed in the scent of purple heather on the warm air, relishing this opportunity to be a part of something so special. She was loving every minute, and the wedding hadn't even begun.

She and Emma followed Hannah and her father up the aisle, arranging the lace train of her dress, taking the bouquet of roses from her and stepping into their places. She folded her hands in front of her and looked up.

Just as Robert had promised, the best man had arrived, in the nick of time. He stood, shoulder to shoulder with the groom, each dressed in the tartan of their clan. He was half a head taller than Robert, his shoulders a little broader, his calves a little more muscular. He turned to survey the congregation, pushing long fingers through his dark hair, which fell in unruly, thick curls to his shoulders.

Isabella sucked in a breath. Ross Maclean was Ross Poldark, on steroids. She pictured him stripped to the waist... But her attention snapped back to reality as his dark eyes, restless as the sea on a stormy day, locked onto hers like a heat-seeking missile and suddenly she had to think about breathing because all her natural reflexes had stalled.

An audible rustle of anxiety rippled through the congregation as he patted his pockets, searching for the ring. When he located it, he acknowledged the collective, muted sigh of relief with a rueful half-smile. It was obvious that he courted disaster, with what appeared to be deliberate relish.

The whole package of a hot best man, wrapped up in Highland dress in an impossibly romantic setting, was exactly what she'd dreamed of.

She knew, right then, that she'd found her distraction.

CHAPTER ONE

BELLA GLANCED AT the antique clock on the marble mantel-piece and then back at her father. He sat in his usual position at the head of the long boardroom table, immaculate in a fine wool three-piece suit. He'd occupied that place for fifty years, since he'd taken over the business from his own father, and she couldn't believe that he was contemplating this radical change.

Uneasily, she thought of how little she'd engaged with him recently. As she'd taken on more and more responsibilities at work, she'd seen less of him, and their frequent conversations had dwindled to infrequent, snatched chats. Should she have seen this coming? Probably, she thought, if she'd been paying more attention, but she'd dismissed his vague reference to retiring, a couple of months ago, as not worth thinking about

'We could still cancel the meeting. Or at least postpone it.'

It was only twenty-four hours since her father had dropped the bombshell that an offer for half the business had been made and, according to him, it was too good to refuse. He would retire, leaving Bella with her half of the company, and a new business partner. Ross Maclean.

Her father met her eyes across the table and shook his head. 'At least meet him, Bella, before you dismiss the idea out of hand.'

He removed his glasses and began to polish the already

sparkling lenses with the silk square from his top pocket, and Bella knew she'd lost this first round. That gesture meant the discussion was closed. For now.

'Ross Maclean has a brutal business reputation.'

Her father looked up again. 'You know him?'

She glanced away, towards the tall windows which looked out over a London square. 'His reputation is no secret. And yes, I've met him, but I couldn't say I *know* him.'

Her mind rewound, at warp speed, to that wedding, two and a half years ago.

From the moment their eyes had locked, the eventual outcome had been inevitable. She had been on a mission to cut loose and have fun, and he'd seemed hell-bent on helping her.

He'd moved like a stalking panther: slowly, but with the pent-up promise of lightning speed in his limbs and she'd been willing prey, eager to play at being stalked. When he'd concluded his best man's speech, perfectly judged to be only just on the right side of acceptable, he'd raised his glass in those strong fingers and toasted the bridesmaids, his dark eyes on hers, one corner of his mouth kicking up into the hint of a smile, as if at a shared secret.

Bella had been happy to be complicit in the secret, and, afterwards, she'd kept it. What she'd done had been so out of character for her that she'd felt unable to explain it to anyone else.

The ceilidh had been exuberant, and the dancing had grown wilder as the night wore on. Their eyes collided, over and over again, across the room of swirling bodies, and when the beat of the music eventually slowed and guests returned to their seats to slake thirsts and recover, the only place either of them wanted to go was into each other's arms.

Much later, in her room, he'd cupped her face in his broad hands and studied her, as if he was trying to commit her to memory.

'Isabella,' he'd murmured, his forehead resting against hers. 'Are you sure?'

She'd nodded. 'Yes.'

'It can only be for tonight. I can't...'

'Perfect,' she'd whispered. 'One night is all I need.'

When she'd woken the next morning, her bridesmaid's dress had been hanging neatly from a hook behind the door, her underwear on a chair. She'd turned, looking for Ross in the dim light, but he'd gone. The place where he'd lain beside her had been cold.

There'd been a scrawled note on the bedside table.

Thank you for being with me, Isabella.
R x

At breakfast he was nowhere to be seen, and then she learned, from a chance remark, that he'd left, to catch an early flight back to London. She'd dipped her head and bitten her bottom lip, annoyed at the feeling of disappointment and loss which swamped her, and then she'd raised her chin and smiled.

'Bella?'

She dragged her thoughts back to the present. Her father was frowning at her.

'Yes?'

'Are you all right?'

She shook her head. 'No. I'm not all right with this sudden decision of yours, or with the person who has made you this offer. He'll take Thompson's Textiles apart and sell off the profitable bits. It's what he does. The company as we know it will no longer exist. And we're doing so well now, since the changes we made.' She stood up and paced across the room, the heels of her court shoes clicking on the old wooden floorboards. 'And I've given everything to make those changes happen.'

'I know you have, and that's one of the reasons behind my decision.' Albert Thompson tucked the silk square into his pocket and put his glasses back on. 'You've taken far too much on yourself. Your talents lie in design and innovation, yet you're spending most of your time on the management side. You need to…'

'I love what I'm doing, Dad. Surely you can step back without retiring completely. You can advise me, when necessary.' She knew she was clutching at straws, but she couldn't stop. 'I just don't want…*this.*'

It was impossible to explain to her father how much the idea of seeing Ross scared her. They'd spent one night together, and they'd agreed it would be only that.

'Perfect,' she'd whispered against his mouth. And it had been perfect.

So perfect that it had been impossible to forget. She'd allowed work to occupy even more of her life, hoping the memories would fade and become manageable, but Ross had been in her dreams, waking and sleeping, ever since that one night they'd both agreed on. Countless times, she'd been on the verge of asking Hannah for news of him and how to contact him. But he'd said one night was all he could give to her, and she'd said one night was all she needed.

If he'd wanted more he could have found her, which meant he wasn't interested in seeing her again. The fear of his likely rejection, if she found him, stopped her from trying.

Perhaps she didn't want to know his reasons for walking away. He hadn't asked why she only needed one night.

She'd tried dating. Dave, whom she'd met at a trade exhibition, had been fun to meet for dinner a few times, but when she'd cancelled an arrangement for the third time, citing work commitments, he hadn't contacted her again, and she found she hadn't really cared. She wondered if she'd ever again experience that shock of recognition which had hit her when her eyes had connected with Ross's that summer's afternoon. The idea of love at first sight had always seemed ridiculous. Now she wasn't so sure.

It would be impossible to build a professional relationship with him, feeling as she did, but she didn't know how to stop her father from going ahead with his plan.

'Try to relax. You're stressed.'

'*Relax?* Dad...'

She took a deep breath, and then another. She smoothed her hands over her black pencil skirt and straightened the cuffs of her ivory silk shirt, then fingered the single strand of smooth pearls she'd inherited from her mother. Like worry beads, rolling them between her fingers sometimes had a calming effect.

'I *am* stressed, Dad.' She patted the neat French knot at the back of her head, checking that no stray strands had escaped. 'I haven't had enough time to process this. If you'd discussed it with me before setting up this meeting, I could have...'

What could she have done? Told him she'd refuse to meet Ross Maclean, the CEO of a mega successful company, because she'd been the idiot to almost fall for him after an agreed no-strings one-night stand?

A feeling of disloyalty flickered inside her and she tried to stamp it out. But if her father did retire, she wouldn't miss the way he sometimes highjacked the business, making decisions without consulting his senior employees. Old habits die hard, she thought, and always assuming there'd be a business left, if Ross Maclean got his hands on it.

She heard her PA Jess's voice outside the boardroom, and the door opened.

Twenty-four hours had not been enough time to prepare for seeing him again, but, she thought, as Ross walked in, neither would a million years. It seemed as if all the air had been sucked out of the room. She'd heard, she thought absently, how it felt in the aftermath of an explosion, and she wondered if a bomb had gone off somewhere nearby and she'd hear the *crump* of it in a few seconds. Everything seemed to be happening in slow motion, and to someone else, while she looked on from outside herself. Was this what was called an out-of-body experience? Shock was the accepted explanation for that phenomenon.

Because he'd changed.

Jess stood, smiling, in the doorway, her father rose from his chair, extending a hand, but Bella felt paralysed.

The first thing she would ask him, when everything went back to normal, was why he'd cut his hair. She remembered running her fingers through his shoulder-length curls, and the way he'd pushed them off his forehead as he'd bent to kiss her, but they were gone. Instead, his thick coal-dark hair was slicked back off his forehead, neat and sober. She wondered, absently, what he would do, and what her father would say, if she gave into a crazy urge to push her hands through it, muss it up a little, so that he'd look more like the man she remembered, rather than the businessman who'd walked into her life—*this* life—ready to throw all the elements she was familiar with up into the air and have them come down in a different, unwelcome pattern.

His charcoal suit had definitely been tailored for him, possibly from one of Thompson's own fine woollen fabrics. Just the acceptable amount of white shirt cuff showed beyond the sleeves, and heavy silver cuff-links gleamed at his wrists.

Even in her state of shock, she could see that he bore all the hallmarks of success and that he carried them with effortless ease.

He shook her father's hand and turned to her.

'Isabella.'

'Ross.'

'My daughter,' said her father, 'and my partner in Thompson's Textiles, Bella, but I believe you've already met.'

Bella saw the door closing and had the wild idea that if she launched herself across the room she might just make it through the gap before it shut out the life she knew forever, leaving her to learn her way around this new one, without a map.

'Yes,' said Ross. 'We have.' He extended a hand, and she took it, remembering the breadth and strength of his warm grip.

'At Hannah's wedding.' Bella pulled her eyes from Ross to look at her father.

In the space of a few seconds, Ross Maclean had been swept back two and a half years. He'd been prepared for this meeting, knowing he was going to see Isabella again. When Thompson's Textiles had been flagged by his team as a company of interest, he'd done his research and found that she owned half the business. The other half, owned by her elderly father, was potentially for sale.

That was when he should have stepped away, but he wanted this deal. There were numerous companies available for the sort of deals he did, but Thompson's intrigued him. It was a family-owned-and-run business which had been established by the Thompsons over a century ago. He wondered how it felt to be a part of such a solid enterprise and a family which stretched back for generations and could look to the future with certainty. And given those facts, why was Albert Thompson considering selling his half?

When he'd discovered that Isabella was a part-owner, the idea of reconnecting with her had overridden his common sense. Thompson's represented an unbroken line of ownership, their reputation for caring for the staff and promoting family values was well-known and the company adhered, with passion, to producing products of only the highest quality. What had made Isabella, from that traditional, rather conservative background, want a one-night stand at a wedding?

He'd thought he could handle seeing her again, but sudden doubt made him wish he'd thought it through more carefully.

She'd been the one-night stand he'd been unable to let go. He'd wanted, very badly, to see her again, and that had rung all sorts of alarm bells in his head. He'd listened to them, until now. Early in life, he'd learnt that commitment was unreliable and love, when given, was not necessarily returned. Even worse, a twist of fate could snatch certainty and happiness away in a flash.

Business deals were solid and reliable, distilled down to a bottom line of figures. He was good at them, although he'd seen himself described as ruthless, and brutal. His reputation for seeing opportunities and taking them was well-deserved, and nowadays his bank account and lifestyle were testament to the success he enjoyed.

Feelings, commitment, love, were something altogether different. Indulging in them was unpredictable and dangerous. The idea of giving his heart to someone else, believing they would care for it with unstinting love, scared him witless. He'd fought for control over his life from a young age, and again as an adult, when he'd come to within a breath of losing everything. Loving someone would mean relinquishing that control. He never planned to do that again. The pain of loss was too great and the responsibility of looking after someone else you loved was too dangerous.

Now holding her hand in his, he thought he'd made a massive mistake, because the impact of seeing her again sent all kinds of need on a route march around his body.

He'd been at rock-bottom when they'd met. But something about the grace with which she'd accepted him for what he was, the way she hadn't asked for more than he was capable of giving, her pure enjoyment in being with him, had made him rethink his lifestyle. She'd been kind and thoughtful and unlike anyone he'd ever known. He'd found himself with space to consider, and the will to turn things around.

Right now, after two years and some months of punishingly hard work, things were as he wanted them to be. The business was flourishing, he had rebalanced his life and so when the prospect of seeing her again had presented itself, he had hesitated but then decided it would be fine. He'd never yet allowed his heart to rule his head.

He'd got it wrong. He inhaled a breath, that perfume he remembered with such sharp clarity invading his senses. Floral and woody, with a hint of exotic spice, it made him want to stay close to her, to breathe in her essence, study the creamy curve of skin where the sweep of her neck disappeared beneath the silk of her shirt. Shock sent his legendary control into free fall. She looked as shocked as he felt and he did look different, he remembered grimly. They'd connected when he'd been fighting hard to stay afloat, with each day a challenge just to get from morning to night, only then to toss, unsleeping, for hours, his mind a treadmill of regret and grief.

She looked different, too. She was thinner and looked taut. Her blond curls, which had floated down her back, tamed only by a circlet of wildflowers, were smoothed into a French knot at her nape, and her slim black skirt and ivory silk shirt gave her an air of gravity, at odds with his memories of her flushed cheeks and grey eyes sparkling with anticipation.

He'd been wild, he knew, because that was how he'd kicked back against life and its cruelties. He should never have agreed to be Robert's best man. There'd been a chance that he might have behaved spectacularly badly. But Isabella had carried him through the evening and night, with her free-spirited attitude and capacity for enjoyment. They'd felt like a perfect match and he'd never expected to feel that again, with anyone. In her arms that night he'd felt safe enough to imagine himself loosening the tight tethers which bound him, and so he'd torn himself away before she woke in the morning, for her sake and his. If he'd stayed, he'd have broken his rules and asked to see her again and then he would have hurt her. It's what he always did.

Ross spent much of the next hour trying to block the memories of the night they'd spent together and concentrate on the business aspects of the meeting. He wondered if her lips would still taste as sweet as they had back then, and if the rather severe image she now presented hid the soft, passionate girl he'd been unable to forget.

Was he crazy to pursue this? To become her business partner would be to put himself in a position, day after day, where he'd have to curb this intense desire, which had flared into life again the moment he'd seen her. Working together would be impossible. He'd have to consider his next move with care and detachment.

He drained his cup of excellent coffee, served by the staff member who'd greeted him and shown him into the boardroom, and closed the folder which lay on the table in front of him.

'All the details of my offer are in here.' He handed it to Albert Thompson. 'There is a duplicate copy of everything for you, Isabella. I hope you'll think over the options but do take your time. Having had this opportunity of a face-to-face meeting, I also have aspects of my proposal to consider.'

Sharply aware of the palpable waves of antagonism coming off Isabella, he stood. He shook Albert's hand and then turned to Isabella, steeling himself to deal with the rush of emotion he knew would ambush him when their hands touched. He made sure the contact was brief. 'Good to see you.' His voice felt tight. 'And,' he cast about, looking for a suitable exit line, 'I understand we're going to reprise our roles at Emma's wedding, next weekend.'

Isabella was catapulted into autopilot mode. She hoped she'd kept her expression impassive but she was sure shock showed in her eyes.

'Are we? I hadn't realised.' She was pleased that her voice sounded cool even though heat flowed through her and her heart bumped. Just exactly *how much* did Ross expect to reprise?

Thankfully he'd turned to leave before the flush which had been building in her reached her cheeks. Somehow, she'd missed that piece of information about the forthcoming wedding. She knew she hadn't paid enough attention to the excited posts on Emma and Andrew's wedding website, but she'd been too busy. This time it was Emma, Hannah's twin sister, getting married at the Castle of Muir.

When Emma had asked her to be her bridesmaid, she'd hesitated, afraid that the memories of Ross would be too disturbing, but then telling herself she was strong enough to deal with them. Now that she'd seen him again, she knew how unrealistic that had been.

She'd been looking forward to the weekend. The pressures of work had become even greater since the previous wedding and she'd planned to take an extra day off and stay until the Monday, but she mentally adjusted that plan.

She picked up her phone and sent a message to Emma explaining that, due to an unexpected development at work, she'd have to leave on the Sunday, after all.

Knowing she was going to have to be the bridesmaid next to Ross as best man again filled her with trepidation. Hannah and Emma had no idea about the night they'd spent together, or the feelings about him which she'd taken away with her.

Afraid they might show, she'd taken care never to mention his name to them.

Her father had opened the folder Ross had given him and was extracting the copies of the documentation which were meant for her. She might as well put them through the shredder, right this minute. There was no way, at all, that this deal could go through. She'd cited Ross's reputation as a reason why his methods were unsuitable for a company like Thompson's, but after this morning that was the least of her concerns. Even if their night of passion had meant nothing to *him*, the way *her* body had lit up when she'd seen him walk through the door meant she could never contemplate a business partnership with him. If she reacted to him like this, after burying her feelings for two and a half years, what hope could she have of keeping them hidden if she had to interact with him every day?

CHAPTER TWO

BELLA VOWED TO herself that this time it would be different.

She took a breath, hoping to calm the nerves fluttering in her stomach. So much was the same. The chapel had stood on this ancient Scottish estate, unchanged, for four hundred years and Emma, the bride, was Hannah's identical twin.

But this time would be different, because this time she would not be having a one-night stand with the best man.

'Bella!' Hannah, now the maid of honour, hissed in her ear, nudging her shoulder. 'They're about to begin.'

Bella smoothed her hands over the amethyst silk dress and reached down to take the hands of the little flower girl and pageboy on either side of her. 'Ready?' she whispered.

Rosie and Dougal nodded solemnly. 'When do we get to throw the confetti?' Rosie looked longingly at the baskets of dried petals clustered at the door behind them.

'Later, Rosie. After we've all been quiet and not wriggly during the ceremony.' Bella put a finger to her lips.

The ancient oak doors in front of them creaked open and the first chords of 'The Arrival of the Queen of Sheba' soared into the shadows of the vaulted roof. Every head in the congregation turned in the direction of the entrance as Emma, her hand looped through her father's arm, began the slow walk up the aisle.

Bella lifted her chin, pinned on her best smile and hoped it radiated a confidence she did not feel. Did anyone else know that she and Ross… She shut down the thought. All eyes in the congregation were on Emma and her joyful smile. No one was looking at her.

Emma and her father halted at the foot of the chancel steps, where the groom and best man waited. Bella handed Rosie and Dougal over to their parents in the second row, took Emma's bouquet of pink and cream roses from her and slipped into her reserved place at the front.

She'd been dreading this moment. Just being here, in this almost déjà-vu situation, was triggering an avalanche of memories. Knowing it was going to be Ross standing next to Andrew, the groom, had almost made her want to dream up a reason to pull out altogether. But only she was to blame for not paying proper attention to the wedding plans, and loyalty to her friends meant she couldn't possibly let Emma down at such a late stage. There was no option but to go through with it, with her courage screwed up tight and her head held high. She could do this.

She *had* to.

At the meeting with her father and Ross, earlier in the week, her normally clear head had apparently been colonised by cotton wool and she'd found it almost impossible to concentrate on what either of the two men were saying. She'd felt resentful of her father for springing this on her, and angry with herself for allowing Ross's presence to affect her so badly.

Every movement of his expressive hands, every tilt of his head, or intonation of a word had resonated with her memories of him. She'd clenched her fists beneath the table, digging her nails into her palms, to try to sharpen her attention. How could so much of his essence have been so deeply imprinted on her soul in such a short time?

She bent to place Emma's bouquet safely on the pew beside her, picked up the order of service, printed on heavy cream paper, and straightened as the organ music began to fade and an expectant hush replaced the buzz of excitement. Andrew and Ross stood tall in their kilts, their backs to the congregation. The heady perfume of flowers mingled with the scent of beeswax from the candles flickering in iron sconces on the walls. Low rays of afternoon winter sun slanted through the old stained-glass windows, pouring jewel-coloured pools of warm, liquid light onto the worn stone floor.

Bella breathed out, dropped her shoulders, and wished she could relax.

Yesterday, her train had been delayed for hours, causing her to miss her connection to the small station deep in the Scottish Highlands. When she'd finally climbed out of the taxi which had brought her to the Castle of Muir, she'd been exhausted. The rehearsal and the rehearsal dinner were over and everyone had gone to bed. The staff member who'd waited up for her had offered her a sandwich and a cup of tea and directed her to her room in a turret, a hike away along silent, stone passages.

She'd hoped for an opportunity to have a short conversation with Ross, to agree that the spectre of a business deal shouldn't be allowed to intrude on this very special wedding. The last thing she'd wanted was for this moment, in the chapel, to be the first time she saw him again. Anticipating it had kept her awake into the small hours. Morning, with its attendant wedding frenzy, had come far too soon.

But today everything had gone like clockwork, and she was determined that this wedding would be memorable, for all the *right* reasons. She squared her shoulders.

Ross turned his head, and as their eyes met her determination crumbled. The breath she'd been taking, ready for the first hymn, stopped in her throat.

His expression was serious. His dark eyes were thoughtful and calm, and he was cleanly shaven, his thick black hair neat.

And yet something about the tilt of his head, the way his

wide shoulders filled the tailored jacket and his long, tapered fingers—*those fingers!*—which felt around absent-mindedly in his pocket, no doubt checking on the ring, landed a punch below Bella's ribs. She did her best to breathe. Her own fingers, suddenly nervous, allowed the order of service booklet to flutter to the floor as they stared at each other.

She was pinned by those eyes, dark as the moat which lapped the castle walls and just as deep. She saw a flame flare briefly in them before his gaze dropped down the length of her body and that feeling of being fully clothed but stripped naked of any sense of self-preservation, swamped her.

He took a quick step towards her, scooped up the booklet and pushed it into her hands, inclining his head towards hers.

'Isabella,' he murmured, 'are you okay?'

Ross turned back towards the bridal couple, determined to keep a clear head and to carry out his duties as a best man with faultless care. This time round he was better placed to do that.

He'd been surprised when Andrew had asked him, even though they'd been friends for decades. After all, as a groomsman at that wedding two and a half years ago, Andrew had first-hand experience of the last time Ross had fulfilled this role, in this chapel. On that occasion, his head had been anything but clear, from the very beginning.

He'd been on a path to raising hell, searching for the quickest route to a state of sweet oblivion, and when his eyes had landed on Isabella, he thought he'd discovered how to find it. She'd looked like someone intent on having fun and he'd been more than willing to provide some. He'd needed to drown out the voice which had pounded in his head, reminding him that he wasn't worthy to be standing there, beside the groom, and Robert would have done well to have chosen someone…anyone…else.

The previous wedding at which they'd all been present

had been his own, to Georgina, and the memories of that day had threatened to overwhelm him, alongside the memories of how he'd failed to keep her safe.

Isabella's wide grey eyes had sparkled with excitement as she'd gazed at their surroundings, fussing with Hannah's train and adjusting the thin straps of her own shell-pink silk dress. When he'd winked at her, she'd angled a glance up at him through her thick lashes, a dimple denting her cheek, and winked back.

Looking at her now, he noted again the changes in her. A trace of fatigue lingered around her eyes, and he wondered what time she'd eventually arrived last night. He'd briefly considered waiting up for her but had dismissed the thought before it was fully formed. He was, he felt sure, the very last person she wanted to see, judging by her reaction to him earlier in the week. But he'd have liked to see her before now, to try to reset the atmosphere between them.

Her hair had been bound, again, in a sleek knot at the nape of her neck, decorated with clips of seed pearls. She exuded a cool reserve, despite that intense look they'd exchanged.

He regretted the person he'd been when they'd first met. He wished that his attempts to bury his own pain had not led him to behave as he had and leave her asleep as he returned to London. He should have had the courage to wake her and say goodbye properly, explaining that one-night stands were his way of keeping himself, and others, safe. But the effect she'd had on him had been so confusing it had short-circuited his brain and his one thought had been to escape.

Besides, her words echoed in his head.

'Perfect. One night is all I need.'

She probably wouldn't have welcomed being woken at the crack of dawn to listen to his garbled and inadequate explanation.

CHAPTER THREE

ISABELLA.

It had been two years since anyone had called her that. She'd made the decision to shorten her name around the same time everything else about her had changed. A fresh start was what she'd needed, and, trying to find it, *Bella* had felt like a new beginning.

After her night with Ross, she'd felt she had to become a different person. She'd thought a one-night stand was what she needed, to forget the stress of work for a few hours. The very last thing she'd been looking for was a relationship. She was far too busy for that. But the feelings Ross had aroused in her had been unfathomably deep and long-lasting. He'd taken a piece of her away with him and she'd had to rebuild herself so the gap didn't show.

Her parents' relationship had been deeply loving. Their commitment to each other, to her and to the family business had been immovable, and so when her mother had died, when Isabella was twelve, the shock of her loss had shaken the foundations of her family life, and the company. Coping with the aching chasm in her life, she'd flung herself into keeping the promise she'd made to her mother, to look after her father and to always be the best she could be. She'd tried to emulate her mother's degree of perfection in everything and that habit had persisted. She'd tried to look after her father, make sure he was never lonely, always strove to be the best in her class at school and later at college, and then insisted on joining Thompson's Textiles and becoming the perfect employee.

The fling with Ross, the agreed one-night stand, had been a deviation of massive proportions from the standards of perfection she set herself. She'd been ready for a few hours of fun, but the pull between them had been more powerful than anything in her experience to date, and knowing she was capable of that depth of feeling, that simple, pure *desire*, had shaken her. Too busy trying to keep the company viable, persuading her father that they had to embrace new methods and meet new challenges, she'd had no room for thoughts of a relationship, but a glimpse of the happiness and the feeling of being absolutely at one with another person she'd experienced in Ross's arms had made her crave more of it. Suddenly, her parents' perfect marriage had become something she could imagine for herself. Her own standards of perfection may have slipped, but the lapse had enabled her to see what she wanted in her future.

But she hadn't been enough for Ross. He'd walked away, their time together evidently just another hookup for him, and she'd been left feeling as if she could no longer believe in herself. She'd made an error of judgement, thinking she could cope with a fling, and she'd had to try to restructure her life. The easiest way to do it, she reasoned, was to persuade her father to invest in the necessary changes so that Thompson's could compete in the current market, and then to redouble her efforts to make a success of the initiative. Surely, the harder she worked, the less potent the memories would become.

The results of her work paid off in excellent results for Thompson's and she'd told herself that it was enough. She'd tried to bury her dreams of the perfect relationship and partnership while she concentrated on making Thompson's ever more successful. One day she'd be able to unearth them again and hope to turn them into a reality, with someone else, when her feelings for Ross had faded away.

It had taken a while—okay, a year—before she'd acknowledged another reason behind her need to be known as someone different. The memory of hearing her name on Ross's lips, whispered in the dark, against her skin, into her mouth, was one she was desperate to preserve, even more than all the other memories which went with it.

Nobody else had ever been able to say her name like he had, and hearing him murmur it again, like a caress across her cheek, had sent her tumbling back through time, to those crazy, heady few hours when they'd had eyes only for each other, and, much later, in the hot, unbearable excitement of each other's arms, it had felt as if he alone could complete her, and she him.

His ramrod-straight back, his steady hand holding the order of service, were at odds with the look of dark intensity, full of shared secret knowledge, they'd shared. The flames which had flared in his eyes had not been in her imagination.

Surely, he wasn't expecting an action replay of Hannah and Robert's wedding? The idea was laughable. Even with *his* reputation for wildness, he wouldn't expect to mix business with pleasure. Would he?

And anyway, he now seemed far from wild.

Perhaps this would be her opportunity to let him know that his proposed deal was dead in the water. She'd explain that she didn't need a partner. If her father was serious in his intention to retire, she could run the company on her own, with occasional help when needed and possibly a new assistant. If he'd accept that, they could go on to enjoy the afternoon and evening, keeping each other at arm's length while they carried out their duties as bridesmaid and best man. But before that could happen, they had to get through the rest of the ceremony without looking as if they were ready to kill, or devour, one another.

Because very soon, when he'd handed the ring to Andrew, he'd step back and take up his position beside her, and she'd be fully occupied in keeping her breathing and her hands steady. And at the end of the service, she'd have to follow the newlyweds down the aisle knowing how close he was behind her, those dark eyes trained on her back. At least this time she knew she wouldn't feel the electrifying sensation of his fingers tracing small circles over the thin silk at the base of her spine, signifying his intention, confirming that he'd received her positive signals and that he intended to act on them as soon as possible.

A curl had somehow escaped from the miracle the hairdresser had accomplished on her usually wayward hair. She smoothed it back, tucked it behind her ear, turned a page in the booklet and tried to find her place. She should at least go through the motions of joining in the service, applauding the bridal couple when they kissed and making sure Emma had her bouquet when they turned to leave the chapel and walk down the aisle as man and wife.

She knew that the reception and ceilidh would last into the early hours. There'd be reels to dance, singing and raucous celebrations, but after the champagne toast she'd switch to the safety of a glass of water and a clear head.

She was relieved she'd changed her plans and would be leaving the following day. The Sunday rail service might be sparse and slow, but she'd prefer to spend extra hours on a train than be forced to spend any more time than was absolutely necessary in Ross Maclean's orbit.

Judging by his previous behaviour it would be Ross who would lead the dancing, call for more champagne and insist on louder, faster music. She wondered which girl he'd set his sights on this evening. Who would he single out to be the focus of his irresistible but dangerous charm? The idea of having to watch him fix his intention on someone else caused her to feel a strange, twisting pain in her heart.

But his serious demeanour and clean-cut appearance were at odds with the behaviour he'd exhibited last time. Then, it had felt as if he was permanently on the brink of doing something outrageous and shocking, and getting away with it, and Isabella had found the prospect of being his partner in almost-crime irresistibly exciting. Suddenly, her life of striving for perfection, for her mother, her father, *herself*, had felt distant and irrelevant. The opportunity to throw off all her conventional restraints and simply let go was within her grasp and although she'd never believed she would, she'd seized it. Determined to forget the pressures of work for a weekend, she'd revelled in daring to play with the fire that was Ross's attention. His focus had been intense, and she'd returned it willingly, but like the rays of the sun through a magnifying glass, it had burned her.

All the evidence pointed to the fact that he'd settled down and changed his ways, but Bella was not about to accept him at face value. Would all the single girls be safe from Ross tonight? At least she knew she would be. Forewarned was forearmed and she'd be keeping him locked out and her own fragile heart locked in.

The rings had been exchanged and Ross turned and took up his position beside her. He was so close he'd notice if she began to do mindful breathing to calm herself and since there was no way she was giving him the satisfaction of knowing she needed to find a way to bring her racing heartbeat under control, she kept a careful distance between them and her eyes fixed on the stained-glass window above the altar.

The fine wool of his black jacket brushed against the skin of her bare arm and she moved a little further away from him, dismayed at the instant reaction of her body. After all this time, for one shocking moment, she yearned to lean into him, to increase that contact, to feel again that intense, unstoppable rush of desire. But she held herself rigid and dropped her eyes to the print of the final hymn. Despite her determination, the words blurred as the warm pine and cool leather scent of his cologne caught her unawares, wafting over her and transporting her back to a place she'd forbidden herself to go, ever again.

The thunderous notes of Mendelsohn's 'Wedding March' brought her crashing back to the present. She fumbled for Emma's bouquet, to find Ross had already picked it up and was holding it out to her. Almost snatching it from him, she gave it to the bride, forcing a smile before ducking her head and stepping back.

'Are you all right?' His voice, quiet but touched with concern, was at her ear.

She nodded, not trusting her voice, and took her place behind the bridal couple, gathering Rosie and Dougal to either side of her and holding onto their hands. They negotiated the walk back down the aisle, making sure that neither she nor the children, who wanted to skip, stepped on the hem of Emma's dress. Then she gave them each a basket of petals and urged them forwards to the chapel steps.

The congregation poured past her, out into the fading light of the winter's afternoon. They gathered on the granite path, seized fistfuls of confetti and showered Emma and Andrew with fluttering petals as they emerged, laughing, their happiness and joy plain to see.

She watched them descend the steps to be mobbed by family and friends, hugged and kissed and smothered with congratulations. Phones and cameras clicked as the skirl of bagpipes cut through the cold air and a piper stepped forward to lead the procession across the wide courtyard to the grand entrance of the castle.

The winter dusk was encroaching quickly, filling the corners with shadows. Frost, bringing the promise of a freezing night, already sparkled on the grass in the flickering light of the flares which lit the way.

Bella shivered in the chill air, searching the last of the crowd for a sign of Hannah, so she could walk with her and not with Ross. But Hannah was already halfway to the castle doors, caught up in the excitement of the surging crowd.

'You're cold.'

She stiffened at the sound of his measured, deep voice. She could feel him beside her, but she did not turn her head. 'It's December. In Scotland.'

'And you're in a thin, silk dress. Who thought that was a good idea, at this time of year?'

'It's Emma's wedding day. I was happy to wear whatever she chose for me. And it'll be warm inside.'

'Let me put my jacket over your shoulders.'

Bella jerked away. 'No!'

The refusal came out too quickly, with too much weight behind it. 'No, thank you,' she repeated, more quietly. 'I'll hurry.'

'Then I'll hurry with you. Come on.'

To shake him off would be too obvious. She could never let him know how badly she didn't want him to touch her, because of how badly she did.

Bella set a brisk pace across the courtyard, focussing on the wide-open doors of the castle, where warm light flooded down the stone steps and the last of the guests were finding their way in, out of the cold, towards the great hall. Once there, she'd be able to separate herself from Ross, put distance between them.

Except she was the bridesmaid, and he was the best man. Ignoring each other was not going to be possible, or acceptable.

Even though she knew what to expect, the spectacle of the

great hall momentarily took her breath away. Swathes of the tartans of Emma and Andrew's clans hung from the walls, interspersed with banners displaying their ancient coats of arms, the warm, plaid colours glowing in the golden light of hundreds of candles. This setting, she thought, might have been taken from any one of five previous centuries. Long tables lined the sides of the hall, decorated with Christmas roses, holly and more candles, leaving the floor in the middle clear for the dancing.

She wished she could avoid the dancing. Bella swallowed, her mouth suddenly dry. She and Ross would be expected to follow the bridal couple onto the floor, when it began.

The piper had made his way up to the minstrels' gallery and now he stood, serenading the guests who milled about below, studying the seating plan and finding their places. Behind him, Bella could see the assembled instruments the band would play later.

She clasped her hands together in front of her, smiled, and risked a sideways look at Ross.

He was looking at the seating plan, his straight brows drawn together in a slight frown. His eyes lifted and caught hers before she could look away.

'This may not be what you want to hear,' he said, 'but we are seated next to each other.'

Bella shrugged. 'Considering our roles in this wedding, I suppose that was inevitable.'

Despite all the promise the evening held of being a wonderful celebration, she couldn't wait for it to be over.

Antagonism, reminding him of that uncomfortable meeting in the boardroom of Thompson's Textiles earlier in the week, radiated from Isabella as Ross ushered her towards their seats.

He found he had to actively refrain from touching her, and the restraint felt unnatural. He wanted—*needed*—to feel if her skin was as smooth and silky as he remembered, and he wanted to slide his hand along her forearm to her slender wrist and then interlace his fingers with hers. He fought against the urge to slip his arm around her waist as he guided her towards her chair.

It was perfectly clear from her whole demeanour that the greater the distance they kept between them, the happier she'd be. Touching her was out of the question.

It had been his intention to forget that night with her, just like he put any other one-night stand behind him. He always made the rules clear beforehand: no commitment, no relationship, and that night had been no different.

'One night is all I need,' she'd whispered.

But one night had turned out to be not enough for him. Against all his principles, he'd found himself wanting more. He craved that unique sensation of belonging he'd felt in her arms. Could a feeling like that be repeated? Could something so deep that it felt infinite ever last, or would its intensity cause it to burn out in a white-hot flame of passion?

CHAPTER FOUR

'LADIES AND GENTLEMEN, the bride and groom!' The booming voice of the master of ceremonies rose above the hum of voices.

Emma and Andrew appeared in the doorway, wreathed in smiles. They made their way towards their seats, amidst thunderous applause, whistles and foot-stamping. Then there was a general noise of chairs being pulled back and the swish of silk, satin and velvet dresses as the guests settled at the long tables. Bella half turned away from Ross, towards Hannah's husband, Robert, as he sat down on her other side.

'That went well,' he said.

Was it her imagination, or were his eyes searching her face for some sort of telltale reaction? Ross had been his best man, too. Had he shared the fact that he'd had the almost ubiquitous fling with the bridesmaid? She pinned on a practised smile, keeping her expression bland.

'Such a beautiful ceremony,' she agreed, her voice cool. 'It's wonderful to be back here, and to see everyone—again.'

She'd have to maintain this pretence of being *fine*, through the dinner and the toasts, but she longed for the moment when she'd be able to slip away, back to her bedroom in the turret.

She raised her glass in a toast after each amusing, emotional and heartfelt speech, being careful to take the tiniest of sips, keeping a tight grip on the slender stem of the crystal flute, and her spine straight, her poise in place. A waiter, stiff with starched uniform and formality, offered to recharge her glass but she laid a finger across the top of it and shook her head.

When all eyes turned towards Ross, as he rose to speak, she lifted her chin and smiled, although her determination to remain cool and aloof threatened to disintegrate at the sound of his deep voice, as he called for the attention of the guests.

She gripped her hands together in her lap, out of sight, and risked a glance up at him. He appeared to be unhurried and at ease as he cleared his throat and surveyed the gathered guests. There was no sign in him of the restless body language she remembered. Everything about him, apart from his voice and his eyes, seemed to have changed.

Those dark eyes, which she recalled as being watchful and unashamedly appreciative, met hers and held her gaze for a moment with what appeared to be steady reassurance. Was he telling her their secret was safe? *Nobody knows?* Then he looked away, briefly running a broad hand across his thick, black hair, leaving it slightly ruffled.

Back then, his hair had been long, falling in thick curls to his shoulders. The style had suited him, adding emphasis to the swagger with which he'd worn his kilt and jacket, at odds with the formality of the traditional occasion. His tall, broad frame had radiated manic energy coupled with a mesmeric magnetism which had proved irresistible.

Resistance had been the furthest thing from Bella's mind, that night.

It had been her gaze he'd held across the table.

'…and so please raise your glasses in a toast to the maid of honour and the bridesmaid, Hannah and Bella.'

Captivated by her memories, Bella realised she'd missed almost everything he'd said. She lifted her head and smiled, looking up at him as everyone would expect and feeling thankful that he'd got her name right, even though a rebel-

lious part of her wanted to hear him say her other name—
her *before Ross* name—again.

What she found, when her eyes connected with his, was
unexpected. His serious gaze was fixed on her face, and a
question lurked in the depths of his dark eyes. He swallowed
a mouthful of champagne and resumed his seat as the applause died down.

'How did I do?' His voice in her ear was quiet enough so
that only she could hear the question. Was this what his eyes
had been asking her?

'I… Oh, fine. Very well, I think…'

He replaced his glass on the white linen cloth. Resting an
elbow on the table, he turned towards her. A small crease
appeared on the left side of his mouth. She remembered how
it preceded his smile.

'Did you, Isabella, hear anything I said?'

She'd longed to hear him say her name again, but the
unique intonation and hint of intimacy only he could give it
drove away any possibility of making up an answer. She felt
caught, in the warmth of his gaze and the sound of his voice.

'Actually, no, I don't think I did.'

'Why?' His thumb smoothed over a small crease in the
surface of the cloth. With a jolt, a memory shifted into sharp
focus, of that same thumb brushing across her lower lip. His
touch had been gentle as a breeze, but it had sent a shiver
of anticipation through her which had raised goose bumps
across her arms and woken something powerfully insistent
in the pit of her abdomen.

'I suppose I was…distracted.' She swallowed. The shield
of cool demeanour she'd constructed for herself with pains-
taking care was not supposed to shatter like this. Not seeing
him for two and a half years should have been long enough
for her to learn to manage her feelings, but now they felt
as fresh as ever. His arm resting on the table, inches from

her, sent the same sizzle of awareness across her skin. She threaded her fingers together under the table and shook her head, determined that no one—*no one*—would see the confusion that was scrambling her brain, robbing her of the ability to make coherent conversation.

Their situation was almost identical to the one in which they'd first met, but he looked and behaved like a different person, and she *felt* like a different one. How was he expecting her to behave? The way he'd walked away, obviously considering her as just another brief fling, had hurt, even though she'd said one night was all she wanted. The feelings of rejection and of not being good enough had made her even more obsessive about striving for perfection at work. And then, after she'd achieved her goal and the business was booming, Ross had reappeared, intent on taking over half of it and becoming her partner.

She'd like to be able to tell him that the deal was off, but she hadn't had the opportunity to discuss it with her father, and anyway her friend's wedding was no place for a business discussion. She felt disadvantaged and undermined.

The space between them was tiny, but even if it had been much bigger, the feelings she'd had last time would have all come racing back. She'd revelled in his touch, drowned in his gaze, all before they'd even danced. Then, she'd allowed herself to be enfolded in his arms on the dance floor, their bodies joined from chest to thigh, their eyes locked.

This time, those feelings had to be controlled. For a start, he didn't look any more pleased than she was to be near each other. Letting herself go around him and enjoying herself felt unthinkable. At Hannah's wedding he'd been wild and unpredictable, his rejection probably simply a casual habit. This time, it would be far more considered, and the hurt would be much greater.

'I was just wondering how many people here were at Hannah and Robert's wedding, too.'

'Mmm.' Ross pulled a hand across his jaw. 'Quite a few, I should think. But Isabella, none of them…'

To her intense relief, he was interrupted by the arrival of the dessert. Bella ate half of her chocolate mousse and then eased her chair back. She could hear the band tuning their instruments in the minstrels' gallery above their heads.

The voice of the master of ceremonies boomed out again. 'Ladies and gentlemen, the "Grand March"!'

The bagpipes, backed up by the country band, struck up a stirring march and within seconds the beat had been taken up by stamping feet and clapping hands. There was a loud, whooping cheer as Emma and Andrew rose from their places at the table and made their way, his arm around her waist, onto the dance floor.

Bella turned towards Ross. 'We'll be expected to dance.' She rose from her chair. 'Shall we?' The quicker she could get through these difficult but necessary few minutes, the better it would be.

Ross stood up and held out a hand towards her. Her instincts screamed at her to step back, not to take his hand, because once she crossed that barrier she didn't know if there'd be any going back.

She bit her lip, hesitating. He dropped his hand and crooked his arm instead and after a moment she slipped her fingers through it, allowing them to rest as lightly as possible on his forearm.

'I'm sorry. I know this isn't what you want. But follow me,' he murmured in her ear, 'and it'll be fine. As you say, we'll be expected to dance.' He turned to lead her onto the dance floor.

Bella shivered, despite the warmth of the room. He looked down at her, concern creasing his forehead. 'Try to relax, Isabella, and not look as if you're being kidnapped. I'll make sure you're okay.'

As Hannah and Andrew completed their first circuit of the dance floor, Ross pulled Bella in behind them. The rest of the bridal party fell into step next, Hannah laughing as she and Robert linked arms. The clapping and cheering increased as the volume from the piper and the band swelled. More couples joined the throng, and they peeled off to left and right at the top of the dance floor, until everyone had joined the march.

The pace of the music picked up and suddenly Bella felt her mood lift slightly. It was difficult to be unaffected by the exuberant, joyful atmosphere and as long as she remained in control of the situation—of herself—nothing could possibly go wrong. Her feelings were hers to contain and she'd had a lot of practice at it. She should be able to enjoy herself without them getting the better of her.

Ross felt the almost imperceptible change in her. The fingers, which had been rigid on his arm, softened. He looked down at her, in time to see her shoulders drop a little and her hips sway into the rhythm of the march. Best of all, that cultivated smile had gone from her lips, to be replaced by a wider one of enjoyment. One that he remembered.

As the march came to its rowdy conclusion, the band in the gallery struck up a polka and all the couples separated out from the line and began to whirl around the floor. He turned Isabella to face him.

'One proper dance?'

Her wide, grey eyes shone up at him, her lips parted in surprise. The exertions of the march had brought warm colour to the cheeks which had been cool and pale earlier but then he saw the moment when she realised she had a choice. They'd danced their dutiful dance together and she could walk away from him, if she wanted to.

He saw the rigidity in her body dissipate slightly. Other couples swirled past and around them, the music growing louder and faster, laughter ringing to the rafters of the ancient great hall. It felt as if they stood in their own private bubble, separated from the noise and music, for minutes, but it may only have been seconds. He bent his head towards her.

'I'd love to dance with you, Isabella. But if you prefer, I'll take you back to the table and I won't trouble you again.'

The tip of her tongue moistened her bottom lip as her chest lifted on a deep inhalation and then fell as she breathed out. The woman who had enchanted him two and a half years before was no less mesmerising now. It was all he could do to stop himself from dropping his head a little further and brushing his lips across hers.

He dragged his eyes away from her mouth and raised his head, hoping that the brief flash of insanity which had engulfed him had not been readable in his eyes. If it had, and she turned her back on him and walked away, he wouldn't be surprised.

It was madness to even think of kissing her, even if it was a light, friendly peck on the cheek. Obviously, she wanted to keep a safe distance between them. He'd left her asleep and disappeared. It had felt wrong, but he'd done it for the right reasons. He wouldn't have had the determination to leave her, if she'd woken, because of how she'd made him feel, and if he'd stayed, all his resolutions about only one night would have crumbled. He couldn't offer her what he knew she deserved—a loving, passionate relationship with a trustworthy and steadfast man. If she turned her back on him now, and walked away, it would be no more than he deserved.

Bella read the intention in Ross's eyes as clearly as if he'd spoken it out loud. Her heart kicked against her ribcage, her lips parted on a small gasp of protest, not at Ross, but at the traitorousness of her own body. She shouldn't want to feel his mouth on hers, ever again, but she did. Just as she'd longed to hear her name on his lips, once more, she wanted to feel that bewitching sensation of surrender, just one more time.

But that was impossible. She would never, ever give in to those impulses again, and risk that crushing rejection, the feeling of not being good enough, when being better than good enough was what she'd strived for almost all her life. The noise of the party receded, and she could hear her mother's voice in her head.

'When you find love, grab hold of it and hang on to it forever, because you might not find it again.'

Ross had never said he loved her, but in those intense hours, when he'd occupied her life, possessed her, body and soul, she remembered the words she'd whispered as she lay wrapped in his arms, not wanting to be anywhere else in the world, ever again.

It had simply been infatuation, driven by the memory of the way he'd made her body sing with desire and passion so intense she'd begged for more, but she hadn't been enough for him. He'd done what he'd said he would do and walked away, while she slept.

With time had come the realisation that her feelings for him ran deeper than she could fathom, into a bottomless well of desire, need and simply wanting to be with him. With care and effort, she had learned to put a lid on it, imprisoning the memories in the dark, trying to deprive them of the light and air they needed to survive, but she'd never be able to forget their existence.

So right now, she should step back. She should shake her head politely and decline to have one proper dance with him. She was sure he wanted this to be over just as much as she did, and his request for a dance was simply another example of the scrupulous good manners he'd displayed all afternoon.

She nipped her lower lip between her teeth. He raised his head and his lids dropped briefly over his eyes. His breath hissed as his chest expanded.

'Isabella…'

'Okay,' she said, nodding once. 'One proper dance.' It would be rude to refuse.

Ross slid an arm around her waist and pulled her closer towards him, until she could feel the warmth of his body through the silk of her dress. His chest was a solid expanse of muscle, his abdomen hard and flat. She had to smother the flash of need that scorched through her before it became addictive. It was simply the position they needed to adopt for the dance, nothing more.

The hand which was not exerting a light hold on her waist came up to cover hers, where her palm rested against his chest. He slotted their fingers together, curling his thumb into her palm and holding their joined hands against the shoulder of his jacket.

'Ready?'

Bella nodded again, releasing her bottom lip. 'Ready.'

Ross turned her slightly, fitting her more closely to his broad frame, and swirled her into the throng of quickly moving couples.

It was fast and it was fun. He moved with a grace which belied his height and breadth, spinning them around, weaving in and out of the other dancers, steering a practised path with the lightest of touches on her back. For a few heady minutes Bella lost herself in the music and the movement, forgetting that she shouldn't allow herself to melt into his arms like this, that she needed to keep her cool and her distance.

When the music stopped, she was breathing quickly, her chest rising and falling against him. The hand which rested on her shoulder blades slipped down to her waist, his long fingers spreading across the small of her back. He kept her fingers enclosed in his, bringing their joined hands to rest against his chest, between them. She tipped back her head, laughing, but the laughter died as she read the intention in his deep eyes.

'Ross…'

He dropped his head and then hesitated, his eyes searching her face, before touching his lips to her forehead. It was a gentle, chaste kiss but the sensation of his mouth on her skin sent a current of awareness and desire fizzing through her, weakening her resolve to keep away from him. Her fingers clenched on the sleeve of his jacket, gripping the fabric, and every muscle in her body went rigid. She knew he'd be able to feel the hard peaks of her nipples, separated from him only by the silk of her dress and the cotton of his shirt. Dazedly, she wished he'd kept his jacket buttoned up, but then she dismissed that wish and sank into the exquisite sensation of being close—so close—to him.

Then he straightened up, loosened the hold on her waist, let go of her hand, and reality exploded all around her.

She stepped backwards.

'No, Ross,' she whispered. 'We mustn't do this.'

CHAPTER FIVE

ROSS STOOD WITH his hands clenched into fists at his sides, using iron willpower to stop himself from pulling Isabella back into the circle of his arms. Holding her, feeling her supple body against him as they danced, then becoming aware of her reaction to him as they stood still, oblivious to the crowd around them, had reawakened the potent desire for her that he'd spent so much energy trying to subdue.

Apparently expending all that energy had been a waste of time. One dance, one moment spent holding her pliant body against his raging one, one touch of his mouth against her forehead...

He did not know from where he'd summoned up the strength to let her go. In the few seconds during which they'd touched, he'd been almost overwhelmed by the need to take possession of her mouth, to imprint his lips on hers so that whenever she kissed anyone else, she'd remember *him*.

The idea of her kissing anyone else was suddenly unbearably painful. He would never be the man who could put his arm around her waist and hug her against his side, drop a kiss onto the top of her head, whisper something to her which would make her laugh, or would make her eyes darken with desire. They would never share that unspoken language in which a touch, a glance could speak volumes.

He would only ever be the man who had caused the death of his partner and who had almost lost the company they'd founded because he'd neglected it in favour of indulging in a lifestyle which had numbed his grief and sent his moral compass veering so wildly from his true north that he'd lost his way.

While lost, unfocussed, drowning in grief and self-accusation which ate at him during every waking moment and robbed him of sleep...*what if he'd done something different?*...he'd found Isabella.

It had seemed so simple, until it hadn't at all. His interactions with women had been limited since that awful day in the Alps when Georgina had died, and his world had disintegrated, and he should have stayed away from Isabella. She'd looked so natural, without artifice or pretence, just as if she was looking forward to enjoying herself. Suddenly, the possibility that the wedding could be something he might enjoy, rather than simply get through, had occurred to him. If that thought hadn't been enough of a warning—when last had he allowed himself to enjoy anything?—then the heart-stopping intensity of the moment when their eyes had first connected should have told him that with her he'd be getting into something too deep and too dangerous. It had taken his breath away, and he should have seen sense and stopped what was happening between them. But he'd bolstered his courage with a dram of whisky, which had taken the sharp edge off his habitual watchfulness, and the hip flask, in case he needed it, was a cool presence in his pocket. The wedding, full of love, had made him feel indescribably lonely. All that joy had just made him sadder, and he'd needed someone to hold him that night and help him to forget. Isabella's openness, her eyes which seemed only to be for him, the willing way she'd gone into his arms, had promised all that.

She'd asked no questions and had been happy to accept him for who he was. They'd been two people both looking for an escape for a few hours, and he'd felt safe knowing she wouldn't ask him for more than he could give.

He'd been unable to stop himself from wanting her too much, and when he'd woken the next morning, he knew he was feeling too much for her, too.

That had scared him. He couldn't put himself at risk of wanting more. She'd said one night was all she needed and that was how it had to be, for him, too.

He'd had to walk away from her that morning. The vision of her sleeping form, her cheeks flushed, and her lips swollen from his kisses, remained imprinted on his memory. She'd looked perfect and he'd known he had to leave her there.

She needed to find someone honest and steadfast, who would care for her as she deserved—a man as different from him as possible.

He'd never asked anyone how to find her. He'd had to find himself, first, but to do that he'd known he had to change.

Ross watched Isabella turn away from him. He had to let her go.

Then she stumbled and in two long strides he closed the distance between them, wrapping his fingers around her upper arm in a light grip.

'Are you all right? Let me take you back to your seat. The dancing might have made you dizzy...'

She swayed towards him slightly, shaking her head. The expression in her eyes was conflicted.

'No. Yes...' She swallowed. 'That is, yes, I'm all right, thank you. And no, I don't want to return to my seat.'

'It's warm in here. Do you need some air?' He moved in front of her, shielding her from any curious gazes which might be directed towards them. 'Can I take you outside for a minute or two?'

Isabella raised her chin. 'Outside, I think I might freeze,

very quickly. As you pointed out earlier, I'm in a thin silk dress.'

'And it's winter, in Scotland.'

'It is.'

He ran his free hand across the back of his head. 'I apologise. That was a foolish suggestion. I thought you were feeling light-headed from the dancing. I was afraid you'd fall.'

'I was,' she said, a slight frown creasing the smooth skin between her brows. 'But it was not from the dancing.'

She stepped sideways, around him, and Ross watched her walk away, straight-backed and purposeful, towards the door.

Bella passed through the stone arch of the doorway and paused. The room hummed with wedding guests, uniformed catering staff weaving between them balancing trays on their hands. Deep sofas and vibrant rugs lent the space a feeling of opulent comfort, enhanced by soft lighting and bowls of white roses, holly and ivy.

A fire blazed in the wide hearth at the far end of the room. Beside it, Bella could see a single, unoccupied armchair. She lifted a glass of water from the tray of a passing waiter and made her way towards it.

What she needed was to sit somewhere quietly and try to unpick what had just happened between her and Ross.

The depth and intensity of the feelings their brief contact had aroused in her had shocked her to the point of knocking her off balance.

They were feelings which she thought she had rationalised and controlled, but they were there, waiting to be aroused by the simple touch of his hand on her back, or his mouth brushing her forehead. Being near to him had sent her heart into a frenzy of beating. That same heart, which he had unknowingly bruised, seemed ready to open itself to him again with a reckless lack of constraint.

She could not, would not, let it happen. She'd learned her lesson and she wasn't about to repeat the mistake she'd made. She'd told him one night was all she needed, and she'd never let him know how wrong she'd been. Their lovemaking had been so intense, so perfect. Their ability to anticipate each other's needs had been extraordinarily satisfying and, during the course of the night, she'd come to assume that the ever-deepening feelings she was experiencing must have been mutual. How could they not be?

But she had been wrong, and then she'd begun to doubt herself about other things, too. Had she really fulfilled the promise she'd made to her mother, all those years ago? Had she earned the position she'd attained at Thompson's or was she only there because she was her father's daughter? And had she worked hard enough to justify his faith in her?

To prove to herself that she was good enough at her job, if not for Ross, she'd worked harder, trying to emulate the way her mother had taken a personal interest in all the employees. But there were twice as many now, spread over the office in London and two factories in Yorkshire, and she had her design team to run, as well as management issues to address. She couldn't say if she'd justified her father's faith in her, because their relationship had become more distant, which meant she wasn't looking after him, as she'd vowed she'd do.

If she'd misread Ross that night, so badly, how would she ever have the confidence to form a lasting relationship with anyone? Her mother had urged her to seize love, when she found it, and never let it go, but she doubted she'd ever have the courage to do that, if she even recognised love when it came along.

Isabella settled herself into the soft velvet of the chair's cushions and took a sip from the glass. The water was cool, soothing her throat which she found was tight with the threat of tears. She swallowed and pressed her lips together, re-membering.

He could easily have found her, but he hadn't looked, and pride had forbidden her to ask about him in the months that followed. If he hadn't wanted to find her, she'd obviously meant nothing to him. It was easier to try to suppress her feelings than to find him and have to face rejection again.

She'd told nobody what had happened between them. She'd buried herself in her work, taking on more and more respon-sibility, encouraging their designers to invent new patterns in unlikely colours which the decorators loved and bought by the roll. She'd travelled to the factories, getting to know all the workers and their family stories, trying her best to remember them all.

Two senior managers had left, one resigning through ill health and one retiring, and she'd convinced her father that she could absorb their roles with only a little extra help. He'd made her his partner when he'd said he could see that she meant it.

The workload had been, and still was, punishing, but the sheer number of hours she spent in the office and at the fac-tories had its own unexpected reward. It reduced the time and energy available to dwell on how Ross had invaded her soul. Work was something she could control. Learning to con-trol her emotions had been much more difficult. She thought she'd succeeded, but her reaction to seeing Ross again had allowed new doubt to erode her confidence.

Ross had ignited something primal in her which she didn't recognise, and then left it to burn itself into cold ashes. She'd buried those ashes, refusing to believe that she'd ever allow them to trouble her again.

So much for that, she thought, sipping at her glass of water. One touch of his lips and *whoosh!* The embers, which she'd believed to be cold, had reignited, her feelings reappear-

ing, fully formed, like some sort of tormenting Phoenix.
How could she possibly work with him when her reactions
to him were so extreme? It would be completely impractical
to believe that they could avoid each other, if he owned half
the business. Even if they weren't together, he'd occupy her
thoughts, as he was doing now.

But this time it was she who had walked away and she
allowed herself to feel a brief moment of triumph. It would
have been easy—so easy—to stay there, in his arms, and...

Ross appeared in the doorway on the far side of the room
and Bella ducked her head, pulling her feet up beneath her,
onto the chair. He had his phone in his hand and was frowning down at it, possibly reading a message. Then he tapped
the screen and held the device up to his ear.

The realisation that he most likely had a partner back in
London hit Bella like a ton of bricks. In fact, he'd probably
had a partner before. Was that why he'd walked away from
her, vanishing without a trace? Why he only ever indulged
in one-night stands?

If he'd been cheating on a girlfriend at home, it was no
surprise he'd left her asleep in bed and escaped.

Bella felt faintly sick at the thought. Was this the reason he
had changed so much? Her imagination began to run away
with her. Perhaps his partner had issued an ultimatum. Perhaps he'd confessed that he'd had a fling with the bridesmaid.
She'd been so willing. So available. She'd just wanted one
night of fun, nothing more.

She watched Ross as he spoke on his phone, his expression serious. He shook his head, as if denying something, and
then the call seemed to end while he was in mid-sentence.
He pushed a hand through his hair in a gesture of frustration
and then his eyes connected with Bella's across the room.
He turned, his kilt swinging about his hips, and disappeared
through the door.

Quite clearly he wanted to stay away from her just as much as she wanted to avoid him.

Hannah walked into the room, her eyes scanning the occupants. They landed on Bella and she threw out her arms.

'Bella, I've been searching everywhere for you. Emma and Andrew are leaving and we need to give them a fitting send-off.'

When she eventually climbed into bed, the linen was crisp and cold. Bella propped herself up on the mound of pillows, tugged the duvet up to her chin, reached beyond the cocoon she'd created for herself and lifted her phone from the nightstand.

There'd been a time when she'd spoken to her father every day, but the habit had slowly fallen away as she'd grown older and busier. Nowadays, she was often so tired by the time she allowed herself to stop work that she barely had the energy to eat, and certainly did not relish a roundup of his day. She knew that lately he'd taken to spending less time in the office, which was perfectly understandable for a man of eighty-one who had worked for sixty years, but she never seemed able to find the time to catch up properly with what he'd been doing.

The more responsibility she'd taken on, lightening the load of his work, the fewer opportunities there'd been to interact with him. While she was used to his habit of making decisions without consulting her or the senior management staff, the fact that he was seriously considering another company's interest in Thompson's had been a shock. If she'd made more of an effort to communicate with him, it might have been different.

When her mother had died, eighteen years ago, Bella's surviving grandparents had been able to offer emotional support, ensuring that she felt loved and valued, but they were physically frail. A housekeeper, Beryl, had come to live with them so that Bella would never come home from school to an empty house and would always have an evening meal prepared for her. At first, she'd resented the presence of another woman in their home, anxious that the memories of her mother might become dimmed.

Reflecting on that time now, Bella could see that her response to losing her mother had been to try to keep everything unchanged. She tried to look after her father when he was home, making him cups of tea and baking the biscuits he liked, as her mother had taught her. It felt as though, if she maintained those rituals over which she had control, she'd be able to keep her mother's presence alive. She was still doing it, only now through her work at Thompson's. She'd never allowed herself to let go and accept the loss, but over the months she began to look forward to knowing the scent of beeswax polish would greet her when she came through the front door, and there'd be a home-baked cake for tea, which she hadn't made herself. A companionship had developed between her and Beryl which had deepened into friendship over the years.

Now she realised she'd all but lost the close and precious relationship she had shared with both her father and Beryl.

She tucked her hair behind her ears and pulled up her father's contact details on her phone, her finger poised over the call button. She wanted, rather badly, to touch base with him. They hadn't spoken since the meeting with Ross and they hadn't resolved their disagreement about his proposed retirement when they'd parted. She told herself she needed to steady his response to Ross's offer for half the company, so that when she returned to the office on Monday she could dissuade him from accepting it. But mostly, she wanted to begin to restore their relationship to what it had always been. She wanted to hear the familiar voice which represented the unmoving point at the centre of her universe; a universe which had spun her around in the past few hours, leaving her feeling unsure and wildly confused.

But if she called him at this hour of the night he'd immediately think something was wrong. Even if she denied it, her uncharacteristic behaviour would worry him. Sighing, she switched off her phone and turned out the light, wishing she could expect to sleep soundly.

CHAPTER SIX

THE LIGHT WHICH filtered around the thick curtains looked as if it had been muffled with cotton wool. Bella stretched and turned over, feeling for her phone on the bedside cabinet. It was nine o'clock and morning had only just broken on this early December day in the Highlands.

Sleep had been elusive, with her mind a shifting kaleidoscope, revisiting the events of the day and evening. She'd finally dropped off, exhausted, in the early hours. She felt muddled, and thankful that she'd only drunk half a glass of champagne.

After the way she'd reacted to Ross, her decision to leave this morning instead of tomorrow felt like an even better idea. She thought she couldn't have been more sure of the fact that she wanted distance between them, but being close to him had roused that fathomless longing which she'd banished with such determination.

The memory of how he'd held her while they danced kept playing on her mind. She'd melted against him, loving the sensation of being in his arms, being guided by him around the floor with effortless grace, and for a few moments, after the dance had ended, she'd been lost in the moment, trapped by his gaze.

Had she unwittingly sent the wrong signals in those few seconds? She'd seen in his eyes that he'd read them, but thankfully he'd chosen not to respond to them and had stayed away from her for the rest of the evening.

She slid out of the narrow bed and padded across to the window. The curtains were heavy, and she had to tug at them to pull them aside. She rubbed a hand across her eyes.

She rubbed again, but the scene beyond the ancient, pebbled glass of the window didn't alter.

Overnight, the landscape had been transformed from the drab colours of a Scottish winter to a startling monochrome. Fresh, unmarked snow covered the ground, far below her turret, and from the glimpse she could catch of the moat, it seemed even that had frozen over. The usually sharp outline of the mountains, which rose up all around the glen, had blurred into indistinct shapes and it was difficult to tell where they finished, and the sky began.

The stone crenelations of the castle and gatehouse were padded with fat cushions of snow and big, soft flakes were still drifting lazily to the ground. Nothing moved apart from the sifting snow, and the atmosphere was still and hushed, as if a giant, muffling blanket had been silently dropped over the world during the night.

There had been no sign of snow last night, in spite of the bitter cold, and the depth it had already reached was an indication of how quickly it was building up. Suddenly, Bella's plan to leave this morning took on a new urgency. It could only be a matter of time before the road down to the station would become impassable, always assuming the trains were still running.

There was no time for a shower or make-up, she decided. She dressed hastily, pulling on her jeans and boots and digging in her coat pockets for her gloves. Her sweater was warm, although not warm enough for this turn in the weather, but her coat, scarf and woolly hat would help to keep the cold out, for a while, at least.

It took a few minutes to pack her remaining clothes and toiletries into her overnight case. Her hair would have to do, pulled into a messy knot at the nape of her neck. She'd worry about eating once she'd boarded the local train, perhaps only once she was safely on the express train from Edinburgh back to London.

The most important thing, by far, was to get away while she could. If spending forced time with Ross was bad enough, then the prospect of being stuck here with him, for who knew how many days, was much, much worse.

The chatter of excited voices reached her before she descended the final flight of stairs into the hall. Guests and family members who had stayed the night were layering up in coats, scarves and hats. She saw Rosie and Dougal bundled into adorable snow-suits, ready to face the outdoors. There was talk of sledging, snowball fights and building a snowman.

It seemed she was the only person intent on leaving.

'Bella!' It was Hannah, striding towards her. 'Isn't this just amazing? Rosie and Dougal are super-excited and their mum says we can take them sledging. Will you come with us? They asked especially if you would. You're flavour of the month…'

'I have to go, Hannah. I'm sorry.' She shook her head. 'I did let Emma know I'd be leaving today, but I should have told you too. I need to get back.'

Hannah's forehead creased in concern. 'Oh, Bella, I'm sorry. Is someone ill? Your father…?'

'No, no, nothing like that. Just a problem at the firm he needs to talk about.'

Hannah's face cleared and she broke into a smile. 'Oh, well, that's okay then. You can stay. The problem will wait, won't it?' She took Bella's arm. 'Come on. There'll be breakfast waiting for us when we get back. The children won't be outside for long. It's too cold.'

Bella shook Hannah's hand off her arm, digging her phone out of her bag. 'I'm sorry, Hannah. I really need to go. I'll call a taxi.'

'Taxi?' Someone laughed. 'Don't waste your battery. We've already tried, and no one is prepared to take a chance in these conditions. They might get stuck up here with us. But hey, what's not to like about that?'

Bella ignored the advice and dialled the number of the taxi company whose driver had brought her from the station to the castle late on Friday night. The call went straight to answerphone, the message informing her that there would be no taxis available until the snow had thawed.

She dropped the phone back into her bag and bit her lip, her mind turning over the options, of which there was only one—she'd have to stay. The idea of retreating to her bedroom, climbing back under the warm duvet, and waiting there for the noise and excitement to subside was hugely attractive but she knew how rude that would appear. From somewhere, she would have to produce the energy to be cheerful and upbeat about the wedding and the snow, to be the perfect guest and post-bridesmaid helper. She would make cups of tea, invent games for the children and wait for this all to end. She straightened up, squared her shoulders, and felt a hand on her arm.

She knew it was Ross before she had glanced down at the long, strong fingers or heard his low voice. She'd recognise his touch in pitch darkness, and it would send the same signals racing around her body: desire, need, excitement. Danger.

'If you're looking for a way out of here, Isabella, you can come with me. I have my four-by-four outside. I can get you to the station.'

Bella turned to find Ross close behind her. She stepped back a little, trying to put more space between them.

'I... Yes, I am.' Hannah was nearby, probably listening.

She could hardly declare that she'd changed her mind and was now able to stay, when she'd been emphatic about needing to leave, a moment ago. How strange would that seem? Hannah would suspect at once that she was trying to avoid Ross, and she would wonder why, ask questions. 'I need to get back…'

She looked up at him. His eyes held hers, and he nodded slightly, as if he understood exactly what she was thinking, and why.

'Yes. So do I.'

Bella hesitated. She could refuse, saying she'd changed her mind, but then she really might be snowed in here for days, having to explain to Hannah why she'd refused his offer. She needed to get away, to put some distance between herself and the events of the past twenty-four hours and try to make sense of her feelings. It was a thirty-minute drive down the glen to the station. Thirty minutes in a car with Ross and then, as long as she could persuade her father not to accept his offer, he'd be out of her life. Getting him out of her mind would be more difficult.

She nodded. 'Thank you.'

'Follow me.' He picked up her bag.

Bella gave Hannah a quick farewell hug and started towards the entrance doorway, but Ross turned in a different direction. He pushed against a small, oak door, held it open for her and then let it swing closed behind them. The passage he took emerged into a boot room next to the vast castle kitchen, and then through a door which opened onto a stable-yard.

The blast of freezing air which hit her made Bella gasp. She buried her hands in the pockets of her coat and tucked her chin into the scarf she'd wound around her neck.

A grey Land Rover Defender was parked at the foot of the steps.

She followed Ross down the slippery stone flight. He slung her bag onto the back seat and held open the passenger door for her while she climbed in and then he pulled the seat belt from above her shoulder and handed the buckle to her, waiting while she slotted it in safely. It was freezing cold inside the big vehicle and she shivered, her outbreath condensing in a cloud in front of her face.

He slammed the door and strode around the bonnet of the car. Bella wondered about what she'd done, having serious second thoughts. She'd made a snap decision to come with him, but was this really her best option? If she'd known for certain that he was leaving she could have stayed. But if he could get her to the station, surely that would be the best outcome of all? She'd taken a chance and had to hope it would work.

He swung his long body into the driver's seat and buckled up his own seat belt. Then he turned towards her, his eyes questioning.

'Okay?'

She nodded. 'Yes. Except…'

'Except what?'

'Are you sure you can get me to the station?'

He pressed the ignition button and ducked his head to peer through the windscreen before flicking the switch which turned on the wipers. The blades scraped across the glass, sweeping aside the accumulated layer of snow, squeaking on the thin layer of ice left behind.

He frowned. 'That will melt as soon as we get moving and I turn up the heating.' He pressed the clutch down and slid the gear lever forward. He wore faded jeans and a thick sweater under a waxed jacket. 'If we leave now, I'm fairly sure we'll get to the station. And if the trains aren't running, I'll drive you to Edinburgh. I have a flight to catch.'

'Oh.' So he'd always intended to leave this morning. 'What about the car?'

'The car? I'll leave it in the garage at the airport.' His knee flexed as he released the clutch, the muscles of his thigh bunching under the denim. 'I spend a lot of time in the summer at the lodge I own, up another glen, not that far from here.' His big hands eased the steering wheel around and the vehicle moved forwards, the tyres crunching on the snow-covered cobblestones. 'It's convenient having the car readily available when I fly in.'

'What about the other guests? Couldn't you have offered anyone else a lift too?' She remembered how those hands had felt last night, at her shoulder blades, her waist, folded over her fingers. And how they'd felt on her naked skin, in that other life. She dragged her eyes away from them, focussing on the way ahead and the snowflakes which seemed to be swirling ever more thickly all around the car.

The lift of his shoulders was slight. 'I could have, but everyone seemed happy to stay here and play games in the snow. Not really my idea of fun, and I have business meetings in London tomorrow.'

She looked across at his severe profile; the frown of concentration as he guided the car; the faint lines at the corners of his eyes, as he narrowed them and peered ahead; the shadow of stubble across his jaw. Just as she'd been in too much of a hurry to shower or wash her hair this morning, he hadn't bothered to shave. He looked like she felt: as if fun had been in short supply for a long time. Their dance last night had been a brief, magical few moments for her, and she wondered if he felt the same.

They bumped across the courtyard, beneath an arch and across an ancient stone bridge.

'And besides,' he continued, casting a sideways glance at her, 'there was no one else I wanted to offer a lift to.' The back of the vehicle swung out slightly as the tyres hit a patch of ice. Bella gripped the handhold at her shoulder. 'Only you.'

CHAPTER SEVEN

ROSS REGRETTED HIS words as soon as they were spoken, but they were out there, hanging between them, in the cold air, and it was too late to take them back. After dancing with Isabella last night, and coming within a breath of kissing her, he'd needed to put distance between them while he tried to come to terms with the way his feelings had deepened since they'd last seen each other. This morning he'd wanted to help her, but he'd also seen the drive to the station as an opportunity to talk to her, free from the heightened emotions surrounding the wedding. But he'd made it sound as if he'd deliberately got her alone in his car. She might feel he was being too forward. Was it his imagination, or had Bella shifted slightly further away from him?

He decided the movement he'd caught from the corner of his eye was her turning her body slightly towards him. The need to look at her overcame his determination to concentrate on the treacherous road ahead of them, and he threw a quick sideways glance across at her.

Gone was the sophisticated make-up and the artful hairstyle of yesterday. Her skin glowed clean and her hair was falling in silky, untidy curls from the messy bun she'd tied it into, underneath the pale blue bobble hat she wore, pulled down over her ears and forehead. She'd tucked her chin into the folds of the matching scarf around her neck. Grey eyes regarded him steadily, but a trace of anxiety stirred in them.

He remembered his first glimpse of her, walking up the aisle behind Hannah, her eyes alight with excitement.

Robert had been his best man when he'd married Georgina and they had always known that their roles would be reversed, one day. He'd been kind, insisting Ross was under no pressure to agree to the role, that he'd absolutely understand if he felt he couldn't do it. He'd asked him because he'd promised he would.

Ross had thought, in the tormented way his mind was working at the time, that being surrounded by the goodwill and joy of a wedding might make him feel better, but it had simply sharpened his anguish. The memories of his own wedding, two years before, were still so fresh, it felt incomprehensible that he'd had a beautiful wife and lost her in such a short space of time.

He'd been in a dark, terrible place. He'd neglected his business and dropped out of his social life, but he'd been determined to honour his promise to his oldest friend.

Somehow, he'd got himself to that wedding, to Robert's side. It had involved what had felt like an impossible effort of will. He'd been late. He'd locked himself in his bathroom, digging deep to find the courage to stand by his friend. Without knowing the hip flask of Scotch was in his pocket, if needed, he believed he wouldn't have made it.

Then he'd seen Isabella, and he'd known he could be okay. With her to distract him he might stand a chance of getting through what felt like a nightmare.

He just hadn't allowed for the possibility that he might develop feelings for her which would threaten to shipwreck the way he'd planned his life.

The car slid sideways, and Isabella gasped, her free hand gripping the edge of her seat. Ross flicked his eyes back to the road, correcting the skid and swearing under his breath. These conditions demanded his full attention, and he'd let it wander. Perhaps this had been a huge mistake. Just another one to add to the list of mistakes he'd already made with Isabella.

Unfortunately, he was understanding, too late, that where Isabella was concerned his mind, and his body were on different planets.

While his mind was firm in its knowledge that he had to stay away from her, to protect her from the man he was, his body had other plans. He'd remembered her, longed for her, ever since he'd walked away from her. Her sweetness and kindness had seemed like some magic elixir from another world, calming him and giving him space to think, after all he'd been through.

But he hadn't seen the repercussions coming, by a country mile. Isabella had come into his arms with no pretension or reserve, and he'd been desperate to keep her there, just as she was. Walking away, for her own good, had been one of the hardest things he'd ever had to do, and he hadn't had any inkling at all, that while he might be leaving her asleep in bed, the memory of her would persist in every one of his waking moments, and many sleeping ones.

Now he needed to use every ounce of concentration to keep her safe. The icy road was more slippery than he'd anticipated, the snow was falling more heavily than ten minutes previously, and from the look of the leaden sky it would not be letting up any time soon.

The road dropped away in front of them, the incline increasing sharply, with visibility reduced to almost nothing. He engaged a low gear and then pressed the hill descent control button. A green icon lit up on the dashboard and he removed his feet from the pedals and concentrated on steering.

Isabella wore gloves but from the tension he could see in the grip she had on the edge of the seat he knew her knuckles would be bone-white beneath them. Resisting his instinct to cover her hand with his, to reassure her, he kept both hands on the wheel, where they needed to be.

Handing over the descent of a hill as steep and as slippery as this one to the automatic control of the car took courage. Ross was familiar with the technology but acutely aware how unnerving it could be for a first-time passenger in such hazardous conditions. Keeping his eyes on the way ahead and his hands firmly in place, he fixed his attention on the task.

Snow. He'd loved it once. The biting cold, the vivid blue of a deep winter sky, the promise and challenge of deep, fresh powder. The air like sparkling champagne, sharpening the senses, filling the lungs to bursting. There'd been no other feeling in the world to compare with that moment of anticipation, pausing at the top of a black run, or plotting a route off-piste, through the virgin white, savouring the moment when he'd fling himself downwards, bent forwards over his skis, digging the ski poles into the snow to achieve the maximum speed in the shortest possible time. Then there was nothing but the rush of air and the exhilaration of speed, when every faculty had to be razor-sharp and co-ordinated to take the line which got you to the bottom in one piece. Alive.

He'd always treated snow with respect. It was unpredictable. Vengeful. It held death in its soft, pure beauty. In a few minutes of mayhem it had swept away love and his future—everything he'd thought of as certain—in a roar of wind and tumbling chunks of ice. Then afterwards, nothing had remained to show what had happened. A mist of snow drifted in the air, while an eerie silence settled. All that was left was his own voice, shouting for help, and his hands digging down into the drift, long after he knew it was much too late to save Georgina, his wife and the love of his life.

But he'd refused to give into the dread. Against all his instincts for survival, swallowing down the fear, he'd made himself return to the slopes the following season, tackle the black runs with gritty determination, ski off-piste. He knew he could never enjoy it wholeheartedly again, but he would not let fear shape his decisions, or his life.

The car lurched and Isabella transferred both hands to the handle above her shoulder.

'Ross…?'

'It's okay. The car can handle worse than this—'

There was a rumble from somewhere ahead, and a ripping, tearing sound. Ross tapped the brake pedal, but the heavy vehicle continued downwards, swinging sideways and sliding around a corner, coming to rest against the massive trunk of a pine tree which had fallen across the road. Five seconds later there was a *crump* as a load of snow, dislodged by the impact of the tree, landed in the road behind them.

The only sound that broke the silence was the growl of the engine.

Ross swore softly. It was his responsibility to keep Isabella safe and to do that he had to figure a way out of this. Forwards was not an option. Turning his head to look back up the way they'd come, he pretty much ruled out that route, too. Trying to do a three-hundred-and-sixty-degree turn on the ice could land them in the ditch he knew ran along one side of the road. And even if he achieved that, trying to climb out of this deep lane, with ice beneath the wheels, now made more hazardous by several feet of snow, might not be possible.

'Ross?' Isabella's voice was quiet. 'Are we…stuck here?'

'No,' he said. He shook his head with a lot more conviction than he felt. 'I'll get us out.'

He wasn't yet sure how. The snow continued to fall relentlessly. Already their tracks had been covered over. If more drifts collapsed from the banks onto the road the vehicle could be half buried in a short time. He closed his eyes and pushed his hands into his hair, berating himself for landing them in this situation. A glance at Isabella's suede, wool-lined boots confirmed that getting out and attempting to walk back up the glen wasn't going to be a possibility. They looked beautiful and warm, but they were not fit for heavy snow and they'd be soaked in minutes.

His own clothing was more robust, and he was tough, but he couldn't leave her here alone and go for help. He checked his phone, but the signal was non-existent. The more he thought about it the more convinced he became that no trains would be running from the little Highland station. If this weather was widespread, there'd be no trains or flights from Edinburgh either, even if they did get there.

Next to him, Isabella shivered.

'I'm sorry,' he grated, unable to mask the annoyance he felt at himself. 'You're cold and you must be hungry, and anxious.'

'I'm a little cold but not at all hungry. And I do trust you to get us out of here.'

He remembered how her lack of pretence had been one of the things which had attracted him. If she was anxious, she'd say so.

But had she seriously just said she *trusted* him? Was she crazy? Anyone who trusted him did so at their peril. Hadn't George done that? A shaft of pain made him inhale sharply at the memory.

He turned his head to look at her. 'You *trust* me? Isabella…' Her gaze was direct, her expression calm.

She nodded. 'Yes. In…this situation… I do.' She released her grip on the handle and the seat and tucked her hands into her pockets. 'What are you going to do?' She sounded genuinely interested.

'I'm going to get out of the car and have a look around, to figure something out. Stay here.'

He tried to open the driver's side door, but it was wedged against the trunk of the fallen tree.

'I can get out on my side and have a look.' She unfastened her seat belt and opened the door, swinging her legs out of the car.

'I don't think that's a good idea. Your boots...'

'Will be fine, for a few minutes. They're flat with grippy soles.'

Before he could protest further, she'd slid to the ground and was walking, kicking her feet through the fresh snow, along the edge of the road. She stopped and called over her shoulder.

'There's a gap in the drift where the snow fell into the road. I think you'd get the car up this way.'

'Okay.' He released his seat belt and clambered over the passenger seat, his long legs making it an exercise in contortion. 'I'll have a look.'

He looked up at the bank. While there was still a layer of snow on the ground, rapidly building up as the flakes continued to settle, he could see that it might be their way out. He knew the car could easily climb the slope and driving through unpacked snow, uphill, would be less treacherous than downhill, on ice. And once they'd climbed out of the hollow made by the road, he knew the route he would take.

'Do you want me to guide you out?' The last few words were blurred by Isabella shivering again.

Ross shook his head. 'Thank you, but no, you're freezing already. I think you should get back into the car before you get even colder.'

It would require careful navigation in this whiteout, and they'd have to hurry before the northern afternoon began to fade into night, but he could get them to shelter, food and safety, at the lodge.

CHAPTER EIGHT

BELLA BRACED HERSELF and pressed her head back against the seat. Ross revved the engine, releasing the clutch slowly, and she felt the moment when the wheels gripped and they began to climb.

She didn't dare speak. She hardly dared to breathe. The incline felt impossibly steep. Seeing the high drifts of snow on either side of them was frightening so she turned her eyes to Ross's hands, where they kept a firm grip on the wheel. His hands, so good at so many things—she swallowed—would surely be capable of guiding them out of this, too.

He knew how far he could push the four-by-four. He must be aware of its limits. She had to trust him to do this.

He muttered something under his breath as their momentum slowed, his legs and feet adjusting the pressure on the accelerator and the brake.

She squeezed her eyes shut. After what felt like an age the car gave a lurch and leapt forwards, levelling out and coming to a stop. That was when she realised she'd been holding her breath, and she exhaled and inhaled noisily, her eyes snapping open on a landscape of snowy desolation.

Moorland, glimpsed through the swirling blizzard, stretched into infinity in every direction. But although the sense of isolation should have been scary, Bella felt curiously safe, cocooned in the warm car with Ross's big, secure presence at her side. It had become rare for her to rely on anyone but herself lately, and she wondered if she could get to like it, in limited doses.

She rubbed at the foggy window with her gloved hand, but the visibility hardly changed. Ross slipped the gear lever into neutral and switched off the wipers. In a matter of seconds snowflakes began to settle on the glass.

'I'm sorry,' he said.

'Sorry? Why? You got us out.'

'Yes. But I'm sorry for getting you into that…this…in the first place.'

Bella folded her arms and regarded him. A line creased the space between his brows. The hand he pulled across his jaw rasped against the unshaven stubble.

'Why did you do it? You could have left me at the castle.' She tipped her head in the direction in which she thought the castle lay, but she wasn't at all sure she was right.

Ross glanced through the windscreen. 'It's that way, so you're almost right.' He turned back to look at her and, for the first time, she noticed the fatigue etched around his eyes. Perhaps sleep had eluded him, too. 'Yes,' he continued, 'I could have. But I knew you wanted to leave, and I think I was the reason why, so I felt responsible.'

She tucked her hands into her pockets again and stared out through the windscreen. 'When I knew you were going to be the best man, I changed my plans to leave earlier. Originally, I was going to leave tomorrow.'

'So was I.'

Isabella jerked her head round to look at him. 'You said you had meetings in London tomorrow.'

'I do. I brought them forward, so I had a reason to leave.' He dropped his shoulders, his exhaled breath vaporising in the cold air. 'After the way you reacted to me at the meeting, I figured you'd want to see as little of me as possible, once we'd fulfilled our wedding duties.'

She smiled. 'I thought the same about you. The wedding was no place for arguing over a business deal, but the subject felt too big to be ignored. And anyway, you didn't want to spend time with me after Hannah and Robert's wedding, either.'

She turned away from him, staring out of the side window. 'I want to apologise.'

'You just have...'

'No.' He pushed both his hands into his hair, leaving it more tousled than before. 'No,' he said again, 'not for...this.' He made a gesture which encompassed both the interior of the car and the wilderness beyond it. 'Although this merits an apology all of its own. I need to say sorry for how I behaved...before.'

Bella stilled, withdrawing herself a little, immediately regretting her words. She didn't want to go back there. She needed to leave the past where it belonged, and, whatever her feelings for him might be, the past included Ross.

Digging it up would only make it more difficult to bury again, and she had to move on. But now the present, in the form of Ross possibly becoming her business partner, had handed her its own new set of difficulties, because if she'd learned anything over the past day, it was that the feelings she had for him were not under control, at all.

At Hannah's wedding, she'd accepted the idea of a one-night-only fling with Ross, believing it was what she needed, and wanted, to relieve her stress and give her a break from work. But she'd lost control, misjudging how it would affect her and allowing herself to be swept into a whirlpool of emotion and feelings which Ross had not returned.

The changes she'd insisted needed to be made at Thompson's had been successful. Furious hard work, driven by her need to prove herself to be good enough, after his rejection, had taken the company forwards to greater productivity and profit.

Now, by a twist of circumstance, it looked as if she might lose control to Ross again, but this time in the form of half the company.

She'd fought to mould Thompson's into the shape she wanted. With her father reducing his involvement, she'd been the major driving force behind decisions over the past two years, and she'd come to regard the company as *hers*. She didn't relish the idea of sharing it with anyone, but most of all she couldn't contemplate Ross being a part of it.

Accepting his offer of a lift down the glen to the station had been an error of judgement, but if the journey had gone smoothly, she would have been congratulating herself on making the right decision.

Perhaps they should have taken better note of the weather, but who was she to judge that? He'd also been anxious to leave. Here they were, and he'd extricated them from a tricky situation, so far. She needed no apology. She'd had her reasons for what she'd done, and she didn't doubt that he'd had his.

If she'd known she wouldn't be able to forget him after he left, would it have made a difference to her decision to spend the night with him?

No, it would not.

Why would Ross feel the need to apologise for something they'd both agreed they'd wanted?

She sat up straighter, resting the back of her head against the window.

'There is no need to apologise.'

Ross mirrored her position, turning his body to face her.

'Yes, there is.' He rested his forearm across the steering wheel. 'I walked away from you without saying goodbye or checking that you were okay.'

Bella shrugged and tried to keep her voice cool, remembering the disappointment she'd felt when she'd discovered

that he'd gone. 'Should I have expected you to? I…wasn't familiar with the etiquette around one-night stands.'

'No, I didn't think you were, which was all the more reason I should have taken better care of you.'

'I was glad that you left me a note.' What would he think
if he knew she'd kept that scrap of paper? 'Otherwise, I might
have thought I'd dreamed you up.' Her attempt at light-heart-
edness coaxed the corner of his mouth into the slightest lift.
'Anyway, if you'd wanted to apologise, you could have done
it last night. There was no certainty that we'd see each other
this morning.'

'Last night…' He shook his head a little. 'Isabella…'

She drew a deep breath, the way he said her name rock-
ing the resolve she clung to, to keep safe distance, physically
and emotionally, between them.

'Have you noticed that I call myself Bella now?'

'Yes, I noticed when your father introduced you to me, and
I thought it might be his name for you. But everyone else calls
you Bella, too.' He folded his arms across his chest, shifting
his position. 'Why is that?'

Bella lifted her shoulders. 'I felt like a change.'

He nodded, his eyes on her face. 'Would you mind, very
much, if I continue to call you Isabella? It's how I think of
you, and I don't know if I can change that.'

Her eyes snapped to his.

'You think of me? That's…surprising.'

The atmosphere between them sharpened.

'Yes,' he said, after a pause. 'I do. Last night,' he went on,
'I wasn't in any sort of state to talk. I needed to get my equi-
librium back. Seeing you again was…'

'We'd already seen each other, earlier in the week, remember?'

'I know, but I was prepared for that. It was business. Nothing could have prepared me for seeing you yesterday, as a

bridesmaid again. It brought back a lot of memories. Did it for you, too?'

'Of course it did, but it's in the past.'

'You've changed.'

'*I've* changed?' Her laugh was incredulous. 'I barely recognised you when you walked into our boardroom.'

'I'm sorry if our fling was the catalyst that caused it.'

Bella bit her lip, considering her response. 'Don't bother yourself over that, Ross,' she said, folding her hands in her lap. She turned, settling herself back into her seat, remembering the phone call of the previous night. 'Are you trying to absolve yourself of guilt?'

'What do you mean?'

'I saw you on the phone last night. You didn't look happy. Is there someone checking up on you? Was there, even before? Is that why you've changed so much?' She could hear the trace of bitterness in her own voice. She found her fingers were digging into the palms of her hands and was grateful for the protection her woolly gloves gave.

A brief flash of understanding lit his dark eyes, and Bella felt a stab of pain. If she was right, even though there was nothing between them, apart from one shared night, she didn't want Ross to be the man who had cheated on his partner, with her. The memories of that night were whole and precious. She didn't want them shattered.

'No.' His denial was firm. 'That's not true. I turned my life around myself. There is no one else in it. The way I was living was dishonouring my…past. I decided I needed to change that.' His voice dropped so that she could barely hear his next words. 'I'd done enough damage.'

Bella could feel his eyes on her, willing her to look at him, but she was determined to resist the pull. She stared through the windscreen, feeling disoriented by the dizzying fall of the snow. The wind had picked up and the Land Rover rocked on its wheels, while eddies of snowflakes whipped into a frenzied dance all around them. She let her eyelids drop, suddenly weary.

'Where,' she asked, 'do we go from here?'

'I don't think we can make it back to the Castle of Muir. We'd have to rejoin the road before the bridge over the river, and that section is covered in ice and very steep. But I know a track that joins the road up the glen, if I can find it.'

'What other option is there?' she asked. 'Do you know an alternative route to the station?'

Ross pinched the bridge of his nose between his thumb and middle finger, eyes closed.

'No. And anyway, I don't think there'll be trains running now.'

'What do you think we should do?'

'I can take us across country. It'll be rough, and slow, but we'll get there before darkness falls.'

'Get where?'

'To the lodge I mentioned, where I spend time in the summer. It's at the top of the glen, in that direction.' He gestured through the windscreen. 'It'll be warmer than this, and there's a freezer full of food.'

'It sounds like the only choice. We'll both be hungry by then.'

'Yeah.' Ross engaged first gear, switching the wipers on again. 'You haven't answered my question about your name. Can I call you Isabella?'

Bella shrugged. 'The answer's yes.'

'Thank you, Isabella. Now, there's only one flaw in my plan to get us to the lodge.'

'Which is?'

'We could be stuck there. For days.'

CHAPTER NINE

THE ACHE IN his eyes was the worst. The cramped muscles of his thighs and arms, even his hands, would ease quickly once he stopped driving, could climb out of the car and stretch, but his eyes would take longer to recover.

The falling snow had threatened to be mesmerising at times. It would be easy to become distracted by its endlessly changing patterns and lose his way. Now the relentless staring into the blinding, shifting whiteness was taking its toll in the form of a headache thumping at his temples.

Landmarks which were as familiar as the backs of his own hands in summer took on alien forms in this world where the land and the sky merged and every shape he thought he recognised shifted and changed the longer he stared at it.

Bella had been quiet. A quick glance at her showed she was awake, despite her stillness and silence. She must be as hungry as he was, but she'd never once complained.

This journey had already lasted half an hour longer than he'd calculated and the sky above had darkened from the threatening grey it had been to a forbidding shade of iron. Soon it would be impossible to orientate himself in their surroundings at all.

The track, faintly discernible between the drifts of snow on either side of it, bent towards the right, climbing again, and the headlights swept across a clump of snow-laden Scots pines.

Ross hissed out a long breath of relief. It was the shelter belt to the north of the lodge, he was sure. They crested the hill and there it was, tucked into the top of the glen, with the steep slopes of the mountains rising around it, their craggy peaks disappearing into the low cloud.

He'd left this place at the end of the summer, not intending to return until the spring, but never had he been so glad to be here. This was his safe space, where he sought and found a degree of solace, but he'd stopped coming here in winter after the accident.

He swung the wheel to the right and circled to the front of the house. Its whitewashed walls almost disappeared in the surrounding white landscape and its stone-tiled roof was covered in a thick blanket of snow.

He cut the engine and leaned forwards, resting his forearms on the steering wheel, turning his head towards Isabella.

'Welcome to Innes Lodge.'

Ross led Isabella around to the back of the house, ready to catch her if she slipped on the icy ground. He felt under the boot scraper for the key and was relieved to find it exactly where he'd left it three months ago. The door creaked open, and he ushered her ahead of him into the shelter of the big kitchen.

If possible, it was colder inside than out. Although the heating system was programmed to kick in when the temperature dropped to prevent disasters like frozen pipes in the depths of winter, the depth of the cold made it obvious the space hadn't been warmed recently. He reached for the light switch and flicked it on. Nothing happened, and he swore softly. The power supply must have been interrupted by the snow. Up here, at the top of the glen, they were at the end of the line and would be the last to have electricity restored. He hoped the additional insulation he'd had installed last summer would prove its worth now.

Could this day get any worse? Seriously?

Asking Isabella to stay where she was, he found his way to the boot room, and the torch in the drawer by the door. Then, although he knew he should not touch her, muttering 'sorry' under his breath, he cupped her elbow and guided her through the hall, past where the stairs wound up into the cavernous darkness of the first floor, to the sitting room.

'Sit here, Isabella.' He pointed to a deep sofa, picking up a tartan rug which was folded across the back of it, and dropping it around her shoulders. 'I'll get the log burner lit.'

She moved away from him but pulled the rug more tightly around herself, clutching it in her fists under her chin.

'I'd rather keep moving, thanks.' She bounced on her toes a couple of times. 'I've been immobile for hours. If I sit down, I think I might freeze and never be able to move again.' Ross caught the gleam of her eyes in the torchlight. 'If you'll show me where there might be candles and matches, I'll see if I can get some lit.'

By the time he returned with a basket of logs from the store at the back of the house, three fat candles which stood on the mantel above the fireplace glowed and the dim room had sprung to life in isolated pools of wavering light and dancing shadows. He fetched oil lamps from the kitchen while the fire flickered into life and Isabella found a kettle on the kitchen range and placed it on top of the wood burner.

The mug of hot chocolate she eventually produced, from cocoa and powdered milk which she dug out of the larder, was the best he'd ever tasted. There was an unopened packet of shortbread biscuits in a tin, and Ross went to the tall cupboard in the dining room and pulled out a bottle of whisky.

He raised an eyebrow at her, proffering the bottle. She held out her mug and he tipped a generous measure into it, before helping himself.

His eyes met hers and he held up his mug. 'We made it.'

'Did you doubt that we would?'

The way she licked traces of sugar from her fingertips made him take an extra breath before he could reply. 'Did you?'

She shook her head, her curls gleaming like spun gold in the candlelight. 'No. I had to trust in what you were doing. I didn't allow myself to doubt.'

'Thank you.' He wrapped both his hands around the warm mug, wanting to reach out and brush the strands of hair off her face but knowing he could not. It was one thing, guiding her through the dark house with a light touch, but quite another to indulge in an intimate gesture like that. It would anger her, and it would make keeping his enforced distance from her almost impossible. 'That must have been a leap of faith on your part, given our past.'

Why, in God's name, had he said that? He'd apologised. Now he had to learn to leave the past alone.

The atmosphere in the room suddenly felt weighted and she stared at him over the rim of her mug. She swallowed a mouthful of chocolate and then brushed the tip of her tongue across her bottom lip. He was aware of his breathing deepening again, his blood heating and his shaky control slipping.

'I'm sorry, Isabella. I shouldn't have said that.'

She shrugged and sat down in the corner of the sofa. 'I chose to come with you. I could hardly complain.'

'Do you regret it?' He stood with his back to the fireplace, feeling welcome warmth beginning to filter into the room. 'You could have been back at the castle, warm, well-fed...'

'And having to be sociable and chatty.' She pulled off her bobble hat and ran her fingers through her hair. 'Play *games*. No. I do not regret it. The drive gave me time to think.' She frowned. 'I don't think it's warm enough yet.' She pulled the hat back on, tucking her hair behind her ears. It settled over her shoulders and Ross tightened his hold on his mug, and on his body. But his mind rewound, to a memory of that hair spread across a pillow, his own face inches from hers, their eyes locked.

Deliberately, with effort, he dragged his thoughts back to the present, but the present did not provide much respite, it simply reinforced his predicament. He was marooned in a cold, dark house with the girl who had haunted his thoughts, fuelled his regrets and who had been the catalyst to him dragging himself up from a place where he was intent on self-destruction. Put simply, she had saved his business, his *life*.

He should be thanking her, but that would involve too many explanations, too much soul-baring. Too much emotion and he didn't do emotion. It was too dangerous.

Under different circumstances, he knew he'd take the quickest route to warming them both up, but they could never do that again.

The air between them snapped with tension. Ross sat down in one of the armchairs and leaned back, trying to defuse it.

'I'm glad you don't regret it,' he said quietly. 'I don't, either. But what thoughts kept you so quiet?'

Her eyes turned towards him and the corners of her mouth lifted. 'Oh. I thought you were wishing you'd left me at the castle and made your escape on your own. And there's that offer you've made for half of Thompson's Textiles. That's given me a lot to think about. I'll be discussing it with my father next week, but I'll have to get there, first.'

He wanted to say that he'd sacrifice a lifetime of comfort for these few precious hours with her. He was sure she'd hoped never to see him again, but they'd been thrown together by a series of circumstances, and he would treasure this time forever. All he had to do was not wreck it by saying the wrong thing, or, God forbid, letting his body overrule his mind.

They found a collection of food in tins, agreeing not to

open the freezer in the larder during the power failure, and they ate in front of the fire, the room slowly warming around them. Isabella leaned down and unzipped her boots, easing them off and rubbing her feet before folding them underneath her on the sofa. She wriggled out of her coat and discarded her hat, loosening her scarf.

Every movement she made captured Ross's attention, watching her relax as she warmed up, feeling her tension ease. She crooked an elbow onto the arm of the sofa and rested her cheek in her cupped hand, her eyes fixed on the flickering flames behind the glass doors of the log burner.

'Nobody knows where we are,' she murmured.

'Does that bother you?'

She straightened up, studying him. 'No. It doesn't.' Her look sharpened. 'Should it?'

Ross shook his head, enjoying her directness. 'No. You're safe here and when the thaw comes, we'll leave.'

'It's strange, isn't it?' Her teeth nipped at her bottom lip.

'The way we've ended up here. Yes, it is.'

'That's not what I meant. I meant it's strange feeling safe with you. Before, being with you felt dangerous and wild. That was part of the…excitement. I'd never met anyone like you.'

He forced a smile. 'Are you saying I've become boring and tame?'

'Mmm…no.' She slanted a look at him. 'But you feel more…dependable.'

He stood up, needing to move, shoving his hands into the pockets of his jeans and walking to the window, keeping his back to her.

Bella watched as Ross rolled his shoulders, stress radiating from the tense muscles of his broad back, his knees braced, legs taut.

His voice was so low she had to strain to hear his words, even in the stillness of their surroundings.

'Isabella, don't make that mistake. I'm not dependable. I'm all right in a crisis and I can think on my feet.' He laughed, with little humour, and his voice rose. 'I've had lots of practice at that.'

He turned to face her, one booted foot tapping the floor, dragging a hand from his pocket and spiking his fingers through his hair. '*Lots* of practice,' he repeated. 'But I'm untrustworthy and unreliable. I've had lots of practice at that, too.' He dropped his head so that his face was in shadow. 'I'm not a safe bet.'

'Going on experience, I'd prefer to say you were wild, Ross, and perhaps unpredictable. But you've changed. I get a different vibe from you now.'

He took a step towards her and instinctively she stretched out an arm, palm facing him. He stopped, regret flashing in his eyes, his lips pressed together.

'That's exactly how you should react to me, Isabella. With extreme caution. I hate to say it, but it's true.'

The silence stretched. Bella dropped her hand to her lap, the movement making Ross's eyes flicker downwards, following it, before lifting again to bore into hers. The moment felt supercharged with danger, as if they teetered on the edge of a chasm from which they both knew they had to step back before the pull of it overwhelmed them.

Bella could see a muscle jumping in his jaw, his chest rising and falling, too quickly, beneath the cabled sweater that stretched across his wide shoulders. She wanted to reach out again, but this time not to stop him. She ached to cup his jaw in her palm, to soothe away the tension with her fingers and then slide her hand around the back of his neck, to massage the muscles at the base of his skull.

An instinct for self-preservation stopped her. She couldn't

go back there. One wrong movement, and all the effort she'd put into trying to forget him would go to waste. Dancing with him last night had shown her how very fragile the barrier was which she'd put up between them. It could so easily have crumbled, leaving her vulnerable again to the powerful feelings their night had triggered. Those unstoppable waves of emotion had seemed to come from nowhere, and they'd left her weak and unable to offer any resistance.

It had been a hard lesson, discovering that she could be caught off guard so easily, and she'd vowed she'd be ready to protect herself better if it ever threatened to happen again. Ross had the ability to make her heart race and all her nerve endings sizzle with anticipation, with that quirk of his mouth, or soft glance from his dark eyes, and she had to stay away from him to have any hope of staying in control of herself and of Thompson's Textiles.

That intoxicating, wild, exhilarating time with him would not, could never, be repeated. She'd felt as if she could have handed over her heart and soul to him, if he'd asked for them.

'What happened to you, Ross, to make you like you were?' she eventually whispered. 'And to change you to what you are?'

He rocked back on his heels, raising his eyes to the ceiling, breaking the thread that seemed to connect his gaze with hers. 'I may have changed outwardly.' He dropped his head, and his fingers went to his temples, massaging them in a circular motion. 'I've got a respectable haircut, and I've stopped depending on the wrong kind of high to get through the days…and nights.' He closed his eyes for a few seconds and Bella remembered the hours of driving, the unrelenting landscape, the concentration he'd never been able to let slip. He must be exhausted.

Then he went on. 'I know I've changed, but you've changed, too, Isabella. You wanted to have fun. We met, and we fitted. I needed something to get me through that wedding, and I found you.' He shook his head. 'We just…we just…for that night, it was perfect. It terrified me, because something so perfect wasn't sustainable. Not by me, anyway. And then you said, *"I want to freeze time, so that I can stay here, with you, forever."'*

'I know I shouldn't have said it, Ross, but it was just what I *felt* at that moment.'

'You were impulsive, and so honest. But you've developed a guardedness, a cool demeanour and an air of detachment, which I think is a sign that now you're assessing everything around you, all the time, for risk.' He pulled his hands over his face. 'Was it the way I left you, or did you discover that one night was not all you needed, after all?'

Bella pushed herself upright, her eyes trapped by his. Her breath caught somewhere in her chest as she tried to breathe. She pressed her hands to her chest.

'It's not like that.' She hated feeling the tremor in her voice. 'I had difficult decisions to make about the business. It was a stressful time, insanely busy and pressurised. Our night was perfect, but afterwards I had to go back to reality, and it wasn't…' Her voice caught and she swallowed. 'It wasn't… nothing was easy.'

'Can you tell me, Isabella, with that honesty and candour I remember, that I didn't hurt you?'

'I…' She tried to speak, to deny his words. To tell him he'd never meant anything to her, at all, because to admit her feelings to him would put her at their mercy, again. The words jammed in her throat.

'Tell me, Isabella,' he said softly.

She shook her head, feeling the tears she thought she'd exhausted years ago drowning her eyes.

'I…can't,' she whispered. She tipped her head back in a futile attempt to stop them from spilling, then she swiped at her cheeks with the heels of her hands and blinked, digging in a pocket for a tissue. 'Sorry.' She swallowed hard.

Ross shook his head. 'It's okay.' The husky gentleness of his voice surprised her. 'I'm the one who needs to say sorry.'

'No, you don't. It wasn't your fault. I knew what I was doing, and I wanted… I *needed*…to do it.'

'I sensed that you weren't a one-night stand kind of girl, and now that I know something about the traditional background of Thompson's, I feel sure you aren't. Why was someone like you, with your close-knit family background and strong values, so intent on a no-strings fling at her friend's wedding?'

Isabella rested her head against the back of the sofa and looked beyond Ross, to the window. It was fully dark and impossible to see if the snow was still falling. She tucked her hands into her armpits and sucked in a deep breath. 'I'd had an argument with my father the night before—the only argument we'd ever had—and I felt bad. It was a disagreement over something to do with the company and I was so frustrated by his intransigent attitude that I walked out.' She pulled her gaze back to Ross. 'I was strung out, exhausted, and I decided, on the train to Edinburgh, that I was going to forget about work for the weekend and try to have some fun.' She shrugged. 'You know the rest. I wanted fun and you looked like a suitably reckless way to have it. The combination turned out to be the perfect solution.' She dropped her eyes, focussing on the flames behind the glass door of the wood burner. 'Afterwards, I found myself working even harder. I've taken the company forward and it's doing very well, but my relationship with my father has become distant and I haven't allowed much time for my friends. It's been all-consuming.'

'What forces you to work so hard? There's a strong workforce and Thompson's success shows how efficiently it's managed. It can't be entirely necessary.'

Bella pulled her feet out from under her and wrapped her arms around her shins, resting her chin on her knees. 'It is entirely necessary. For me.'

The memory of finding him gone still hurt. She preferred not to dwell on how the strength of her feelings had confused her. Added to that had been her bewilderment. How could she have felt so deeply, while he'd been able to walk away, without even saying goodbye. Reinventing herself, becoming someone different from the person Ross had met, had been the only way to keep going.

Ross usually loved her honesty and her inability to be anything but utterly straightforward, but right now he hated it. Hearing her confirm what he'd suspected since he'd seen her again, in the company boardroom and then in the chapel, formal and stiff behind Emma, made his heart ache.

It had taken a few seconds for him to register that this was Isabella, when he'd walked into that room, and he'd had to work quickly and hard to mask his shock and surprise.

In his mind he kept the image of her as he'd left her asleep in her bed. He'd convinced himself that she wouldn't care when she'd found him gone. She'd understand that was how he operated. They'd agreed on it.

He'd left a note which he believed had drawn a line under their night. He'd had no intention of trying to contact her again—the feelings being with her had uncovered were far too frightening to risk it.

She'd touched something in him he'd buried deep. Caring for someone—*anyone*—was dangerous. Either they hurt you or you hurt them. It was a risk he couldn't afford to take.

The lesson had been drummed into him, by the casual cruelty of the universe. Nothing was certain, especially when you relaxed and thought it was.

He cared about Isabella. She'd helped him through one of

the most difficult days and nights of his life, and he was not going to let anything hurt her, if he could prevent it. First and foremost, that meant staying away from her.

Just this once, he wished she'd lied.

He slapped that thought away because he knew he only wished she'd lied to make him feel better. He didn't deserve that.

After his night with Isabella, he'd wanted more but he knew he would eventually hurt her. He'd failed to protect Georgina and he knew he could never dare to risk another relationship, or commitment. No one would be safe with him. Leaving her without saying goodbye had hurt her anyway, but he saw it as damage control. Seeing her again, allowing her to think they might have a future, would have been dishonest, and the hurt would ultimately have been much deeper.

But being with her had given him space to think about how he was busy trashing his life and he'd pulled himself out of the black hole of depression and addiction, got a haircut and saved his company from bankruptcy.

He'd screwed up with Isabella, and the universe didn't offer second chances. That wasn't how it worked.

CHAPTER TEN

Ross PICKED UP the torch and strode out into the cold hall, closing the door behind him to keep the warmth in. He unlocked the front door and took the steps down two at a time, ignoring the danger of the slick, icy surface.

The freezing air hit him in the chest and he struggled to breathe, feeling as if he was drowning in dry ice. He stopped and bent, putting his hands on his knees and coughing until his breath steadied.

He'd had to put a safe distance between them. The sight of her eyes brimming with tears had been too much for him to bear. Knowing the part he'd played in causing her distress made it ten, a hundred times, worse. All he'd wanted was to cross the space between them, take her hands and pull her up against him, wrap her in his arms and comfort her. He wanted to tell her it would be okay, but he couldn't lie to her. It would never be okay between them, because he couldn't risk it.

Good things didn't happen to people like him.

He pulled their overnight bags from the back of the Defender and carried them into the house, dumping them at the foot of the stairs. Then he returned to stand in the sitting room doorway.

'Isabella?' She was crouched down in front of the hearth, putting another log in the wood burner. She closed the glass door, dropping the catch into place and straightened up, turning towards him.

Her face was a mask of composure, her eyes cool grey pools. All trace of her tears had been erased.

'Yes?'

'I... I've brought your bag in. I'd show you up to a bedroom, but it's much too cold upstairs.' He stepped back and she walked across the room, back straight and head high. 'I think you should sleep here, on the sofa. I'll take one of the bedrooms. There's a bathroom off the landing, but obviously there's no hot water.'

She picked up one of the oil lamps. As she passed him, he caught a hint of the scent of her warm skin, and damask roses. It was as alluring in the depths of winter as it had been in summer. She gathered up her bag and started up the stairs without looking at him.

'Let me.' He reached for the bag, but she shook her head.

'I can manage, thank you.'

Ross busied himself adding more logs to the fire, hoping it would burn for a good few hours. Then he ran upstairs and pulled pillows and a duvet off one of the beds, returning to arrange them on the sofa.

Isabella reappeared, shivering. 'Upstairs is like an ice house, Ross. You can't sleep up there.' She glanced at the sofa. 'Thank you for the duvet. You could pull the cushions off the armchairs and make a bed on the floor. Are there more duvets upstairs?'

He nodded. 'There are, but...'

Her gaze was direct. 'I really don't mind. It's the practical solution.'

'If you're sure I won't disturb you. I'll try to keep the fire going through the night.'

Bella wrapped the duvet around herself and lay down on the sofa with her back to the room. She could hear Ross arranging cushions on the floor. Warmth began to seep into her body and the tension in her muscles gradually dissipated, but although she was bone-tired, sleep felt a long way away.

She was acutely aware of every move Ross made. He was so close she could reach out and touch him if she wanted to. She thought back to the wedding reception, and of the end of the dance, when they'd stood, touching, their eyes locked. The helpless attraction between them was so forceful, but the reasons she couldn't give in to it more potent still.

He was the very last person who should arouse these feelings in her. If he succeeded in buying out her father it might signal the end of Thompson's Textiles, the company she'd been fighting to save with every ounce of her strength and every minute of her life. Even if he didn't rip it apart and sell it off in bits, she could never work with him.

Where she saw a family-run enterprise, in which she knew all the employees and each of their roles, he would see opportunities to make it more profitable and streamlined. Jobs would be lost, along with the personal feel, instituted by her mother and so important in maintaining the ethos of the company. It was something she'd done her best to preserve.

Yet he'd shown none of his ruthless business side today. He'd been considerate and kind, thoughtful about her needs and taking care to keep his distance.

Just being near him, hearing his voice, kick-started her imagination. How would it be if he felt differently about personal commitment? She'd never be able to maintain a business relationship between them. She'd want all of him, but none of him was available.

Her mind turned in circles, growing more exhausted, but no less active. He'd got past her defences, when she'd admitted he'd affected her badly at Hannah's wedding, and she regretted letting him see her distress, but seeing it had affected him, too. She'd seen it in his face and in the way he'd abruptly left the room, giving her time and space to recover.

She must have drifted off eventually, because something woke her.

She was chilled to the bone, and shivering. The fire must have gone out. She'd have to get up and relight it.

The room was filled with an unearthly white light. The time on her phone, which was showing five percent of battery, was 1:15 a.m.

There was a new, brittle sharpness to the cold.

Only half awake, she slid off the sofa, wrapping the duvet around herself while she made her way, teeth chattering, to the window.

The sight which confronted her when she pulled the curtain aside was dreamlike.

The lowering clouds of the previous day had almost cleared. A few pale wisps scudded across the inky backdrop of the sky, across which thousands of glittering stars were scattered. The crescent moon hung low on the horizon, spilling silver light across the frozen mountain peaks and into the glen. Every surface glittered with frost, as if a giant's hand had sprinkled a dusting of sparkling crystals over the world.

'Oh!' Bella gasped. It felt like standing in the middle of her own personal snow globe, in that moment of stillness before someone picked it up and shook it.

The air seeping in around the old sash windows was exquisitely icy. She drew back, shaking with cold, chilled from her toes to her ears, the possibility of returning to sleep now an impossible hope.

'Isabella? Are you okay?'

'N-no. I'm…n-not.'

'What's wrong?' His face was briefly illuminated by the lit-up screen of his phone. 'It's the middle of the night. What is it?'

'The fire has gone out and I'm…so cold.' A huge shiver

shook her. 'The s-snow has stopped. But everything…everything is frozen, including me.'

A match scraped and the oil lamp flared. Ross pushed the duvet back and stood.

'Let me light the fire. Are you properly awake?'

'If I wasn't awake how would I know how cold I am?'

He laughed, his voice rough with sleep. 'I can't argue with that.' He crouched in front of the hearth and pulled fresh logs from the basket.

Bella shivered uncontrollably, pulling the duvet around her shoulders. Ross struck a match, and a flame flared, briefly illuminating his face. He closed the glass doors as the logs caught.

'I'm so tired but I won't be able to sleep until I'm warm again.' She yawned.

'Shall I make some more hot chocolate and whisky? Would that help?'

She shook her head. 'I just want to go back to bed.' She turned and wobbled, the duvet tangled around her legs. Ross put out a hand to steady her and she leaned into his side. His arm went round her shoulders.

'Let me help you.'

'How come you're so warm?' she asked. 'When it's cold enough to freeze…'

'Possibly,' he replied, settling her into his side, 'because I haven't been standing in front of a leaky window in a freezing room at after one o'clock in the morning.'

She sighed. 'Mmm. Maybe.' He'd kept his thick sweater on and she dropped her head onto his shoulder, feeling its rough, comforting texture beneath her cheek.

His chest rose in a deep inhalation. 'Isabella?'

'Mmm?'

'Two duvets are warmer than one. Would you like to come under mine and yours, with me?'

'I think that's a bad idea, but I'm so cold.'

'Just to get you warm again, I promise.'

Isabella felt as if she'd been fighting the cold and her attraction to Ross forever. Fatigue fogged her brain, and her willpower flagged. She nodded against his shoulder. 'Okay.'

She folded herself down onto the deep cushions Ross had arranged on the floor, pulling her duvet with her. Ross tucked the second duvet over her and slid in beside her, putting an arm around her waist and pulling her towards him.

'Your feet are like blocks of ice, Isabella,' he muttered, as he tucked her back against his chest. 'Where are your socks?'

'They were wet, remember? Where're yours?'

'Damp.' He rested his chin on the top of her head.

Slowly, his warmth enveloped her. Her tense limbs released, inch by inch, and she began to feel her stiff body relaxing against him and sinking into the soft cushions. He must have moved over a little because the patch where she lay was warm from his body. She turned her face towards the pillow and breathed in the scent of him.

Somewhere in her brain a voice tried to tell her that this was, indeed, a bad…a very bad…idea, but her need for warmth and sleep made her ignore it. His chest rose and fell with comforting regularity against her back. The weight of his big hand, spanned across her waist, anchored her in safety.

She flexed a leg, her foot brushing his calf, and she felt, rather than heard, the groan in his chest.

'It's beautiful outside,' she murmured. 'You should look.'

'And end up as cold as you? I'm not going anywhere.'

The last thing she remembered before she sank into sleep was his hand leaving her side and moving up to cover both of hers where they were folded together at her chest, and the feather-light brush of his mouth against her hair.

'I'm sorry I made you cry,' he said.

* * *

Sometime before morning, Isabella must have turned towards him, because when he woke his arms were wrapped around her, her head on his chest.

Not wanting to disturb her or have her waking in a state of shock at finding herself in his bed, he tried not to move. In the half-light of the early morning, he looked down at her.

Strands of her long, unruly hair were spread over his chest. Thick eyelashes fanned against her cheeks. Judging by the faint flush on her skin, he could tell that she was properly warm. Her soft mouth, the lower lip a little fuller than the upper, curved in a slight smile. Her left hand had found its way under his jumper and the shirt he wore beneath it, and he could feel her fingers resting on the swell of his pecs, just below his right nipple.

His hands had remained safely outside her pale blue cashmere jumper. He lifted a hand from the soft wool over her shoulder blades and brushed a strand of her hair away from her face, so he could drink in her beauty more easily.

With sudden relief, he heard the faint flare of the boiler igniting, in the boot room beyond the kitchen. The power must have been restored. Within minutes he could hear the metallic tick of the radiators as they heated up. He and Isabella would be warm and dry, and they could safely wait at Innes Lodge until the snow and ice thawed.

He could charge his phone and make the calls he needed to make.

But his relief was tinged with regret. With the heating working, there'd be no need for a shared bed tonight and although the knowledge should be a relief, it wasn't.

Once she woke, this time of having her in his arms would have to end and he'd have no further reason to hold her, however much he wanted to. Being with her brought with it an unfamiliar sensation, as if something inside him was being unlocked, allowing unhappiness to escape and contentment to fill its place. He searched his heart for the guilt he knew it carried, but he couldn't conjure it up.

Was this how it felt to be at peace with oneself, he wondered.

He'd lain awake for hours last night, listening to her steady breathing, unable to relax with her so near. He'd been aware of the fire dying down, the air in the room cooling, and the change in the light outside, but he hadn't wanted to risk disturbing her by adding more logs to the stove.

The memory of the night they'd spent together played havoc with his mind. She'd slept in his arms, and he'd lain awake, confused by the emotions which swirled through him. Guilt had fought with utter, boneless contentment, the battle seizing his thoughts, pitting them against each other, for hours.

Guilt had won the battle, but the words she'd whispered as she'd lain in his arms, drifting in and out of sleep, had found their mark.

'I want to live forever, so I can stay here, with you.'

He'd realised that he wasn't living, at all. He was existing, and wasting everything he and Georgina had achieved. She would always have a place in his heart, but if he wanted to live, he was going to have to change.

Now, the tightening of his body as Isabella slept against him made his breath hitch. She looked just as she had when he'd walked away from her that summer morning, but the memories of their lovemaking that night were indelibly etched in his memory. She'd been eager to please him, but it had been so easy to please her, too. He'd never been able to blot out the little sounds of need she'd made, her gasps of pleasure, her moans of release.

They'd lost themselves in each other and for a few hours his guilt and grief had been forced into the background.

His brain slammed shut on the memories, but his body wasn't so biddable, hardening further against her. She shifted slightly, her breath sighing, her hand coming to rest on his abdomen. He knew he had to move while he could still summon up a fraction of willpower.

He'd prefer not to witness her reaction if she found herself in bed with him, even if it was a makeshift bed on the floor.

Very carefully he eased her off his chest, settling her against the pillows and tucking the double layer of duvets around her. Once her breathing had subsided back into an even rhythm, he slid onto the floor and stood up.

The heating had already taken the chill off the air and the remains of a log glowed in the wood-stove. He scooped up his boots and left the room.

It took Bella several minutes to surface, swimming up through the layers of deep sleep. As she woke, she shifted, revelling in the warmth of the bed and the comfort of the duvets around her. Slowly, jagged memories of the night returned, and her body tensed with embarrassment as the pieces began to fall into place.

The ice-cold hours at the dead of night, her desperate, all-consuming need for warmth; the sparkling vision of the fairy tale landscape in the grip of a hard frost under moonlight.

The gentle way Ross had suggested sharing the duvets and how he'd folded her into the curves of his body, lending her his warmth and comfort.

Carefully, she turned her head and felt a pinch of disappointment before a surge of relief.

He was gone. What the hell would she have done if he'd still been there?

Suddenly terrified that he'd reappear she scrambled to the floor. As she hurried upstairs to the bathroom, she realised she could hear the faint background hum of the heating system and that the house was warm.

When she descended the curved stairs, the aroma of toast and frying bacon enticed her into the kitchen. She raked her fingers through her untidy curls and shoved her hands into the pockets of her jeans, taking a breath, dropping her shoulders.

Ross stood at the range cooker, turning over rashers of bacon in a pan with a fork. A rack of toast was keeping warm at the side and the table was set with plates and cutlery, butter and marmalade.

He turned his head as she came in, but kept the pan handle in one hand, the fork in the other.

'Good morning. Coffee?'

'Hi.' She stopped in the middle of the room, taking in the big table, gleaming with years of polish, the colourful rug on the floor and the array of utensils hanging on hooks behind the range. 'Yes, please.'

'It's in the pot. I was about to bring you a cup.'

'Oh. Thank you.' She thanked whatever it was which had woken her before that had happened. 'But... I'm sorry...' she began. He still wore the dark green cable sweater and his hip-hugging jeans.

'If you're talking about last night, please, don't apologise.' He waved the fork in his hand towards the table. 'It was... the sensible solution.'

'I disturbed you.'

'You were cold. *Very* cold.'

She tucked her hands into her armpits. 'When did the power come back on? The house is lovely and warm.'

He pulled the frying pan of sizzling bacon off the ring and turned around. 'Sometime early this morning. I took bread, butter and bacon out of the freezer.' The lines of anxiety and fatigue had faded from his face and his eyes looked alive with something. Amusement? The night was a bit of a blur in her mind. Had she said or done something embarrassing?

'It smells delicious. But I must have made you cold, too. In the night.'

'On the contrary, I think I made you warm. You slept.'

Her eyes slid away from his as she remembered the feel of his arm around her, his hand folding over hers, his mouth…

'Did you?'

'Uh…did I what?'

'Sleep. After I disturbed you.'

'Yes. I did. It was the double layer of duvets which did the trick.'

'Oh. Good.'

'Sit down and I'll bring you breakfast.' His voice was warm, a little rough.

But Bella moved across to look out of the window. 'Have you been out? It's magical. I wanted to tell you in the night, only… I think I went to sleep.'

'You did tell me, but I didn't want to…get out of bed. I thought it would wake you up again and you seemed to be very nearly asleep.' He slid crisp bacon onto two plates and set them down on the table. 'And I've only been as far as the car to get my phone charger. Everything is frozen solid. You could probably skate on the loch. Not that I ever do.'

Bella studied the glittering landscape. 'Where's the loch?'

'At the front, on the other side of the track. But it's probably not safe…'

She looked across at him, seeing the frown of anxiety returning to his forehead.

'I won't go onto the ice. I wouldn't be that silly, Ross.'

'No.' His face cleared. 'Of course you wouldn't.'

Bella walked through the door into the boot room. 'Do you think there're boots here that might fit me?' She looked at the neat row of outdoor boots. 'Oh, there's a sledge!'

He was in the doorway behind her.

'I think most sizes are catered for so I'm sure there'll be boots to fit you. And, yes, there is a sledge.'

Bella picked up a boot and turned it over, looking for the size. 'These should do. It's the perfect day for sledging. I'll go out after breakfast.'

He took a step into the room, looking from Isabella to the sledge and back again. 'Isabella, I don't know... The temperature outside is arctic. You'd be frozen in no time. And what if you fall off and hurt yourself? We're stuck here. I wouldn't be able to get you to a doctor.'

He folded his arms, the movement pulling his sweater tightly across his broad shoulders. Heat flared in her abdomen, along with the desire to measure that breadth with her hands. She tried to shut the feelings down.

'I wasn't aware that I needed your permission or that sledging required a risk assessment.'

The boot room suddenly felt too small for both of them. She stepped round him, back into the kitchen. 'Anyway, I'm not going to hurt myself. The snow is so deep, if I fall it'll be like landing on a great, big, fluffy duvet...'

Their eyes met, and something arced between them. She stopped, too close to him, the flash of heat in his gaze intense. Had mentioning the duvet triggered the memory of how he'd held her, that lightest of kisses? Perhaps having her in his bed hadn't been quite as practical and easy for him as he'd made out. She felt her cheeks warming. When he'd clasped her hands and kissed her hair, had he thought she was already asleep?

'Let's talk about it after breakfast. You must be hungry. I am.'

They sat at the table, and she extracted a slice of wholemeal toast from the rack and twisted the top off the jar of orange marmalade.

'I am hungry. And I want energy to have some fun in the snow.'

Then she remembered his comment of the previous day. *'Not my sort of fun.'* She'd decided he looked as if he hadn't had any fun for a long time. Perhaps it was time to change that.

'I love sledging. My father used to take me on the heath near our house when I was little.'

'Did he? The last time I went sledging was at school.'

Except for the Cresta run and you could hardly call that sledging.

He poured two mugs of coffee and slid one across the table to her. She added milk and lifted it to her mouth, keeping her eyes on him.

'Thank you. At *school*? Not with your family?'

He swallowed a mouthful of toast. 'No. We… I didn't really get to do those kinds of things, and then I lived with my grandparents from the age of seven.'

Isabella put down the piece of toast she was about to bite into. 'Oh. What…?'

'My parents split up. Neither of them wanted custody of me. I don't think they'd ever really wanted children. According to my grandparents, my arrival was a bit of a surprise, and their marriage eventually couldn't stand the strain.'

'Oh, Ross, I'm sorry, that's…' She thought about her loving parents and the gaping hole her mother had left when she died, and how her father had done his utmost to fill it, trying to be everything to her. 'Your grandparents *said* that to you?'

He shook his head. 'I heard them saying it to someone else. They didn't want their retirement plans disrupted by a seven-year-old, so they sent me to boarding school.'

Isabella swallowed and pressed a hand to her chest. The reasons behind his self-sufficiency, his insistence on control, his resistance to commitment shifted into focus.

'Ross…'

'It's okay, because I loved it. There were ready-made friends, organised games, even sledging in winter. All those things I'd never had.' She sensed a thread of tension under his flippancy.

'But what about love? Did you have that? And it was not okay for you to have heard that you were unwanted. Surely you went to your parents in the holidays? Or to your grand-parents?'

He leaned his forearms on the table, looking relaxed, but she saw the tension in the fingers which gripped his elbows.

'Love?' There was a note of dismissal in his tone and she wished she hadn't asked the question. 'That's not some-thing… Anyway, there were always a few of us who didn't go home in the holidays. Children whose parents lived abroad, for instance. I saw my parents occasionally. They both remar-ried. My grandparents have died but they left me the house. I used the proceeds from the sale to found my business.'

Bella picked up a piece of bacon in her fingers. 'This is perfect. So crunchy. Thank you.' She studied her plate. 'Do you have any contact with your parents?'

'No. Not anymore.'

She glanced up at him. 'You must wonder about them? How they are?'

Ross pulled a hand over his jaw and she noticed he'd shaved. 'No…yes, I suppose I do. But they've never tried to contact me, and I'm…busy. And as you know, I went through a bad time when I didn't connect with anyone much.'

'But things are better now. *You're* better now. Maybe they tried to contact you and then gave up when you didn't re-spond. Have you thought of trying to find them?'

'I have a phone number for my father. I got it from the solicitor when my grandfather—his father—died. He was living in Spain and didn't manage to come to the funeral.'

'So you could simply call him. I used to talk to my father every day…'

'Used to? Why don't you, now?'

'Only because work became so busy, and he's started to slow down a little. He doesn't come into the office as much as he did.' She considered her words and how they must sound, as if she didn't have time for her aging father. 'I thought of phoning him on Saturday night but it was late.'

She hated that she'd walked out of the meeting after Ross had left, angry with her father, and they hadn't spoken since. When she'd wanted to call him on Saturday night, she hadn't really known what she would say.

'Were you going to tell him you'd seen me again? Persuade him I'm not the business partner you need?'

Bella chewed her lip. Ross's eyes were on her, serious, but a muscle at the side of his mouth jumped in an almost-smile.

'Possibly, but I didn't. There'll be time for that when I get back.'

'Is that what you'll say?'

The atmosphere in the kitchen thickened as the silence between them grew. Bella thought about the man who'd walked into the boardroom, with whom she'd spent the past twenty-four hours, and the evening before that at the wedding. It was difficult to absorb the changes in him. The man for whom she'd fallen had been wild and intense, who'd since cultivated a reputation in business for being tough. The Ross who sat at the table opposite her now had been kind, serious and thoughtful. The situation was confusing, the facts impossible to compute.

'You can charge your phone now. Perhaps you can speak to him today.'

'Perhaps.' Would she still tell her father that he had to turn down Ross's offer? Yes, because her feelings for him simmered, ready to ignite at the touch of a hand or a smile, but he'd made it clear he'd never return them. Eventually it would break her heart. Having to work with him, see him every day, but never be able to tell him how she felt would be torture.

'Perhaps you could phone your father, too.'

Ross looked shocked, caught off guard. 'That's never going to happen. And it's not a subject I care to discuss.'

'Why, Ross?'

'I have nothing to say to him, and if he had anything to say to me, he could have said it, years ago. And anyway, now is not the right time.'

'Will there ever be a right time?'

'Possibly not.'

There was a steel edge to his voice. Bella could suddenly imagine what it'd be like to face him in a hostile negotiating environment.

'Maybe,' she said, softening her voice, 'he's as stubborn as you are. Perhaps he also thinks there'll never be a right time.' She pushed back from the table and stood up. 'If I speak to my father today, I'll be able to tell him about going sledging. And after today, you'll be able to remember very clearly the last time you flung yourself down a snowy hill. Unless you want to be boring and just watch while I hurtle down the slope at breakneck speed...'

He was quiet and he looked pale. 'So you think being aware of things that could go wrong is boring?' But then he nodded. 'Maybe it is. Yes. Perhaps I'll just watch you.'

Like the proverbial hawk.

CHAPTER ELEVEN

'JUST ONE MORE go and then I'll stop.'

'You said that three times ago. You must be getting cold.'

'Did I? I've lost count, but this time I really do mean it. And I'm not cold.' She clapped her hands together, a shower of snow flying off her gloves. 'Not *too* cold. Are you?'

Was he imagining the faint challenge in her tone?

She hadn't tried to persuade him to join her on the sledge and he'd stood at the bottom of the hill, hoping he'd be able to catch her if she fell, his heart pounding with anxiety every time she flew down the slope.

Her face glowed with the cold and the exertion of pulling the sledge up the hill. Their frozen breaths mingled in the crystal-clear air. It was a perfect day.

Despite worrying that she'd injure herself, he found he liked seeing Isabella so relaxed and obviously loving it. Since wrestling the sledge off its hook on the wall and dragging it outside, refusing his offer of help, she'd sparkled with excitement.

He'd decided not to argue with her about sledging, in spite of his misgivings. She'd have gone, anyway. She wasn't going to let him stop her.

She'd shed her aloofness and returned to being the woman he'd tried so hard to forget, out to have fun and ready to engage with him on his terms, because they'd been her terms, too.

And being together in the house, with the memory of the

night in which nothing had happened hanging between them, had begun to feel dangerously intimate. He thought they'd both needed to escape their thoughts and unspoken words.

He needed a distraction from wanting to feel the softness of her pale blue cashmere sweater again, and the shape of her shoulder blades beneath it. Her hair, which she'd woven into a thick braid, hung heavily over her shoulder and he longed to feel the weight of it in his hands.

'Well, if you don't stick to your word this time, I'll toss you over my shoulder and carry you back to the house.'

She bent to pick up the rope of the sledge and slanted a look up at him.

'Do you promise?' She straightened up, renewed tension suddenly crackling in the air between them. 'That's almost enough to make me...'

'Stop it, Isabella.' His voice sounded rough to his ears. 'I'm being serious.'

'Just *how* serious?' Her smile softened the challenge in her eyes.

'It's getting colder.' He changed the subject, trying to neutralise the potent chemistry which simmered between them.

'I don't feel cold. I've been towing the sledge up the hill. You should try it.'

'You refused my offer of help.'

'That's because you only get to pull the sledge up the hill if you're going to ride it down again.' She stamped snow off her boots. 'My rules.'

Ross glanced up at the sky, where a bank of cloud was encroaching from the north, obliterating the blue. 'Once the sun goes behind those clouds the temperature will plummet even further and your lips are already almost purple.'

Of all the damned stupid things to say. Isabella frowned and pressed her lips together, then nibbled at them.

'Are they really?'

Now he had to look at her mouth. His own lips didn't feel cold, at all. They burned with the desire to cover hers and restore warmth and colour to her mouth.

'Yes.' He nodded. 'Go on. One last go.'

She dug in her back pocket and pulled out a stick of gloss, smoothing it over her lips, leaving her mouth with a silky sheen, and the faint sweet summer scent of strawberries on the wintry air.

He needed this to be over, preferably now, while he still had a faint grip on reality, but he also wished he could make this moment last forever.

He watched her as she set off again, dragging the sledge behind her. She'd found winter boots which fitted her and a down jacket which was too big, the sleeves half hiding her gloved hands. The gleaming rope of her hair hung down her back from beneath her bobble hat, the end fastened with a red velvet scrunchie.

The sledge had carved tracks into the snow, cutting through the frozen crust to the softness below. He'd encouraged her to take roughly the same line each time. That way he knew there were no hidden dangers waiting to cause mayhem at the bottom.

To his surprise, she'd listened to his advice.

She waved at him when she reached the top, shouting something which he couldn't hear. By the time he realised what she was signalling to him, it was too late to do anything about it.

She'd taken a few steps to the side and chosen a new line. She probably thought it would be faster, and she was right.

The untouched snow was smooth and perfect. It looked soft and innocent, but Ross knew about the gullies and rocks which crossed and dotted the hillside. He'd calculated the route which Isabella should take, making sure it was the safest, as far as he could remember. The way she was going now, on this last run, would take her away from him, veering to the north. She'd reach the bottom near the track which ran up the glen, and he knew about the ditch which followed alongside it. It gurgled with clear mountain water in the summer, but now it was filled with snow.

This was going to be her last run, no more questions. If necessary, he'd put his threat into practice and carry her home. The stress was getting to him, putting him on edge.

He tried to jog along the bottom of the hill, but the snow was deep and soft and the best he could do was wade through it. The hill was steeper where she was coming down and he watched, helpless, as the sledge picked up speed, the hiss of the runners over the snow cutting through the silence of the sharp air. Then it veered to the right and disappeared behind a shoulder of the hill and the sound stopped.

'Isabella!' He tried to pick up his pace through the snow, scrambling over the brow of the hillock, his feet slipping. Reaching the top he stood up, scanning the landscape in front of him. The sledge lay, overturned, some distance away but Isabella had vanished.

Instant panic gripped him, panic, and the awful, slow-motion sense of having been here, done this, before. He could see the tracks of the sledge, and where they abruptly ended, and the disturbed patch of snow beyond. Was that where she was? Buried in that soft, pure blanket of white which held death at its heart? This couldn't happen again. Could it?

Yes, he thought, it absolutely could. He'd let his guard slip. He'd allowed himself to imagine being with her, again, even if it had only been for a few seconds, in bed this morning. Was this the price he was going to have to pay for that? And Isabella, too?

Immobile with shock, he called her name again, but all he heard was the echo of his own hoarse voice off the crags across the glen. Then he plunged into the snow, fighting his way to where she might be. He remembered digging in the drift which had buried George, with his bare hands, shouting for the help which had taken too long to come.

He should never have let George go first down that lethal slope that day. It should have been him.

And he should never have allowed Isabella to go sledging this morning. Was he crazy? He should have seen this coming. He *had* seen it coming but she'd been determined, and he hadn't argued. He'd wanted her to have some fun, to make up for upsetting her last evening. And anyway, she would have gone, whether or not he'd wanted her to.

The snow was waist-deep where he began to dig, scooping armfuls out of the gully, his breathing laboured, his arms refusing to move fast enough.

How soon would it be too late to save her?

There was a glimpse of bright red and his heart lurched, thinking it was blood, but then he remembered the red velvet scrunchie and his hands hit the fabric of the down jacket and he felt her move. He scooped away more snow and managed to get his hands under her armpits, pulling her upwards. The relief which surged through him when he heard her rasping breath was huge, almost making his knees collapse. He pulled her upright. Her hat was missing, and her hair was soaked. He brushed snow from her face and heard her take another wheezing breath, and then...was she *laughing*?

'Oh, Ross!' She clung to his shoulders, her eyes shining. 'That was the best fun. It felt like flying, even before the sledge went one way and I went the other. Then I really *did* fly.' She coughed. 'Sorry. I was winded when I hit the snow, but it's okay now. Thank you for digging me out, though I would have been fine once I got my breath back... What's wrong?'

Bella gripped Ross's arms. His face was as white as the surrounding snow and she could feel him shaking beneath her hands. 'Ross?' His eyes, darker than she'd ever seen them, with an expression she could not decipher, roamed over her as if seeing her for the first time and not believing what he saw.

His curled fingers bit into her upper arms, through the padding of the jacket, so firmly that it hurt.

'Ross,' she said again, more urgently. 'What's wrong? Let me go. You're hurting.' She shook his shoulders a little, but his muscles were rigid, his whole frame in the grip of a tremor.

Bella lifted a hand, gripped her mitten in her teeth and pulled it off, dropping it in the snow. Then she curved her palm around his jaw and smoothed her thumb across his cold cheek. One of his hands released her arm and came up to link with hers, clenching over her fingers.

'Isabella?' His voice cracked. 'Are you...?'

'Ross, I'm fine. It was nothing. Just snow.'

He shuddered as he filled his lungs. 'You were buried. I couldn't find you. I thought...'

Bella frowned, tipping her head back to look at him properly.

'It was only for a minute. What did you think, Ross? Tell me what's wrong and I'll try to fix it.'

'It...felt like much longer. And it can't be fixed.' He released her and pulled both his hands down over his face, shaking his head. 'I thought... I was afraid I'd lost you. Like I lost George.'

Bella stilled, searching her memory for a mention of George, and finding none.

Ross looked profoundly shocked. The exhilaration of the sledging and the rush of adrenaline from the fall forgotten, she knew she needed to get him indoors, to a warm, safe and familiar environment.

'It's okay, Ross. You haven't lost me. I'm fine.' She tried to keep her voice light and not allow her sudden anxiety to show. 'But I'm cold. You were right to say we should go in. Come on. I'll make us some tea.'

Bella left her boots and jacket in the boot room and filled the kettle. Then she went in search of Ross. She found him in the sitting room, his back to the fireplace where the log burner smouldered, giving out steady heat. His fingers were pressed into his temples, his eyes closed, but they opened when she walked in. He stared at her, following her movements as if he needed to map them in his mind.

She stopped in front of him. 'You should take your jacket off, Ross, and your boots.'

He nodded and tugged down the zipper of his jacket, tossing it onto the window seat and easing his feet out of his boots. He looked around the room, frowning, then fixed his gaze on the window.

'I'm sorry,' he said. 'I panicked.'

The desolation in his voice tore at her heart and Bella pressed her hands flat to his chest. The thud of his heart beneath them was quick and his breathing was shallow. Lines of anxiety which she hadn't noticed before were etched into his pale face.

'You're shocked, Ross. I'll bring you some sweet tea. Sit down.'

But his hands came up to fasten loosely around her wrists. 'Don't go just yet. I need to see you. To make sure…'

Bella curled her fingers into the dark green wool of his jumper and rested her forehead against his chest. He smelled of warm pine and cool leather and the need for comfort radiated off him like an ache.

'I'm here, Ross. I'm not going anywhere,' she murmured into his sweater. Then she lifted her head to look at him again. His eyes seemed to be fixed on something distant yet turned inwards on a memory which caused him terrible pain. 'Tell me, Ross.' She smoothed her hands over his shoulders. 'Who was George? How did you lose him?'

* * *

He'd never spoken about the accident. He'd answered the questions the emergency services had put to him. He'd written a detailed statement for the police. Officially, he'd been cleared of all blame. It had been a tragic accident. The avalanche risk that day had been rated 'low'. The skiing conditions had been perfect.

Who knew what had triggered the deadly slide of snow and rock? Sometimes it simply wasn't possible to pinpoint the cause. It was a case of wrong place, wrong time. It was the risk you took for the ultimate thrill, going off-piste.

Ross never doubted that he was to blame. He must have dislodged a rock, somewhere higher up. Perhaps the downdraft from the helicopter which had dropped them off, which he had booked, had set the snow in motion. Or perhaps it had been him, calling to George, saying he'd be following right behind. He remembered how his voice had echoed round the valley and how he couldn't make out the shouted reply. The sound of it had stayed in his head for four years, and he hadn't stopped trying to decipher the words.

He dropped his head and looked into Isabella's anxious grey eyes.

'George,' he said, 'was my wife.'

He saw the look of confusion cross her face. She frowned. 'Your *wife*…? Oh, Ross. I didn't… I never knew…' She shook her head, bewilderment transforming into shock.

'It's okay. I'm okay.' At least he could try to make it better for her. He didn't think it'd ever be better for him.

He'd never felt he deserved Georgina. She was beautiful and clever and loved by everyone, whereas at the age of seven he'd learned he didn't deserve any love at all. He'd been a nuisance to his parents and a hindrance to his grandparents, but at school he'd discovered that the way to earn praise and recognition was by trying to excel at everything. The rugged good looks and sharp intelligence, along with a lack of concern for his own safety he'd inherited from his parents had meant he'd succeeded, on the sports field and in the classroom. But he'd had to keep making himself do better, the fear of failure a relentless goad at his shoulder. He hadn't been good enough as a son or grandson, but he could be good enough at other things if he pushed himself to the limit, and beyond.

When he'd discovered the adrenaline rush which speed could deliver, he was hooked. Balanced on the knife-edge between winning and self-destruction, he felt enough. That feeling, longed for as a child, became his addiction as an adult.

Georgina and he had recognised that same drive to win in each other and the competition between them had spurred them on. He'd let her ski first that day because it was what she'd wanted. If he'd been more secure in their relationship he'd have taken better care of her.

George had been swept away and buried, and Ross had been powerless to save her.

In a flash his life had changed utterly.

Isabella took his hand and guided him down onto the sofa. She sat cross-legged near him, but not touching him, and waited, and when he began to speak he wasn't surprised to discover that she was a good listener.

'We met,' he said, eventually, 'at a graduation party, and that was it. We were an item. We had similar ideas and ambitions. We set up the company together, and when we'd made our first million we celebrated by getting married. George— Georgina—became the fourth member of our group.'

'You, Robert and Andrew?'

'Yes. She was as addicted to extreme sports as I was and probably more daring. She refused to be left behind.' He pushed his hands into his hair, rubbing his scalp. 'She even did the Cresta run, when the ban on women was lifted.'

'She sounds…amazing.'

'She was. But she also challenged me. That was what first attracted me to her. And she was demanding. That's why I let her go first that day, even though I won the toss.'

'Won the toss? What do you mean?'

'It was the last day of our annual "boys'" skiing holiday. A Sunday. George had flown out to join me for the week-end.' He gave a half-laugh. 'Like I said, she was never happy being left behind. Robert and Andrew had opted to stay on the black runs. We'd been heli-skiing earlier in the week and George wanted a go at that, so we went.' He gripped his hands together in an attempt to hide their tremor. 'My friends used to tease me about how she always got her way. We tossed a coin for who'd go first on the powder, and I won. So, it should have been me.'

Isabella raised a hand, but he shook his head. 'No. Please don't touch me.' He kept his eyes on his gripped hands. 'She wanted to go first. I saw her disappointment, and I knew she'd resent it if I didn't let her. She could kick off when things didn't go her way. And so I let her go. I'd already had my turn at being first on powder, and the price of not going first was a small one, in exchange for keeping George happy. As it turned out, the real price was…' He closed his eyes, spreading his hands, palms up.

It should have been the perfect last run of the holiday, and since that day he'd been suspicious if life began to feel good, because he knew it couldn't last. *Good* was an illusion, and a warning. It was the universe setting you up, beguiling you into thinking you could have it all, be happy, before knock-ing you down again.

So he began to wreck things which felt too good before they could wreck him, just to be safe.

He'd been deep in that wrecking phase when he'd met Isabella.

When he finished speaking there was no sense of relief or catharsis, just the feeling that he'd now burdened Isabella with a story which would mean nothing to her.

She shifted on the sofa. She was probably looking for a reason to get up, leave the room. He'd discovered how difficult people found it, being confronted with his pain and loss. They couldn't meet his eyes, and would avoid having to speak to him, if possible. Robert and Andrew had been his support, always there for him, but even they had not been able to stop him when he embarked on a path of self-destruction. It must have taken huge courage on Robert's part, to ask him to be his best man.

'Thanks for listening.' He glanced sideways at her. 'You may not believe this, but I've never actually told anybody how it happened.' Then he felt the shock of her touch as her hand came to rest on his shoulder. Her fingers slid down his arm until she could weave them through his. Her hand was warm and soft and the contact felt amazing, as if he'd been wandering alone for years but had suddenly found someone to connect with.

He took a deep breath. 'So you see, like I said, it can't be fixed.'

'No,' she said, her voice quiet. 'It can't be fixed. But you can.'

CHAPTER TWELVE

ROSS TURNED AND Isabella saw the shock in his eyes. He shook his head. 'I don't know what you mean. It's the same thing.'

'No, it's not. Not at all.' She smoothed the pad of her thumb over the back of his hand, 'What happened to George was an awful, tragic accident. There was nothing you could have done to prevent it.'

She felt the tug as he tried to remove his hand from hers, but she hung on to him.

'If I'd got to her more quickly, even though she had multiple injuries…'

'I can't imagine how awful it must have been for you, Ross, but even if you'd got to her in half the time, it doesn't sound as if it would have made any difference. Yet you still choose to believe it was your fault.'

'I do believe it was my fault. The burden of it sometimes feels unbearable and I turned to ways of coping I'm not proud of, now, but I had to find a way to numb myself.'

'Did you allow yourself to grieve? To lose the love of your life like that isn't something you can get over. You have to learn to live in a different way. Did you take time off work? Have counselling?'

He laughed. 'Are you kidding me? That would have been self-indulgent.'

'No, Ross. It would have been self-care, and consideration

for others. If you'd destroyed yourself the business would have collapsed and people who depend on you would have suffered.'

'Such clear-sighted logic was frankly beyond me at that time. I was barely able to function on any level. And the business...' He turned away from her, chewing his lip. 'I just wanted to be able to bury the guilt and escape from myself.'

'Is that what you were doing when we met at Hannah and Robert's wedding? Escaping from yourself?'

Ross nodded. 'The last wedding at which we'd all been together had been mine. Robert and Andrew had been my best man and groomsman. I could have turned his wedding into a complete disaster. But...'

'You met Robert at school?'

'Yes. And Andrew. I spent some of my holidays with them, up here in Scotland, near to where my father had grown up. It was idyllic, when I think about it. Too perfect. It was never going to last forever.'

'Do you think you blame yourself for the accident because you were allowed to blame yourself for your parents' divorce? For putting too much strain on their marriage? Do you blame yourself for everything that goes wrong?'

'I... No... Perhaps.'

'And the accident, and the loss you suffered, has reinforced your belief that you're not deserving of love. So now you don't dare to commit to a relationship because you're determined it's going to fail before it's even started. Why would you commit to anyone or form a relationship if you were certain you were going to lose them?'

'Probably the only commitment I ever made was to Georgina, and to setting up our company. We were hungry for success, and we were also lucky with our first few deals. We soon became sharp at spotting companies which would respond positively to a buy-out offer, and even better at splitting them up and selling them off.'

'And you're still doing that? You didn't think of changing your direction, after Georgina died? Having a fresh start? There must be so many opportunities for someone like you.'

He rolled his shoulders, tension still radiating off him. 'No. I felt I had to keep going. The company was the one real link I had to her. But after a few months I began to realise how hard I'd had to work at keeping her happy. Just acknowledging that piled on the guilt even more so I worked even harder.'

'And that's what you've done ever since?'

'Not entirely. I needed to work. I still do, all the time. I had to prove I could still succeed and that I didn't need anyone else after all, but in doing that I almost destroyed myself. I took to sabotaging things in my life that meant anything to me—friendships, relationships, anything that felt good.

'Robert and I had always promised we'd be each other's best men, but when he asked me, I was reluctant at first. He must have known there was a possibility I'd ruin his wedding day and the fact that he'd kept his promise, even though I was a ticking time bomb, made me want to go through with it. As the day approached, though, I couldn't imagine how I'd get through it, until...'

'Until?'

'Until I saw you.'

She felt as if the world stopped in that moment, but she forced herself to remain calm. She registered the stroke of Ross's thumb across her wrist. It sent small shocks of sensation up her arm to gather in her chest, her heart swelling with emotions which were hard to identify and harder to contain.

'I heard that by the time you saw me...' she paused to swallow, unable not to relive the shock of the moment his smouldering eyes had first connected with hers '...you'd already entertained the congregation with a mini stand-up routine which involved arriving late and mislaying the ring.'

He blew out a breath. 'I was good at that. I could be the life and soul of any party, even if I was drunk and high. By the time I saw you, walking up the aisle behind Hannah, radiating excitement and the expectation of a good time, I was a little drunk.' He leaned back, resting his head against the sofa cushion, rolling his face towards her. 'I was spellbound by you. You were enchanting.'

'That night...' Bella felt her voice falter, remembering the intensity of it and how her emotions had shocked and overwhelmed her, even though she'd only wanted one night of escapism. Her eyes stung. She'd had practice at keeping those emotions under control, and she needed to draw on that practice right now.

She blinked and looked away, but Ross had seen.

'Isabella, look at me.' He put an index finger under her chin and tilted her face towards him. 'Please don't cry. In a sea of regrets, the fear that I may have hurt you has been one of my most acute. I should have been more careful to explain to you what I was like.'

She sniffed and rubbed her eyes. 'It's okay. We agreed it would be one night, Ross. We both knew the score, even if we didn't know the reasons behind our needs. What I felt—what I *thought* was between us—was something I'd never felt before. The intensity of it swept me away, completely, and it's remembering that which brings tears now. Yes, I was sad and hurt when I realised that you'd walked away and weren't ever coming back, because I thought something so intense must be mutual.' She dug in a pocket for a tissue and blew her nose. 'I just wanted to be enough for you.'

She brushed the back of her hand across her eyes. 'I wish I could have been there for you, all those times when you've felt alone and unable to talk about what happened, when you needed someone to be with you to help you through the dark times.'

Ross circled her wrists with his fingers. Her grey eyes, soft with compassion, gazed into his and the strength of their connection shook him. Such honesty and empathy were a rare gift.

She leaned forward and cupped her hands around his face.

Somewhere in his brain, a message bleeped at him to stop this. He'd walked away from her before, to keep her safe from him, and he had to do that again.

'I can't do this, Isabella.'

Their lips hovered close to each other, almost touching. He was drowning in her eyes, her scent, and he was afraid he lacked the strength of will he needed to save them both.

'I know, but I want to. So much.'

'I'm not who you need. I'm damaged, and I care about you too much. I refuse to risk hurting you again.'

The tip of her tongue brushed across her bottom lip, leaving it gleaming. He longed to taste her again, to see if she was as sweet as he remembered, but he had to find the will to resist the temptation. Like an addiction, one taste would be all it would take to sweep away his reason and give into the need which roared through him. He'd never be able to get enough of her, and addiction led irrevocably to destruction.

She rose up, kneeling next to him, and moved her hands from his face, pushing her fingers into his hair, her thumbs massaging his temples where the headache, precipitated by the shock of losing her in the snow, had throbbed earlier. He tipped his head back and closed his eyes, giving in to the sweet pressure of her fingers on his scalp. His fists clenched at his sides as he forced himself to keep his hands away from her, his body threatening to outrun his iron control.

Control was everything to him. The thought of relinquishing it scared him. He couldn't afford to let go of it, to let fate loose on his life. He'd already lost so much, and if he gave into this need, which was thundering towards him like an express train, he'd lose the one thing he suddenly knew he cared about more than anything else.

'It's very difficult,' Isabella whispered, 'not to be able to have what we both want so much, but I know we can't. One night wasn't enough then and it wouldn't be now and I know you aren't free to give more than that.'

Ross released his fists and moved a hand up, tentatively resting it against her cheek. 'You're so beautiful, Isabella, and so kind and forgiving. Yet I can't let myself want you. I can't let myself hurt you again, so I have to let you go.'

'I know.'

She turned her face and pressed her lips to the centre of his palm. Their touch was silky and tender and his intake of breath was sharp. He buried his fingers in her hair and then slid his arms around her waist and pulled her against him, cradling her head on his chest.

'You smell so good. Roses and strawberries. Like summer in winter,' he murmured.

'And you. Warm pine and cool leather and something spicy…'

'I'm so sorry.'

'Don't be sorry, Ross. We had one perfect night. We must never regret it.'

'You have the loveliest soul of anyone I've ever known.'

Isabella eased herself upright. The feel of his jumper beneath her cheek was so comforting that she wanted to stay there, feeling his chest rise and fall and hearing the steady beat of his heart, but she knew she had to put space between them.

They were stuck here, trying to manage this intense attraction and it would be so easy, and so wrong, to give in to it. What would happen when they returned to their real lives? For all she knew, her father had decided to accept Ross's offer. She wanted nothing more than to be with him, now, but the consequences would be disastrous. If he was imposed on her as a partner, by her father's decision, she'd have to resign from Thompson's, sell her half of the company, and start a new life. It wouldn't be possible to work with him when every fibre of her being wanted him.

Everything she'd worked towards and achieved would be wasted; her parents' legacy would be destroyed. She couldn't risk allowing any of that to happen.

Ross scrubbed his hands over his face and stood up, looking down at her. Her eyes were wide.

'I'm sorry I scared you when I disappeared into the snow. If I'd known how you felt I would never have gone sledging.'

'But then I would never have told you about George.'

'Are you pleased you told me?'

He thought for a while, wondering how to express his feelings. He felt relaxed in a way he couldn't articulate. A weight he carried seemed to have shifted, making it a little easier to bear.

'Yes. I'm glad I told you. It's made me feel...somehow lighter.'

'I can't begin to know how you feel, but I'm glad you told me, if it helps, and just so you know, I love your jumper.'

'You do?'

'Mmm.'

'I'm pleased about that, because I don't have another one with me. And I think we could both do with tea, now.'

CHAPTER THIRTEEN

THE MORNING'S EXERCISE, dragging the sledge up the snowy slope behind the house, over and over, had tired Bella out. Her arms and legs ached and she felt emotionally drained. Her body felt primed, needing only a touch or a look from Ross to ignite it, but her mind had prevailed.

The sound of Ross's voice came from the kitchen, sounding as if he was on a business call. When silence returned, she swung her legs to the floor, headed for the door and cannoned into Ross, coming the other way.

'Hey.' He clasped her shoulders, steadying her. 'Are you okay?'

'Mmm.' She dipped her head. 'Are you?'

He dropped his hands. 'I'm fine.'

One corner of his mouth twitched, a smile ghosting across his features. 'Thank you for listening to me. It's not a good story.'

'No. But I think you could feel better, perhaps with help.'

Bella sensed his slight withdrawal. He turned back towards the kitchen.

'It's how I am, Isabella. That is not going to change. Now come and have tea and something to eat. You must be hungry, after all that fresh air and exercise this morning.'

'I thought I could smell food.'

'There's tomato soup and bread. Only tinned. Somehow,

I was clean out of fresh ingredients. And I've been down to the cellar and found a bottle of red.'

'My hair is messy.' She gathered it up in her hands at the back of her neck and let it fall again. 'Diving headfirst into a snowdrift and then falling asleep on the sofa is a sure route to a bad hair day.'

'It's beautifully messy.' He gave her a gentle nudge. 'I'll put a couple of logs in the burner and join you in a minute.'

Bella lifted the lid of the saucepan on the range, inhaling the peppery sweet scent of the soup. She was ravenous. As she stretched up to lift bowls off the dresser, her phone began to ring. Still not fully present, it took her a moment to locate it, in her bag on the worktop.

It had stopped by the time she'd dug it out and it was the third missed call from her father.

'Your phone rang a couple of times. Were you meant to be back at work today?'

'Mmm. I was originally going to stay until today, but then…'

'Then you found you were bridesmaid next to that best man again, and you decided to cut and run.'

'Got it in one. Look where that has landed me.'

'Yeah, look. Do you mind, or do you wish yourself some-where—anywhere—else? Be honest.'

She looked up at him. 'I'm always honest.'

'I know. It's one of the innumerable qualities about you which drive me crazy.'

'You'd rather I wasn't?'

'No, I wouldn't want you to be anything other than what you are. Last night, when I asked you if I'd hurt you, a part of me really wanted you to deny it, but then I knew you'd be lying to protect both of us, and although I'm sorry I made you cry, I'm glad you told me the truth. But you haven't explained why it is still necessary for you to work so hard, when Thompson's is doing so well.'

Bella pulled in a long breath, then walked across the room and sat down. 'You said you'd never told anyone about how the avalanche happened.' She folded her arms on the table, her shoulders lifted. 'Well, this is something I've never told anyone, either.' Ross placed a glass of wine in front of her and she ran her fingers down the delicate stem. 'I was eleven when I realised the seriousness of my mum's illness. Life should be simple, at that age, but it became complicated for me.' She lifted the glass and took a sip of wine. 'I began to make bargains with myself. If I did well in my school tests, or ate all my cabbage, she'd get better. Things like that. None of my deals worked, obviously, but before she died I promised her I'd always do my best, at everything.'

Ross pulled out a chair and sat opposite her, keeping his eyes on her. 'I'm sorry, Isabella. If this is difficult for you, please stop.'

She shook her head. 'It is difficult, but I need to tell you, so that you can try to understand. My life without my mother was frightening. Even though my father did his best, he was dealing with his own grief. I felt as if the world was out of control, that the order of it had been upset, and so I began to control the things I *could*. As long as I felt in control, I could negotiate life, and I succeeded in doing what I wanted to do, eventually, working my way up through the ranks at Thompson's, establishing a design team and taking on a management role, too. All the time, I told myself I was fulfilling the promise I'd made to my mother, to do my best. My long-term relationship broke up because I never had enough time to devote to my boyfriend. That hurt, but I kept going. I never stopped for long enough to examine my life and discover that by trying to control every aspect of it and make it the best, I'd lost control of the balance.'

She tipped her head back to study the ceiling. 'The argument I had with my father before Hannah and Robert's wedding was to do with changes I knew had to be made at the firm, and you know how I was feeling when we met.' She lowered her chin and met his eyes across the table. 'I lost control of my feelings that night, Ross. They were too powerful for me. And when I realised you didn't feel the same, I had to do something to numb them. I hadn't been good enough for you to break your habit of one-night stands, even though I'd thought I wanted that, too. We'd felt perfect together and perfectionism was already my habit, but I had to admit that I'd got things very wrong, with you. I had to guard against it ever happening again, and prove I was good enough at something else. Work was all I knew.' She raised her glass and took a gulp from it. 'That is why I could not deny that you had hurt me, or that you weren't part of the reason behind the changes in me.'

Bella's phone began to ring again.

'I'm sorry, Ross. I must take this. It's my father.'

He nodded, lifting the wine bottle and stretching across the table to top up her glass.

She swiped the screen to accept the call. 'Dad?'

'Bella. Are you all right? I've seen reports of the blizzards in Scotland. When do you think you'll get back?'

Holding the phone to her ear, she rose and paced across the room.

'I don't know, Dad.' She glanced across at Ross. His look was impassive. 'It was still snowing earlier and last night there was a hard frost. I don't know when we... I'll...get back. The weather has taken everyone by surprise.'

'But you're safe, and warm, I take it?'

'Yes, perfectly, thank you. I'll let you know as soon as I'm on my way.'

'It must be fun, being snowed in at a castle.'

She smiled, glancing across at Ross, who was ladling soup into bowls at the cooker. 'Mmm. How are you, Dad?'

'Oh, fine, darling. Just uncertain what to do about this offer. It still stands. I heard from them this afternoon. I know it's not what you want but I feel it'd be the right thing, in the future.'

'Just hold on until I get back, please Dad. Promise?'

'I will, if you insist.' She could hear the smile in his voice. 'We need to discuss it again.'

'We do. I'll talk to you soon. Love you. And love to Beryl.'

She ended the call and sighed. 'I should have called him this morning. Somehow, with the sledging and...everything else...it slipped my mind.'

Ross put a bowl of soup in front of her and pulled a loaf of French bread from the oven, slicing into its crisp crust and sliding a chunk of it onto her plate.

'Surely you're entitled to a couple of days away?' He put bread on his own plate. 'It is...or was...the weekend.'

'He was just checking that I'm okay.'

'Is *he* all right?' He sat down opposite her. 'This is a rather basic meal, but the wine is good.'

'It smells delicious, thank you. I don't need anything more.' She sipped the soup. 'He's okay. Just stressed about the firm and where to go with it. He said your offer still stands.'

'It does. I talked to my team a little while ago and asked them to communicate with him. You didn't tell him where you are.'

She paused, the spoon halfway to her mouth. 'No. I thought it best not to complicate things. It might make him anxious.'

'About you?'

'Yes. He knew my travel plans and where I'd be. Telling him it had all changed would just have made him worry. I hadn't spoken to him since...our meeting. If he knew I was snowed in with you, he'd have all kinds of extra worries.

He might think I'd do the deal with you without consulting him.' She smiled. 'It's the sort of thing he's inclined to do. He gets an idea in his head, and he wants it all done and dusted by lunchtime. Power-sharing is still an unfamiliar concept to him.'

'Who is Beryl?'

'Beryl? She's my father's housekeeper. I don't have to worry about him as much as I might because I know she's there.' She smiled. 'She came after my mother died and she's been with him ever since. She's…wonderful. She's been like a second mother to me, but she took care to keep my mother's memory alive for me. Thanks to Beryl, I was never a latchkey kid.' She swallowed another mouthful of soup and broke off a piece of her bread. 'She gave me lots of praise and said how proud my mother would have been of me. I loved hearing that. It made me feel that I was doing what my mother would have wanted.'

'Don't you think your mother would have wanted you to be happy, above all?'

She put down her spoon and pressed her lips together, thinking. 'Yes. And I think she'd be happy with what I've achieved, too. My father thinks selling his half of the firm to a younger, more dynamic partner would make me happy because it would allow me to expand my life, beyond work. But I don't know if I want that. It feels…scary.'

'Is that how you felt when you found I'd walked away from you? Scared?'

Bella felt a stillness settle over her, as if she'd stumbled across something which she was afraid to disturb.

'Yes, I think so,' she said, after a pause. 'It felt scary to have opened myself up to someone so completely. I had no defences against you.'

'You don't need to be afraid of me, Isabella.' He picked up a piece of bread and tore it in two. 'I will never risk hurting you again.'

She put her spoon down, her soup only half finished but her appetite for it gone.

'Ross, what I felt this afternoon… I was so close to taking that risk, even though it might have ripped me apart.'

Ross pushed back his chair and stood, raking a hand through his hair, gripping the back of his neck.

'What we feel is dangerous. This afternoon, I wanted to take you to bed to make love to you. I still do. The night we spent together was the only time I've felt a measure of peace, and I crave that again. But I care about you too much, Isabella. I can't take anything from you, because I can't give anything back, and you deserve to have everything.' He left the table and crossed the room, leaning his hands on the worktop and staring out into the dark. 'We're trapped here, in a bubble of unreality, and it would be easy…*so easy*…to lose ourselves in each other. But reality is waiting for us, just as soon as this,' he gestured towards the window and the snow, 'weather changes. And then what will happen? An affair that cannot last, because I cannot commit to a relationship. It would leave you hurt, and I can't… I *refuse*…to do that to you.' He dropped his head.

Bella pushed her chair away from the table and stood up. 'Yet we've come to know each other over the past two days, Ross. You've shared things with me you say you've never shared before, and I've done the same with you. We're irrevocably linked by that knowledge, even if we walk away, and having that closeness would make a business relationship even more difficult.'

He swung round, his face taut with stress. 'I wanted you to understand why I can't allow myself to need you. I'm not worthy of you, and I can't be trusted to keep you safe.' He gripped the countertop beside his hips, his knuckles white, and shook his head. 'You deserve to be happy and fulfilled, to have it all. One day you'll find someone who can give you that.'

Darkness was creeping up the glen and fog had rolled down from the mountains behind. Bella could not see if the snowfall had stopped. Ross's words had found their mark. The real world was only just beyond this bubble where they found themselves. Even though the atmosphere between them felt charged and angry, she felt it would be easier to stay here, with him, shut away from their lives where difficult decisions had to be made.

'No.' She pulled her braid over her shoulder and tugged on the end of it. 'I don't think I will.' She scooped up their bowls and carried them to the sink. 'If I had all of someone, I'd have to give all of me in return. I'll never have the courage to do that.'

CHAPTER FOURTEEN

Ross WONDERED IF Isabella was lying awake, too.

She'd carried her duvet and pillows up to the spare bedroom he'd shown her and closed the door. He'd heard the distant sound of the shower and when he'd come upstairs to his own bedroom, he'd paused on the landing, listening. There was no sound from beyond the door, and no strip of light shining beneath it.

That didn't mean she was asleep. He'd already stopped himself, numerous times, from climbing out of bed to go and check that she was okay.

He turned over, again, and punched his pillow, anger and frustration a coiled spring inside him.

This afternoon it had taken all his willpower to keep his feelings in check. He'd wanted Isabella, in his arms, in his bed, in his heart. They'd wanted each other.

It was so tempting to snatch one or two nights together, cut off from reality, and for the first time he acknowledged that it would damage him as well as Isabella, because the feelings he had for her were deepening. He'd never been able to forget her, unlike all the other hookups he'd had. The more he'd learned about her over these few days, the more he'd come to respect her work ethic and admire her resilience. Allowing their relationship to progress would ultimately hurt them both. He'd want to stay with her, but he could never commit to that, especially if they were to become business partners.

There was no place for personal feelings in business. There was always collateral damage, in every deal, but he didn't want it to be Isabella who suffered.

She made him feel things he wasn't allowed to feel. With her, he saw the possibility of a future where pain relaxed its grip on him, a future he didn't deserve. Like a stone in a shoe, or pressing on a splinter, he had to keep the pain alive because that's what kept him going. He'd seen what had happened when he'd dulled it with substance abuse. He'd gone into free fall. Meeting Isabella had forced him to see what he'd become, because in her arms he'd felt the bands of guilt and remorse loosen, giving him space to think. He'd saved the business, but he'd never recover from the loss of Georgina. He had nothing to offer anyone else.

If he allowed the feelings Isabella stirred in him to take hold, if he let go of the pain and guilt, he'd have nothing to hold onto. Who would catch him if he fell again?

He thought of the relationship she had with her father, the warmth in her voice when she spoke of Beryl. She understood loyalty and integrity, the importance of friendship and family values.

His friendship with Robert and Andrew upheld those qualities, but his family values were lacking, apart from his brief marriage to Georgina, and sometimes he'd wondered if even that would have lasted if she'd survived. They'd been a volatile couple, burning with the need for success and for each other. Would they have flown too close to the sun and burnt out? Would she have tired of him and ultimately rejected him, too?

Isabella was already in the kitchen when he went downstairs in the morning, and the aroma of coffee helped to clear his head. He stopped in the doorway, looking at her standing at the window holding a steaming mug, sunlight glinting off her hair.

'Good morning.'

She turned, giving him a tight smile. 'It's a beautiful morning. Perfect for—'

'Not for sledging,' he interrupted. 'Please.'

Her smile softened, a little. 'For a walk down to the loch. If you can dig us out of the front door.'

'After a cup of coffee and a slice of toast, I'll be ready for anything.'

She moved around him stiffly, the ease between them gone. The shape of their conversation of the previous day hung like a shadow, just out of sight.

It took him half an hour with a shovel to dig a path through the fresh snow from the house to the track. The loch, frozen over and covered in snow, lay beyond, down a slope. Isabella rubbed her upper arms with her gloved hands.

'Where's your hat?'

She put a hand up to her hair. 'I lost it in the snowdrift yesterday. Afterwards there didn't seem to be a right moment to hunt for it.'

'Wait here. I'll see if I can find it.'

Minutes later he jogged back towards her, holding the frozen hat aloft.

'Not exactly wearable, but it'll thaw.'

Isabella took it and shoved it into a pocket. 'Thank you.' Her dimple appeared as she smiled. 'I'd have been sorry to lose it.'

She strode off quickly along the shore, stopping to admire the view of the mountains, and the snow-laden pine trees, and to exclaim at the sight of a rare red squirrel darting across the path ahead of them.

They walked further, and their silence felt comfortable to Ross, the noise of their breathing and their boots crunching in the snow the only sounds in the crisp air.

'Did you sleep well?' Her question caught him off guard.

'No. Why do you ask?'

'You look tired. I didn't sleep, either.'

'What kept you awake?'

'Oh, worrying about the business. There was a message from my father which posed a few questions. That's nothing new.'

'Want to tell me about it?'

'About Thompson's?' She threw a sideways glance at him. 'Surely you know everything there is to know, if you're prepared to buy half of it.'

He nodded, burying his hands in the pockets of his jacket. 'I know all about the balance sheets, the numbers of employees, the factories, the suppliers, the clients.'

'So, like I said, everything.'

'But I don't know the personal side. What it means to you, and your father, and why. *Your* side.'

'Are you interested? I thought your business dealt in hard facts and figures. Not personal stories.'

'Yes, that's true.' Ross wondered if he'd regret asking the question. 'But I'd like to know what drives you. After all, you know what drives me.'

She was silent for a few more steps.

'Okay.' She puffed out a steamy breath. 'My family set up the firm more than a century ago. We source, spin, dye and weave wool into fine cloth for the garment industry, or yarn for the knitting industry. But you must know all this?'

'Mostly, but carry on.' He liked listening to her voice and hearing the note of enthusiasm which had already crept into her tone.

'Traditionally, we've supplied many well-known labels. Top names that have been around for a long time. Our wool has kept many famous names warm, from royalty downwards.'

'Is your blue jumper made from Thompson's wool?'

'Naturally. I always wear our products when I can.'

'It's beautiful. The colour is a perfect foil for your eyes, and the wool is as soft as…almost as soft as your skin.'

'Ross.' Her throat felt tight. 'I thought you wanted to know about Thompson's?'

'I do. But I'm admiring your product.' He glanced at her. 'Is that okay?'

'Yes. Thank you.' She adjusted her scarf, tugging it more closely around her neck. 'A few years ago, we had decisions to make. I'd had to work insanely hard to keep the business afloat. I knew we had to change, embrace more modern methods, experiment with new markets and products.'

'But?'

'But I couldn't make my father see that change was vital. I think he felt if he let go of the way things had always been done, in his lifetime, he'd be letting go of my mother. She'd been closely involved in the business, and he relied on her insight and vision, especially in staff matters.'

Ross bent to pick up a pine cone, tossing it from one hand to the other.

'What happened?'

'I almost burnt out. I was exhausted and stressed and…' She lifted her shoulders. 'I was trying to be everything, to everybody. I felt I needed to live up to my mother's legacy, connecting on a personal level with the staff. I'd promised her to always do my best, and to care for my dad. I didn't know… I couldn't judge…if my best was good enough, so I tried harder, striving for perfection in everything. It felt relentless, but Thompson's needed to change and I knew I'd have to instigate that, too.'

'Is that when we met?'

She stopped and turned to look at him, biting her lip.

'Yes. It was. I hadn't had a day off in months. I needed a…distraction…that weekend.'

'And you found me.'

'We found each other, Ross, and for a few hours I forgot everything except being with you, in the moment. It was afterwards, when I knew you'd meant what you said about one-night-only, that I realised life could be more beautiful, if it could be shared. Our night had felt perfect to me, but it wasn't enough to make you want to stay with me.' She turned back in the direction from which they'd come. The lodge, smoke curling from the chimney, was distant, at the foot of the hills. 'I'm getting cold. I'd like to go back now.'

'What did you do?'

'Do? I did the only thing I knew how. I worked harder so that I had no time or space to think, or regret. While I held onto the memory of *us*, I needed a new…*identity*. It felt like I'd…given mine to you and you'd taken it away with you. I could no longer recognise myself. I don't mean literally. When I looked in the mirror I still looked the same. I mean emotionally.'

'Isabella…'

'I didn't want to be Isabella anymore. I wanted to be a tough businesswoman my father could rely on and who didn't have to depend on anyone else. I succeeded, but at a personal cost which I'm only just beginning to count.'

Her words made him ache, somewhere in his chest. He wanted to take her hands and tell her she was amazing, but their chemistry was already off the scale and touching her risked causing it to ignite into something beyond their control.

He pulled in a breath, trying to order his thoughts. 'I also had a fresh start. After us.'

Surprise sparked in her eyes, but she blinked, and it was gone.

'You did?' The scepticism which coloured her voice didn't surprise him, but it hurt. Whatever their relationship might become, he wanted to be the person she always believed… the person *in whom* she could always believe.

'You remember what I was like.'

She gave a low laugh. 'Ross, doesn't everyone? It's impossible not to remember, especially given the change in you now.'

'I suppose I'll always be best remembered as the hell-raiser. I'm sure that version of me was more fun, for other people.'

'Not for you.'

'Not for me, no. Because I was lost. I was desperate to find something to hang on to, to save myself from drowning.'

'And then we happened.'

'You happened, Isabella. I saw you at Hannah and Robert's wedding and I wanted you. You looked so…perfect. Wholesome, delighted with your role as bridesmaid, fresh…eager to have some fun. I wanted a part of you to be mine, because I had this crazy notion that you could fill the void that had been at my core, most of my life, and light up the darkness.'

'You had me, Ross.' Her voice was barely above a whisper. 'All of me.'

'I know. And when I realised that I had what I wanted, I was terrified.'

Two faint lines between her brows deepened. 'I don't understand why.'

'I told myself I was afraid of hurting you. My family had disintegrated, for which I blamed myself, and I lost Georgina, whom I loved so deeply. I couldn't accept that her death was just a freak accident. I had to find someone to blame, and that was myself. In the grip of grief, I decided that my love was somehow tainted. Whoever I gave it to would leave me or be hurt, or worse.' He rubbed his eyes. 'So when I…felt what I felt for you, that night, I had to stop it. I had to keep you safe from me.'

'Ross.' She stretched out a hand and touched his forearm. 'Those losses were not your fault.'

He shifted sideways a little, beyond her reach.

'The idea was so deeply embedded in my mind, I couldn't shift it. I didn't want to continue running the business without Georgina. I couldn't bear to deal with the projects which had sprung from her initiative. The idea of profiting from them felt wrong. When I met you, the business was teetering on the edge of failure.'

The compassion he admired so much was back in her eyes.

'In my other life I was good at deals, and the peace and space I found with you enabled me to think clearly and I made a deal with myself. I vowed not to see you again, so that I wouldn't hurt you, and I wanted to honour Georgina's life and everything she'd achieved...*we'd* achieved together. So I promised myself I'd turn things around.'

'And that's what you did.' She nodded and he saw the depth of understanding which settled on her face, in her eyes.

'Yeah. It is.'

'It must have been tough.'

'It was more than tough. Sometimes it felt impossible and unreachable. Sometimes I felt desperate, but I'd made a promise to myself, and I had to keep it.'

They walked on in silence. Ross moved closer to her and her shoulder bumped his upper arm.

'And yet,' she said, after a while, 'discovering I'm a partner in Thompson's didn't bother you. You knew you'd see me at that meeting.'

He nodded. 'It bothered me, but it intrigued me more. Your insistence that you only needed one night with me didn't fit. And I made the ultimate business error. I let my heart rule my head. I wanted to see you again.'

'I was thrown off balance by the idea of seeing you, when

my father revealed the identity of the prospective buyer. But you were so different.'

He laughed. 'You were, too. How did you get around your father's opposition to the changes you wanted to make to Thompson's? He must have already struggled with the new version of you.'

'I presented him with an ultimatum: change or I'd have to rethink my position. Luckily, he decided change was the better option.'

'And now?'

'Now, I continue to try to keep the personal touch in the business alive. I try to know everyone's name, and the names of their children. Their dog, if necessary. I tour the factories frequently so that I notice any changes which might have happened. I build personal relationships with clients and suppliers. I...'

'But you have no time for a personal life.'

Bella stopped and turned away from him, looking out across the frozen surface of the loch.

'The one personal relationship I haven't been so good at has been the one with my father, and Beryl. There hasn't been time, and he's pulled back. Sometimes I don't speak to him for days, but I always think tomorrow will be quieter.' She shrugged. 'It rarely is.'

'And now he's considering selling his half of the business. No wonder you aren't happy about it.'

She hissed out a frustrated breath. 'I've shown him I can do it. I've run the company practically on my own for two years. He could retire but still provide backup when necessary. I don't...*need* anyone else.' She turned, looking at him over her shoulder, her chin high. 'Especially if that person is you. How could it possibly work, with...*this*?' Her hands moved, making a gesture which encompassed the space between them, one of them landing on her heart. 'Surely you can see that?'

A note of desperation threaded through her words and Ross frowned. Thompson's meant everything to her. It provided a link to her mother and a happier time of her life and she'd almost burned herself out, turning it into the profitable company it was today. There was an irony to the fact that her work and vision had made it an attractive investment proposition to people like him. It was his intention to try to gain a controlling stake in the company, then split it, sell off profitable parts, but for the first time he wondered if there might be another way: a way that would help Isabella, rather than break her.

He approached business deals with clinical detachment, with little thought for the human consequences, but this was different. He was aware how unprofessional it was to mix business and personal lives and he'd have to try to think outside the usual box.

'Perhaps your father is anxious about the toll this is all taking on you, Isabella. Have you thought of that?'

'Then why would he pull back? Even retire? He's always said he'd never retire.'

'Maybe he thinks it's the only way to help you get some sort of life back. If you had a partner, who wasn't intent on breaking up the business, you'd be freed up to do other things.'

She pushed her hair off her forehead, increasing her pace. 'Like what? Working at Thompson's is all I know. I don't do anything else.'

'That,' said Ross evenly, 'is exactly what I'm getting at. You could take up a sport.'

She laughed. 'Whatever makes you think that? I walk and run a lot already. It's good thinking time. I often come up with a work solution when I'm out running on the heath.'

'Okay. Something unrelated to work or thinking about it.' He took a breath. 'You could date.' He found those words difficult to say.

Isabella stopped and kicked at the snow with the toe of her boot. 'No,' she said. 'I couldn't. I definitely couldn't.'

Back at the lodge, Bella made cheese sandwiches and two mugs of hot chocolate. 'There's not much left.' She peered into the jar of drinking chocolate. 'Enough for two more. After that it'll be coffee or tea, without milk.'

They settled on the sofa by the fire and Bella wriggled her toes in the warmth.

'Was it always a foregone conclusion that you'd join the family firm?' Ross stretched out his legs and crossed his ankles.

'No, it was my decision entirely. Thanks to my mother, the company is quite unique in the way it's run, with an emphasis on staff care and family values, and I wanted to continue that. I studied textile design at art school and after working for a few years in the design and product development department, I did a management degree.

'But I started at the bottom, and I've worked my way up. I know and understand every stage of the process, and I love it. *Really* love it, even though it's been a struggle for the past few years.' She drained the last of the chocolate from the mug and put it down on the tiled hearth. There was real passion in her voice. 'Dad was nervous about expanding into overseas markets, but it's been a success. He also didn't like the idea of using Alpaca wool alongside our more traditional products, but it's been a huge hit. It's soft, light and very warm.'

'So you've won some of your battles. How do you rate your chances in this next one?'

Bella folded her arms. 'I don't know. He seems very determined.'

'Would it help,' Ross asked, after a silence, 'if I said I'd keep the company up and running, as it is now? You could have a partner to take some of the pressure. From what I understand, even though you legally own half of it, your father has always kept a controlling vote on major decisions? I could change that. Make it equal.'

Bella turned her head, but he kept his gaze away from hers, staring out of the window, tapping the side of his mug.

'Why would you do that? You're in this to make a profit, aren't you?'

'The bottom line is not always the most important thing. And I'd be doing it to help you.'

'That would be a generous gesture. But we'd still have to work together. And we can't.'

'What if I took a much less hands-on role? Put in a partner who'd report to me, but who worked with you?'

She shook her head. 'You'd still be there.'

'And that's not what you want.'

She stood up suddenly, picked up her mug and swung round to face him.

'No, it's not. I don't need help.' Her voice shook. 'I've proved I can do this on my own and I need to keep on proving it. Otherwise I'll have failed and I can't do that. I have to keep succeeding, doing better, not handing over responsibility to someone else…to *you*. Especially not to you. I've already failed with you.'

'Isabella, listen…'

'No.'

'Please.' Her eyes snapped to his. 'You haven't failed with me. My reasons for leaving you were *mine*. I was trying to protect you. It wasn't as though you didn't match up to some mythical standard you seem to think I might have set. But that's what you're doing. You're constantly measuring yourself against perfection and finding yourself wanting. No one's perfect. No life is perfect. All you're doing is setting

yourself up to fail, over and over again, and you deserve so much more than that.'

She stepped back and sat on the edge of the sofa. 'No.' Her voice was low. 'I don't. Not if I'm not good enough.'

'Don't you see, Isabella, it's not that you weren't good enough for me. You were too good. I was intent on sabotaging any relationship that felt right, or too good, because I believed I could never make it last.'

'You don't do relationships.'

'Precisely.' He pushed a hand through his hair, frustration tugging at him. 'How can I help you to feel better?'

'Stop trying to make it better,' she almost shouted. 'It can't be better. I may have been too good for you, but I wasn't good enough for *me*, and I hate that. I failed *myself*.' She walked out of the room, but he followed her into the kitchen. She stood at the window and dropped her head, her shoulders hunched. When she spoke again her voice was quiet. 'I was twelve when my mother died, but something she said in the last days of her life has stayed with me.'

'Can you tell me what it was?'

'"*Seize every opportunity that comes your way. You can always change your mind if you decide it's not for you, but if you hesitate, that chance may never come again. And when you find love...*"' Bella swallowed, her voice husky '"*...hold on to it with all your might and never let it go.*" I promised her I would. I've tried to take opportunities. Spending one night with you was a daring one, out of my comfort zone. I wasn't looking for love or commitment, just a break from the pressure I was under at the time, and afterwards, when what I felt for you didn't fade away, I didn't try to find you because we'd agreed on one night only. I was afraid you'd reject me. I wondered if you'd even *remember* me. But I thought—I *felt*—there was something special between us...

and I'm very much afraid that it's never going to… I'll have let it go and I'll never…find it again.'

Ross stepped up behind her and put his hands on her shoulders, half expecting her to flinch, but she leaned back against him as if she needed his support.

'I know,' he said quietly. 'I felt it, too, and it scares me because it feels beyond my control. I couldn't forget you, but I couldn't look for you, either, because I'm not what you need. You deserve everything good that life has to offer.'

She shook her head. 'I don't feel like I do. I promised to do my best, but my best wasn't good enough.'

His eyes connected with hers in the reflection in the window and the look of tenderness in their depths made her lungs squeeze and her heart thump.

'I'm sorry.' His warm breath whispered against her hair. 'It's I who has never been good enough. Not you.'

Isabella felt his hands slide down her arms and loop around her. 'My weather app shows a warmer front coming in from the west, overnight.'

She stilled, her stomach tumbling into free fall, because she knew what that meant.

'The snow will melt,' she whispered. 'Tomorrow, we'll be able to leave.'

He nodded, his cheek brushing against the side of her head. 'This will be over. You'll be able to get away.'

'I should be pleased. But I'll be…empty. You'll be relieved.' In the reflection, she watched him shake his head and his arms loosen. His hands spread across her ribcage and his thumbs drifted upwards, settling just beneath the swell of her breasts.

'No. I won't be.'

'Why not?' Her eyelids felt weighted.

With the lightest pressure, he turned her in his arms and eased her backwards until her hips connected with the edge of the sink. She moved, restless, but he settled his hands on her waist, gently holding her still. She reached up to cup his face between her hands as he pinned her in place.

'We shouldn't be doing this, Isabella.' His voice whispered across her forehead. 'I can't give you what you need.'

'I know we shouldn't. I can't be what you want,' she murmured against his jumper. She slid her hands around the back of his neck, burying her fingers in his thick hair. 'Do you want to stop?'

He bent his head and pressed his forehead to hers and their eyes locked. 'No. Do you?'

'I should, but I don't. I want to take this chance to be with you because I know I'll regret it if I don't, whatever happens after tomorrow.'

'Are you sure, Isabella?' His voice was rough as he resisted her pull. 'Are you sure this is what you want? I'm so afraid of hurting you.'

'Don't be.'

He brushed his mouth over hers, nibbling at her lower lip and making her gasp. 'We can still stop.'

She shivered as his fingertips probed beneath her sweater and traced a path across her skin, scattering a trail of burning imprints wherever he touched her. 'I don't think I can...' Heat spiralled through her body, leaving no room for thought, just an intense, white-hot need.

He wrapped an arm around her shoulders and put the other behind her knees, lifting her up against his chest. 'Tomorrow we'll have to face reality, but we can have tonight.'

Soft grey light softened the dark. Isabella lay curled into his side, one arm across his waist. The bedclothes were a pale tangle of linen and a cashmere throw, and one of her long legs lay, uncovered, across the bed.

He gripped the edge of the duvet and eased it up over them,

letting it fall lightly around her shoulders. She stirred, rubbing her cheek against the side of his chest before settling again, her breathing falling back into a deep, steady rhythm.

They had hardly slept. Exploring every inch of her, finding what would elicit her sighs of delight and moans of pleasure and then discovering what an instinctive and generous lover she was, as she did the same for him, had been exquisite, tender and, at times, wild.

It had been better—infinitely better—than before. His mind was clear, and there was none of the frantic urgency of their previous encounter, when he'd been desperate with the need to find the oblivion he'd craved, and achieved, for a few short hours.

Then he'd woken, the morning well advanced, and the need to escape had been all-consuming. Lying beside her, he'd been the happiest he'd been since... He wasn't going there. He didn't dare to be happy. She was beautiful, fun, kind and good. Too good for him. *Too good.*

He'd had to stop it or he'd be tempted to make promises he knew he could never keep. His love was tainted. It had driven his parents apart and Georgina...

What the hell have I done? he thought now, looking down at her sleeping form.

Because the realisation, which hit him in the chest with the force of a small meteorite, was that he *needed* her and he could never let himself have her, again.

He couldn't imagine a scenario in which he would be able to watch her walk away from him. Each time he tried, she turned, in his imagination, and came back to him, her grey eyes alight with compassion, her body, when he pulled her into his arms, warm and yielding.

Nothing good ever lasted. He knew that for a fact, and he was never, ever going to take a chance on it, especially not if Isabella was the collateral damage.

To give into this would be selfish in the extreme. He'd finish up destroying them both. He'd screwed up his chance with her the first time, and second chances were the stuff of fairy stories. They just didn't happen, in the real, brutal world.

Why would a woman like Isabella ever want to be with someone like him? She was kind and compassionate, listening to him and trying to help him, insisting that he wasn't to blame for the losses he'd experienced in his life, when he knew he was.

It was lighter now. He hadn't heard the central heating boiler come on, which was strange because he could hear the ticking of the radiators and the pipes, as they warmed up.

Then he realised it wasn't the heating he could hear. It was the steady drip, drip, drip of the ice melting on the roof and dripping onto the window ledge, like a clock, measuring out the minutes he had left with her.

Isabella stirred against him, splaying her fingers across the taut skin of his abdomen. He sucked in a quick breath, knowing he should leave the bed, now, before this went any further. He shifted his position, ready to separate himself from her, but her eyes fluttered open and she turned her head and pressed her mouth to the side of his chest, her hand slipping lower, her fingers scraping over his skin.

'Isabella.' His voice felt rough. 'We should get up. The snow is melting. We can leave.'

She pushed herself up on one elbow, her hair falling across her face and onto his chest, dropping a kiss onto his mouth. He brushed the tangled mass back from her forehead and held it behind her head, drawing her mouth down to his again, for one last kiss.

'I don't want to leave,' she murmured, 'not just yet. It's barely light.'

Ross felt his resolve weakening, his control shredding. What difference could one more hour make?

She slid a leg across his thighs, bending her knee and moving over him.

One more hour with her, before he'd have to watch her walk away.

One more chance to lose himself in that blissful oblivion, where his body told him he belonged. But his mind knew better.

When he next woke, the space beside him was empty. He pushed himself upright, looking around the dim room. Her clothes, which they'd left strewn across the floor, were gone. He walked to the door and smelled coffee.

Isabella sat curled in the corner of the sofa, her hands wrapped around a mug. She'd braided her hair. His fingers flexed with the desire to undo it and run his fingers through it, making it look wild again.

She turned her face towards him as he stopped in the doorway.

'Hey.'

She nodded. 'Hello.' Her eyes dropped. 'Perhaps you should get dressed. We'll need to get going.'

He'd pulled on his jeans but nothing else, in his hurry to find her, and he saw her eyes warm as they rested on his chest, then she turned away.

'Isabella? Are you okay? I thought…' He wanted to say he'd thought they could share a shower, but he felt the distance she was putting between them and stopped.

'I'm fine.' She sounded cool. Distant and unreachable, barely recognisable from a few hours ago. He wanted to turn back the clock to the dark hours of the night and relive them.

They got ready to go in near silence, Isabella moving stiffly around him, avoiding his touch.

Once in the car, he turned to her. 'I can take you to Edinburgh. Come on the flight to London with me.'

But she shook her head. 'I'll go to the local station, Ross. Thank you, but I think that's best.'

Ross pulled up the train information on his phone. 'The trains are running on a reduced schedule, but you should be in time to catch one. If you're sure I can't change your mind.'

'I'm sure.'

He checked the rearview mirror as he pulled away from the house and onto the track. The image of Innes Lodge was perfectly framed, against a backdrop of snowy peaks and a pale blue sky. In his mind he took a snapshot of it. In that picture was encapsulated everything that had made the past three days so sweet. And so bitter. He loved the Highlands, and he loved Innes Lodge. It was the place where he found a measure of contentment and peace but now, he wondered when he'd ever be able to come here again.

If he returned, would he be able to revisit his memories of Isabella with detachment, recalling the sweetness, or would the bitterness of loss and regret overwhelm him?

He glanced across at her. Her expression was detached, and she was quiet. He wondered if she would turn her head and look in the wing mirror for one last glimpse of the lodge, but as the image of the house behind them grew smaller, his hope shrank with it.

They pulled into the small station car park with time to spare. Isabella pulled her hands from her coat pockets and turned towards him.

'Ross.' Her eyes roamed over his face. 'I…'

'Please, Isabella, let's see each other again.' The words had been beating in his brain throughout the journey, but he'd been determined not to say them out loud.

She shook her head. 'That would be a really bad idea.'

He gripped the steering wheel, his knuckles whitening. 'There must be a way we can make it work. I'll… I'm going to contact your father as soon as I get back to London and withdraw my offer for Thompson's. I know it's not what you want.'

'That won't change my mind.'

'Then please, *please* tell me what will.' He hit the flat of his hand on the steering wheel, trying to quell the panic stirring in his chest.

She was quiet for so long that he thought she wasn't going to speak to him again, but then she sighed out a breath and half turned in her seat, towards him.

'I have a few specific memories of the time my mother died, but the overall feeling was one of vulnerability.' She leaned her head back against the window, twisting her fingers together. 'Even though my father was so caring, the feeling of insecurity is impossible to describe. The fixed point, around which everything in my life revolved, had vanished and there was nothing holding me steady. I felt exposed, stripped of protection, as if my nerve endings had all developed extra sensitivity and my skin hurt at the slightest touch. I wanted to make myself smaller, to take up less space.'

'Do you still feel like that?'

'With help from my father, and Beryl, and remembering that I had to be brave, I learned to adjust. I was able to achieve my ambitions and lead the life I wanted, but then I met you. I'd never opened myself completely to anyone, before. I'd always held something back, to keep my heart safe, but with you, all those restraints crumbled. I was bereft of the self I knew and the vulnerability flooded back. I had to reinvent myself into someone who wouldn't fail again.'

'I'm so sorry. I wish…'

She held up a hand. 'This morning, I felt…amazing. I thought of what we shared last night—your tenderness, your strength, your willingness to let go completely with me, and how I had laid myself completely open to you, again, and suddenly I didn't feel amazing anymore. That feeling of spinning out of control with nowhere safe to land, swamped me. Being with you is exquisite and beautiful, but the price is too high. I'm not brave enough to risk exposing myself to that vulnerability, knowing you can't be there for me.' She put her hand on the door handle.

Ross felt a fist around his heart, squeezing until he struggled to breathe. He shook his head.

'Let me try to care for you. I'll do anything…'

'In that case, there is something.'

'What?'

'Until you learn to forgive yourself, and to love yourself a little, your heart will never be open to accepting love from someone else. You deserve happiness, Ross. Please, give yourself permission to find it.'

She pushed the door open and swung her legs out of the car, sliding to the ground. Ross pulled her bag from the back of the Defender and carried it onto the platform as the track began to hiss with the approach of the train.

She stretched up and brushed her lips across his cold cheek. Then he lifted her bag up the steps and into the carriage and ducked his head to watch as she made her way to a seat, but as the train pulled out of the station and began to gather speed, she didn't turn her head to seek him out.

CHAPTER FIFTEEN

ROSS SLUICED THE rain from his face and shoved a hand through his hair, yanking open the door of the Defender.

They'd only been together for three days but parting from her felt like losing a part of himself. The memories of the previous afternoon and night were vivid. She'd started tugging his sweater over his head before they'd reached the top of the stairs, burying her face in his chest, her fingernails digging into his arms.

He rubbed his fingers across his biceps. He had the marks to prove it.

Their desire had been so hot, so desperate, they'd barely made it into the bedroom, never mind the bed.

The thought of not seeing her again aroused the beginnings of panic, and that was dangerous. There'd been a flash of surprise in her eyes when he'd said he was going to withdraw his offer for Thompson's, but even that hadn't changed her mind. Where in hell had the skewed logic come from that buying into Thompson's was a good idea?

If he wanted her to be okay, he had to cancel the deal, now.

He parked in his reserved space at the airport and walked away. When he pushed through the door of the coffee shop, he almost knocked a tray from a waiter's hands.

'Sorry. I'm sorry.' There was a vacant table in the corner by the window and he threaded his way towards it. Dumping his damp coat and cabin bag on the second chair, he sat down and buried his face in his hands.

How, in the name of anything, had he got himself into this unholy mess?

'Sir…?'

He looked up at the young man holding a menu, but he waved it away.

'Espresso, please. Double shot.'

He knew the caffeine hit would make his hands shake, but they were shaking already, so what the hell. He needed the intensity of the black, powerful coffee to pull his focus back to reality, and think clearly. He needed to concentrate on the dark, bitter liquid tracking heat down to his stomach to take away the memory of her words, and the look on her face as she'd turned away from him and boarded the train.

When the coffee arrived, he swallowed a mouthful, pleased when it burned his mouth, and all the way down, too. It was the distraction he needed. When he'd drained the small cup he put his forearms on the table and peered through the misted-up window, watching the rain patter against the glass, hearing the muted roar of a jet as it sped down the runway. He felt the effects of the caffeine begin to take hold, seeping through his veins, making his heart thump and sharpening his awareness.

He was not in the habit of giving in to fear. He faced it down and defeated it. But this little twist of unease which flickered in his gut was different. It was elusive and he couldn't pin it down. He closed his eyes.

Rejection. His thoughts stopped, as his mind found what he'd been looking for. Since the rejections of his childhood, he'd made sure nothing like that would ever happen to him again. He'd loved Georgina, and her death had been a different kind of loss, as if his love hadn't been strong enough to keep her safe.

Isabella had rejected him, because he made her feel vulnerable. Fear stopped him from being the person she needed to care for her. He'd told himself to stay away from her to avoid hurting her, but all the time he'd been afraid of being hurt, himself.

On Thursday morning, as she stepped off the bus and walked to the offices in Bloomsbury, Bella acknowledged that not even the bright Christmas lights could lift her mood.

London in December was grim, despite the hype around Christmas. Grey skies, grey streets and the stark outlines of bare trees in the parks were a miserable contrast to the towering beauty of the Highlands and the dazzling landscapes of snow and ice the blizzard had delivered.

She'd worn her scarlet wool coat in a fruitless attempt to cheer herself up. She still felt connected to Ross, to Innes Lodge, and the intensity of their time together, but she had to believe it would lessen.

Climbing the steps to the glossy blue door which faced out over the square, she shook the drops from her umbrella.

Jess, at her desk outside Bella's office, looked up.

'Hi, Bella. Welcome back. How was the wedding?'

'Good morning, Jess. The wedding feels like a long time ago now, with the extreme weather that came after it. But it went very well, thanks. I'm sorry I wasn't back on Monday.'

Jess nodded towards the closed door of her office. 'Your father is here to see you.'

Bella frowned. 'He usually plays golf on Thursdays. Perhaps the weather… Did he mention what it's about?' She'd learned to treat any deviation from her father's normal routine as potentially suspect.

'No, but he's very cheerful. Full of the joys of spring, even though it's only December.'

'Mmm. Thanks for the warning. Hold my calls.'

Bella found her father standing at the window of her office, looking out over the wet square, his hands clasped behind his back.

'Dad?'

He turned. 'Bella. Did you have an enjoyable time away, despite the weather?'

She dumped her work backpack on her desk. Then she hung her coat on the stand near the door, along with the umbrella, giving herself time to prepare for whatever was coming next.

'Yes, thank you. How has your week been?'

He crossed the room and kissed her on the cheek. 'May I?' He gestured towards the chair in front of her desk.

'Of course. Is everything all right?'

'Yes, yes. Fine. I've had a good week, thank you. But there is something I need to tell you.' He steepled his fingers under his chin and looked at a point somewhere above Bella's head.

The faint alarm bell ringing in her head notched up the volume. He was finding this talk awkward. Had he gone ahead and accepted Ross's offer?

'Is this to do with the meeting we had last week?' She rested her elbows on her desk.

He dropped his hands and smoothed a palm over the knee of his fine woollen trousers. 'Yes,' he said, and nodded, 'it's related.'

Bella sat back in her chair, clasping her hands in her lap and braced herself.

'I… I don't really know how to say this, Bella.'

'I suggest you just spit it out, Dad, whatever it is. It doesn't matter how you say it.'

'Ah. Well, you see, there's someone…'

Bella sighed inwardly. It seemed they were going to go over all this again.

'Yes, Ross Maclean, who wants to buy you out.'

'No. Not someone who wants to buy me out. Someone I'm going to marry.'

'Marry?' She felt as if she'd been hit, hard, in the chest, and all the air had left her lungs. She tried to fill them again, but her normal physical reflexes seemed to have shut down. Words formed in her brain, but her mouth would not articulate them.

'I'm sorry, Bella. This is obviously a surprise for you. There was no other way to put it.'

Bella thought she was probably doing a good impression of a goldfish. She tried again to breathe and heard herself gasp but finally, *finally*, the power of speech seemed to drift to within her grasp again.

'Dad,' she said at last. 'I think *surprise* hardly cuts it. Last week we discussed a possible buy-out, but you promised not to rush things.' She took a huge breath. 'The same principle applies to other aspects of life. You need to think things through carefully. If this is someone you've just met...'

All sorts of possibilities raced through her mind. How had he met someone? At the golf club? Playing bridge? Or, God forbid, *online*? Was he being scammed?

His face split in a smile, a look of happiness so profound settling on his features that Bella felt her heart squeeze, despite her shock.

'Oh, no, it's not someone I've just met. I've known her for a very long time. It's Beryl.'

'What?' She gripped the arms of her chair. *'Our* Beryl? How on earth has this happened, Dad? After all these years...'

'I don't know another Beryl.' He smiled. 'Although she is ten years younger than I am, she raised the question of her own retirement a few months ago. When we discussed it, we both realised that the idea of no longer being near each other really wasn't something we wanted to contemplate. It's taken all the years you mention for us to slowly grow close.' He re-

moved his glasses and pulled his ubiquitous silk square from
the top pocket of his jacket and began to polish the lenses.
'And we decided, six weeks ago, to get married.'

Thinking back, Bella calculated that 'a few months ago'
would have been about the time her father had first raised the
possibility of perhaps selling his half of the business and retiring. She wished she'd listened to him with more attention,
but she'd dismissed the notion as just another of his ideas.
He'd always had an endless fund of them. Now, she began
to understand, a little.

'This is the most wonderful news, Dad.' She stood,
rounded the desk and bent to kiss him on the cheek. 'I'm so,
so happy for both of you. It's a big step.'

'Not when you're my age. I loved your mother dearly, and
that won't stop when I marry Beryl. She'll always be in my
heart, as I know she is in yours. But finding someone who
wants to share their retirement with me, who knows me and
loves me, as I know and love her, is a thing too precious to
deny. We wanted to tell you the news together. We made two
dates for you to come to supper, if you remember, but you
cancelled both. And then I decided I'd tell you after the meeting last week, but…well, it didn't feel like the right time.'

Bella pressed the heels of her hands into her eyes. She
knew she'd smudge her eye make-up, but that was a frivo-
lous concern in the face of this momentous announcement.
Shame and regret at how angry she'd been with him hollowed
her stomach. He'd been preparing to share this amazing news
with her and she'd spoiled the occasion, more than once. But
even so, he'd contacted her in Scotland to see if she was all
right. She made a silent promise to herself that things would
change from today.

'Is this what prompted your decision to retire, Dad?' If
selling to Ross would give her father the peace of mind he
needed for a happy, stress-free retirement, opposing him was

going to be even more difficult. Perhaps she shouldn't allow her own personal feelings to interfere. Ross's words, in the car in the station car park, rang in her head.

'I'm going to withdraw my offer for Thompson's. I know it's not what you want.'

'Beryl and I would like to enjoy the years we have left together, travelling, enjoying trips to the theatre and restaurants without the burden of running a company. In fact, to start with we've booked a cruise, just after Christmas. You're experienced and supremely competent now, Bella, and with the right partner...'

'Dad, you're not to allow worries over the future of Thompson's to interfere with your plans. I'm thrilled that you and Beryl have found each other, even though you've been practically living in each other's pockets for years. Are you planning to marry before the cruise, or after it?'

'Oh, before, of course. There's no sense in having a long engagement at our age, and we want to get on with life together. But we want to do things properly. After all, I've booked the Honeymoon Suite.'

Bella shut her eyes. *Honeymoon Suite!* Her world had been turned upside down in a few short minutes and it would take time to get used to the new order of things. Her heart swelled with happiness at the thought that her father had found love again after all this time, and with the knowledge that he and Beryl would provide love, companionship and care for each other.

'Dad, that's...*so* exciting. I must call Beryl now, to tell her how pleased I am.'

She took her father's hands, pulling him to his feet.

'Steady on, Bella. I'm eighty-one years old. I need to stand up slowly, or I'll immediately fall down again.'

'When have you ever done things slowly, Dad?' She gave

him a hug. 'You're eighty-one years *young*, and you and Beryl are going to have a marvellous time together.'

'I'm so glad you're happy for us, my dear, but I knew you would be, once you were over the surprise. Now I'm going to take the rest of the day off. It's too wet for golf but Beryl and I have a table booked for lunch at our favourite Italian restaurant.'

He started towards the door.

'Dad, it's one of the best surprises I can imagine.'

From her office window she watched her father leave the building and walk away towards the bus stop. He could easily have asked his driver to pick him up and take him home, but he saved that privilege for what he called 'extra-special events'. Bella hoped his marriage to Beryl would qualify, and that he wouldn't decide to travel to his wedding by bus or expect Beryl to do the same.

In his belted coat and felted wool fedora, he walked with vigour, his rolled-up umbrella tapping the pavement at his side. He had a spring in his step which she envied.

Her heart, which had felt so bruised until an hour ago, overflowed with joy for him and Beryl. She reached for her phone to call her.

After congratulating Beryl and having a lengthy conversation about plans for the wedding, she made herself address the question of what to do about Ross's bid. Should she explain to her father why she could never work with him? He'd know she'd been hurt and hadn't turned to him for comfort. That might cast a shadow over the happiness he and Beryl had found together and she wouldn't allow herself to be the cause of that.

Or could she persuade him that it would be better to consider any other possible offers before accepting this one? Her father had always been decisive. His mind, once made up, was difficult to change.

She thought about the drive from Innes Lodge to the station and how Ross had brushed his hand over hers and she'd moved away. Was that the last time she'd ever feel his touch?

As she grappled with her feelings, there was a tap at the door. She dragged her attention back to the present, imagining how excited Jess would be, when she told her the news of her father's engagement.

'Bella?'

'Jess, I have something wonderful to tell you...'

'Bella, I'm sorry, but I've just had a call...from the Royal Free Hospital.' Bella's world shrank around her to this precise place, this moment. 'Your father has been taken to A&E. I've called a taxi for you.'

CHAPTER SIXTEEN

BELLA STARED DOWN at her father's still face, his skin as white as the sheet beneath him. A dressing had been pressed to the left side of his head and she could see the purple stain of a bruise spreading across his temple. His left arm was strapped to his body in a temporary sling and his head and neck held immobile in a brace.

'Dad?' It came out as a whisper, and she tried again, bending over him, bringing her mouth closer to his ear. *'Dad?'*

There was no response. She took the thin fingers of his hand in hers, stroking her thumb across his knuckles.

'Dad, It's me. Bell... Isabella.' She swallowed, trying to swallow her tears of shock and fear.

The taxi ride up to Hampstead had seemed to take forever, the rain reducing the speed of the traffic to a crawl. She'd begged the driver to hurry, and she knew he was doing his best, but she didn't know if that was going to be good enough.

She thought of how she'd watched her father from her office window, walking with such happiness in his step.

What if that was the last time she'd see him walking, the last conversation they'd have?

Guilt burned her insides, and she felt sick with fear. What had he been thinking about when he'd tripped and fallen?

Was the reason her beloved father was lying on a trolley in A&E all her fault? Had she said or done something to upset him and take his attention off the slippery pavement? She knew her logic was faulty, but she couldn't help questioning herself. Perhaps she'd sounded too shocked by his announcement, or not reacted with enough joy? What could she have done to prevent this from happening? While the taxi sat stationary at yet another red light, she had a sudden insight into how Ross must feel about his wife's fatal accident.

If her father had a serious head injury, would he ever be the same again? She'd cope with any outcome, as long as he pulled through, she vowed. Had Ross made those frantic promises, too, as he'd searched for Georgina in the snow?

A doctor, accompanied by a nurse with a clipboard, tapped her shoulder.

'We're taking him for an MRI scan, Ms…?' His voice was kind. 'Then we'll have a better idea of what we're dealing with.'

'Thompson. Bella Thompson. I'm his daughter.'

'Good. Go and get yourself a coffee. We'll call you when we're done.'

Was he insane? How could she drink coffee, while her father lay there, seeming to hover between life and death.

'I… I'll just wait. If that's okay.'

'That's fine.' He glanced at the monitor attached to her dad. It beeped rhythmically and she told herself that was a good sign. She watched as the trolley was wheeled away, around a corner and out of sight and then she called Beryl, for the second time that morning.

When they next saw him, her dad was in a ward, the end of his bed raised. His head had been properly bandaged and his wrist encased in a cast.

Intense relief rushed over Bella as she saw the moment he recognised them. They stood on either side of his bed, but his eyes were fixed on Beryl.

He smiled. 'I'm sorry to cause all this bother. I'm fine, but they insist on keeping me in for a few days for observation. Apparently I have a mild concussion. We've missed our special lunch, and the visit to the venue…'

Bella watched as Beryl took his hand and bent to plant a kiss on his forehead. 'Don't be silly, Albert. We can have lunch any day, and Claridge's has been there since the early eighteen-hundreds. It will still be there when you're better. It's much more important that you get well in time for our wedding, and the cruise.'

Bella swallowed down the lump in her throat, marvelling that it didn't choke her, as she watched the love that flowed between them.

'Yes, you're right.' His eyes twinkled. 'We don't want to waste that booking in the Honeymoon Suite.'

Obviously his memory was fully intact.

Bella kissed his cheek. 'I'm so sorry, Dad. But it's such a relief to see you awake and…remembering everything.'

He shook his head, wincing a little. 'Oh, I don't remember everything. I have absolutely no memory of what happened. My last thought was of how much Beryl and I were going to enjoy our lunch. I'd booked our favourite restaurant. Did anyone think to cancel?'

'I did, Albert.' Beryl patted his hand. 'They send their best wishes for your recovery.'

Bella didn't even know they had a favourite restaurant, let alone what it was called.

'I'm sorry, Dad,' she said again. 'I haven't spent enough time with you lately. I promise that's going to change.' She would find time, from now onwards, to speak to him every day. They'd always maintained close contact, but she'd let it become distant. Working too hard, to try to excise her own hurt and be the forceful woman she thought she had to be, had unravelled the precious ties they shared. Nothing was worth compromising a loving relationship for, but it had taken this accident for her to realise that. She couldn't prevent mishaps or difficult times in the future, but she could make the most of the present by always being available for her father and Beryl, if they needed her.

Work would always be there, waiting for her, but in future the people close to her would take precedence.

Her father raised his good hand. 'Nonsense, Bella. I know how busy you've been. This was just a silly accident because I'm just a silly old man who didn't look where he was going. I had other things on my mind.'

'You're definitely not silly, Dad.'

She thought about the advice her mother had given her twelve-year-old self and for the first time she wondered if she'd encouraged him to look for love again. It was not something she would ever ask, but she'd like to think it was true.

How much had she missed, while she'd worked twelve-hour days, refused social invitations and not engaged properly with her father for months on end?

He had quietly allowed her to assume the role she'd grown into at the company and had stepped back. He'd aged, she realised now, although he'd lost none of his business acumen or zest for life. He'd found someone to love and care for. They had a favourite restaurant, and holidays planned. How had she missed all that? While she'd had her head turned the other way, determined to bury her own hurt, her father and Beryl had made plans to embark on a shared life. They weren't worrying about their ages, or how much time they might have together. They were enjoying their new-found love and fulfilling each other.

Her father's eyes looked tired. 'I'll leave you two,' she said, giving him another kiss on the cheek. 'Don't worry about the office, Dad. I'll keep things going until you feel like coming back in. And if you don't, that's okay, too.' She walked around the foot of the hospital bed and wrapped her arms around Beryl. 'You will call me if there's anything I can do, won't you?' She drew back, holding Beryl's hands. 'I'm so happy for you.'

Beryl's eyes misted. 'Thank you, Bella. I love you both, you know.'

CHAPTER SEVENTEEN

IT WAS MONDAY afternoon before Ross extracted a sensible answer from Thompson's Textiles and when he did he was shocked to learn that Albert Thompson was in hospital.

'Is he ill? Or injured? Where is he? I need to speak to him.'

He wished he could contact Isabella. She'd had some differences of opinion with her father which had caused her worry, but this was much worse. She must be beside herself with anxiety and as far as he knew there was only Beryl, her father's housekeeper, to offer her support. Examining his reaction to the news, he found his need to help her and offer comfort far outweighed his need to discuss the deal with her father.

But it seemed impossible to reach her, because while her PA was happy to talk to him, she managed to tell him very little.

'He's not dealing with any business matters, for the foreseeable future,' she said. Was her voice always that husky or was she going down with a cold?

Not getting answers to his questions infuriated him. He was used to getting what he wanted, be it service, information or his own way. He needed to speak to Albert Thompson and to withdraw his offer, otherwise Isabella would think he hadn't been sincere when he'd told her he planned to cancel the deal.

Her opinion of him mattered, more than anything else he could think of in his stressed state.

When he'd left her, that first time, he'd hated himself. Not for leaving, but because he knew she'd be hurt by his behaviour. He'd tried, in vain, to put her out of his mind, to treat the encounter like the dozens of others he'd had, and still intended to have. It had proved impossible. In the end he'd made a deal with himself: get a grip, give up the mind-altering substances, get cleaned up and never, ever do anything again that was going to mess with his mind so badly. He'd come close to losing control of his life completely, and now it felt as if it was happening again.

'What about Isa—Ms Thompson?' he'd asked, trying to keep his voice calm. 'Can I speak to her?'

'Ms Thompson is travelling in the north of England, visiting our factories. I'll tell her you called.'

'With her father in hospital I'm surprised she's left London. Was that wise?'

He'd counted on the PA's loyalty to Isabella outweighing her discretion, and he was right.

'Mr Thompson will be discharged from hospital tomorrow to continue his recovery at home. Care for him is in place to enable Ms Thompson to handle the running of the business for as long as necessary.'

'Well,' he said, gritting his teeth, 'that's excellent news, but I'd like to send my good wishes to Mr Thompson.' He changed tack and dropped his voice to the smooth baritone which usually guaranteed results. 'Could you possibly help me to do that, Ms...?'

'Jess,' she said. 'I'm Ms Thompson's PA. And yes, Mr Maclean, I'll certainly try.'

'Thank you, Jess. Your help is much appreciated. However, I'd like to have something delivered—a wellness package? If you could let me have an address...'

It worked. Armed with an address, he got hold of his own PA and asked him to arrange something suitable, and then made himself wait.

Those few days felt like the longest of his life.

He'd expected a note of thanks, or an email, so he was surprised when he received Albert Thompson's phone call on Saturday morning. He listened while he expressed his thanks for the gift and good wishes, and then introduced the real reason for needing to speak to him.

There was a short silence while Albert considered what he'd said.

'Will you come to see me, Mr Maclean? Perhaps this afternoon?'

'I wouldn't want to intrude, or take up your time, and I really don't think it's necessary. I just wanted to tell you that I don't intend to sign off on the deal.'

'Humour me, Mr Maclean. Having to take things easy while I recover means I have too much time on my hands. I enjoyed meeting you and I'd like to see you again. Besides, I'd like to know why you've changed your mind.'

'I don't…'

'About three o'clock? Looking forward to seeing you.'

The call ended, leaving Ross wondering how he'd just been outplayed.

The weather had turned bitter. Sleet, instead of rain, sifted down, freezing even on contact with the heated windscreen of Ross's black Aston Martin, as he eased it into a parking space on the wide street. Red brick Victorian houses, with complicated roofs and stained-glass window panels, marched up the hill into the mist.

He checked the address on his phone and pushed open the iron gate of number twenty-three.

The woman who opened the door to his knock was trim and attractive, her grey hair cut in a bob. She introduced herself as Beryl, took his coat and showed him into a study across the hall. Albert Thompson sat in a wing-back chair, watching a sports programme on a widescreen television.

'I see you've met Beryl, my fiancée,' he said, stretching out a hand.

Ross paused, glancing between them, unable to disguise his surprise.

'I… I didn't know. Congratulations.'

'Thank you. How could you have known? Take a seat.' He pressed the remote and the screen went black. 'Tea?'

'Yes, please. How are you feeling?'

'Not bad, considering how I look.' Albert touched his fingers to the bruise on his temple. 'My main aim is to be better in time for our wedding. Impressive bruise, don't you think?'

Ross nodded. 'It is. When will you be getting married?' He glanced around the room, and out into the hallway, thinking that this imposing, elegant house was where Isabella had grown up; where she'd lost her mother.

Despite its grand proportions, it felt homely and comfortable. Newspapers lay on the ottoman in front of the fireplace and framed family photographs crowded a side table. He searched them for pictures of Isabella and then dragged his eyes away.

Remembering her as an adult, in his arms on the dance floor, in his kitchen, in his bed, was painful enough. He didn't need to add pictures of her as a child or young student to the collection in his head.

'The Friday before Christmas. We're having the wedding breakfast at Claridge's.'

'Wonderful. May I wish you both every happiness? Isabella didn't mention your engagement…' He stopped, hoping he hadn't prompted questions about the weekend in Scotland.

'Thank you.' Albert nodded. 'Of course, you were at the same wedding. How well do you know my daughter, Mr Maclean?'

The question caught Ross off guard. He rubbed a hand over the back of his head, playing for time.

'I… We first met two and a half years ago. She was the bridesmaid at a wedding for which I was the best man. But we didn't see each other again until the meeting at your head office, and then again in Scotland, last weekend.'

'So not very well.'

Ross wanted to say he felt as if he'd known her all his life. He wanted to explain how, when their eyes met in that chapel, he'd been overcome with a longing to know her that was more profound than anything he'd ever experienced before. How the idea of having feelings for anyone, ever again, had scared him and how he'd walked away.

'So, no, not well.'

Understatement of the century. He linked his hands between his knees and made himself meet Albert's eyes.

The older man nodded. 'Mmm. Yes. Obviously, I know her, very well indeed, and I'm worried about her. She's taken on far too much at Thompson's. She's working much too hard, and now that I'm planning to retire, she'll work even harder. That's why your offer interested me. I saw it as a way to reduce the workload on her, but she is fiercely independent and insists she can manage on her own.'

Ross let out a long breath. 'I'm not an easy man, Mr Thompson. I'm driven and relentless and exacting to work with. I've been considering the offer I made and I've reached the conclusion that I'm not the man best…suited…to take Thompson's forward in the way you envisage.'

'May I ask why?'

'I have a complicated past. There was a lack of care in my childhood, which has impacted on me emotionally, and I lost my wife in an accident, which I should have been able to prevent. At the moment, at least, I'm not in the right place for this particular challenge.'

Isabella was one of the few people he'd spoken to about his past, but something about the warm, comfortable atmosphere of the room was conducive to sharing. The house, although large and lived in by only two people, felt filled with something with which he was unfamiliar, but which felt as if it might be addictive. Was it love?

'I was disappointed to hear you're reconsidering your offer. I'm looking forward to my retirement with Beryl and I'll only enjoy it fully if I know Thompson's, and therefore Bella, are in safe hands.'

'Thompson's is a thriving business. I don't think you'll have trouble attracting other investors. Now, if you'll excuse me…' He stood up. 'I don't think there's anything to be gained by taking up any more of your time.'

He needed to get away from the beguiling atmosphere which he felt surrounding him in this house, in the company of Isabella's charming father and his fiancée. It was too comfortable. He could begin to need it, and what was the point of allowing himself to need something he couldn't have?

'You won't stay for tea?'

Ross shook his head. 'No, thank you. After all, I won't.'

He shook Albert's hand and turned away.

'Ross?'

He turned back.

'May I call you Ross?'

'Of course, although…'

'I wish you well, and I'll be happy to hear from you if you change your mind. Tragedy can shape us in many ways, but the outcome depends on which shape we choose to accept. I lost my wife to illness, when Bella was twelve. I never thought I'd have the courage to open myself to love again.' He shook his head. 'You're an entrepreneur. You understand about risk. Falling in love is probably the biggest risk any of us ever takes. But where would we be if we were all too afraid to take it?'

Ross retrieved his coat from the stand in the hall and shrugged himself into it. It was still damp despite the warmth of the house. He stood for a minute, absorbing the smell of beeswax polish and the scent of roses from a silver bowl of red blooms on the circular table in the centre of the room. The perfume of roses would now always remind him of Isabella, as if he'd ever need reminding.

He knew Albert's words were going to settle in his mind and bother him. Yes, he was a risk taker, but was risking his heart a step too far into the unknown? Were the stakes too high?

There was one thing about which he had absolutely no doubt. He would never, ever accept an invitation to be a best man again.

He let himself out of the ornate door and pulled it shut behind him. The sleet continued to drift down, visible in the halos of yellow light surrounding the streetlamps. He'd stop on the way home for a drink at The Hollybush, his favourite pub. There'd be people to chat to, and he'd be able to put some distance between himself and the past two weeks.

On second thoughts, he'd go straight home. He didn't feel like chatting to anyone, even though his Battersea penthouse, with its view of the Thames, held no attraction for him at this moment at all.

He latched the gate and ducked his head into the sleet, walking in the direction of his car and sidestepping the person, hidden under an umbrella, coming towards him.

'Ross? What are you doing here?'

Despite her umbrella, moisture sparkled on her hat and coat, and on the curls which lay over her shoulders.

'Isabella. I… I thought you were in Yorkshire.'

She nodded. 'I was. I got back last night. How did you know?'

'Your PA told me.' Ross rolled his head towards the house. 'I came to see your father.'

Her grey eyes widened, disbelief flashing in them. 'He hasn't…you didn't…'

'No.' He shook his head. 'No, we didn't. I contacted him to tell him the deal is off. As I said I would. He asked me to visit him, to explain…'

The last time he'd seen her in London she'd been dressed for business, in a pencil skirt and silk shirt, heeled court shoes. He much preferred the skinny jeans and quilted jacket she wore now.

'Your bobble hat survived.'

'It did.' She raised a gloved hand and patted the damp wool, then ducked her head to peer past him at the house. 'How is he?'

'Bored, I think, which is probably a good sign. It means he's getting better.'

'For no logical reason, I felt it was my fault.'

He frowned. 'Why? How could you have prevented it?'

'I couldn't have, but I felt—I *know*—I've neglected him. He and Beryl had been engaged for six weeks and they hadn't been able to tell me because I kept cancelling plans. I felt guilty.'

He nodded. 'I know how irrational guilt feels.'

'This accident was such a shock. It made me realise how distant I'd become. I didn't even know about Beryl, or that they have a favourite restaurant…'

'They seem very happy. It's wonderful for them.' He brushed moisture from his face. 'Perhaps you can take something positive from this, if it's brought you back in touch with things.'

'Maybe it's brought me back in touch with *myself*.'
The self that I love.

Shock at the realisation fused his thought process so he had to kick-start his brain and drag it back to the rain-drenched street. 'Can I give you a lift somewhere?' Stupid question. She must think he was an idiot, along with everything else.

'Hardly. I've only just arrived.'

'Of course. Well, it was good to see you…' He pulled the key fob from his pocket and pressed the button. The lights of the Aston flashed as the locks clicked. She looked from him to the car and back again.

'You too.' She put her hand on the gate. 'Ross?'

He looked across at her from the driver's door. 'Yes?' His misguided heart leapt. Was she going to ask him to stay? To come back in for tea? The idea of returning to the warm, inviting house was so tempting. The idea of spending time with Isabella was alluring.

'Did my father accept your decision?'

He paused, swallowing down his disappointment, mentally berating himself for his reaction. She didn't want to see him. She was hardly going to invite him in for tea.

He opened his mouth to say yes. But then he realised that wouldn't be true.

'Not absolutely,' he said. 'Isabella?'

She latched the gate closed behind her. 'Yes?'

'I… I contacted my father.'

Her eyes searched his face, lighting up, and she smiled.

'I'm so pleased, Ross. That must have taken courage. Was he…?'

'He seemed glad to hear from me.'

'And your mother? Could he tell you how to contact her?'

'Yes. They're back together.'

CHAPTER EIGHTEEN

THE WEEKS BEFORE Christmas were always busy, but Bella made them busier still. Flinging herself into overdrive, she tackled every task at breakneck speed and with ruthless efficiency.

She returned to Yorkshire to visit the Thompson's factories, personally touring the facilities, chatting to as many employees as she could during a working day and then working on her laptop in the evenings, setting up new targets for the New Year and scrutinising the accounts, even though she had rock-solid faith in the accountants.

She was relentless in her determination to stay on the move.

The nights weren't so easy. Ross disturbed her sleep, visiting her dreams so that she woke, turning towards him, to find the space beside her empty and cold. At three o'clock in the morning the future felt dark and lonely.

The high street was especially fun in the weeks before Christmas, with the quaint shopfronts decorated in holiday themes. The scent of ginger wafted from the door of the bakery as a family came out, the children nibbling gingerbread biscuits. She stopped at a stall selling spiced, mulled wine and wrapped her hands around the warm cup, inhaling the smell of cloves and cinnamon, and thinking how much more fun this would be if she could share it with someone else.

Arranging the wedding with Beryl took extra time, and

Isabella loved seeing how much fun her father and his wife-to-be had, discussing the details of the ceremony and celebratory lunch. Her father was determined to stick to their original date, despite the remnants of the bruise on his head and his arm in a sling.

'Then,' he said, 'we can have a family Christmas and Beryl and I can fly off to join our cruise on Boxing Day.'

In the Honeymoon Suite!

On the day of the wedding the simple service made Bella's throat thicken with emotion and her father's speech, at the lunch party afterwards, brought hot tears to her eyes. He spoke of love. The love he'd had for Bella's mother, his love for Bella, and the amazing good fortune he'd had in finding love again, late in life, with Beryl.

They drank a toast to love, and to the happy couple.

At four o'clock, when the lunch had been rounded off with tea and cake, Bella kissed her father and new stepmother before they took the lift to the suite they'd booked for two days, holding hands, looking as happy as newlyweds should.

She said goodbye to the remaining guests as they left, and then stood on the hotel steps and wondered what to do. She'd completed her Christmas shopping, and the office had closed for the holidays, but she felt too full of excitement to go home. She wished she'd stayed behind at the hotel and asked a few of the guests to join her for a drink, but they'd all seemed to be heading off in groups, with their own plans.

There was nobody she could think of to call and meet up with at such short notice. Her insane schedule of the past few years had meant friendships, apart from Hannah and Emma, had faded into the background, and they'd both already left for Scotland with their husbands to spend Christmas and New Year with their families.

She wandered along the pavement, admiring the sparkling Christmas lights which decorated the trees and shops and hung in garlands and festoons across the street. The dazzling window display of a small, boutique chocolate shop caught her attention and she stopped to look at it, and then, as she looked up, her eyes connected in the shadowy reflection with those of the tall man standing beside and a little behind her.

She spun round, her hands flying to her mouth.

'Ross.' Her pulse rocketed, adrenaline kicking in instantly, preparing her for fight or flight. She took a step backwards, dropping her hands and wrapping them both around the strap of her cross-body bag.

'Isabella, please stay.' He raised a hand but dropped it to his side. 'Please, will you listen to me for a minute.'

She stepped back a little further, putting more space between them. 'Are you *stalking* me, Ross?'

'Technically, I think I probably am, but I wanted to speak to you, and this was the only way I could think of making it happen that didn't involve turning up at your office, and I didn't think you'd want that.'

'No, you're right. But…how did you know…'

'I visited your father, remember? He may have mentioned the date of the wedding, and the venue.'

Isabella nodded. 'They've both been so excited. Of course he would have mentioned it.'

'Did it go well?'

'It was brilliant. They both just seem to glow with happiness…' She stopped, feeling awkward, tucking a strand of hair behind her ear and dropping her eyes from Ross's face.

'Isabella.'

She angled a glance up at him. 'What are you doing here, Ross?' Her voice didn't sound like her own. She swallowed, crossed her arms and tried again. 'What do you want? If it's to talk about the deal…'

'No.' He shook his head and rubbed his hands over his face. She heard the sound she loved, of palm across stubble.

'That's not why I'm here. I'd... Will you come out to dinner with me? I'd like to take you on a date. A proper date.'

'A date?' Her thoughts whirled, trying to find a steady point but looking at him made it difficult. His eyes, fixed on her face, were midnight-on-a-moonless-night dark, and his hair looked as if he'd spent the afternoon pushing his fingers through it. The line of his mouth was straight, his lips pressed together as he continued to stare at her. 'A *date*?' she repeated. 'I thought you didn't do dates. Only hookups.'

His expression relaxed a fraction and one corner of his mouth lifted slightly. The crinkle lines at the corner of his eyes deepened, hinting at the smile he so rarely displayed. 'I don't. Not ever. And the only hookups I've ever truly enjoyed have been with a bridesmaid.'

'Oh. Then why...?'

His eyes left hers for a moment, as he glanced around, stepping aside to allow a group of pedestrians to pass. 'I just want to have a conversation with you. There're things I need to say, if you'll listen. And I don't want to say them here, in the street, in the cold. I want to take you somewhere quiet and comfortable where we can pay each other proper attention.'

'I don't know. I don't think it's a good idea.'

'Mmm.' He bent his head and unfastened the top button of his long woollen coat. 'Under this coat I'm wearing your favourite sweater.'

'Well...' Bella felt her lips twitch and she tried to suppress a smile. 'In that case, maybe.'

She thought she saw twin, dark flames flare in his eyes, but it might have been a reflection of the Christmas lights. 'I can work with "maybe", but first, may I congratulate you on your father's marriage?'

'Thank you. They're so happy and I feel so happy for them, taking a chance on love late in life.'

Seeing him, hearing his voice, made her feel boneless with

relief, as if she'd been holding herself together by sheer will-power and now she could let go for a little while, and allow his presence to support her.

He moved closer. 'May I?' He cupped her elbow. 'The pavement is a little treacherous.'

'Where are we going?'

'It's not far at all. We need to cross the street, but if you decide you don't want to come with me, I'll understand.'

CHAPTER NINETEEN

THE RESTAURANT WAS hidden behind a door on a quiet cobbled mews. It was one of Ross's favourites, where he knew the service would be discreet and the food delicious.

Even though he hadn't made a reservation, feeling that would be tempting fate, the concierge led them to his usual table, in an alcove.

'It's early,' he said, once they were seated opposite each other, 'so it's quiet, but later it'll be buzzing.'

'I prefer quiet. And I'm not that hungry. I've already had a wedding breakfast, remember.'

'I do remember. You can have something light, or just a drink, if you prefer. Tell me more about the day.'

A waiter brought menus and filled glasses with water.

She sat back on the velvet banquette, fingering her pearls. 'It was beautiful. They looked wonderfully happy, and my father spoke so movingly. I suddenly felt as if there were parts of him I don't know at all.'

He watched her fingers and wanted to reach out and take them in his, to quieten their agitation, but he kept his hands firmly on his side of the table. One wrong move could have her getting up to leave.

'When I left you at the station I felt as if…you'd taken an essential part of my being with you. I didn't know how I'd continue to function. I had a while to wait for my flight and did a bit of soul-searching.'

The waiter arrived to take their order, but he waved him away, draining his water glass.

'You'd rejected me, refusing to see me again.'

'I said you had to learn to love yourself a little.'

'Yes. The idea was alien to me, but I realised that what you said was true. How could I expect you to want to be with me when I wouldn't promise to be there for you? I'd told myself to stay away from you, to prevent you from getting hurt, but in those few minutes I realised it was myself I was protecting.'

Her eyes seeming to be everywhere but on him, but at last her gaze connected with his.

'I've realised I've been doing the same thing. I've allowed my fear of feeling vulnerable again to stop me from reaching for what I want and seeing where that takes me.'

He nodded. 'The day I went to see your father, he said something which stayed with me.' He tapped his fingers on the table, trying to release some of his tension. 'He said, *"Falling in love is the biggest risk most of us ever take, and where would we be if we were too afraid to take it?"*'

'Is that what you are, Ross? Too afraid?' she murmured.

He had to hold her gaze, to give him the strength he needed. 'I thought I was strong, able to stand up for what is right. I take calculated risks in the deals I do. I steer clear of commitment outside the workplace so I can never be accused of breaking a promise. But...'

He stopped, and Isabella reached across the table and brushed her fingers along his jaw. 'But?'

'But I've been afraid to take the most important risk of all, of loving someone and being loved in return. I'm afraid of being hurt, again, by someone I love.'

'Ross, are you saying...?'

He held up a hand. 'I need to finish, otherwise I'll lose my courage. That's when I knew I'd already taken the risk. I was deeply in love with you, and I was trying my best to sabotage it, like I'd sabotaged other things in my life. I don't want to be in that place, where I'm afraid, any longer. I realise I can try to forgive myself for wanting to heal and allowing myself to want to be with you, if you'll have me, and I promise to love you, and care for you, as you deserve to be loved and cherished. If you'll take the risk of loving me back you will never need to feel vulnerable again.'

Isabella bowed her head. He reached across the table and tipped her chin up so he could see her face and his heart dropped. Tears flooded her eyes and then one escaped and trickled down her cheek. He swiped it away with his thumb.

'Please, Isabella, don't cry. I'm sorry. I shouldn't have said all this.'

She reached up and circled her fingers around his wrist, pulling his hand down to wrap it around hers and stretching across the table to seize his other hand.

'Please don't say you're sorry.'

'I'll get the concierge to call a taxi for you, if you want to leave. I knew you didn't want to see me again. I should have stayed away from you.'

'No.' She disengaged a hand and wiped her fingers across her cheeks. 'I've let my fear of being vulnerable stop me from falling in love. The fear of losing someone I love, again, is frightening and I haven't seized the opportunity. But I *want* to be brave. I might feel vulnerable and afraid, but if I know you're there to catch me and hold me, I can be strong and courageous and love you, as you deserve to be loved.'

Somehow, Ross was on his feet, and then sliding onto the seat beside her. His hands cupped her face, his fingers slipping into her hair. Gently, he angled her head so that his mouth could find hers with no restriction.

'You love me?' he whispered, incredulous. He felt her nod, but his mouth had covered hers before she could utter another word.

She tasted sweeter than he remembered. He tried to keep it gentle, but the way she buried her hands in his hair and pulled him towards her made that difficult. Nothing mattered, except the taste of her, the feel of her body pressed against his, her heady, achingly familiar perfume and the emotion which swelled inside him until he wondered how he could contain it.

'Isabella…' He lifted his mouth from hers. 'I can't guarantee to keep control of this kiss.'

'Perhaps that's a risk we should take,' she whispered.

'When I saw you there, in your amethyst silk dress, it felt like torture, because second chances don't happen in the real world. But the universe has given me one. I intend to hold you and love you forever—'

'Sir?'

Dazed and confused, Ross turned his head towards the interruption.

'I've taken the liberty of bringing over a bottle of your favourite champagne,' said the concierge, 'since it seems celebrations are in order.'

The rain had cleared overnight, leaving a pale blue, rinsed sky. Across the jumbled rooftops, the trees of the heath sparkled with a sharp frost in the low winter sun.

Isabella stood at her window, thinking about the unexpected directions life could take, when you thought your course was set. A glance across a chapel, an overnight blizzard…

'Are you wearing my shirt?'

Ross wrapped his arms around her waist, pulling her back against his chest, resting his chin on her hair.

'Yes. You weren't going anywhere, so I thought you probably didn't need it.'

'Just for the record, it looks much sexier on you than on me.'

'I think I should be the judge of that.'

'The speed with which you managed to get it off me made me assume you didn't like the look.'

He dropped a kiss on her cheek.

'Mmm. There might be some buttons missing.'

'And I do need it. I need it off you.' He began to slide the too-large shirt off her shoulders. 'But before I get lost in the moment, or preferably the next few hours, I have a question. Do you have plans for New Year?'

Isabella shook her head. 'No. My dad and Beryl will be away on their cruise. Are you thinking of Hogmanay in Scotland?'

'Uh-uh. I'm thinking of somewhere more exotic. And warmer. The frost is pretty, but so is the ocean.'

'Where exotic?'

'My house in the Caribbean—if you'll come with me? We can lie in a hammock and sip cocktails. You can wear a bikini and I can...'

He turned her in his arms, crushing her against him, kissing her hair, her forehead until he found her mouth, and then travelling further, down the column of her throat as she tipped her head back.

'You can what?' Her voice felt light and breathy.

He picked her up, cradling her against his chest, his mouth finding the supersensitive place where her pulse beat at the base of her throat. 'Let me show you.'

EPILOGUE

THE ANCIENT STONE walls of the Castle of Muir were bathed in golden September sunshine, the gilded, sharp edges of the turrets and battlements etched against a perfect blue sky. The delicate, honey-sweet scent of heather, in its final flush, drifted down from the purple clad slopes.

Isabella's two maids of honour, Hannah and Emma, tweaked her ivory silk dress and made last-minute adjustments to her hair. Hannah tucked a sprig of white heather into her bouquet.

'For luck,' she whispered, 'not that you need it. Ready?'

Isabella nodded. 'Oh, yes.'

The organ music swelled, and she tucked her hand through her father's arm to begin the walk up the aisle. He patted her hand. 'What a wonderful day this is, Bella.'

As they entered the chapel all heads turned towards them, but it was Ross's intense gaze that she sought, and held. His dark eyes, always filled with love when they rested on her, today held a passion so deep it threatened to steal her breath.

Jess, her bridesmaid, fussed with her dress when they reached the chancel steps, took her bouquet and stepped back. Andrew and Robert stood next to Ross, his best man and groomsman, and family and friends filled the chapel. For Isabella and Ross, two of the most important guests were his mother and father, who had travelled from Spain for the wedding.

Ross took her hands in his and held them throughout the service, and when he kissed her she could feel pent-up emotion thrumming through him.

'I love you,' she whispered, against his mouth, 'so much.'

When the speeches had been made, the wedding breakfast eaten, and the dancing was in wild, full swing, they slipped away. The Defender was parked, waiting for them, at the steps.

The long September twilight still lingered in the western sky, but an autumnal mist was creeping up the glen. Ross pressed the ignition button and eased the vehicle into gear, then he put his hand on her thigh, his thumb tracing a familiar pattern. She was sure he could feel the heat his touch generated through the silk of her dress.

'Ready?'

'For anything. For everything life has in store for us, as long as we can do it together.'

'Don't you want to know where we're going?'

He glanced across at her and she put her hand up to cup his jaw, seeing a flicker of uncertainty cross his face.

'If you want to tell me.'

'We're going to Innes Lodge. Is that all right?'

Isabella smiled. 'It's the most beautiful place in the world. I can't wait to see it again.'

'I hoped you'd feel that way. Somehow, I didn't think a luxury hotel would be what you wanted. This time there'll be no snow, and I've had the larder and kitchen stocked with everything we need for as long as we want to stay. No meals from tins.'

'Although that was one of the best meals I've ever eaten.'

He'd proposed in the hammock, by the pool of his beach-side house in the Caribbean, surprising her with an antique ring of amethysts and pearls. When they'd phoned her father with their news, Albert had apparently treated their fellow passengers at the dinner table to the ship's finest champagne.

Their partnership was developing into a great success. Ross understood what needed to be done to take the company forward, without compromising their traditional methods and values. His latest initiative had been to form a co-operative with a group of sheep farmers in Yorkshire. Farmers were hard-pressed and investment from Thompson's could prove to be a lifeline to some of them. In exchange, they would rear sheep and produce wool fleeces under strict conditions of welfare which would mean that Thompson's woollen cloth and yarn could be certified organic.

Isabella knew she would never have had the time or resources to set up this scheme without Ross's knowledge and negotiating skills. Knowing the business was in his safe hands gave her the space to concentrate on the aspects of her work which she was best at, encouraging innovative ideas and developing new designs with the creative team. Their new, organic product was generating lively interest in the fashion industry and the order book was filling fast.

Ross had taken on most of the factory visits, although Isabella still accompanied him when she could, determined to keep in touch with their employees. When possible, they combined the trips with visiting the farms on which their wool was grown, getting to know the farmers and their families and learning about their way of life, in the glorious setting of the Yorkshire dales.

Tramping across fields bordered by low stone walls and glittering rivers, in wellington boots and country clothes, the air sharp and fresh, was an exhilarating change from boardrooms and business suits. Meeting the flocks of quizzical sheep and the earnest black and white sheepdogs which looked after them, was becoming one of Isabella and Ross's favourite ways of relaxing together.

'You'll be twitchy after a week at Innes, wanting to get back to work, putting the business world in order,' she teased.

'I disagree. There is unfinished business at Innes Lodge which we need to attend to, first, and after a week we'll just be hitting our stride.'

She covered his hand with hers as the low buzz of awareness she always felt when they were together began to turn into the fizz of anticipation.

'This is our opportunity to make the absolute most of our second chance.'

'It is, and we will,' she said, and smiled.

* * * * *

*If you enjoyed this story,
check out these other great reads from
Suzanne Merchant*

Cinderella's Adventure with the CEO
Heiress's Escape to South Africa
Ballerina and the Greek Billionaire
Off-Limits Fling with the Billionaire

All available now!

MILLS & BOON ®

Coming next month

HOW TO WIN BACK A ROYAL
Justine Lewis

It was a face she knew well. One that was tattooed on her heart.

She recognised the frown, the narrowing of his light brown eyes and the sudden tenseness in his shoulders. But there were differences as well. The beard for starters. Auburn, like the rest of his hair, thick and well established. It was clipped neatly and well groomed. Not the result of neglect, but purposeful.

He *wanted* to look different.

She didn't blame him one bit. She'd often toyed with the idea of dying her own light brown hair to see if she'd be able to go unrecognised.

Beard or no beard, she'd recognise this man anywhere.

Why here? Why now? Why him? This was her 'get out there and forget Rowan James' weekend. This was *not* meant to be her 'run into your ex unexpectedly' weekend.

They were separated by two metres but an ocean of grief and pain. She stepped towards him, half wondering if he would simply turn and flee. She wouldn't blame him if he did. Her instincts told her to do the same.

Continue reading

HOW TO WIN BACK A ROYAL
Justine Lewis

Available next month
millsandboon.co.uk

COMING SOON!

We really hope you enjoyed reading this book.
If you're looking for more romance
be sure to head to the shops when
new books are available on

Thursday 24th April

To see which titles are coming soon, please visit
millsandboon.co.uk/nextmonth

MILLS & BOON

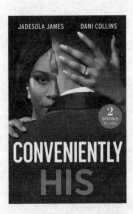

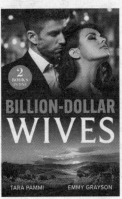

afterglow BOOKS

Afterglow Books is a trend-led, trope-filled list of books with diverse, authentic and relatable characters, a wide array of voices and representations, plus real world trials and tribulations. Featuring all the tropes you could possibly want (think small-town settings, fake relationships, grumpy vs sunshine, enemies to lovers) and all with a generous dose of spice in every story.

♪ @millsandboonuk
⊙ @millsandboonuk
afterglowbooks.co.uk
#AfterglowBooks

For all the latest book news, exclusive content and giveaways scan the QR code below to sign up to the Afterglow newsletter:

SCAN ME

afterglow BOOKS

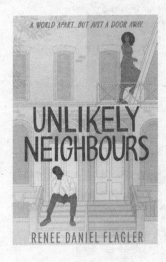

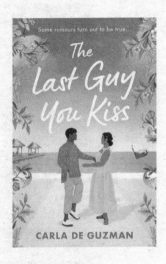

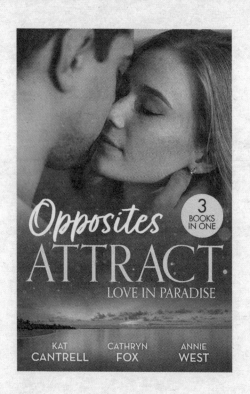

OUT NOW!

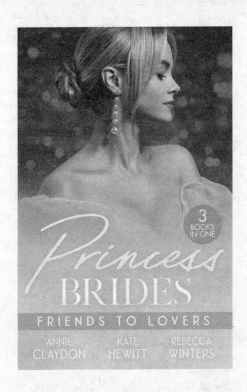

Available at
millsandboon.co.uk

MILLS & BOON

LET'S TALK

Romance

For exclusive extracts, competitions and special offers, find us online:

f MillsandBoon

X @MillsandBoon

⊙ @MillsandBoonUK

♪ @MillsandBoonUK

Get in touch on 01413 063 232